THE FORBIDDEN HEIR

A Novel of the Four Arts

M.J. SCOTT

emscott enterprises

PRAISE FOR M.J. SCOTT

The Shattered Court
Nominated for Best Paranormal Romance in the 2016 RITA®
Awards.

"Scott (the Half-Light City series) opens her Four Arts fantasy
series with the portrait of a young woman who's thrust into the
center of dangerous political machinations... Romance fans will
enjoy the growing relationship between Cameron and Sophie,
but the story's real strength lies in the web of intrigue Scott
creates around her characters."
—*Publishers Weekly*

"Fans of high fantasy and court politics will enjoy The Shattered
Court. Sophie is such a great heroine..."
—*RT Book Reviews*

Fire Kin
"Entertaining...Scott's dramatic story will satisfy both fans and
new readers."
—*Publishers Weekly*

"This is one urban fantasy series that I will continue to come back to...Fans of authors Christina Henry of the Madeline Black series and Keri Arthur of the Dark Angels series will love the Half-Light City series."
—*Seeing Night Book Reviews*

Iron Kin

"Strong and complex world building, emotionally layered relationships, and enough action to keep me up long past my bedtime. I want to know what's going to happen next to the DuCaines and their chosen partners, and I want to know now."
—*Vampire Book Club*

"Iron Kin was jam-packed with action, juicy politics, and a lot of loose ends left over for the next book to resolve that it's still a good read for series fans."
—*All Things Urban Fantasy*

"Scott's writing is rather superb."
—*Bookworm Blues*

Blood Kin

"Not only was this book just as entertaining and immensely readable as Shadow Kin—it sang in harmony with it and spun its own story all the while continuing the grander symphony that is slowly becoming the Half-Light City story. . . . Smart, funny, dangerous, addictive, and seductive in its languorous sexuality, I can think of no better book to recommend to anyone to read this summer. I loved every single page except the last one, and that's only because it meant the story was done. For now, at least."
—*seattlepi.com*

"Blood Kin was one of those books that I really didn't want to put down, as it hit all of my buttons for an entertaining story. It

had the intrigue and danger of a spy novel, intense action scenes, and a romance that evolved organically over the course of the story. . . . Whether this is your first visit to Half-Light City or you're already a fan, Blood Kin expertly weaves the events from Shadow Kin throughout this sequel in a way that entices new readers without boring old ones. I am really looking forward to continuing this enthralling ride."
—*All Things Urban Fantasy*

"Blood Kin had everything I love about urban fantasies: kick-butt action, fantastic characters, romance that makes the heart beat fast, and a plot that was fast-paced all the way through. Even more so the villains are meaner, stronger, and downright fantastic—I never knew what they were going to do next. You don't want to miss out on this series."
—*Seeing Night Book Reviews*

"An exciting thriller . . . fast-paced and well written."
—*Genre Go Round Reviews*

Shadow Kin
"M. J. Scott's Shadow Kin is a steampunky romantic fantasy with vampires that doesn't miss its mark."
—*#1 New York Times bestselling author Patricia Briggs*

"Shadow Kin is an entertaining novel. Lily and Simon are sympathetic characters who feel the weight of past actions and secrets as they respond to their attraction for each other."
—*New York Times bestselling author Anne Bishop*

"M. J. Scott weaves a fantastic tale of love, betrayal, hope, and sacrifice against a world broken by darkness and light, where the only chance for survival rests within the strength of a woman made of shadow and the faith of a man made of light."
—*National bestselling author Devon Monk*

For everyone who kept asking me about this book

ACKNOWLEDGMENTS

This book has been a bit of a journey. And it might not be here if lots of the usual suspects hadn't been there for me. Thank you to Kate, Allison, Sarah, Lissa, and Alyssa for awesome feedback and Ainslie the blurb goddess. Thank you, as always, to my lovely Lulus for writer sanity and to Bec for motivation, info, and travel adventures. Love always to my folks who always cheer me on. And finally, all praise to Katie Anderson for my beeyootiful cover.

Deep the earth
      Its harvest life
      Bright the blood
      Sharpest in strife
      Swift the air
      To hide and fool
      False the water
      The deadly pool

CHAPTER 1

"Welcome to Illvya."

The words echoed around Sophie Mackenzie's head and she suddenly felt oddly detached from her body. "I think—" She took a step forward, swayed, and then steadied as her husband's arm came around her waist.

"Sophie?" Cameron said urgently at the same time as Henri Matin said, "Madame?"

"I am quite—" Sophie started, but the room spun around her and she squeezed her eyes shut against the sensation.

"Lord Scardale, perhaps you should help your wife to a chair," Henri said. His voice was deep, the musical tones of the Illvyan accent underscored with concern or something close to it, which eased the swirl of fear in her head and stomach somewhat.

The next moment, Cameron swung her up, around—which made her head whirl faster—and then settled her into a chair. She kept her eyes closed, still feeling as though the room was spinning around her, focusing on trying to convince herself she was sitting still and safe. The knot in her stomach had loosened into a writhing sensation that was far more unpleasant. She breathed through her nose, determined not to throw up.

"It's been a long journey," Cameron said, sounding fierce. "She needs to rest."

No. She needed to know that they were safe. She couldn't rest until they were safe. They had fled from the palace in Kingswell in the dark of night, leaving a dead assassin behind them. They had risked everything to leave Anglion and cross the ocean to the country that was Anglion's sworn enemy. It was entirely possible they had merely jumped from frying pan to fire, and she could not let her guard slip until she knew if that were the case.

She opened her eyes. "I am quite well." There. She managed the entire phrase that time, though the sentiment was no truer than it had been on her previous attempt.

Cameron's face came into focus, above her. He stood by the chair, clear blue eyes darkened by fatigue and worry. Henri stood next to him. His eyes, lighter by several shades than her husband's, were a blue closer to the pale silver of his hair. And they were, in comparison, far more composed. But there was an equal amount of skepticism in each of their gazes. Clearly neither man believed her claim. She couldn't fault them for that. She didn't believe it herself.

But she was determined to go on. "Mis—I'm sorry, I do not know the correct form of address," she said to Henri apologetically, struggling for the words. Her Illvyan was not fluent by any stretch of the imagination, and her education in the language had definitely not included the finer details of wizardly protocol. Given that Anglion considered the wizards of Illvya to be anathema and heretics, her teachers presumably hadn't thought such things necessary.

"The correct term is Venable, for a wizard. Venable Matin. I'm not sure how you would say it exactly in Anglion—no, you say Anglish, do you not? Mine is not perfect," Henri said with a small flick of his fingers, as if to indicate that he took no offense in her ignorance.

"Since we are in your country, it does not seem to matter

what we Anglions call the language," Cameron said. "And your grasp of it, however you name it, seems admirable."

Henri nodded once. "That is kind of you to say. Perhaps it will improve further on your acquaintance. Still, I do not know the precise translation of Venable. Honored wise one would come close, I suppose. And, if you do not care to correct me on what your language is called, then I shall not quibble over my titles tonight. Besides, as I am master here at the Academe, you may call me Maistre Matin, to be more exactly correct. It is simpler."

Sophie smiled, hoping the expression didn't reveal the depths of her exhaustion. Her stomach was settling, but that only left her more aware of how much the rest of her ached for sleep. "Maistre Matin, then. I would like to know where my husband and I stand. We are seeking asylum here in Illvya. At least for a time. We need to know if it will be granted to us. And under what conditions."

Henri pursed his lips. "It is a long time since an Anglion witch—at least one of your status—made her way to these shores." His eyes looked oddly dark for a moment. Then he blinked and they were as before.

"My status? I'm not sure I understand you," Sophie said.

"We get a small number of Anglions arriving here, of course. It is not common but it does happen. Though, more often, men than women. And of the women, more often those without any power, or only some small power, already dedicated to your goddess. But I do not recall the last time there was a royal witch on our shores. Let alone an unbound one. I imagine we'd have to dig into the history books quite far back to find someone in that state." He pushed the fabric of his robe back from where it had fallen over his arm and the cloth seemed to shimmer slightly, catching the light with a dark rainbow gleam that was echoed in the black jewel in his heavy gold ring.

"Unbound?" Her stomach clenched again. How did he know

that? What did an Illvyan know of the rites of the goddess? Or that, in her case, they had failed.

"Is that not the right term? Undedicated, perhaps?" The maistre pursed his lips, gaze intent on her. Then he glanced at Cameron. "Though perhaps . . . not entirely unentangled."

Unentangled. Cameron went tense beside her. Sophie didn't let her gaze stray to her husband. Could Maistre Matin sense the bond between them? If he could tell that she was not bound to the temple, then the answer was almost certainly yes.

"Relax, Lord Scardale, I mean no harm to you or your wife. And, to be frank, my fam would stop you before you could draw your sword or your gun. They are very fast, the familiaris sanctii."

"You have a demon here? In this room?" Sophie's heart began to pound and only the fact that she was so tired kept her seated. A demon. The stuff of every tale of horror she had ever been told as a child. A creature like the one that had greeted them at the door to the Academe, skin the color of stone and dark metal, eyes black and knowing. It was a measure of how exhausted she was that she hadn't managed to react with more than mild alarm at the sight. Or stepped within the doors of L'Academe di Sages at all.

"Do not look so worried, Lady Scardale. I assure you that Martius is perfectly safe. And as for what unbound means, well, I'm sure you know that as well as I. Though, I will confess, I am intrigued to learn how a royal witch in full possession of her powers did not undergo your temple's so-called ritual." His lips pursed again, as though he had tasted something sour.

Sophie swallowed, unsure what was safe to tell him. She needed time to think. To adjust to their new reality. To rest. But there was no rest if there was no safety. "I—"

"That is a story for another time," Cameron interrupted. "My wife asked you a question. Do you grant us asylum?"

Henri shrugged. "Asylum is not mine to give, Lord Scardale. For now, I will grant you the safety of the Academe and such protection as we can offer. Other details will be . . . decided later."

"Decided by whom?" Cam demanded.

Henri looked amused. "By those who rule here in Illvya. Or rather, those who make decisions. Namely the emperor and his parliament. The latter like to think they wield some influence. Though I'm sure you are familiar with that idea from your home country."

"Queen Eloisa rules alone," Cameron said stoutly.

"I hope for her sake that that is true," Henri said. "Though your presence here may suggest otherwise. Unless—" He broke off. "But come. Your lovely wife needs sleep and food, Lord Scardale, and I imagine that such things would not be unwelcome for you either."

"Our safety?" Sophie managed, even as visions of a soft place to lie down began filling her head, so enticing that she suddenly wanted to cry. She swallowed. She could endure a little longer.

"Is guaranteed for tonight," Henri said. "In the morning, I will have to inform the emperor of your arrival."

"But—" Cameron started.

Henri cut him off with a gesture. "It cannot be avoided, my lord. And it is better that he hears it directly from me rather than from rumor."

"What happens then?" Cameron demanded. He looked poised to . . . what? Fight his way out? That couldn't possibly work. Not when the venables had demons at their beck and call.

"The emperor will decide what happens next. But he is not in the habit of harming Anglion refugees. I doubt he will change his methods with the two of you. But for now, the best thing you can do is rest. You have my word, no one will harm you under my roof. So come, Willem will take you to your accommodations. You can eat and sleep and bathe, and perhaps, in the morning, you will do me the kindness of telling me news of my daughter."

He looked suddenly wistful and Sophie hid a wince. Chloe de Montesse had been a refugee in Kingswell for close to ten years.

That must be how long it had been since Henri had seen her. Might be how long it had been since he'd had any news or word of his daughter at all. Was that how it would be with Sophie's family? Would she never see them again?

No. She couldn't think about that. If she did, then she would definitely cry. She formed a polite smile with an effort and the instincts ingrained from her time at court. "Of course, sir. I only know your daughter a little, but I would be glad to tell you what I can about her."

"As will I," Cameron said. He touched Sophie's shoulder lightly and then offered his hand to help her up. "But for now, we would be grateful for that food and a chance to sleep."

The young man—Willem—who had shown them to the maistre's chambers was waiting outside the door when Henri opened it again to usher Sophie and Cam out. Perhaps he had been waiting there, he and the two young crows who had accompanied them on their journey through the Academe, the whole time.

At the sight of Sophie, the smaller of the two crows squawked, sprang from Willem's shoulder, and flapped five or six feet to alight on her right shoulder.

"Tok!" Willem said, despairingly.

Henri looked curious and tilted his head, pale eyes fixed on the crow. It squawked at him defiantly, the noise ringing in Sophie's ears, and its claws suddenly gripped her shoulder more firmly, the power in them clear despite the thick weight of her woolen cloak padding her.

"You have made a friend, Lady Scardale," Henri said, still speaking Anglish.

"Sorry, Maistre," Willem muttered in the same language. "He is overly curious, that one."

"It is often so with ravens," Henri said. "And often that is a sign of a good familiar. That one is from Scilla and Tieko's latest clutch, isn't he?"

Willem nodded. "Just as willful as them."

"Hopefully just as strong," Henri said with a small smile. He clucked his tongue at the bird, extending a finger to touch its beak.

Sophie felt the weight of the bird shift on her shoulder as it cawed at the maistre. Familiars were another strange Illvyan thing. She had heard tales of animals working with mages but knew nothing of how such things might be achieved in practice. The crow, however, seemed harmless enough. Though harmless was perhaps not the best description for something with claws that gripped so tightly and a long, pointed beak that was mere inches from her eyes.

She decided to ignore it. There were more dangerous things than crows in this building, and she was still feeling lightheaded. And she would happily murder someone to feel clean. She had not bathed or changed her clothes for several days. Goddess knew what she smelled like. Maybe that was why the crow—raven, whatever it was—was attracted to her. Crows ate carrion, didn't they?

"Willem, take Lord and Lady Scardale to one of the guest chambers. Perhaps the Bleu," Henri said.

Willem gave a shallow bow and then nodded at Henri. "Of course, Maistre."

"We will talk more in the morning, once you are rested," Henri said, nodding at Sophie. "Willem will organize a meal for you tonight, if you wish, and bring you to break your fast in the morning."

"Thank you, Maistre Matin," Sophie said. "You have been very kind."

"You are most welcome," Henri said with a slight emphasis on "most" that made Sophie's unease rise again.

But she was too tired to try and work out any hidden meaning behind his words. She knew so little of Illvya. Only the tiny pieces of information that the temple, and the royal family, allowed to be included in Anglion lore. From such scant knowledge, she doubted she had any hope of deciphering the maistre's intentions, even if she were in full command of her faculties rather than half-asleep on her feet. The man was right. There was nothing more they could do tonight. They could begin to understand their new circumstances in the morning. She merely offered a small curtsy to Henri and then turned back to Willem.

Cameron tucked her left arm through his. She leaned into him gratefully, her stomach twisting again as they began to follow Willem's pale head along another series of corridors and stairways that left her completely bewildered as to where they were in the building. She couldn't focus enough to notice any particular details of the route they walked. She was vaguely aware of soft carpets beneath her feet and patterns and colors on the walls, but it took all her energy to keep placing one foot in front of the other. It seemed as though they were walking miles, though it couldn't be nearly that far.

The length of their journey through the building left her in no doubt that the Academe was a sizeable structure. Not quite as large as the palace at Kingswell but definitely heading toward that scale. The Illvyans took the teaching of magic seriously, it seemed.

She wondered how many of the Arts were taught here. In Anglion, the temple oversaw all three branches of the Arts to a degree but was really only involved in teaching earth witches like Sophie. The military took care of the blood mages and the practitioners of the Arts of Air had their own schools and secrets. But maybe in Illvya all magics were studied under one roof? Certainly the presence of the familiaris sanctii they had encountered on arrival suggested that all four branches of magic were taught here. Including the water magic that was anathema in Anglion because it involved the strange creatures.

Anglions were told that Illvyan wizards were secretive and that the demons they commanded deadly, but that did not appear to be the case so far. Though the mere fact that Henri hadn't imprisoned or killed her and Cameron on sight didn't mean that the Illvyans were allies. Far from it. She was under no illusion that she and Cameron were safe. But as the maistre had said, there was nothing to be done about that tonight. All she could do was follow Willem through the endless halls and face whatever came next.

Cameron didn't think he'd ever been quite so grateful to see a bed in his life. Not even after coming off weeks of sleeping rough on patrol in the Red Guard. For a moment it was all he could think of, the sound of Willem closing the door as he exited the chamber registering only vaguely. There was nothing he wanted more than to crawl into the bed fully clothed and sleep for several days. But sleep was going to have to wait.

He remembered the key Willem had handed him, the one currently biting into the hand he was clenching too hard. Turning from the bed, he crossed to the door to turn the key in the latch and test the handle.

Locked. Good.

He left the key in place and turned to study the room. It was sizeable, nearly equal to the main room of his brother's apartment back in the palace in Kingswell.

And his brother, Liam, was the Erl of Inglewood, one of the highest-ranked men in the kingdom. The space the Mackenzies were allocated in the palace reflected that power. The fact that this, a mere guest chamber, was so large made Cameron uneasy. Illvya was rich, drawing its wealth from the empire it controlled as well as its own resources, and the size of the Academe demonstrated that the mages enjoyed their share of that wealth.

With wealth and magic came power.

And with power came politics, intrigue, and ambition.

Exactly the same things that had endangered them in
Kingswell. Only here, the players were unknown.

And those unknown players now held his and Sophie's fate in
their hands.

There hadn't been much time to think when they'd made the
choice to leave Anglion. Now they were going to have to deal
with the consequences of that choice. Beginning tomorrow.
Neither of them was capable of strategizing tonight. But he
wouldn't rest until he was satisfied that this room was as secure
as he could make it.

He walked a circuit of the room, noting bars over the
windows that ran in a tall row along the far wall. The glass in
several of them was ajar slightly, allowing a breeze that carried
the unfamiliar fragrance of the city beyond to enter. Some of the
notes in the scent were familiar—the smells of too many people,
horse dung, and wood smoke. Bread and roasting meats. A
distant hint of water from the harbor he knew lay to the northeast. But the familiar was mixed with a strange oily smell and
unknown spices, enough to drive home the stark reality that
they were no longer in Anglion.

He stared through the glass. The black metal barring it was
cunningly wrought, shaped into ornamental figures that softened
the impact somewhat and obscured part of the view of the dark-
cloaked city. The bars were clearly meant as a barrier. The question was whether they were intended to keep the occupants of
the room in or some threat from the world beyond the
window out.

Either way, the bars didn't move at all when he reached
through the window to test a set with a few fierce pulls. It would
take explosions or some magical attack to shift them. There was
little he could do to ward against either of those eventualities, so
for tonight he would have to hope they would be protection
enough. As for keeping him and Sophie in, well, he doubted
either of them would make it more than a few hundred feet
down the road before keeling over from exhaustion. Nor did

they have any notion where they might escape to. He intended to start rectifying that ignorance as soon as possible. Knowing the terrain was the basis for any good strategy.

The breeze had a cool edge to it and he closed the windows. The last thing either of them needed was to catch a chill. Illvya was supposed to have a similar climate to Anglion, but the days had still held the last heat of summer when they'd left Kingswell and here it felt more truly like the early weeks of autumn that it was. He stared down at the strange cityscape a few seconds more, then drew the curtains across to block it from sight. It was an odd kind of relief when the view—and all it represented—was hidden.

The vivid blue and silver fabric of the curtains was heavy in his hand as he tugged them into a better position, the floral pattern on it more intricate than any he'd seen in Anglion. Similar fabric formed the layers of covers on the bed. More strangeness. Instead of carved wood, the bed frame was made from black metal, curved into arcs of artful branches and flowers at either end in an impressive display of skill.

He made himself look away from the bed, lest he give in to the temptation it offered, and continued his inspection. There was only a single door. Willem had mentioned a bathing room farther down the hallway. They were both filthy from their journey, but he hoped Sophie was as tired as he was and would be willing to forego a bath until morning.

A servant had delivered a small meal of bread, ham, cheese, and a selection of fruit only minutes after Willem had left. Jugs of water and beer and a pot of steaming tea of some sort rested on a low table set near the fire. He was hungry, but the thought of eating made him feel even more tired. Sophie had ignored the food, too, though he'd coaxed her into drinking a little tea.

The only other pieces of furniture in the room were a large armoire where their inadequate bags were now stowed and a cluster of three chairs arranged around the table. The fire was alight. Good, and not only for the warmth the flames provided.

The flames would also be a deterrent for anyone who might try to enter a room through a chimney flue. Not that he had any idea how the Illvyans built their buildings compared to Anglion structures.

Inspection completed, and his immediate concerns about potential entry points for attackers quelled, he walked over to collapse onto the bed, tempted to groan in sheer relief at the fact that they were both still alive and he was finally horizontal on a surface that didn't sway like a ship beneath him.

But there was no answering flop from Sophie following his lead. She'd been silent while he'd prowled around the room, standing by the fire in her wrinkled and stained gray dress, sipping her tea until she'd finished the cup and put it down. He lifted his head, propping himself up on his elbows. Sophie was staring at the door as though she expected it to burst open, hands fisted in her skirts.

"What is it?" he asked. Her face was too pale, too drawn. Shadows the same color as her dress pooled beneath her eyes.

"They have demons here."

True. And that thought should have been disturbing. But his body was at the point of being unable to truly process their new circumstances. "Yes. But so far they don't seem inclined to . . . ." He hesitated, trying to make sure he didn't frighten her. Demons, if the tales were true, could kill a man in seconds. Without so much as touching him. But he was not about to remind Sophie of that. "Maistre Matin guaranteed our safety."

She threw a glance back at him that made it clear that she was not heartened by Henri Matin's words, or overly inclined to trust the Illvyan. He forced himself back to his feet before the siren song of the well-padded mattress could lure him down to unconsciousness. Obviously he wasn't the only one in the room thinking of their vulnerable position.

"Sophie, love, you need to rest."

"And I suppose you can just sleep knowing a demon could walk through this door any second?" Her voice was too high.

She'd been so steadfast in their headlong journey from Anglion, but apparently she had reached the point where she was struggling to continue to maintain her composure.

A demon could do more than walk through the door. They could probably move through the wall. Water magic was strictly taboo in Anglion, and while he had been a member of the palace's Red Guard, not even that position allowed him access to any detailed knowledge of what a water mage was capable of.

The tales he had been raised on painted demons as near-invincible forces of mayhem and destruction, limited only by their aversion to salt and the will of the mages who controlled them. The salt part was true. The familiaris sanctii could not travel by sea. That fact, and the resulting inability for Illvya to bring them in force across the strait that separated the mainland from Anglion, was perhaps the sole reason that Anglion was not part of the Illvyan empire.

But as for the rest, well, he did not doubt demons were powerful—there had to be a reason that Anglion had forbidden the use of the magic that summoned them so many centuries ago—but he didn't know truth from fiction beyond that.

But he did know that his wife was afraid. And that he did not want that to be true. He couldn't completely remove the fear—they had just abandoned everything they knew and fled to a country where they were alone and, apart from his soldiering skills and their combined magic, relatively defenseless—but he could try to make her feel safe for the night. If she slept, she would regain her strength. She would face what came in the morning. They both would.

He moved to her side. "We'll set wards."

She shook her head. "I'm too tired."

"There must be a ley line here," he said. "Illvyans practice three of the same magics we do. They need ley lines to draw on. I can't imagine they would build the school for their mages where they couldn't access one."

He sent his senses out and down, seeking the ley line. He

hadn't noticed one before now but he hadn't been looking for it, having more immediate concerns. The room they'd been given was several floors above the ground, but the ley line would most likely be a strong one. It would have to be to serve so many mages in one place.

In Kingswell, finding the ley line would be as easy as reaching out for the hand of a lover or an old friend. He knew every inch of the palace and the countryside surrounding it. The thought of it gave him a sudden sharp stab of grief, the knowledge that he might never see it again sinking like a knife through his chest. Pain that only sharpened with the realization that never seeing the land or the palace also meant never seeing the people who lived within the palace walls or anywhere else in Anglion. Including his family.

But he couldn't afford to think about them now. He had to focus on here and now. His only priority was protecting Sophie. Right now, that meant finding the ley line.

He searched farther down still, following the stone of the walls, layer by layer toward the earth.

And there—a buzz of magic. Faint, and a somewhat different sensation to the lines he was used to, but that might be because he was exhausted. His fingers wrapped around Sophie's as he reached for the source of power. She was stronger than him, and together they were stronger again. If they could connect with the ley line, if nothing else, it would restore some energy to them.

The first time he'd touched Sophie after she stepped onto a ley line had changed both of their lives. One could almost consider it the moment that had led to this one they found themselves in now. Caught up in the intoxication of that first headlong, uncontrolled rush of power, they'd had sex. Something unmarried royal witches were definitely not supposed to do.

That moment of madness had led to their marriage, to the discovery that Sophie's power could not be bound to the goddess as every other royal witch's power was, because she and Cameron had formed some sort of bond between them during that first coupling. It was the root of their troubles. Had earned them the hostility of the Domina and of Queen Eloisa, to whom both Sophie and Cameron were sworn. Sophie's status and untamed power—a threat to the throne given she stood sixth in line to the crown—had presumably led to the attempt on her life that had convinced them both that they needed to flee the country.

But here, in this place, the ley line was something to help solve their problems, not cause them. Or so he hoped.

"Can you feel it?" he asked as he stretched his senses deeper into the earth. The ley line, unfamiliar as it was, felt strong. Strong but distant. But still usable, as far as he could tell. He eased his power toward it. There was an odd sensation, as though the line itself was pushing back at him, resisting his demand for access, but then it yielded and warmth flowed through him as the magic let him in.

Sophie's fingers tightened around his. "Yes," she said, sounding spent. But there was a sudden flare of power through his fingers as she added her strength to his. Then a second jolt, far stronger than the first, as she made the connection to the ley line.

The fog of fatigue clouding his head eased as the power began to flow faster. The reviving effect of the magic would be temporary, but it should last long enough to let them do what was needed. "Good. Let's set the wards."

They worked together, laying the wards over the door and windows. Sophie's were unsophisticated—after all, she was still new to her power and her training was far from complete—but strong. He added some tricks he'd learned from his time in the Red Guard and hoped the combination would be enough to put her mind at ease. He didn't know if the wards would actually stop a demon, or even one of the Illvyan mages, but the important thing was for Sophie to believe they could.

"There, that's enough." He let go of her hand and stepped back. "Time to rest, love."

There was color in her cheeks again and the shadows under her eyes seemed lighter. The magic had done her some good, but she needed sleep. And food. His stomach was growling now that some of his energy was restored. Sophie would be starving, too.

"Ground the magic back into the stone," he prompted. Too much power from the ley line would make her restless.

"I know," she said. She sounded annoyed at the reminder, but annoyed was better than scared. He let the magic he'd been holding go, and it rushed away from him, as though the ley line —stronger here than those he'd used in Anglion—was pulling it back. The sensation wasn't entirely pleasant. Did it feel the same to Sophie? She was stronger than him, which made her more sensitive to the ley lines. The first time she'd seen one, she'd said it looked like a river of golden light, whereas he saw it only as a faint shimmer.

But if the difference in the ley line had disturbed her, her face didn't show it. He decided not to ask, merely took her hand and led her over to the table, determined that she should eat. And then, at long last, they could sleep.

CHAPTER 2

A low chiming noise startled Sophie out of a sleep so deep she didn't even remember having laid her head on the pillow. She blinked in the darkness, uncertain where—or even who—she was. Beside her, Cameron stirred, and the memory came back to her.

The Academe.

Illvya.

"Sweet goddess, what is that noise?" Cameron muttered, pushing up onto his elbow.

"I don't know." She shoved the covers back and climbed out of the bed. The room was dark, but a faint light showed around the edges of the curtains. Perhaps it was morning. If it was, they must have slept for at least twelve hours already. Which didn't dim her desire to sleep longer still.

She groped her way to the curtains and pulled them back, revealing a just-rising sun beyond the window, sending arrows of golden light spreading across the buildings of Lumia. A city she'd never expected to see for herself.

Anglion history said it was corrupt and dangerous. Full of

wickedness, and users of depraved magic. Though it didn't deny Lumia was beautiful.

On the first two points, she had no idea what the truth was. On the third, it was clear that Lumia was indeed as fair as the light it was named for.

Looking down from the height of their room revealed it to be a city of taller buildings than she was accustomed to. In Kingswell, the largest building was the palace. Here though, the buildings all seemed to be at least three or four stories high, many of them taller still. She couldn't remember how many sets of stairs they had climbed to reach their room the night before, but she thought they too must be on a fourth floor or higher.

The skyline spread before her was sketched in curving domes that nestled together in groups, narrow spires spiking toward the sky, and less ambitious buildings that combined odd angles and made the golden light gleam brighter against the deep shadows. Reflecting off the glazed tiled roofs and arched windows, the gilded light seemed almost tangible, oozing over the city, the color near to that of the honey her mother's bees produced on their estate. The shining city looked like something half-imagined, a glimpse of a place that belonged in a dream. Or perhaps a nightmare.

She suppressed a shiver and turned back to the room. The chiming continued, growing more urgent in tone. The light revealed no clue as what the source of the sound might be. Eloisa's palace had a system of bells that could be used to summon servants, but there was no sign of anything like the levers that operated those.

While she searched, the volume of the chime increased again. Cameron was glaring around the room, looking far from awake, dark hair spiking up in all directions, and his blue eyes slitted. "Make it stop."

"If you can tell me what's causing it, that would be a good first step," she retorted.

He grimaced. "Goddess knows in this place."

"Maybe—" She broke off as a knock—loud but somehow politely cautious—sounded.

She looked at Cameron.

He shrugged. "If they were coming to do anything bad to us, I doubt they'd knock."

"Maybe that's what they want us to think," she said with more bravado than she felt. She tugged one of the many layers of quilts off the bed and wrapped it around her shift in lieu of taking the time to dress. She moved to the door and put her hand against the wood to take down the wards so she could open it.

Willem stood on the other side, his pale curls flattened back against his head by wont of being wet. "Madame Mackenzie," he said. "I came to collect you and your *mari* for breakfast. I have been waiting for an age. Did you not hear the chimes?" He spoke mostly Anglish again, for which she was thankful.

She shook her head apologetically. "We heard them. We didn't know what they were."

Willem looked puzzled. "We use the chimes to request entry when a room is warded. It is not always wise to knock on a warded door, no?"

"I suppose not," she said, feeling slightly foolish that such a simple thing had not occurred to her. "But we don't use such a system where we are from."

"Anglions must be brave," Willem said, looking as though he thought perhaps "crazy" was the correct term.

The fact that most Anglions didn't ward their doors at all—either from lack of magic or lack of need for such protections—didn't seem like a thing to mention. Willem had clearly never contemplated such a situation. Which meant she needed to remember not to knock on any doors here without checking for wards first. Another reminder she was no longer in a familiar—or safe—place. "Perhaps you would show us how to work the chimes?"

He nodded at her politely. "After breakfast, please. I shall wait while you dress. The meal will be underway, but we can still eat if we are quick."

There didn't seem to be any hint of whether or not to partake in breakfast being a choice, and it was clear that it was Willem's priority just now, so Sophie merely returned the nod and closed the door.

"Well, I guess this means the emperor hasn't sent a troop of soldiers to take us into custody," she said, trying to sound cheerful.

Cameron paused in the middle of buttoning his trousers. "Not yet, at least." Then he smiled. "I think the best plan is to just take one thing at a time for now. Food first. Then we can start to make a plan." He picked up his shirt and drew it over his head.

Despite her continued nerves, she couldn't deny that her stomach was demanding food, so she followed his example. The resulting outfit of rumpled, travel-worn gray dress and hastily pinned hair was hardly impressive, and she was uncomfortably aware that neither she nor the dress smelled particularly pleasant. But it was the best she could do at short notice. Cameron needed a shave and his clothes were as wrinkled as hers, so at least they were a matched pair.

When they rejoined Willem in the hallway, he beamed happily at them. "Very good," he said. "Now, breakfast. This way."

They set off at a fast walk that Sophie suspected would be closer to a run were Willem on his own and late for breakfast. He looked younger this morning with his hair still damp. She judged him to be thirteen, maybe fourteen. At that age, every boy she'd ever known had been preoccupied with food, eating quantities fit to feed armies. Which explained the pace he set as they moved down the lengthy hallway to the nearest set of stairs.

Unlike the previous evening, she was awake enough to pay attention to her surroundings and the route they were taking through the building. Thick carpet muffled their footsteps, the patterns woven through the muted green and gray shades forming sprays of delicate filigree that it seemed almost a crime to walk on. The walls were fashioned from paneled wood for the first four feet or so from the floor, then changed to broad tiled borders for several feet more before changing again to plain painted plaster. The tiles were, like the carpet, covered in small, carefully detailed patterns that grew more vivid in shades as they progressed up the wall. The plaster above the tiles in the corridor where they walked was a bright leafy shade of green, but as they descended the stairs to the next floor, the paint, and the predominant colors in the tiles and carpet, changed to a deep blue. Did the colors indicate something? Was it rude to ask? Perhaps it would be wiser to start with a different line of inquiry first. "No ravens today?"

Willem shook his head. "They will be breakfasting, too. In the Raven Tower."

"The Raven Tower?"

"Where the rookery is." He looked at her curiously, clearly wondering how anyone could not know such a basic fact.

"You breed the birds?" Cameron asked.

Willem nodded. "Yes. Ours are the best. Some take wild crows or other animals as fams, but the Academe ravens are prized." He turned at the bottom of the staircase and started down another long corridor. "The young ones not yet bonded or the breeding pairs who have fledglings and are not with their masters—if they have such—are cared for in the rookery."

She supposed it was no different from raising chickens or ducks or geese. But for some reason, the thought of large numbers of the big black birds in one place was disturbing. All those sharp beaks and claws. But she didn't think Willem would appreciate that particular thought so she merely smiled at him.

As they reached the next staircase, there was a squawk and a flap of wings above them and then a bird settled on Willem's shoulder, twisting its head to peer at Sophie. She thought, though she could not be certain, that it was the same one—Tok

—from the previous night. If not him, then another young one, something about it a little ungainly—if a bird could be said to be such a thing—that told her it was not yet full grown.

She nodded at it as it studied her, and it tilted its head and cawed back but, to her relief, didn't move from its perch.

Willem twisted his head to frown at the bird. "Tok, you should be in the tower."

The raven cawed again, fluffing its feathers, claws denting the fabric of Willem's robe forcefully enough that she wondered why it didn't tear.

"If you're hungry later, don't blame me," Willem muttered, twisting his head toward the bird as he walked.

Tok made no reply, merely bobbed his head and settled his feathers before fixing his gaze on Sophie.

Sophie tried to ignore the bird and the intensity of its gaze. The walls on this floor were a cheerful yellow but otherwise similar in design to the ones above them. Very different from the stone walls, softened by silk hangings and tapestries, that she was used to in the palace in Kingswell. And Anglion houses generally had wooden floors and small rugs, the walls painted white. They echoed—the sounds of those living in them plain to anyone in the house. Here, however, the carpets muffled their footsteps and, it seemed, most signs of habitation. There were no telltale noises to suggest that there were any other humans anywhere in the entire Academe. The silence and the unfamiliar surroundings made her skin prickle uneasily.

She could, however, smell hot bread, fried meat, and something greenly herbal in the air. Apparently the demands of her body were winning over the undercurrent of fear that threaded her stomach. She was starving. In this very moment, she'd happily have taken food from anyone—even a demon—if it would ease the gnawing in her belly.

"How many students are there at the Academe?" Cameron asked from beside her.

Willem shrugged. "Somewhere around one thousand."

Sophie halted, startled. "So many? All . . . wizards?"

"Not all of us," said a dry voice from behind her.

Sophie spun on her heel. A woman dressed in the same swirling black robes as Willem—though hers seemed to be made of a much finer fabric—had stepped out of one of the many doors lining the corridor and was pulling it closed behind her. She laid her hand against the wood and then clucked to herself before turning back to Sophie.

Her hair was silvery. Not the white blond of Willem's, but rather the true silver of age. Her face was very pale, the years written on it in an infinite number of fine wrinkles. She cocked her head, bright blue eyes fastened on Sophie's face. Her hands gripped the handle of a black cane but she didn't seem to be leaning on it heavily.

"Madame Simsa," Willem said from behind Sophie in a tone that suggested he was nervous.

The old woman's gaze didn't move. "I know my name, Willem. What I don't know are the names of our . . . guests?"

"This is Lord and Lady Scardale," Willem said. "From—"

"Anglion. I have eyes in my head, child."

Did their clothes so clearly mark them as Anglion? Yes, many of the people they'd seen as they'd passed through the streets of Lumia on the previous day had been wearing bright colors, but there'd also been a good number dressed in sensible, sturdy working clothes in duller shades. Sophie would have thought hers and Cameron's fell into that category. Admittedly, they were currently looking somewhat worse for wear, but that shouldn't give them away.

Could Madame Simsa, like the demon who'd answered the Academe door on their arrival, sense something about their magic? Either that or she had a sanctii whispering in her ear. A sanctii not currently visible. Sophie fought the urge to step back and put a little more distance between herself and the older woman.

Willem had addressed the woman as Madame, but somehow

Sophie doubted that was the whole truth of it. This woman had some sort of power.

"Venable." She bobbed a shallow, cautious curtsy, keeping her gaze on Madame Simsa. There was intelligence and confidence in her blue eyes. The expression of someone used to commanding respect. Here at the Academe that had to mean being a magic user of some kind. A strong one. Not that Sophie could sense Venable Simsa using any magic. Back in Kingswell, she had been able to feel the chill of Illvyan magic amidst the damaged stones of the palace, but here she couldn't isolate the same sensation. Maybe because she was surrounded by that very magic? She deepened the curtsy. Politeness seemed wise.

Particularly when she had no idea how the hierarchy of the Academe—or indeed all of Illvya—might work. The age-white of Venable Simsa's hair left no clue as to what magics she might wield. The Arts of Air and the blood magic that battle mages like Cameron wielded didn't mark their users like earth magic did, but working with the demon sanctii did—as the black streaks mingled with red in Chloe de Montesse's hair had proven. But perhaps those faded with time. Earth witches' hair eventually turned gray like anyone else, though more slowly, unless they were particularly strong. Which in Anglion currently meant only a few of the royal witches.

Venable Simsa nodded in return, not denying the title. "Lady Scardale." Her eyes flicked to Cameron. "Lord Scardale." Her mouth quirked and she gestured to herself, the movement making the fabric of her robes gleam briefly, a hint of color rippling over the black like light catching a raven's wing. "As you can see, we are not all wizards here."

"So the Academe teaches all of the Four Arts?" Cameron asked.

"Just so." Her gaze sharpened and Sophie felt like she was being examined from the inside out.

"Still, one thousand students is a large number," Cameron said.

It was. The Red Guard might have close to a thousand blood mages, but she didn't think there were anything like that many earth witches in Anglion. Not those with power enough to do anything above herb witchery anyway. Nor were there so many brothers of the Arts of Air. And those here at the Academe were just the current crop of students. How many mages were there across Illvya and the empire?

"Younglings, many of them," Venable Simsa said, flicking a hand as though to dismiss Cameron's assertion. "Like Willem here. Remind me how old you are, Willem?"

"Fourteen, Madame," Willem replied promptly, with a small bow. "Not so young."

"You start learning magic younger than that?" Sophie said. "That is a long time to study something without knowing if you will have any power at the end of it."

That earned a shrug of Venable Simsa's black-clad shoulder. "We believe in giving students a good grounding. Magic is safer if those who wield it know what they're about."

"And what happens to those who do not manifest?"

"We do not only teach magic here," came the reply. "Our students study many things. They get the same education as normal students in languages and literature and mathematics and such. As well as some more advanced subjects for those who show an aptitude for a particular topic. We do not believe in keeping our population ignorant. Those students who fail to manifest any power go on to have useful occupations. Advocates and scholars and engineers. That sort of thing."

"I see," Sophie said, though she didn't entirely. She didn't even know what an advocate might be. Behind her, Tok cawed, there was a rustling whistle of feathers, and then the bird thumped onto her shoulder. She went still and Venable Simsa smiled.

"The bird likes you."

"So it would seem."

"Good breeding, that one. He will be a good familiar."

"Earth witches don't use familiars," Sophie protested before she could think. "At least not in Anglion."

The smile widened. "Ah. But you are not merely an earth witch, are you, child?"

"I—" Sophie stopped. There was no obvious answer to that particular statement. Or to the challenge in those blue eyes that for a moment seemed to shine with a rainbow gleam.

From behind them a bell rang several times.

"Breakfast is almost over," Willem said. "Madame, excuse us. Maistre Matin asked me to escort the lord and lady to eat and then to his study."

"And no one must keep the maistre waiting, I suppose," Madame Simsa said with an edge to the words. "All right, on your way. Though you should send the bird back to the rookery. He is too young to behave himself in the dining hall. And someone might take it amiss if he steals their sausages."

Tok squawked in what sounded like a protest at this and Sophie nearly smiled at the indignant tone. Willem smiled outright, glancing at Sophie.

"No one would dare harm a feather of one of our ravens," he said. But he inclined his head toward Venable Simsa. "I will try to convince him. But he is not likely to listen."

"Not if he's got his eye on Lady Scardale here, no," Venable Simsa agreed with a nod. She moved her attention to the bird and made a swift shooing gesture. "Off with you. The lady will still be here in a few hours. One hopes. And if you are, Lady Scardale, come and find me."

Tok's claws dug into Sophie's shoulders and she thought the bird was going to ignore the command. But then he launched into the air, circling their heads with one last protesting caw before he swooped over the venable's head and disappeared down the hall, heading back in the direction they had come from. Venable Simsa, it seemed, was not to be disobeyed. Even by a raven. Sophie filed that piece of information away and bobbed another curtsy before turning to hurry after Willem, who was once again in motion.

Willem hustled them along until they arrived at a pair of huge wooden doors, standing open at the end of one of the corridors. Judging by the noise issuing from within, this was the dining room. As they stepped across the threshold into a room startling in its sheer size, the dull roar of voices felt almost like a blow after the silence of the corridors.

One thousand students, Sophie reminded herself as she stared down the length of the room. It was nearly as large as the Salt Hall in the palace in Kingswell had been before it had been destroyed. But rather than a grand palatial structure like the Salt Hall, this was merely a very large room filled with rows of long tables. It was more simply decorated than any of the rooms she had seen in the Academe so far. The walls were white, the floor tiled in black and white.

That was about all she had time to take in. The shock of the sound hitting them didn't last long. It took no more than a second or two for quiet to descend as the attention of those gathered along the lines of long tables focused on the trio standing in the doorway.

The absence was as startling as the wall of sound had been. In the depths of the silence, Sophie was abruptly aware of the hum of the ley line far beneath her feet, its subtle vibrations filling her mind like the purr of a large but very distant cat. Other than when she and Cameron had strengthened the wards in their room, she hadn't yet paid much attention to the power of this place.

She was used to the sensation of ley lines now, of magic running beneath the earth. After all, the palace at Kingswell was built over several of them, as were most important buildings in Anglion. Obviously the Illvyan architects took advice from their wizards as well. The ley lines in Anglion had felt like rivers of power running beneath the ground. This one felt more like the

sea they had crossed to reach Illvyan. Deep and full of hidden
dangers. She couldn't quite shake the sensation that it wanted her
to dive into its depths. Or that she might be engulfed if she did.

The hum of conversation starting up again shook her out of
her reverie and she blinked. Many heads were still turned toward
them, and the sounds had the tone of whispered questions and
speculation.

Not so different from a dinner at court.

And she knew how to handle a court. Keep your smile polite,
your words careful, and your thoughts and emotions to yourself.
She squared her shoulders, arranged her face in the polite,
neutrally friendly expression she had perfected during her years
as a lady in waiting, and gazed back at those staring at her. Quite
a few of them looked away.

Willem had apparently spotted an empty table or people he
knew, because he pointed at a spot somewhere off to the right
and then began to move rapidly in that direction. She slanted a
glance at Cameron, who merely smiled and offered his arm.
Together they followed in Willem's wake, passing between two
of the rows of the long, solid tables.

With every table they passed, the whispers behind them
grew louder. Sophie's spine prickled, the sensation of all those
eyes watching her tangible. Almost everyone in the room wore
the loose black robes as Willem and Madame Simsa did,
covering whatever clothes they wore underneath. She thought
she caught a few glimpses of color at the throats of some but she
couldn't be sure. Passing through the sea of black was like
moving through a frozen flock of ravens. If ravens could grow to
be human-sized. Which didn't make the experience any less
unnerving.

Ahead, Willem had found a mostly empty table. The man
and woman already seated looked as though they didn't know
whether to stay or go, expressions frozen in odd half smiles. Was
it wrong to hope they would leave? She wanted to ask Willem if

he knew why the maistre wanted to see them, but she wasn't going to do that in front of an audience.

"Good morning," Cameron said in Illvyan.

Or she thought that was what he said. Her Illvyan was not as fluent as his, but just then she didn't think she could have spoken a word of it if she'd tried, nerves driving all memory of the language from her head. Still, she smiled at the two strangers as they returned Cameron's greeting, then took the chair that Willem held out for her.

The woman sitting opposite her, who looked like she was Sophie's age or perhaps a little younger, smiled tentatively back. Her golden hair—a shade rare in Anglion—was tied back in a precisely elegant arrangement of braids that made Sophie wish she'd had more time to bathe. She resisted the urge to tug at the wrinkled sleeve of her dress, wishing she had one of the all-enveloping black robes to cover the state of her clothes.

The man seated beside the golden-haired woman had bright blue eyes and dark hair. He rubbed his close-cropped beard with one hand, the other hovering near the edge of the table. For a moment, Sophie thought he might be about to stand and leave, but then his posture eased and he said, "I am Simeon. This is Magritte."

Damn. They were going to stay. But at least he spoke Anglish. Which was a relief. Though that feeling dampened when she realized that his doing so meant word of who they were had spread. Apparently gossip traveled just as quickly in the Academe as in Kingswell.

"Hello," she said. "I'm Sophie. Sophie Mackenzie. This is my husband, Cameron." She didn't want to complicate things with titles.

Magritte's brows drew together. "I thought your name was Scardale. That's what—" She stopped speaking as Simeon nudged her with his elbow, the movement visible despite the cloaking folds of the robes.

Before she could begin to offer an explanation of titles versus personal names, Willem reappeared, a laden plate in each hand. The smell of warm bread, melted butter, and some sort of fried meat reached her nose and her stomach rumbled. She almost snatched the plate out of his hands as he offered it to her, only years of etiquette lessons preventing her from cramming the food into her mouth as fast as humanly possible. Instead she waited, hiding her impatience by reaching for the tea—she hoped it was tea—that Magritte had poured for her while Willem passed the second plate to Cameron and left to obtain his own meal.

She sipped the liquid. It was tea, though the same unfamiliar brew she'd had the night before. Tart yet faintly sweet.

Whatever it was, it was delicious and she drank gratefully, the heat and tang scalding away some of the foggy feeling from her head and easing the hunger pangs. She'd almost finished it by the time Willem returned, his plate piled higher than hers and Cameron's put together. The last two mouthfuls occupied her while the boy slid into a chair and picked up his knife and fork. Sophie took that as a sign that there were no further ceremonies to be observed before the meal could begin, reached for her own silverware, and applied herself to her meal.

When she was halfway through the pile of toast, fried ham, and some sort of green vegetable that tasted like a spicier version of spinach, her hunger began to ease. No longer quite so distracted by the food, she realized the Illvyan pair were watching her and Cameron with expressions somewhere between curiosity and wariness. Well enough, then. Perhaps it would be wiser to talk to them if she couldn't question Willem. She and Cameron needed knowledge. They may as well begin with the Academe itself, seeing as that was where they found themselves.

She put down her knife and fork reluctantly. She was still hungry, but perhaps it would be wiser to try and form some connection with others at the Academe than just continue to eat in silence.

"Are you students here?" she asked. With everyone they had met wearing the same dark robes, she had no idea how one might tell student from master other than age. Nor did she know how long Illvyan mages might train for before they were considered no longer students.

Simeon's brows lifted. "Can't you tell?"

"Should I be able to?" She returned his stare. In Anglion, she could feel when someone was using earth magic nearby or had set a ward, and earth witches were marked by their reddened hair, of course, but she hadn't been taught to know if someone had power merely by looking at them. "I mean, Willem, he is too young. But you and Magritte . . . I am not sure of your ages."

Or abilities. Magritte and Simeon both looked close to her own age. So they may have manifested or may not yet be twenty-one. But if Magritte was old enough to have power, then surely her hair would not be that shade? Or no, Sophie realized with a sudden start. They did not confine women to just earth magic here. Water magic—demon magic—was supposed to cause your hair to darken. But blood magic and the Arts of Air didn't mark their users in the same way as the other two forms. Nobody knew quite why. Magritte could very well have power. She should tread carefully.

Magritte said something under her breath in Illvyan that Sophie thought might have meant "barbarian," but she wasn't entirely certain. "You do not know how to look for a connection to a ley line?"

Cameron, who had emptied his plate, answered before Sophie could. "That isn't something earth witches do in Anglion."

Magritte raised her eyebrows. "Then how do they work together?"

"They do not need to," Cameron replied. Sophie assumed he was trying to imply Anglion witches were strong enough not to need to work together. Not true. The temple devouts and priors did. But that training was limited to those dedicated to the goddess. She'd never thought why that might be before. Though, if Cameron had decided not to share the information, she would keep it to herself for now.

"How . . . interesting." Magritte's voice suggested "interesting" was more like "backward" or "ridiculous." Sophie focused on her food and sipped more tea, trying not to react. She found it strange here. So the Illvyans would find her strange, too. That was only natural. And keeping the conversation polite was more likely to yield information.

"You didn't tell us what you were studying, Magritte," Cameron continued. Magritte smiled at him, Sophie noticed.

"She is not yet of age," Willem said as he drained his tea. "So she does not know yet what she will be."

This earned him a look from Magritte that would have turned his tea stone-cold if he had not yet finished with it. He ignored her and forked up the last of his food.

"Such an uncertain time," Sophie said, trying to look sympathetic rather than indignant. If Magritte had not yet manifested, then she could no more see a connection to a ley line than Sophie herself could. "It is hard to be on one side of the door and never know if it will open. I was nervous before my Ais-Seann."

"Unnecessarily," Cameron added, putting his hand over hers. "My wife comes from a strong line of magic."

Magritte looked down at her plate. Perhaps she was reconsidering the assumptions she had made about Sophie and Anglions.

That was probably a good thing. Cameron was somewhat overstating things. Yes, she was of the royal line, but Sophie was the strongest witch to come out of her particular branch of it in recent years. In decades, in truth. Another fact she thought she should keep to herself. Along with her place in the Anglion royal succession, which currently stood at sixth in line. Unless, of course, Queen Eloisa had struck her from the line of succession altogether.

Was that possible? Lineage was lineage, after all.

It was a moot point for now. Any claim to the throne she might have didn't matter here. It wouldn't matter anywhere if she never returned to Anglion.

What mattered was surviving the day and starting to make a plan for their future. She opened her mouth to ask Simeon what he was studying when Willem cut her off by announcing that they should go, the maistre was expecting them. She couldn't help feeling frustrated that she couldn't have time to learn more but rose anyway. Whatever Henri Matin wanted from them, it was probably more important than anything Magritte or Simeon could divulge.

CHAPTER 3

Sophie was beginning to regret having eaten so quickly by the time they entered Maistre Matin's office. The food sat uneasily in her stomach as her nerves returned, the hairs on the back of her neck prickling. Her fingers itched to try to rub the sensation away, but her time at court had taught her to hide discomforts and emotions at times when it was not proper to display them. So she kept her hands folded in front of her. Propriety may not have much relevance to the current situation, not when all the rules of protocol and behavior she knew were Anglish, but one of the steadfast rules of navigating court politics was to never give away any more information than you had to. A rule that seemed to apply equally well to situations in which you had no idea if you were safe or not.

Maistre Matin waited for both of them to enter before he closed the door and then gestured them toward the fireplace. The fire, burning steadily, cracked and sent a small spark flying through the space between them. Sophie watched its path toward the beautifully woven rug at their feet but it suddenly winked out of existence when it was a few inches from the floor. The sensation on the back of her neck intensified, turning to a

definite chill, like a finger of ice sliding down her skin. Had
Maistre Matin done something to stop the ember, or had it been
his demon sanctii? Demons could walk unseen through a room.
There could be fifty of them in the room with them for all
she knew.

Hardly a reassuring thought.

With no way of knowing if she was being observed by
demons, she looked around the room. She'd formed only a vague
impression of the maistre's study the night before, too intent on
securing their safety to notice much else. In fact, the whole
memory of standing there the previous evening speaking to
Henri Matin felt more like a dream than reality. Then again,
almost everything that had happened to her since they had run
felt unreal.

Today, she set herself to paying closer attention. To taking in
this new place they had to adapt to. The room was warm from
the fire, other than the lingering chill on her neck. Carved
wooden shelves lined the walls, stuffed to bursting with leather-
bound books and papers. The curtains had been drawn back, the
sunlight streaming in, revealing the colors of the furniture and
carpets to be deep grays and dark blues.

In her memory they were black, the chairs and the curtains
and the rug beneath her feet. But today the only black things in
the room were the robes the maistre wore, and in the daylight,
even those seemed to have the faintest sheen, an iridescent swirl
she wasn't entirely sure was there, just like Madame Simsa
had had.

She curtsied to him as Cameron bowed. "Maistre Matin," she
said, speaking Illvyan. She needed the practice. The words came
that time, unlike in the dining hall, but still unfamiliar and
ungainly on her tongue. To her ear, her accent was passable.
Which probably meant it was dire to a native speaker. "I bid you
good morning."

Henri's pale eyes—so unlike the deep dark brown of his
daughter's—regarded her steadily, an uncomfortable gaze. It was

difficult not to feel that he knew exactly what she was thinking. Perhaps he did. "Good morning, Lady Scardale," he said. "I am happy to see you looking more refreshed this day."

"Thank you," she said. This was a game she was familiar with. The polite small talk of courts and, it seemed, academies of wizards. She schooled herself to stillness. Reached for that court-schooled poise she'd never been entirely sure she'd mastered.

"Was your room quite satisfactory?" Maistre Matin inquired.

"Yes, Maistre. Thank you."

"And you slept well?"

"Yes." The smile she directed at him was calm. "The room was very comfortable."

He looked pleased. She had no idea why. He was master of the Academe but she doubted he had much involvement in choosing the furnishings of its guest rooms.

But perhaps he was only being polite. Still, this man was the father of Chloe de Montesse. Chloe, who had fled to Anglion and managed to thrive as a refugee, in the very capital of a hostile land. She was smart and resourceful and—Sophie had no doubt—powerful, though she was careful not to use her powers in any way that would go badly for her in Anglion. And this man had raised her.

"You are most welcome. And now that we have satisfied the niceties of conversation, perhaps you would be seated and we can discuss more important topics at hand?"

Ah. Perhaps academies of wizards were not quite so polite after all. She smoothed her skirt carefully, watching Henri as he motioned her to a chair. Not what he seemed. She must remember that. Very little here could be as it seemed, and she was in a precarious position for all the maistre's seeming affability.

Trying to look composed, she sent a thread of power down, seeking the security of the ley line. Deep and unknown as it was, it was still less daunting than facing one of the wizards she had been taught to fear all her life. The line was there, a slow pulse beneath her feet. But unlike in their chamber, here her connection to its power felt tenuous at best. As though there was a thick wall of glass between her and the power, blocking her access.

Wards.

Wards laid, most likely, by Henri Matin.

A man who had at least one demon sanctii at his beck and call.

One who may very well be in the room with them, watching unseen.

If the tales of her childhood were to be believed, a demon could kill a man in seconds.

The water magic—demon magic—had been banned in Anglion for a reason. And the destruction of part of the palace back in Kingswell was a reminder of why. Demon magic came with chaos and mayhem. The wizards supposedly had control of the demons, but now and then one might slip free of their restraints.

Free to kill at will.

Sowing disaster and death. Requiring more death to bring them back to heel.

That was supposedly what had happened centuries ago in Anglion. Casting out the water mages the first time was the way Eloisa's family had come to power.

It had taken the combined powers of all the magic wielders of the court and had cost more than that.

But in the end Anglion had been freed.

So the stories had said.

Of course, in the stories, the Temple didn't try to kill royal witches. So who knew what she could believe.

If she couldn't trust what she could believe, then she would try a different approach. Start with what she knew. Build on that knowledge. Then she would be able to determine a plan. Find a way to survive. To keep her and Cameron alive.

Starting now.

Settling her hands into her lap, she made herself smile again at Henri. "What was it you wished to discuss, Maistre?"

"Any number of topics comes to mind, Lady Scardale," Henri replied, switching back to Anglish. He turned his attention to Cameron, who was hesitating beside her chair. "Please, Lord Scardale. Sit. We may as well be comfortable in body for this conversation."

Meaning what? That it was going to be uncomfortable in other ways? Sophie tightened her grip on the thin thread that was all she could touch of the ley line. What exactly she, half-trained and now outcast, might do against a master wizard of Illvya was a question she didn't want to think too hard about. Still, between her earth magic and Cam's blood magic, perhaps they could at least do some damage if they were attacked.

"Have you heard from the emperor?" she asked as Cam settled into the chair beside hers after pointedly moving it several inches nearer to her. The emperor seemed the most likely reason for them to be summoned to meet with the maistre again so quickly.

"No," Henri said. "I sent a messenger to the palace earlier. The message has been received but so far, I have not received a response."

"Is that usual?" Cameron asked.

Henri shrugged. "The emperor is not a hasty man, as a rule. I think if he has not sent for you by now, then it will likely be a few days."

And what, exactly, did he need those few days for?

Cameron didn't look happy with the news. "But he will send for us?"

"Almost certainly," Henri said.

"And in the meantime?" Sophie asked.

"That is what we shall discuss. That and other matters."

That wasn't exactly reassuring. It would be nice to know that Henri was on their side.

"You said you wanted news of Chloe," Sophie said. "Perhaps we could start there."

Chloe de Montesse had never told Sophie much of her relationship with her parents or of her past in Illvya other than her husband had been killed before she had fled Illvya. The fact that she'd chosen to flee to Anglion, where she would be treated with suspicion for life as an Illvyan refugee and marked as a free witch by the colors of her hair, suggested that however her husband had died, it was in a manner that the powers that be in Illvya did not approve of. One that might bring repercussions to his wife.

Had her husband been a traitor? The thought hadn't occurred to Sophie before. Perhaps Henri was not a father seeking news of his daughter but the maistre of the Academe, seeking news of a renegade. After all, a man as powerful as he should surely have been able to protect his daughter when she needed such protection.

Hopefully none of this sudden torrent of speculation running through her brain was apparent to Henri. If it was, he showed no reaction, merely inclined his head and steepled his fingers in front of his mouth. If he was trying to look as though news of his daughter was of little import, the spark of eagerness in his pale eyes betrayed him.

"Chloe was well when we left Kingswell. She was not harmed in the attack, and no sanctions or punishments were being imposed on Illvyan refugees." That she was aware of. Cameron might know more but he was apparently keeping his counsel.

Tall, dark, and silent. She'd forgotten that had been how she had once categorized her husband. She knew a different side of him now, but apparently he could still play the stone-faced warrior when required.

She might need that side of him now. Intimidation and bluff were probably how they were going to survive, if indeed they were going to survive. If they didn't, it wasn't going to be because she hadn't tried to avoid that fate. If she'd wanted to die, she could have taken the easy path and remained in Anglion. Or not fought off the assassin sent to kill her.

"And before that?" Henri asked, leaning closer.

Sophie chose her words carefully. "I have only come to know your daughter recently, Maistre. But she has a business of her own in Kingswell. She is prospering."

"Why did you not know her before?"

"Your daughter's store provides magical supplies, Maistre," Cam said. "My wife only recently reached her Ais-Seann. She had no need of such things. Besides which, women of her rank do not tend to frequent the port. That is where Madame De Montesse has her store. It is in a good street but not somewhere the palace ladies often choose to venture."

"Madame de Montesse," Henri said musingly. "She has not remarried, then?"

"I am not aware that she has a husband," Sophie said. If Chloe was married, she was keeping the man well hidden. And indeed, it would take a brave man to marry an Illvyan free witch in Kingswell. She wondered if the maistre was testing them. Anglion had always been full of rumors that Illvya had spies in the capital. In most parts of the country, even. Did Henri already know about Chloe and just wanted to see if they would tell the truth? "But she seems content."

His expression was both pleased and a little sad, she judged. Which suggested that perhaps he was, indeed, a worried parent rather than the master of wizards, hunting down a wayward witch.

"Thank you, Lady Scardale," he said. "That is . . . a comfort to hear. Chloe always forged her own path. Nothing anyone else could say would ever dissuade her from a plan once she had formulated it. It is hard to have her be somewhere where so little word reaches us. But it will please my wife to have this news. As it pleases me."

"So little word." Not "no word." She wondered where exactly he obtained his information. From whoever the emperor's spies in Anglion were? Or whoever controlled them here, perhaps. Some news obviously traveled between the two countries. Henri had known who they were when they'd arrived. But if the emperor did have spies in Kingswell, she couldn't imagine that he would waste their time on Illvyan refugees who were causing no trouble. No, they would be trying to find out what was happening at court, amongst those with power. "I am glad to be of help. Chloe was always kind to me."

"Was she the one who helped you get to Illvya?" Henri asked, then pursed his lips, holding up a hand with forefinger extended. "Perhaps it is wisest if you do not tell me such things."

"That seems safest," Cameron agreed.

He had been watching their exchange, blue eyes wary. She'd caught him glancing around the room, as much as he could without moving to give his reconnaissance away. Had he the same thoughts about demons as she did?

"Then I suppose that brings us to our next topic of conversation," Henri said.

"Which is?" Cam asked, his voice less friendly.

"What exactly we are going to do with the two of you, of course. You are not naïve, Lord Scardale. Not as young as your wife." He inclined his head to Sophie as if in apology. "I do not mean offense, my lady, but you are new to your power."

"I was Queen Eloisa's lady-in-waiting for several years before I reached my majority, Maistre," Sophie said. "I have lived in the court for all that time. I am not totally inexperienced."

"Ah, so. Yes. But being a lady of the queen—or the crown princess, as she was—offers a degree of protection in a stable court such as the Anglion one has been for some time now. You will find our politics somewhat more . . . robust."

Sophie blinked. "I thought your emperor ruled the entire continent."

"He does," Henri said. "But one man cannot oversee such an empire alone. His Imperial Majesty has a tight grasp on the reins of power, but those reins are attached to many steeds, so to speak. Ministers of parliament. The officers of his armies. The governors of his countries. It can make things complicated."

"I will confess, Maistre," Sophie said. "I do not fully understand what exactly a parliament is." She had been taught to fear the might of the emperor of Illvya, but her education had neglected any details of how exactly he ruled his empire. It had discussed the strength of his army and his mages, not his bureaucracy. And at that moment she would take any scrap of knowledge about either that she could gather.

"In Anglion, your queen has advisors, no? As did her father before her?"

"Yes. But they are advisors only. She does not have to take their advice."

Henri chuckled. "Yes, well. That is perhaps not so different. The trouble is our empire is large, so the number of advisors required to bring the emperor knowledge of all the different lands and their attendant issues is likewise large. So that is the role of the parliament. They represent the people. Both those who have a seat by virtue of title or rank, and those who are appointed by their localities."

"But your parliament does not just advise. It also makes laws, doesn't it?" Cameron asked.

Apparently, the Red Guard educated its officers better in the politics of Anglion's enemy than her tutors had her.

"It can propose laws, but ultimately the emperor approves or disapproves them."

Cameron nodded. "And if he disapproves?" Apparently her husband shared her desire to understand Illvya better.

"Usually the law is revised until his disapproval is reduced. Or until the parliament decides they do not wish to pursue the battle." Henri looked amused. "After all, the emperor has more cards up his sleeve than they do. Ultimately his armies are sworn to him. And then, of course, there are his magic users."

"Are you sworn to the emperor as well?" Sophie asked.

"All Illvyan magic users make an oath to protect the land.

That is generally interpreted as protecting the crown as well. The parliament does not interfere in our business though, and we try not to interfere in theirs unless the situation warrants it. That usually means war. Or something similarly catastrophic."

That was a neat answer. One that did not precisely answer the question she had asked. A fact, she imagined, Henri was well aware of. She decided not to push. If they appeared too interested in any one particular aspect of Illvyan life, Henri might just decide to stop talking. "What about the temple? Where is the goddess in all of this?"

Henri smiled and offered another small shrug. "Well, that is the other thing about an empire, my lady—many countries equates to many beliefs. The earth witches still worship the goddess, of course, but you will find she does not hold such sway here as she does in Anglion."

"Does the temple have a representative in the parliament?" Sophie held her breath. She had no desire to cross paths with another domina intent on power.

"No. The most senior of the dominas, the one who presides over the main temple here in Lumia, comes to court, but I would say her influence is not particularly strong with the current emperor."

Which either meant he was not pious or he worshipped another deity.

"There are many rumors about your emperor. About what his powers may or may not be," Cameron said. The question at the end of that sentence hovered unspoken.

"That, Lord Scardale, is a question you will have to ask him," Henri said.

Another non-answer, Sophie noted.

Cameron nodded, smiling slightly as though he hadn't really expected an answer to the question. "Perhaps I will."

"Which rather brings us back to our topic. About how the two of you intend to occupy yourselves while you wait for His Imperial Majesty to decide what use he wishes to make of you."

Cameron's mouth flattened. "And if we don't wish to be made use of?"

"Then, as I see it, your options are to try to disappear into the empire and see if you can find somewhere where he will not find you. Or perhaps to return to Anglion, where he definitely will not pursue you."

"I'm not so sure about that," Cameron muttered.

"The emperor has larger plans in that direction than the pursuit of one stray witch and blood mage, I would imagine," Henri said.

"What if we do neither of those things?" Sophie asked. She didn't see how they could possibly return to Anglion. And as for the other, well, that would take planning. She imagined if they tried to run now, they would not make it very far. Not with so little knowledge of the empire. Better to be realistic. Or at least appear to be so.

"Then I imagine you will have to deal with His Imperial Majesty and whatever he decides he wants from you. And with what he makes of your explanations in relation to your . . . ambitions."

"I don't have any ambitions," Sophie said forcefully. The last thing she wanted was to be tangled up in still more politics.

Henri shook his head. "I believe, after what occurred in Kingswell, that may be a difficult position for you to convince anyone of. You are now one of those near the top of the line of succession for the Anglion throne, as I understand it. People will expect you to want what most of them want."

"And that is?"

"Power, my dear. Simply put. That is what they will see in you. In both of you. Power. Currently unleashed. Unattached. And perhaps uninformed." He pursed his lips. "In your place, Lady Scardale, I rather think the safest path would be to decide that a few years studying at the Academe was what I wanted."

Become a student? Why?

"Why?" Cameron asked, echoing her thoughts. He had edged forward on his seat.

"If you choose to devote yourself to studies, it would demonstrate that you are not trying to provoke anything. Or anyone. Students are generally not considered fair game in the court's machinations here. Or the parliament's. It is not a complete guarantee, of course—nothing in life is—but it is something to think about."

"Wouldn't studying here be a signal that I wanted to increase my powers?" Sophie asked.

"Perhaps. Most will view it as a sign that you are not wedded to Anglion teachings though. That you are open to other ways of thinking. That is more important, at least as an immediate concern."

"I see," Sophie said. It was tempting. To have more knowledge about her magic. Knowledge beyond what the temple in Anglion would teach her. Beyond that which the Domina had allowed her to know. Which Sophie suspected was less than other earth witches of the Anglion court. But studying Illvyan magic would make it a thousand times more difficult to return to Anglion. Besides which, there had to be advantage to Henri in him offering them the option. Particularly when he had brought it up so readily.

"Lord Scardale is also welcome to continue his studies. Blood mages are valued here."

"I never was much of a student," Cameron said, spreading his hands. "I may not be worth your time."

"You were good enough to be a member of the Red Guard, were you not? That shows some degree of skill. Besides, you may find it interesting to see how our methods differ. And, as I said, becoming a student here sends a message."

Cameron nodded. "We will consider your offer."

"Excellent, we can speak more later. But now I have other duties to attend. The Academe doesn't run itself, unfortunately. I shall have Martius escort you back to your rooms."

A demon? Sophie flinched, unable to control the reaction quickly enough to hide it.

Henri must have noticed her expression. "You will come to no harm from my fam," he said. "And if you are to stay here at the Academe, you must become accustomed to the familiaris sanctii. Petty fams, too. Those, in particular, you will find it hard to avoid." He made a peculiar gesture, an angled sweep of his hand down toward the floor. "Martius, show yourself."

Sophie felt a sudden chill, and then a creature like the one who'd greeted them at the door to the Academe last night stood before them.

It was several feet away but she could still feel the cold rising from its skin. Enough that she was somewhat surprised that it didn't steam slightly in the warm room. She hadn't noticed the same from the creature—what had Willem called it? Bel something? Belarus?—who'd answered the door the previous night, but she had been too exhausted to note much at all at that point.

Martius inclined its head toward her, gray and black mottled skin seeming to soak up some of the light in the room. When it straightened, the black eyes regarded her with something she might have called curiosity, though it was a little difficult to tell. The demon's features were humanlike but not human. There was no hair on its body, for a start. No eyebrows or lashes graced the bald head. And the features were blunter than a human's, the face full of rough planes rather than curves. A black tunic and pants hid most of its body but the muscular arms were bare. Its hands were large and strong, the nails gray. It was a forbidding sight. No less because it was studying her with those large liquid black eyes. What did the demon—no, sanctii. She had to remember that here. Calling these creatures demons in Illvya where they were accepted would not be wise. What did the sanctii think of her?

"Hello, Martius," she managed to say.

Martius' black lips peeled back in what was probably a smile, revealing silvery teeth. "Lady," it said. The voice was harsh, the low tones coming across as though the sounds of Illvyan did not quite suit its throat. It turned to Maistre Matin and said something in another, more guttural language, those words coming faster.

"Show them back to their chamber, please," Henri said, then added something in that same unknown language.

Cameron, on the other side of Henri, was watching this exchange, expression somewhat dubious. But apparently he realized they had little choice in the matter, as he merely moved to Sophie's side to offer her his arm, putting himself between her and the sanctii as they followed Martius out of the room.

"What do you want to do?" Cameron asked when they were back in their room.

Sophie turned from where she was checking the wards. They seemed unaltered, which was a relief. But she sank more power into them regardless, walking around the room, hoping movement would dispel some of the chill that seemed to have sunk into her bones as she had walked beside the sanctii through the halls of the Academe.

What did she want to do? It was a simple question but there was no simple answer. They had had little choice but to flee Anglion after an attempt on her life that she had been fairly certain had been ordered by the temple. And the temple meant Domina Skey, who was the highest representative of the goddess in Anglion.

Domina Skey, who also seemed to have gained the ear of the queen since the attack on the palace in a manner that no one else had managed. If the Domina was the one who wanted Sophie dead, then it was unlikely that they would have found safety anywhere in Anglion. Perhaps they could have found some tiny remote village and lived anonymously, but what kind of life would that be?

So they had fled, and now they were here. Where it seemed only more intrigue and trouble awaited them.

"I'm not sure I even know where to start thinking about what I want to do. Other than I'm wondering whether we have made things even more complicated than they were." She bit her lip, trying not to think that this was all her fault, but somehow she had brought this all upon them.

"Things became complicated when the palace was attacked," Cameron said. "Which wasn't our doing."

No. But what had come since was. If Cameron hadn't been forced to marry her, then he could be happily back in Anglion. Though that would also mean that he could be happily back in Eloisa's bed.

That thought made her shiver.

"Are you cold?"

"A little," she admitted.

"I can build up the fire."

She shook her head. The room was cozy enough, and the sunlight streaming through the windows added to the warmth. But it would take more than that to shake the ice from her skin. "The sanctii. It feels cold to me."

"Cold?" Cameron sounded puzzled.

"Like a chill in the air. Didn't you feel it?"

"I'm not sure," Cameron said. "You were closer to it than I was." He frowned. "Was it like the feeling you had in the palace? When you found the scriptii?"

She'd forgotten about that. It felt like months ago but in reality was it was only, what, three weeks perhaps? The fact that she'd sensed the scriptii that had caused—or been part of the cause—of the explosions that had destroyed part of the palace may have been the final straw in focusing the Domina's ire on Sophie. Not that Domina Skey had liked her before that. Not when Sophie had done what royal witches were never supposed to do and slept with a man before she was married. "Similar. But different. The scriptii felt dangerous. Wrong somehow."

"And the demon doesn't?"

"I don't know," Sophie said. "It's all too new. Its appearance is hardly reassuring, but I didn't get the feeling that it meant us any harm."

"Because Maistre Matin has it under his control," Cameron said. "Who knows what it might be capable of if that were not true?" His face twisted. Then he lifted one of the embroidered quilts from the bed and came over to wrap it around her shoulders. "Here, come sit down."

They perched together on the side of the bed. The sky beyond the barred windows was blue but the sunshine wasn't enough to lift her mood. Indeed, the peaceful sky only emphasized the fact that the city beneath it was an unknown one. Sophie tucked the quilt more tightly around her and leaned into Cameron. "I'm sorry."

"For what?"

"For dragging you into this."

"You did not drag me. I chose to come with you. I wanted to come with you. You're my wife." He slid his arm around her shoulders, drawing her close. She leaned into him, wanting the comfort of how he felt. Warm. Warmer than her. Real. Solid. She wanted to believe the certainty in his voice but it was hard. His life would be completely different if she'd never crossed his path.

"I just wish—"

Cameron's arm tightened. "My father used to tell me that wishing was pointless. That one has to act not hope. He may have been an arrogant bastard, but I think in this case, we should be taking his advice. We are in a situation that can't be wished away, regardless of what either of us may feel. So we have to deal with it."

She hoped he was talking about being in Illvya rather than being married to her. "I know."

"Which brings me back to the question, love, of what you want to do."

"If we had a choice, I'd rather live my life quietly with you somewhere. But I don't think we have that choice." She couldn't stop the small sigh that escaped her.

"No, it would seem not. Even if we were back in Anglion, we wouldn't be able to hide away."

"Then if we can't run, we have to fight for ourselves. And I think that, if we need to fight, then we need to be well-armed. To hone what strengths we have."

"You want to stay here at the Academe and study, then," Cameron said. It wasn't a question.

"I think it's our best option, don't you?" She twisted to look up at his steady blue eyes. "Unless we're going to try to run back to Anglion right away. And I don't see how we can. Unless Chloe helpfully told you how to return? Or Captain Jensen?"

Cameron shrugged. "Chloe, no. The captain . . . well, let's say he mentioned there may be ways to contact him. But we'd need a head start to make it back to the coast and I don't think we'd get one here. Not with demons surrounding us, and wizards using magic we don't understand. I doubt we'd get more than half a mile once someone raised the alarm if we tried to leave."

"So we stay, then." She felt more certain as she said the words, even though her stomach still churned. "And we learn. As much as we can. About magic. About Illvya and the empire. So no one can control us."

"You realize that, if you become a stronger witch, it's only going to make you more of a prize?"

"If I become a stronger witch, then anyone who tries to take me as a prize is going to have to pay a price."

"And when the emperor decides to take an interest in us?" Cameron said.

She shook her head, frustrated. That was the unknown in this plan, what the emperor would do. Or how long they might have until he decided. "Until we know what he wants from us, that's hard to plan for. I think it's best to just focus on learning what we can before then. After . . . well, we can make a new plan. But for now, we need information. And I need more training. So this is the best place for us. Besides, perhaps they can help us understand the bond. How it is I can do blood magic." She looked up at him, struck by a thought. "Maybe whether you can do earth magic."

Cameron frowned. "It may be safer to stay within the bounds of what we know. If you dabble in other magics, then it will be very hard for us to return home."

"Illvyan refugees are not unheard of." Chloe was one, for a start.

"Illvyan refugees. Not Anglions who have gone to the land of the enemy and returned having consorted with demons."

"Hardly consorting." She had no desire to go any closer to any of the sanctii than she had to.

"That's not how the Domina would view it," Cameron said. "Besides which, the average Illvyan refugee is not one of the heirs to the throne."

"I'd rather not be an heir," Sophie said. "The Domina should be happy if I disqualify myself." The Domina was rarely happy about anything to do with Sophie, however. Least of all something she would clearly view as heresy.

"Perhaps. But our families are still in Anglion. I, for one, do not want to give up the chance to get back to them one day."

Guilt twinged again. He was right. She couldn't only think of herself. Or even only of Cameron. There were other people affected by their flight from Anglion. Her parents. Her brothers. Cameron's brothers and their families. People they both loved. If they wanted to be able to see them again, they needed to consider each step they took carefully. "All right," she agreed. "Then earth magic for me. Blood magic for you. Learning about the empire for both of us. The bond, well, that can wait for now. Maybe we can discover more about it on our own."

CHAPTER 4

C ameron watched Sophie straighten her shoulders under the quilt and tried to ignore the sensation of a door closing firmly behind them.

"Agreed," he said. It was a choice. Perhaps not the right one —though only time would reveal that—but a choice. And, in truth, there were no truly good choices in this situation. Only the choice to stay with Sophie and work to make sure they survived. That one day they could have a life that held a greater resemblance to normality than the one that currently lay before them.

He was about to become a student at the Academe di Sages —Maison Corbie, as the Illvyans called it affectionately. Which was something he'd never even thought of imagining, so far was it from the realm of things that were possible or even desirable when he'd been safely back in Anglion.

But they were in Illvya now.

Alive despite the best attempts of their unknown enemies.

He intended to stay that way.

Intended to keep Sophie alive, too.

She still had shadows under her eyes, the darkness draining

some of the golden glow from her skin. Tired from their head-long flight. As he was, too.

The quilt she'd pulled around her shoulders was a rich blue that should have suited her. Instead it served to emphasize how exhausted she looked.

She shivered again, despite the enveloping folds of the quilt, and he made a decision.

First things first.

They needed to tell Maistre Matin of their decision and, after that, there were a hundred details to determine and questions to ask. But now, looking at the edges of Sophie's battered gray dress peeking out from beneath the quilt—and, as he moved to tuck the quilt around her and caught a whiff of stale sweat and salt and smoke wafting from his own clothes—he knew the thing he wanted most of all was a bath. To feel clean and comfortable and not quite so much as though he was running for his life.

If he felt that way, then no doubt Sophie felt the same.

Plus, a bath would help speed the chill she still seemed to feel from her bones.

He stood and held out a hand. "Come with me."

Her brows rose. "Where are we to go?"

"I thought we might investigate that bathing chamber Willem pointed out to us." He lifted an arm and sniffed exaggeratedly. "I, for one, need to renew my acquaintance with hot water and soap."

Her brows rose higher. "Are you saying I smell?"

"You, milady, could never smell." He grinned at her. "Though, right now, I will say you are somewhat . . . fragrant."

Sophie smiled. "I did wonder whether maybe that crow liked me because I smelled like a dead thing."

He laughed. "If that were the only attraction, he would have chosen me first." He pulled on her hand and she rose obediently to her feet, fingers tightening on his, letting the quilt slither from her shoulders to fall back on the bed. She did smell faintly of sweat, and her clothes had the same tang of salt and smoke and too many days' wearing as his, overlaid with the more recent scent of their breakfast. But underneath it all she still smelled warm and female. Like Sophie. A smell he was extremely fond of.

He turned toward the door.

"Wait," she said.

"You don't want to bathe?"

"I do." She glanced down at her dress. "But we need fresh clothes."

He hadn't packed any other clothing in the small bag he'd brought. He'd saved the room for any valuables he could find, ammunition for his pistol, and a spare dagger. Then matches and anything else he'd thought might be useful. "Did you bring any?" He'd told her not to, if he was remembering rightly. To focus on valuables. Clothes could be purchased, if they had the funds.

"Just underthings." She wrinkled her nose. "If we bathe and then put these clothes back on, it will surely defeat the purpose of bathing in the first place."

She was right, but he couldn't see an alternative. Clothing required cash, which would require changing some of the coin or jewels they had brought. That was not a simple matter. For one thing, he had no idea if they would be permitted to leave the Academe to go into Lumia.

"We'll feel cleaner, at least," he said. "Then we can ask Willem for assistance to find new clothes." The boy had told them how to summon him or one of the Academe servants. "We can always bathe again."

Sophie didn't look pleased at the prospect, lips pursing. "We could call for a servant now."

"Yes, but that might take some time. Not to mention all the fussing that would go with finding clothing that may fit. That could take hours." If the maids in the Academe were one-tenth as fastidious as those who attended the court ladies in Anglion, it *would* take hours. "And those hours will be a little more pleasant once we are more refreshed."

Sophie looked torn.

"Nice big bath," he coaxed. "Soap. Clean hair. Warmth."

Perhaps the thought of the simple pleasure of hot water and soap was too much to resist. because her expression eased, and she headed for the door.

Like many of the other rooms in the Academe, the walls of the bathing chamber were tiled. But here the tiles extended all the way up the wall and then covered the floor as well. Like the other rooms, the tiles were painted with intricate designs—in this case fish, watery-looking plants and flowers, and tiny suns. And however they were glazed—was that the right term?—it wasn't simply a layer of shine but instead glimmered somehow, making the tiles look almost like pearls, a sheen of color adding depth and movement to the images painted on them.

Though surely, here in Illvya where the sanctii had free rein, it wouldn't actually be pearl? Anglions wore pearls to protect themselves from demons. Born of the sea, it was said they would keep a sanctii—for whom salt water was anathema—from being able to work their magic on the wearer.

Having seen a sanctii now, Cameron wasn't sure he still believed it.

Still, the tiles gleamed pearl-like before him. Added to the flickering light through the lamps on the walls—the chamber had no windows—and the walls seemed almost alive.

Or maybe that was just his still-tired brain.

Sophie hadn't wasted time staring at the walls. She was bent over the huge bath, working the brass taps. Hot water poured from the faucet. The expression in her deep brown eyes as she straightened to watch the bath fill was near to lust. It didn't change when she turned to study the glass bottles lining the tiled niche in the wall at the end of the bath closest to him.

"You first," he said. Her head twisted, one brow arching as

though she didn't believe he meant what he said. He wasn't entirely sure he did. Just looking at the steaming water made him even more acutely aware of the thin layer of grim and dust ground into his skin.

But she would be more at ease if he watched the door while she bathed, so he just nodded at her and pointed toward the bath. Sophie didn't wait for a second invitation. She fumbled at her dress and soon enough it lay in a puddle of gray wool at her feet.

Cameron's breath stilled. The light of the lamps turned Sophie's skin a deeper shade of gold. And between the lamplight and the steam, her thin chemise was practically transparent. She reached for one of the glass bottles of oil, lifted the stopper, sniffed once and then bent to pour some into the water. As she leaned forward, the curve of her breast was perfectly silhouetted. Something flared in his gut as he watched her, the scent of spice and smoke and flowers rising around them from whatever she'd put in the water.

It made his head spin a little, the sudden fierce heat of longing.

His wife.

The past few days had been fear and flight, and there was maybe more of that to come, but here and now, there was the two of them. He moved toward her without thinking, fingers loosening his own clothes.

"On second thought, that bathtub is big enough for both of us," he said, bending to press his lips to the back of her neck. Her skin was slightly damp, warming from the steam. Salt and Sophie. A heady combination.

They'd had no time for this in their flight. Survival was more important than satisfaction, after all. But now they were safe. And he'd slept and eaten.

Those basic needs satisfied, he found he suddenly wanted to satisfy some other urges.

His wife.

It still surprised him, this strength of wanting when it came to her. Having subsumed it for the last few days meant that it only returned more strongly now as he curved his body over hers, letting his hand stray around to capture the breast that had tantalized him.

Sophie gasped.

There. That sound. That was the one he liked.

Sophie liked it, too. Her nipple had hardened to his touch. But then she wriggled free.

"Bath," she said firmly. "I'm filthy." She looked him up and down with a frown. "So are you."

"You taste just fine to me."

He reached and she dodged. "Bath."

"How about we combine the two?"

The tub was more than big enough for the two of them. Positively decadent. Which made one wonder exactly why the Academe needed such luxurious facilities for its guests. But maybe they were just being hospitable.

"Sounds slippery," she said.

"Slippery is good. If you've forgotten that over the last few days, then I definitely need to remind you."

She shook her head at him. "You have a one-track mind." She pulled her chemise over her head and dropped it. He took a step forward, wanting her more.

"When it comes to you, milady wife, then yes, I am guilty as charged. I want you."

Sophie stepped into the bath and sank down into the water, her face turning blissful. "You'll need to take off your clothes. I don't mind sharing a bath with you, but I'm not doing your laundry."

"Spoiled."

"Not spoiled. I am perfectly capable of washing dirty clothes. But I'm not bathing with them." She reached for one of the bars of soap next to the oil bottles, wet it, and started to wash. Seeing her rub lather into her skin, the movements slow and careful as though she was intent on ensuring that she didn't miss even a single inch of her body, was enough incentive to stop talking about his clothes and just take the damn things off and join her.

He wanted his hands stroking her body. Her hands stroking his.

And that was just the start.

It didn't take long, though he was cursing his long boots by the time he got those free. Sophie looked up as he came back to the edge of the tub and then wriggled backward so he could climb in, passing him another bar of soap. She sluiced the soap bubbles off her arms as he scrubbed himself down rapidly, then ducked under the water to wet her hair.

When she surfaced, he reached for her. "Turn around. I'll wash your back for you. Or your hair, if you'd prefer."

Wet, the long dark lengths of her hair fell around her like dark silk. They caught the light, too, shining with glints of gold and red.

Earth magic reddened women's hair. He didn't know why. It was just one of those facts of life that one didn't question.

The sun rose. The wind blew. Earth witches had hair the color of the deepest heart of a flame if they were powerful.

He had no doubt the unfamiliar red in Sophie's hair would continue to deepen and increase until hers reached that shade.

He reached out and touched a strand, tracing its path down her body.

Sophie smiled, then handed him one of the bottles from the end of the bath. "This says 'hair,' doesn't it?" she asked, pointing at the label.

It did indeed. He opened the glass stopper and took a sniff. It smelled like lemons. And something green. The liquid sloshed in the bottle, moving faster than oil would. It seemed likely it was intended for washing hair.

"Turn around." He poured a little into his hand and then lifted half a handful of her hair and rubbed the liquid in. It foamed like soap and rinsed away clean when he followed with a handful of water from the bath.

Sophie sniffed appreciatively and tilted her head back so he could continue. As he washed her hair, he watched her skin turn pink from the warm water, saw the tension running out of her neck and back as he rubbed slowly and rinsed. He didn't stop when he was done, just transferred his attention to her shoulders, easing the knots he found beneath her skin until she sighed and leaned back against him.

He put the bottle with the lemon-scented liquid back on the shelf, then reached for the oil he'd seen Sophie pour into the bath.

Maybe oil and water didn't mix, but he was going to have fun seeing if that were true.

He dribbled oil into his hands and reached around to cup her breasts. The little pleased sound she made seemed promising.

He continued his explorations, Sophie's skin slick beneath his hands. Soon enough she was breathing hard and making sounds even more pleasing.

He was making some himself as she writhed under his touch, her wet back rubbing tantalizingly against his ever-hardening cock.

He wasn't sure how much longer he could torture himself by focusing solely on her. He wanted more. Wanted to be inside her, to feel her slick against him in more ways than one.

Seemingly she had the same idea because she twisted in his arms, the movement sending water spilling over the edge of the bath. She was kissing him and the need turned to fire.

This. This was the thing they were fighting for. This need between them.

This truth that neither was truly whole without the other. He didn't care if it was the bond or love or both. All he knew was that he needed Sophie like air.

He coaxed her up on her knees, straddling him. Her skin was wet and shining, warming pink across her face and chest, her brown eyes molten as she stared down at him. He spread his thighs a fraction, moving hers wider and slipped his fingers against her. Into her. She was ready. Slicker than oil. Warmer than the steam. She clenched around his fingers and he bit back a groan as he moved his hand to position himself against her

"This, love. This," he said, and then pulled her down onto him. The relief of it almost killed him, pleasure roaring through his veins like a lightning strike. He moved beneath her, or her above him, he couldn't have said which. Didn't care which. Cared only about the sensations. The need. He wouldn't have cared if the room had tumbled down around their ears as they fought this brief private war, both of them fierce and hungry and frantic. Until finally he heard her call his name—the sound seemingly far away from where he was, so lost in her—and then he let himself go as her body tightened around him and drove him over the edge.

It was somewhat surprising to find that they hadn't drowned in the aftermath. As his breath eased, Cameron opened an eye. Sophie was draped over his body, her breathing rapid, her muscles limp. The bath water had cooled though he didn't feel cold. Yet. But he didn't want Sophie to get chilled.

"We should get out, love."

"Only if you can levitate me," she said, sounding more than half-asleep.

"Sadly, no. And I'd be sorry to see you drown." He cupped her ass gently. "It would be a waste of all this."

"Brute," she said. But she wriggled a little—goddess, how could he want her again so soon?—and then rose to her knees, smiling down at him. She looked so well satisfied that he couldn't stop the smug smile that spread across his own face.

Sophie yawned hugely. "I could sleep for days."

"Me, too. And, as we have no pressing appointments, I

suggest we return to our chambers. I could be persuaded to sleep. Eventually." He pulled her down to kiss her, then pushed her away again. "Out you get."

By the time he'd extricated himself from the bath, Sophie was wrapped in a towel and staring down at the floor in dismay. Her dress was sopping wet. As were his own clothes. Well, perhaps the two of them could conjure a drying spell. In the meantime, there were plenty of towels that would suffice for a dash back to their chambers.

He wrapped a towel around his waist, scooped up the sodden clothes, and bowed slightly to his wife. "Shall we retire, milady?"

~

The damnable chiming woke Cameron for a second time. He blinked, then rolled to see Sophie asleep beside him in the bed, lying on her stomach, sheet only covering her from the waist down. She didn't stir as he sat up.

Good, better to let her sleep. He pressed his hands into his eyes, wishing he could join her. His memory of how they'd gotten from the bathing room back to their chambers was hazy, but apparently they'd fallen asleep at some point. It was still bright day outside. And the damn chimes indicated that someone wanted to see them.

He pulled the covers over Sophie, tugged on shirt and pants, and went over to crack the door open just far enough to see who was outside. He'd been half expecting Willem, but instead the mottled gray face of one of the sanctii was peering down at him. He only just managed to stop his instinct to slam the door and grab his weapons.

"Yes?" he said. He had no idea if this was the same creature he'd seen the night before or in Henri's office. He hadn't precisely been paying attention, too distracted by the fact that there was a sanctii in front of him—and he hadn't yet seen enough of them to know how different they were from one another.

"Maistre," the creature said.

"Maistre Matin wants to see me?"

A nod. Which produced interesting effects in the sanctii's skin. Where a human's would have flexed and folded, the gray flesh appeared to almost crack . . . though that wasn't entirely the right word. It formed ridges. Something that suggested that the skin wasn't as supple as a human's. Or else was a trick of the blotches of mingled color.

"Both of you." The demon gestured at the door.

"My wife is sleeping."

"Both. Soon."

No arguing with a summons from the maistre, it seemed. Cameron's stomach made a gurgling noise. How long had they slept? Hopefully not through the appointed hour for lunch, if there was such a thing. He wouldn't last until dinner.

"What time is it?"

"High sun."

Cameron tried not to look blank.

"Noon," the sanctii added.

"Tell the maistre we will be with him shortly." He was fairly certain he could find his way to Henri's office from their chambers now. Hopefully the demon didn't have to wait and escort them. Sophie hadn't reacted well to the presence of the creatures earlier. He'd be happier if she kept her distance until he understood exactly why that was.

The demon nodded. "Soon," it repeated, and then it vanished.

Well, that answered that question.

Now he just had to wake Sophie and go find out what the maistre wanted this time.

~

Sophie was still not sure that she was entirely awake when they reached Henri's office and were admitted to find not only the maistre but Madame Simsa waiting for them.

"Lord Scardale, Lady Scardale," Henri greeted them. "Come in. Madame Simsa tells me that you are acquainted?"

"We met briefly this morning, yes," Sophie said. She dipped a quick curtsy. "Madame."

Madame Simsa, sitting in a chair near Henri's desk, waved off the gesture. "No need to stand on such ceremony." She tilted her white head at Sophie. "Though pretty manners never go astray, I suppose."

"That's what my tutors always told me. My mother, too," Sophie added.

"Tutors?" Madame Simsa asked. "In magic?"

"Ah, no. Before my Ais-Seann. The other ones."

"What preparation came before your—Ais-Seann, is that what you Anglions call it?" The older woman's blue eyes were sharp in her face.

Sophie glanced at Cam. She didn't want to give Anglion secrets away. "My mother has a little earth magic. I grew up watching her. And I had the standard lessons once I came to court. A year or so."

"So little?" Madame Simsa scowled and turned to Henri, spitting something in rapid Illvyan that Sophie thought was "what a stupid"—or maybe that was "careless"—"system" before turning back. "And after?"

"Once I manifested, I had lessons with the temple, as all earth witches do."

"Oh? And what did the temple have to say about your"— Madame Simsa waved a hand at Cameron—"entanglement with this one?"

"They were not pleased," Cameron said. "But I don't believe it impacted Sophie's education. Though there really hasn't been much time since her birthday to judge how she was progressing."

"Madame Simsa has offered to assess you, Lady Scardale,"

Maistre Matin says. "She is one of most our experienced teachers."

"You are an earth witch?" Sophie said, curious.

Madame Simsa smiled. "That is one of my talents, yes."

Meaning that she practiced more than one of the arts?

"I have decided that I only wish to pursue studies in earth magic," Sophie said. "Does that change your interest?"

"Hedging your bets, child?" Madame Simsa said. "Well, that is understandable. But no, I'm sure I can find much to occupy myself with you in earth alone." She turned her gaze to Cameron. "Though, it may take a little more than earth magic to sort out what exactly the two of you have done to yourselves."

"Perhaps we can start with the basics," Cameron suggested. "Sophie and I are happy enough as we are, for now."

"I take it that you are going to concern yourself only with blood magic, Lord Scardale?"

Cameron nodded. "No one ever suggested I had any potential for any other kind."

Madame Simsa snorted. It seemed she didn't think much of the way magic was taught in Anglion.

Henri, on the other hand, merely nodded. "Venable Marignon, our senior blood mage, is out of the city just now. She is due to return tomorrow."

"Women teach blood magic here?" Cameron blurted. He looked shocked.

"Yes," Henri said. "It is not the most common choice, but women are free to study whichever of the arts they are suited to. And believe me, Verite Marignon is well suited to blood magic. I would prefer that she assessed you. So you will have wait until tomorrow, Lord Scardale."

"Does that mean there are female battle mages in the emperor's army?" Sophie asked, fascinated.

"Some," Madame Simsa said. "The army, of course, also has instructors for those who take that path. As do the Imperial Guard."

Madame Simsa snorted again. Did the Imperial Guard not do things to her satisfaction either?

Sophie pressed her hands into her skirts, trying to quell her sudden nerves. She was about to have to satisfy Madame Simsa as to her skills in magic. That seemed a daunting task.

"After we have established your skills with your magic, then we can look at other classes for you," Henri said. "History and geography, at least, I think. And language classes for you, Lady Scardale."

Sophie's cheeks went hot. She knew her Illvyan wasn't as good as Cameron's, but that didn't make it less embarrassing to have the deficiency pointed out. However, it would be stupid to pretend she didn't need instruction. And she would take whatever other classes they offered her. She and Cameron needed knowledge to navigate this place.

"Your husband probably only needs some more conversation opportunities to refine his accent. He'll get plenty of those in his classes, but we will see what else we can contrive." Henri pursed his lips. "How well do you read Illvyan, Lord Scardale?"

"Well enough," Cameron said. "There weren't many books in your language in Anglion."

"We have some texts in Anglion," Madame Simsa said. "But you may need to improve your skills. Perhaps you can join your wife initially. We have students who were born in other parts of the empire, and most of them take Illvyan here. It is taught throughout the empire but more successfully in some places than in others."

"Whatever you think is best," Cameron murmured.

He had his diplomatic face back in place. How did he feel about effectively returning to studies? He'd been in the Red Guard for years. And now to be reduced to being a mere student once more?

"Well, child, no time like the present," Madame Simsa said, rising from the chair. "Your husband should be able to survive without you for a few hours, surely. He cannot have recovered so fast from . . . earlier." She grinned at Cameron, the expression approving.

Sophie felt her cheeks go even redder and pressed her hands to her face. How in the name of the goddess did Madame Simsa know what she and Cameron had been doing in the bathing room?

"Bonds are noisy," Madame Simsa added. "For those who know what they are."

Henri coughed.

Cameron looked like he didn't know whether to be horrified or amused.

"It is an easy enough thing to teach you to shield the noise," Madame Simsa said. "Perhaps we will work on that tomorrow, once Venable Marignon is done with your husband. That will make life simpler—and quieter—for everyone."

Sophie nodded, trying to will the heat out of her face. She wasn't sure what would be appropriate to say anyway.

Nor was she certain what Madame Simsa meant by "simpler". She'd said the bond was noisy. Noisy like sensing a ley line? Or something else?

"Good," Madame Simsa said. "That is settled. Now come along and we will find an empty practice chamber. Somewhere safe for you to show me what your temple witches taught you on your little island."

"Yes, Madame," Sophie said. She took a step. Stopped, turned back to Cameron. They hadn't yet gone anywhere alone since arriving in Lumia and the thought was suddenly terrifying. Cameron was safety, here in this strange place. The one person she could trust. It was possible that all of this was just a ploy to separate them.

But refusing point-blank didn't seem to be an option. Cameron, watching her, seemed to know what she was thinking. He gave her a tiny shrug and then a reassuring nod. She breathed out. If they took her, he would come for her, she knew that much. Find her or die trying.

She was just going to have to trust that it wouldn't be necessary.

"How long will this take, Madame Simsa?" Cameron asked.

"As long as it takes," Madame Simsa said. "Why, do you have another appointment?" She looked amused.

"I was hoping to take Sophie into the city soon. We need clothes and other things."

Henri cleared his throat. "I think it would be preferable for Sophie to stay within the Academe walls for now. You, Lord Scardale, can blend well enough if you don't talk too much, but her accent gives her away. The palace, in my experience, leaks rumors like an ill-tended roof. And your wife is not to be risked."

Cameron's brow furrowed. "Are you saying she's not free to leave?"

"No. If you should choose to give up the protection I have offered you, I will not stop you. But while you accept it, I am asking you not to do something needlessly foolhardy."

And what exactly did he think was going to happen to her in the city? Sophie's fears rose again, but Cameron was nodding as though he agreed with the maistre's assessment. Which left her with little choice other than to follow Madame Simsa out of the room to whatever awaited her.

CHAPTER 5

Cameron made it as far as the front door of the Academe
before Willem appeared at his side, black robes settling
slowly around him, suggesting that he'd moved fast to catch up.

"Are you going out, Lord Cameron?"

The boy didn't sound out of breath but he looked somewhat
concerned.

"What if I am?" Henri had said that Sophie should stay
within the grounds for now, not him.

Willem's expression turned innocent.

Cameron wasn't buying it. "Well?" he prompted.

Willem had been nowhere in sight when Cameron had found
his way to the dining room after Sophie had left Henri's office
with Madame Simsa. Cameron had assumed the boy was at his
lessons like most of the other students. There had only been a
few in the dining room, none of whom seemed all that interested
in speaking to the Anglion stranger in their midst. He'd quickly
gone back to fetch some of the coins they'd brought with them
before he'd headed for the door and the city beyond.

Willem took a moment before answering, pursing his lips
thoughtfully before his expression brightened. "The maistre said

I should go with you if you went out into the city. Show you the way."

More likely watch where he went and report back. Still, Cameron couldn't blame Henri for being cautious. In his position, Cameron would be watching two Anglions washed up on his front door with a certain degree of suspicion as well. Still, how had Willem even known that Cameron was leaving the building? The corridors had seemed empty. Though he wouldn't have necessarily seen a sanctii, he supposed.

"Your Illvyan is good, my lord," Willem said. "But mine is better. I shall find you better deals. Take you to the best stores."

"Who says I was looking to buy anything?" Who said he could afford the best stores, more to the point? Willem might know a money changer. Cameron could exchange some of the Anglion coins he'd brought—the gold would be worth something even if the Anglion currency wasn't. He would wait to sell another pearl from Sophie's necklace. Henri had told him the Academe would feed and house them, so other than clothes, their immediate needs were few. Figuring out a longer-term source of income could wait while they got their bearings and consolidated their plans.

"You arrived with so little luggage, sir. You will need more. Lady Sophie in particular. Women get out of temper when they do not have enough clothes."

Cameron snorted, amused by the boy's world-weary delivery of this particular judgment. "Do they indeed?"

"Well, my sisters did," Willem said with a shrug. "But they were not yet married. Perhaps that matters more to them then. Madame Sophie already has a fine husband." He looked over his shoulder quickly then, expression suddenly guilty.

"Who are you looking for?" Cameron asked.

"Madame Simsa would set me extra studies if she heard me saying that women are only out to catch husbands. My sisters were interested in little else, but Madame Simsa says that is my parents' fault, not theirs. Says they should have been sent to school. But school is expensive."

"How many sisters do you have?" Cameron asked, amused now.

"Five. All older. Many dowries to be considered."

Five daughters could be expensive, if dowries were common here. "What does your father do?"

"He is head clerk for a shipping firm. He works down by the harbor." Willem waved vaguely to his right. Cameron noted the direction. Knowing where the harbor was could be useful.

"They sent you to school though?" A head clerk sounded like it might pay a reasonable wage. But still, six children . . . maybe more if Willem had a brother or two. That would stretch any household.

"There have been many practitioners of the Airs in my family. None of my sisters manifested magic, but my family has hopes of me. If not, well, Madame Simsa says I have some skills with the birds and that there may be hope for me yet if I study hard, regardless of my magic." Willem sounded happy enough with this fate. "Madame Simsa is wise, Lord Cameron."

Madame Simsa, Cameron gathered from this information, was someone that Willem was both a little awed by and a little enchanted with. As she was about to instruct his wife in goddess knew what, he hoped the boy's affection for the venable was warranted. Though hopefully the lessons would focus solely on earth magic as he and Sophie had agreed. He didn't think Sophie would risk their chance to return home by seeking to study beyond that, but he also wasn't sure he trusted the venables not to try and entice her to do just that. Every teacher or tutor or sergeant he'd ever had had been a tad obsessive about any of their charges they deemed to show potential. Always seeking to guide them to greater heights. Sophie had to be very tempting raw material for a mage to mold.

Well, he was just going to have to trust her to keep her head. There was little else he could do.

He turned back to the door. If he had to traipse through a strange city and conduct some business, then Willem probably wouldn't be such bad company. And possibly a very good source of information. The boy was, after all, still young. And eager to please. It shouldn't be hard to get him talking. "Shall we go?"

Willem grinned, then pulled his robes over his head, bundling them into a pile and unceremoniously shoving them into a small cupboard built into the wall. Underneath the robes, the boy wore a plain woolen jacket in a dull sort of gray shade over a white shirt. His pants were black, as were his boots. The clothes were clean and well cut, but Cameron didn't know enough about Illvyan clothing to judge what they said about Willem. For all he knew they were part of the uniform of the school. Henri hadn't mentioned a uniform, but it would make sense for younger students at least, who were living away from their families, to have one. Uniforms did simplify life.

Or complicate it. After all, they often came with oaths. Like the ones he'd broken so thoroughly when he'd fled here with Sophie. Certainly it was likely that he would have been leaving the Red Guard now that he was married and had to manage the small amount of land that came with the title Eloisa had granted him, but leaving was different to desertion. Which was what he had done by coming here.

He shook off the thought. As he'd told Sophie, there was little point wishing for things to be different. He had made his choice.

He followed Willem out the door and along the short path, turning at the gate to look back at the building. Last night it had loomed in the darkness, but it had been hard to get a sense of its size.

Large. Four stories tall and as wide across as the grandest erl's house he'd ever seen. Not as big as the palace in Kingswell, though he had no idea how far back the building went. Or if there were more buildings behind this one. It could be nearly as large if there was more than one building in the complex.

"You must tell me what you want, Lord Cameron. Then I will know where to take you." Willem pushed the gate open and held it, waving Cameron through.

"Some clothes, you were correct about that. For both of us. A map of the city, perhaps one of the entire country, if such things are available." He kept the last part casual. A map of the empire was key, but he didn't want word getting back to Henri that it had been the first thing he'd wanted to purchase.

Willem nodded. "That is easy enough. There are stores that sell small maps for those visiting Lumia, to help them find their way around. It is not so difficult once you know the system though." He launched into an explanation of rings and spokes and quarters that sounded very complicated.

Cameron held up a hand. "Let's wait for the map. A money changer first though. And also, perhaps a bookstore? I would like to get a book that teaches Illvyan. I don't suppose it would be possible to find one written in Anglish?"

Willem frowned. "For Lady Sophie?"

"Yes. Though I also need to improve my skills."

"The best way is by talking," Willem said. "I could help you. You could speak Illvyan to me and then help me with my Anglion in return.

"Anglish," Cameron corrected gently. "That's how we say it. Yours seems quite good."

"I know some. Usually it is only taught to the older students, but my father knew an Anglion man once. He learned a little from him. I have learned more since I came to the Academe. But it is never the same as speaking to someone from the place. My Parthan was terrible until I became friends with someone from there."

Cameron had no idea what country spoke Parthan. Yet another reason to find maps. "Well, if your teachers say it is acceptable for you to learn from me, I'd be happy to help you practice." He wasn't looking to put any noses out of joint by teaching the boy something he was not supposed to know. "Perhaps you can practice with Lady Sophie, too. But a book would also help her." He really should teach Willem about Anglion titles at least, but he liked the more friendly sound of Lord Cameron and Lady Sophie. Hopefully as students, they could drop the titles completely. It might help them blend in.

"If Lady Sophie has trouble with the language, then Maistre Matin might ask a sanctii to help her."

"A sanctii?" He thought of the creature he'd met the previous night and its harsh raspy voice. It didn't seem a likely candidate to help a person perfect their Illvyan accent.

"They have a skill with language. And they can . . . ." Willem waved a hand vaguely in the air. "They can do something to help those who find it difficult."

"Something magic?"

Willem nodded.

Demonic language lessons. Not something Sophie was likely to want to embrace. "Let's start with the book and see how that goes. It's simpler."

"All right. There will also be books on languages in the library in the Academe. Maps, too. Larger ones of Illvya and the empire. So you do not need to purchase those," Willem said eagerly. "You can save your money and buy something pretty for Lady Sophie."

Cameron smiled at that. Perhaps he would. He needed to be careful with their funds so if he could find maps and other books at the Academe, that helped.

They had walked a little way from the Academe now. He needed to start paying more attention to his surroundings. He spotted a familiar-looking building. A portal. Maybe the one they'd come out of the night before, unless he'd completely lost his bearings. "Is that the closest portal?"

"Yes. There is another one a little farther in the other direction from the Academe as well. Those are the closest public ones."

Did that mean there were private portals? Perhaps within the Academe itself? Private portals were not unheard of in Anglion.

After all, they had used the one owned by Chloe de Montesse to escape Kingswell. However, they were not common due to the cost of constructing and maintaining them.

But perhaps Illvyans could build such things more cheaply. The empire was far larger than Anglion. And they had demon magic, of course.

So. Portals. If there were portals within the walls of the Academe, it would be good to find out where. And to find out where one could travel to from them. He knew Anglion's portal symbols, but beyond those Chloe had showed him to get them to Lumia and to the Academe, he had no idea what any of the others for Illvya and the empire might be. "Is there also a guide to your portal system?" Having had to flee in haste twice now, he would make sure he identified the best routes to take if the need should arise a third time.

"Yes. You should be able to acquire one from the sellers who do the city maps. This way."

"Is that the same way as the money changer?"

That drew a frown to the boy's face. "Not to the one who has the best rates. Unless you wish to use one of the banking societies."

"A money changer will do for now." He wasn't entirely sure what a banking society was but it sounded like it might require things like letters of introduction or identification or even sums of money more substantial than he currently had. "That first. Then clothes and a city map." He considered. He had brought a small amount of ammunition with him for his pistol. It wouldn't last long in a fight. But he didn't want Henri to know that, so bullets could wait until he had figured out how to leave the Academe without his little informant by his side.

"Which way do we go?" He went to step out into the street. Willem caught his sleeve and hauled him backward just as a carriage rattled past, drawn by two huge black metal creatures billowing steam. A spark shot up from beneath the carriage, arcing toward Cameron. He slapped at it reflexively as it landed

on his sleeve, still staring after the vehicle. "What in the name of
—" He bit back the invocation of the goddess. He didn't know if
anyone used that language here. He was trying to blend in.
Trying and failing, gaping after the carriage like a Carnarvon
sheepherder come to a city for the very first time. "What was
that?" he said, managing to sound a little calmer.

"Do you not have *fabriques* in Anglion?"

"No. Is that what those things were? Fabriques?" He rolled
the word around in his head, committing it to memory. "What
are they?"

"Metal and magic," Willem said. "Faster than real horses.
They can go farther in a day without stopping."

"Magic? What kind of magic?"

"A little Air, a little Water. Another thing the sanctii assist
with. They are good with machinery and mechanisms and such.
There are other kinds of fabriques but the horses are the most
common."

Demon horses as well as demon languages? What else did the
sanctii do? But no, perhaps better not to think about that
just yet.

But when he returned to the Academe, the first room he was
going to seek out would be the library.

The room Madame Simsa led Sophie to was quite some distance
from Henri's office. In fact, it was in a different building entirely.
They crossed a small wedge of garden—more a courtyard—and
then followed the path down between two buildings away from
it again before Sophie had a chance to do much more than
register flowers in strange colors and unfamiliar shapes. She
would have liked to linger, but Madame Simsa didn't seem the
kind to want to pause and admire flowers.

She also set a good pace for someone who appeared to be in
her seventies, her cane propelling her along with clicks and

thuds. She didn't pause until they reached a row of five small stone buildings, each maybe twenty feet wide and set apart from each other by a similar width of grass. Their walls were made from a pinkish-gray stone, and from the depth of wall that showed around the door frame, they were built very solidly. They resembled nothing so much as the prison building in Portholme. The narrow windows weren't barred, though they, and the rest of the buildings, shimmered with wards piled upon wards, their glow painfully bright. Madame Simsa stopped by the second of the buildings and thumped her cane once against the door. The ward-glow died and she turned to Sophie. "Come along, child."

Not a prison, Sophie told herself firmly. If they wanted to imprison her, they could have kept her in her chambers in the other building with very little effort. After all, the windows of that room were barred. And Madame Simsa seemed an unlikely sort of jailer. No doubt she was powerful or Henri wouldn't have handed Sophie over to her with such alacrity, but she didn't look like the type to do Sophie harm.

"Child. A little caution is a good thing, but I promise I am not going to eat you." Madame Simsa stood in the doorway, looking amused. "My teeth aren't what they used to be, after all." Her smile widened. Her teeth looked perfectly white and healthy to Sophie.

Earth witches generally had excellent health. They were long-lived. As were their husbands, at least in Anglion where the marriage bonds set in place by the temple gave the husbands a little of their wives' power, ensuring good health.

"And there's no sanctii waiting inside to eat you either," Madame said, a little more sharply. "What are you, a witch or a wailer, girl? Come along."

Sophie's head snapped up at that and she marched over to Madame Simsa. She was a royal witch of Anglion. Madame Simsa might learn that Sophie had some teeth of her own.

Inside the room was dim. Madame Simsa gestured toward

the wall to their right. "There are earth stones over there. Can you light those?"

"Yes, Madame," Sophie said. She reached out with her powers, seeking the stones. There. A row of them warmed to life with pleasing speed and the room lightened to a comfortable level. There wasn't much within it: a sturdy-looking square wooden table with four chairs pushed against its edges, a fireplace with a mantle above it, a cupboard squatting into the far left corner, and the shelf that held the earth stones.

"Good. You aren't completely untrained, then," Madame Simsa said. "Come, we will find out what else you can do. Bring two of those stones over to the table."

Sophie obeyed, the familiar light of the earth stones oddly comforting as she carried them over to where Madame sat.

The venable nodded approvingly. "Now, you are to answer what I ask and do as I demand. Do not worry if anything I request of you seems risky. These practice rooms are warded half a dozen different ways and solidly built besides. Plus, I doubt you can start anything I cannot finish if needs be."

The older woman started to grill her, firing questions and setting magical tasks with little pause between each one. Sophie could do some of them she was familiar with, managed a few more through applying things she had read about combined with things she could already do, and failed miserably at others.

She wasn't entirely sure how long this went on but she was growing tired by the end.

Madame Simsa finally nodded and the stream of questions ended. Sophie wanted to slump back in her chair but she kept her spine straight. The ley line beneath the Academe was still strong beneath them, but dipping into the power had not been simple. The unfamiliar line was almost too strong and grasping it had been like being buffeted by strong winds.

"So you are not a weakling," Madame Simsa said. She smiled suddenly. "I imagine your Domina was not well pleased when you and that pretty husband of yours got yourself bound up as you did."

How did she know that? "Are earth witches not bonded to their husbands here?"

Madame Simsa thumped her cane on the floor. "Only if they choose to be. And the bond between the two of you is no marriage bond. I've seen those before. Besides, if the Domina had you neatly bound to Temple and husband, I can't imagine anyone would have been able to do whatever it was that sent you running to the empire. You can tell me that story one day. When you know me a little better."

Know her or trust her?

Maybe both. Only time would tell if either of those things would come to pass. "You seem to know a lot about Anglion," Sophie said.

"I have paid attention over the years. Illvya may be anathema to your country but here in the empire, His Imperial Majesty believes in understanding his enemies. As did his father before him. Illvya has studied your country. Some of that knowledge escapes the emperor's court, particularly when it comes to magic. After all, the emperor can hardly understand the magic your queen has at her command if his own mages cannot explain it to him." Madame Simsa paused. "Knowing your enemies is a strategy you may wish to consider."

Sophie frowned in frustration. "That would be easier if I knew who they are."

"Indeed. So pay attention. Do not take things here at face value. I'm sure Henri has told you that you are safe here at the Academe, and that is most likely true, but you are valuable here in Illvya. Because of who you are and because of what I suspect you can do. The news of the former is probably spreading already. The latter, well, we shall try to keep that to ourselves a little longer. It will only complicate things."

"Yes, Madame." It seemed sound advice.

"A wise woman once told me that in life, you are either a

player of the game or a pawn to be moved about by those who play. This has proven to be true. Doubly so when it comes to magic and the whims of royalty. Remember that."

"Yes, Madame." There didn't seem much else to be said. And she couldn't disagree with Madame Simsa's words. Not from what she learned during her time at court at Kingswell or from what had happened after her Ais-Seann. And after all, back in Kingswell, someone had done their level best to remove her from the board altogether. She did not intend for it to be so easy for someone to try a second time.

"Good. So. I will determine a schedule of lessons for you, based on what I have learned here today. Plus, I think it would be good for us to meet at least once a week. I no longer take regular classes but I tutor some of the more advanced students. Or those who show potential to become so."

Sophie assumed she was the latter rather than the former. "Yes, Madame." She was beginning to sound like an idiot, repeating the phrase over and over.

"Pretty manners, child. But I hope you are not so meek as that court seems to have trained you to be."

"No, Madame," Sophie said. She grinned suddenly, relieved that she had managed to at least demonstrate enough talent to keep the venable interested in her. "I'm sure my parents, my former tutors, and even the chief of the queen's ladies would have no problem telling you that that is not the case."

Madame Simsa looked pleased at that. "Good. So let us return. I, for one, could use some tea. And you will need robes and other supplies for your lessons."

Tea sounded good. A cake or two to go with it would not go astray. Now that her nerves had settled somewhat, her appetite had returned. Between that and all the energy she'd just spent demonstrating her skills, she was starving again.

As they crossed the wedge of garden, a black streak swooped down out of the sky. Sophie nearly stumbled as she ducked.

"Don't worry, Tok wouldn't hit you," Madame said, watching

the raven who was cawing and circling their heads. "They're clever creatures."

Sophie stood where she was, trying to keep the bird in sight. Which became simpler when he suddenly landed on her shoulder, claws biting a little through the wool dress.

"Perhaps we should make sure your robes are padded," Madame Simsa said. "We did not discuss familiars, child, but I think perhaps we must."

"Anglion witches don't have familiars."

"That may be so. But familiars are stubborn things at times. This one seems to be choosing you. He's a little young, of course, so perhaps you could dissuade him."

Sophie turned her head to try and look the bird in the eye. "Shoo."

Tok cawed again, his head tilting at an angle that made it clear he found her amusing.

"You may have to try harder than that." Madame Simsa pointed her cane at the bird. "Back to the tower with you, nuisance. You may see Lady Scardale again tomorrow."

The crow's claws tightened on her shoulder and for a moment, Sophie was sure he was going to stay right where he was. But then he gave an annoyed-sounding croak and took off again.

"I will add a meeting with the Master of Ravens to your schedule for this week."

"I don't want a familiar." She wasn't going to do anything to mark herself as different.

"As I said, you may not get a choice. Besides, it isn't unheard of for an Anglion earth witch to use one. Once upon a time, they were more common. Before your temple grew quite so powerful." Madame Simsa commenced walking back toward the main building.

"What do you mean?" Sophie had never heard of such a thing. Or read about it in any history book she'd been given.

"There is not enough time to explain now, child. For now I

will say that it is wise to always take the tales told by history—or tradition—with a large grain of salt. You will learn more in your classes. So, come. Tea. Robes. Supplies. The sooner you begin, the better."

The following morning, Sophie's head was spinning by the tenth hour. Madame Simsa had turned the remaining hours before dinner the previous evening into a whirlwind of activity.

She'd taken Sophie down to the depths of the Academe to meet a little dapper man named Roberre. Sophie hadn't been able to figure out exactly where this man stood in the hierarchy of things other than he seemed to be a senior sort of servant or hireling. He'd sized her up quickly, walking around her with a studying sort of eye, and then provided her with one of the voluminous black robes. It had a narrow stripe of brown at the edge of the collar which he informed her was for a student studying earth magic. Air was yellow, blood red, and water blue. Those who had not yet manifested wore unadorned black.

"What happens if you are studying more than one?" she'd asked.

Roberre had looked questioningly at Madame Simsa, who had nodded.

"Things become more complicated. Most students begin with one field of study and hence one color on their collars, then add more as they can based on interests and abilities. Once the venables declare a student advanced, the robes change." He gestured at what Madame Simsa was wearing. "See this fabric. It appears black, but as it moves, it catches the light."

So she hadn't been imagining things. "Like shot silk?"

He looked pleased. "Yes. Only we use several colors amongst the black. And patterns."

"In other words, the more complicated the robe looks when the wearer moves, the more they can do?" Sophie asked.

Madame Simsa had nodded. "Yes. Walking rainbows, some of us. If rainbows went about dressed in black. Some of the patterns are only discernible to those who have magic. But the emperors have always considered it to be only fair that the public have some chance to know what sort of magic a mage might wield. If only so that they may afford them the proper respect."

~

After the robes had come books and writing materials, and then Madame Simsa had walked her through several floors of classrooms, pointing out which classes might be held where. She'd allowed only a glimpse into the two libraries she had pointed out, enough for Sophie to register that they were huge rooms stuffed with shelves holding a tantalizing number of books. And then she'd delivered Sophie back to the dining hall, with the final instruction that she would send Sophie a schedule at breakfast and she wasn't to be late to her class, before leaving her with Cameron.

Who had had his own adventures with Willem in the city and had amused her with tales of what he'd seen before they'd gone back to their rooms. Cameron had started studying the city map, but Sophie had been too tired to keep her eyes open for long and had crawled into bed.

Now it was morning again and she was sitting at breakfast with Cameron and Willem once more.

She was just finishing a second cup of tea when a very short girl with brown hair tinged with red approached their table.

"Are you Lady Scardale?" she asked with a friendly sort of smile.

"Sophie," Sophie said, nodding, taking in the stripe of brown at the girl's collar.

"Madame Simsa asked me to bring you this." The girl held out a piece of paper. "Your schedule. And, as it seems we are sharing our first class together, she told me to walk with you to class."

"Oh." Sophie took the piece of paper and unfolded it. "Thank you." She studied the list of classes, days, times, and locations written in tiny precise handwriting. It seemed like a lot.

"Read later," said the girl. "We need to go or we will be late."

Sophie looked up. The girl was practically bouncing on her heels, in a way that would have earned her a severe discussion of appropriate deportment for ladies in public places from Lady Beata. But the Academe wasn't a palace and, whoever the messenger was, she was right. They were cutting it fine to reach their class, if Sophie remembered correctly where the classroom indicated on the list was. She rose, then bent to kiss Cameron.

He hadn't yet received a summons to meet with Venable Marignon, so he was going to be left to his own devices until he was. Sophie had told him where the libraries were, so she imagined he would head there. Just looking at the map of Lumia had reminded them both how little they knew about the country they were now residing in, let alone the empire beyond.

"I'm Lia," the girl informed Sophie as they left the dining hall. She tapped her collar. "Earth witch. My twenty-first birthday was a few months ago."

"Mine, too," Sophie said.

"I assume that was your husband," Lia said. Her Illvyan was a little uncertain, her accent odd. Which, strangely, made Sophie, who was doing her best to decipher it, feel a little better.

"Yes," she replied. "Cameron Mackenzie. Lord Scardale."

"I don't know much about Anglion titles," Lia said cheerfully. "Does that make him important?"

Sophie decided to downplay a little. Cameron, it was true, wasn't one of the senior nobles of the court—though his brother, as Erl of Inglewood, was—but his rank didn't matter so much when Sophie's own position on the line of succession was so high.

Unless, of course, she'd been disinherited. She could imagine Eloisa in a rage, doing just that. "Not very, and as our ranks mean little here, I think it's easier if you just call us Sophie and Cameron. Or do students use their titles here?"

"Not in classes, no. But you will notice a little social dance going on from time to time. There are those who would prefer to, how do you say it? Stand on ceremony?"

"Something like that," Sophie said with a smile. "My Illvyan isn't very good."

"Mine isn't perfect either," Lia said. They had reached the staircase that led to the upper floors. She grabbed a handful of her robe and the skirt of the dress she wore beneath and hitched them up before she started to climb. Sophie, who was finding the combination of the robe and the belled skirt of the dress she wore—one of several Cameron had bought for her—somewhat cumbersome, followed her example.

"Where are you from?" Sophie asked. Lia's skin was darker than hers and also darker than most of the Illvyans she had met so far.

"The Faithless Isles," Lia said with a shrug. Then she paused. "You probably don't know where that is, do you?"

Sophie shook her head. "No, I'm sorry."

"Don't be." Lia resumed climbing. "It's a group of islands off the northeast coast of the mainland, up beyond Partha. Mostly famous for growing cotton and for our king trying to kill the emperor."

"Why would he—"

"Not the current emperor. His grandfather," Lia said. "When he conquered Partha and came to our shores, announcing that he would take us, too, our king tried to kill him there and then in the audience chamber. Of course, the Imperial Guard and their mages didn't let him succeed. But the attempt gave the emperor the excuse to kill the king and take us over a lot more quickly than may otherwise have been possible. And to punish us for the rebellion, he took half the population and sent them to work as servants—slaves, really—across the empire. And renamed us the Faithless Isles as an example to others." She sent Sophie a sidelong glance. "Not known for their subtlety when they wish to make a point clear, the Imperial Family."

Was that a warning? "I will keep that in mind." Her stomach churned. Slavery and conquest. Exactly what Anglion feared from Illvya.

"Do," Lia said. "Though, to be fair, the current emperor has been less aggressive. Maybe because he already has the entire continent in hand so he doesn't need to be. And his father freed the slaves. Though most of our people did not return home after that."

"Why not?"

"They found new lives. They changed, I suppose. Perhaps they thought their old lives would no longer fit who they had become."

Would she be able to fit into her old life if she ever returned to Anglion? It was a disquieting thought. She squeezed the bannister too tightly and then made herself relax. They had reached the top of the stairs and Lia turned right.

"When did you come to Lumia?" Sophie asked to distract herself.

"About a year and a half ago. There isn't a lot of magic in the Isles, but my family has thrown up more than its share of witches over the years. So the governor granted me a scholarship to come here to study and be prepared."

"Governor?"

"The emperor's . . . proxy, I think the word is. He rules the Isles."

"I thought you said you had a king? Did he have no heirs."

" The surviving members of the royal family were amongst those sent away. We do not have kings anymore."

"As slaves?" The thought of a royal family overthrown was somehow shocking. It had happened, of course, in Anglion's history but not for several centuries. She couldn't imagine such a thing.

"So they say," Lia said. She paused in front of one of the doors lining the corridor. "This one. And the chimes have not yet sounded, so we're even on time. Come, you can sit with me."

CHAPTER 6

By the time Sophie returned to the dining hall for lunch, she was exhausted. This day was not letting up when it came to the pace of new information being thrown her way. The first class with Lia had dealt with earth magic. But only from a theoretical point of view. The kind of lessons that Sophie had taken in Anglion just before her Ais-Seann. It seemed Illvyan witches continued their education for longer. It was easier to study if one wasn't immediately married when one came of age, it seemed.

After the first class, there had been a class in Illvyan and one in history, where she was with students who all seemed to be far younger than herself. Which made sense. Judging by what Lia had told her, most of the pupils came to the Academe before they manifested. So those who needed a grounding in things perhaps not taught in all corners of the empire could be brought up to speed as well as prepared for their magic if necessary.

Sophie's head ached from trying to follow the classes in Illvyan. She'd been hoping that Cameron might appear in one of her nonmagical classes, at least, but he hadn't. Being without him put her on edge. Alone, she had no one to watch her back.

Being surrounded by rooms full of strangers didn't make it any
easier for her to relax and pay attention.

And there was still half a day remaining.

Hopefully lunch and more tea would refresh her enough to
concentrate on whatever the afternoon might bring.

There was no sign of Cameron or Willem but she spotted Lia
at a table with Magritte, who had also been in their earth magic
class earlier, near the rear of the hall. Lia saw her and waved.
Magritte didn't look as welcoming, but Sophie was going to
ignore that. If she was going to survive the Academe, she needed
some friends. She was used to having Eloisa's fellow ladies-in-
waiting in her life. Cameron was wonderful, but she had grown
accustomed to spending much of her days with other women.
She wouldn't have called all of them friends, perhaps, but they
were a close-knit group. She missed them, the sudden pain of it a
shock that made her suck in a breath. She tried to ignore it,
summoning a smile as Lia waved at her. There were friends to be
made here, if she made the effort.

"How was your morning?" Lia asked through a half-full
mouth as Sophie sat down.

"Interesting. Tiring. It's hard to keep up in Illvyan at times."

Lia nodded sympathetically. "Yes. I wish I had the money for
the *reveilé*, but sadly my funds do not extend so far. So I shall just
have to study hard."

Reveilé? Sophie didn't recognize the word. "What is a
reveilé?"

Magritte looked at her with surprise. "It is a thing the sanctii
can do. To help you understand a language."

"There are no sanctii where Sophie is from," Lia said to
Magritte.

Magritte's nose wrinkled. "That must make life very difficult." She looked at Sophie. "Are there really no sanctii in
Anglion? Or water magic?"

"No." Sophie suppressed the shudder that wanted to roll

down her spine at the thought. "Water magic is forbidden. So no sanctii."

"Perhaps it is because Anglion is an island," Lia said. "The sanctii cannot cross salt water. "We do not have them in the Fettered Isles either."

Magritte snorted. "The Fettered Isles has no water mages. Just a few earth witches. That is why you have no sanctii."

Lia narrowed her eyes at Magritte. "So you are the expert on sanctii now?"

"No, but I'm good with history," Magritte said. "Water magic isn't so common. And your islands—lovely as I'm sure they are—do not have a history of it."

"Neither does Mesineia," Lia retorted.

Sophie didn't know where Mesineia was. And she didn't want a geography lesson on top of everything else that was being crammed into her head already. It might explode. She felt as though she was back at the court in Kingswell, in her first few months as a very green lady-in-waiting, trying to learn too many new faces and places and rules at once. "I don't understand how a demon can help you learn a language," she said.

Both girls looked shocked at that.

"You can't use that term for the sanctii here," Lia hissed. "It is very impolite."

"Not to mention that if a sanctii heard you they might decide to object. Sometimes they object quite strenuously," Magritte added, glancing around the room as though she expected one of the creatures to appear in front of her any minute and demonstrate. "If any of the vens hear you, you'll be in trouble."

Sophie flushed. "Sorry. It's hard to adjust."

"We will help you," Lia said. "You and that handsome husband of yours." She grinned at Sophie. "I would have been eager to marry young, too, if the men at home looked like him."

It probably wasn't the time to explain Anglion marriage customs or the fact that she and Cameron had had little choice in the matter when it came to their wedding. She just nodded instead. "But the reveilé?" she asked again.

Magritte shrugged. "I'm not sure anyone understands it, not even the water mages. The sanctii can do things to your mind. Not all of them good, but this one is. Apparently."

"Being from Illvya and never having had to study in a language other than your own, the appeal of such a thing has probably never occurred to you," Lia said, shaking her head at Magritte. "I would do it in a heartbeat. Life would be much easier. Perhaps Maistre Matin would allow it for you and your husband, Sophie."

The likelihood of Cameron willingly letting a demon mess with his mind seemed remote to Sophie. The thought didn't exactly appeal to her either, even though the result did. She had to improve her Illvyan somehow. But for the time being she was willing to follow Lia's example and apply some old-fashioned studying to the matter.

Perhaps then her head would feel less like it had been beaten with a stick all morning.

~

"Heads up!"

Cameron ducked as Venable Marignon swung the wooden practice staff at his head with enthusiasm. He twisted away from her, widening the distance between them. His instructor just grinned as she spun to face him, weight distributed evenly over her feet, staff twirling idly between her hands.

She didn't even look particularly out of breath. Whereas he was beginning to tire. Henri had been correct when he had said that the venable was well qualified to teach blood magic. The woman fought like a tiger. A very skillful tiger. Who could use magic.

Well, he could use magic, too. He reached for the ley line, caught at the power, and used it to slide the woven grass practice mat out from under the venable's feet. She slipped backward and fell, though she didn't let go of the staff.

He braced himself for a resumption of the attack, but instead, she burst into laughter.

"No one has tried that move on me for a long time," she said. "Serves me right." She climbed to her feet, dusting off the leather breeches she wore with brisk strokes. "So, Anglion, you are not entirely unskilled."

Cameron kept a wary eye on her. The instructors who'd trained him in the guard had been fond of launching an attack after a bout was supposedly done. Venable Marignon was more than sneaky enough to try just such a thing. He focused on watching her stance and the way she held the staff. It had been a long time since he'd fought with one, though his muscles seemed to remember most of how it was done, even if they protested it. "I was a member of the Red Guard. So I hope not."

"That would be a pity," she agreed. "Though I think you would not argue with me if I said that you are a better fighter than you are a mage."

He shrugged. "I've been told that since I manifested, so no." He'd never been the quickest at magic. But he'd always been good at the other things that went into being a soldier. Though here in Illvya, the differences in techniques were throwing him off just enough to make him feel like the rank green boy he'd been when he'd first joined the guard. It was a disconcerting sensation even though he knew it was really an opportunity to hone his skills.

Venable Marignon narrowed very green eyes at him. She wasn't a pretty woman—striking, perhaps—tall and strong, with jet-black hair braided close to her head and skin somewhere between Sophie's and the color of weak black tea. "Ah, but that was in Anglion. Perhaps here at the Academe, we can teach you a few new tricks."

"As long as they don't involve your fist in my face," he said, rubbing his shoulder where the venable's staff had connected earlier. He would be bruised, the kind of bruising he hadn't sported since those long-ago days of his training. For blood mages, connecting to their power for the first time wasn't as simple as reaching for the ley line as an earth witch did. No, most blood mages required emotion to make the breakthrough. The emotion the Red Guard chose to employ was anger. Achieved by punching their recruits in the face.

Venable Marignon shook her head at him. "I can't say I haven't used that technique with a particularly slow student from time to time, but no, that is not usually how we achieve our aims here. So perhaps there are things we can teach you, if you care to learn."

She was offering more power. More chances to survive. To make sure that Sophie survived. He wasn't in any position to turn that down. "I do," he said simply. "So, shall we spar again?"

For Sophie, the rest of the week moved past in a blur. Lessons. More lessons. Meals. Trips to the library with Cameron to study and to further their knowledge of the empire. The library was vast and well stocked. But most of the volumes were in Illvyan—even the maps were marked in Illvyan—which made her feel like she was trying to push all the information they gained into her brain through a layer of sticky treacle. With every day that passed without the emperor summoning them, she could feel this new world becoming more familiar. But it was still exhausting. She fell into bed at night with an aching head and a desire to sleep so strong she barely had time to kiss Cameron good night before she succumbed.

She felt as though she had been penned in under stone and the odd light from the gas lamps for weeks rather than days. Maistre Matin was still refusing to allow her to go outside the Academe's boundaries, so the only breaths of fresh air she took were when she was walking between the buildings to her classes.

The brief respites were pleasant but came with their own difficulties. The young crow, Tok, had developed an uncanny ability to find her almost anywhere. He often appeared at the window of whatever classroom she was in, squawking loudly until the venable teaching the lesson inevitably shooed him away. He stalked her in the corridors as well and had even appeared in the dining hall three times. Which had caused nothing but consternation. Familiars apparently didn't usually eat with their human companions in such public places. That was sensible. No one wanted to share their meal with a menagerie. The fact that Tok wasn't even her familiar only made it even more awkward.

She suspected many of the students—those who would love to have a familiar—thought she was encouraging the damned bird. Nothing could be further than the truth.

When Tok pecked Cameron's hand, drawing blood, as he had tried to detach the bird from the shoulder of Sophie's robes on their seventh day at the Academe, Sophie decided enough was enough. Tok wasn't going to be dissuaded by anything she could do, so she needed to appeal to a higher authority.

Madame Simsa seemed the most likely to be able to assist. The ravens mostly seemed to mind their manners around her. She'd taken Sophie to the rookery several days earlier and the birds had crowded near to the older woman, angling heads and wings to be petted but taking care not to let their claws or beaks come anywhere near any part of Madame Simsa that might get scratched. Sophie had been more fascinated watching the birds paying court to the witch rather than by the rather dry presentation on the care and breeding of the ravens delivered by the Master of Ravens. That possibly hadn't endeared her to him, but she didn't intend to have a familiar so she wasn't overly concerned.

As she made the way through the Academe to Madame Simsa's rooms, up on the highest floor near the tower that housed the rookery, Sophie hoped fervently that the venable would be able to do something to make sure Tok could be convinced that Sophie was not for him.

He had followed her on her journey, swooping and circling around her as she walked, cawing in what had first sounded like cajoling calls that had grown more strident and indignant as they neared Madame's rooms.

The bird settled on her shoulder again when she stopped at Madame Simsa's door. He clicked his beak as she knocked but settled into silence as the door opened and Madame Simsa blinked at her.

"Sophie. This is unexpected." She looked at Tok, then back to Sophie. "Is everything all right?"

"Yes. My apologies for disturbing you, Madame, but I was wondering if I could speak with you."

Madame Simsa stepped back to let Sophie in, nodding. "I see you still have your friend."

"That is what I wanted to talk you about."

White eyebrows rose. "Then by all means, talk."

Sophie looked around curiously. She knew some of the venables lived at the Academe, whereas others merely had offices with families and homes elsewhere. Madame Simsa, it seemed, was one of the former. The room was a small sitting room, crammed with two small settees, a number of side tables, single chairs, and a desk that hovered on airy carved legs tucked in against the far wall under a window. There was another door in the wall to her right, though it was closed.

Books, inkpots, small glass containers, and framed miniatures littered the surfaces. It was both cozy and a little overwhelming. Judging by the book lying open on one of the settees next to a lap-sized quilt made from patches of silks, it seemed as though she had disturbed the other woman reading. She moved to the other settee, bending to move what she took for a small fur-covered cushion closer to the corner.

The cushion uncoiled with a chattering sound of annoyance and Sophie jumped about a foot.

Behind her, Madame Simsa laughed, the sound cracked but joyful.

Sophie was too busy staring at the creature on the settee to turn around. It stared back at her, its small face screwed up in disapproval before chittering again. It appeared to be some kind of monkey, though an unfamiliar one.

"Riki!" Madame Simsa said. "Manners."

The monkey didn't look apologetic, but it leaped off the settee to one of the chairs and then to the other settee, perching on the rolled arm, one of its hands grasping the cover of a lamp standing on an end table beside it as it fixed Sophie with a disapproving gaze.

Sophie, who'd turned to follow its flight, her pulse still pounding from surprise, wound up face-to-face with Madame Simsa again.

"I'm sorry, my dear," Madame Simsa said. "Riki never did like being woken up abruptly."

Just a monkey, Sophie thought. It had meant no harm. And she was there to ask the venable for advice. Best not to be rude about her pet. "Well, who does?" she said, managing a smile. She tilted her head at the animal. "My apologies, Riki."

The monkey had a shock of white fur around its face, framing eyes and a muzzle a brown close enough to be black. The white continued down its neck and back but shaded to the same dark brown along its arms and legs down to the tiny, clever hands and feet. The tail, which was currently making a sinuous *S* in the air, was brown, too, except for a final tuft of white and black at the very tip. It bared its teeth at her, a flash of pointed white in bright pink gums that was startling against the darker skin as it chattered again.

"Hush, Riki," Madame Simsa said. "Be nice to our guest."

The monkey quieted at that, eyes suddenly intent on Sophie, the expression a little too knowing for her comfort. There was definitely intelligence in the face. Understanding dawned. Not just a pet, perhaps.

"Is he—she—your fam?" Sophie asked.

"She is trouble," Madame Simsa said as she settled down onto the settee and the monkey grinned at her. "But yes, she is a petty fam." She stroked Riki's head. "She keeps me company. Her and Belarus."

"Belarus is your sanctii?" Sophie hadn't realized. Belarus was the first sanctii she'd met the night she and Cameron had arrived at the Academe. She hadn't come face-to-face with the creature since—at least she didn't think she had. She hadn't spoken to any of the sanctii she'd crossed paths with that week.

"Yes," Madame said. "He is mine."

"I didn't know . . . ."

"That I was a water mage?"

"Yes." Sophie nodded. "I was reading about the Academe in the library. There is a book that talks about the venables who teach here. Your entry didn't say you were a water mage."

"Because I don't teach it these days. Earth magic is less fraught. At least when it comes to teaching students how to utilize it." Madame Simsa's expression was frank. "And Anglions are not, in my experience, comfortable with sanctii. Maistre Matin and I thought it would be easier for you to get used to me if you didn't know."

That was true. "Belarus isn't here now though?" She couldn't feel a chill in the air.

"No." Madame Simsa leaned forward. "How did you know that?"

"I thought he would show himself here in your rooms," Sophie said. She wasn't ready to share with the Illvyans that she could sense the demons and their magic. Who knows what that would do to their plans for her? She was there for earth magic, nothing more. Besides, it was never a good idea to give up an advantage if you didn't have to.

Madame Simsa's eyes narrowed.

Sophie tried to look innocent. "Is it usual to have both a sanctii and a fam?" There. A slight change of subject. And a valid question. She hadn't seen any of the other wizards who practiced water magic with a familiar other than their sanctii.

The blue eyes were studying her carefully. "It is less usual now. Some consider it a little old-fashioned." She sniffed. "Though there is nothing wrong with learning to hone one's skills the old-fashioned way. A petty fam is unlikely to tear your throat out, after all. Or consign the world to oblivion." She grinned as she said the last and flapped a hand at Sophie. "Don't worry, my lady. None of the sanctii have managed to do that yet. I won't deny that the odd wizard or two have disappeared in unusual circumstances over the years, and their sanctii along with them, but as you can see, the world remains."

"I see," Sophie said. None of that sounded amusing to her.

"Then again, sanctii don't steal everything shiny they come across." Madame Simsa frowned across at the raven on Sophie's shoulder. "I would advise you to lock away any jewels you might own when that one is around. Never met a raven who could resist a diamond. Makes attending balls interesting at times."

"I don't own any diamonds." She rubbed her fingers over the sapphire in her betrothal ring. "And I don't think it's likely that I'll be attending any balls any time soon." For which she was most thankful. In her experience, balls consisted of too little dancing, too much tedious small talk, and avoiding the grabbier-handed members of the court. Maybe Illvyan men had better manners, but somehow she doubted it.

"I would not be so sure," Madame Simsa said. "The emperor will take an interest in you and your husband sooner or later."

A chill that had nothing at all to do with sanctii ran down Sophie's spine. She didn't want to think about the emperor.

Madame Simsa shook her head, then leaned forward and patted Sophie's knee reassuringly. "But that is a bridge to be traversed when needed. Let us return to the subject at hand." She pointed to Tok, who sat, preening his feathers on the back of the settee behind Sophie. "That one."

"Is there anything we can do? To get him to leave me alone?"

Sophie asked, twisting to study the bird. It wasn't that she didn't like Tok, but she didn't want a familiar. And she didn't need him following her around, drawing attention to her every movement.

Madame Simsa shook her head. "If you do not want him, then the only real chance is to send him away. Otherwise, he will continue to pester you and will not try to form a bond with anyone else."

"Away?"

"To one of the other schools."

"There are others?" Of course there were. Illvya was only one country in the empire. One Academe probably couldn't cover even Illvya's mages, let alone an entire empire.

"Yes. We are the largest. The oldest. Most would say the best, which is why we get our pick of students and teachers, but there are others. And where there are students, there are mages in need of fams."

"Will that work though, to send him elsewhere?"

A shrug. "Perhaps. If he has truly decided that you are the one for him, then it may not."

"What happens then?"

"He can be used for breeding. Or take his place in the flocks that form around the academes. The birds are fed, monitored as far as they can be, but such a life is not risk free."

Sophie looked at the raven. He tilted his head, returning her gaze. It seemed unfair to send the bird away from the place he had been born. Was that odd? To be concerned about the feelings of a bird? But from the little she'd learned about familiars, it was hard to think of them simply as animals.

"Do I need to decide now?"

"That is entirely up to you and how long you can tolerate him annoying you. Or remain determined not to accept the help he is offering." Madame's tone suggested she thought this was foolishness even if she wasn't saying so outright. The monkey, curled in her lap, was also looking at Sophie with what could only be considered disapproval. The expression was far too human, which only underscored that familiars were not normal creatures.

"It is a pity that ravens are not good candidates to become familiaris majus," Madame Simsa said. "He is bright, that one. He could be useful."

"What's a familiaris majus?" Sophie asked. She knew familiaris sanctii. And familiaris, on its own, was the formal term for a familiar. But she didn't know what majus meant.

"Anglions," Madame Simsa muttered. "I don't know what your country thinks it's achieving by keeping the people uneducated." She straightened in her seat, making Riki chatter at her. She stroked the monkey's head soothingly. "A familiaris majus is not a common thing but water mages sometimes attempt it. The sanctii . . . well, in the place that they come from, they are not alone. There are other less powerful creatures there. A familiaris majus is made from bonding an animal and one of those creatures. When it works, the familiar becomes more powerful and more intelligent. Not on the level of a sanctii but still useful. I'm not sure what happens to the creature on the other side. They do not take a physical form here as the sanctii do. But there must be some benefit."

"So they make the mage stronger than a petty fam?"

"Yes. They can amplify the powers of a mage who is perhaps less strong beyond what a familiar only can achieve. The kind of mage who might not wish to attempt controlling a sanctii, for example. But the bonding is complicated, and it is most successful with larger creatures like dogs or sometimes horses. Which can be inconvenient. I knew one water mage who used a darkbear." She paused. "Those are small bears from one of the northern countries, I forget which. They are the size of a large pig rather than a normal bear. Though their claws and teeth are still sizeable. And quite sharp, as I understand it."

Sophie had never seen a live bear. There was a stuffed one in one of the galleries that held the various animal and plant specimens that the Anglion royal family had collected over the years.

That was a vast brown beast, whose fur still smelled musty after all the years it must have stood there. Its claws had nearly been the length of Sophie's hand.

"A dog sounds more reasonable," Sophie said.

"I agree, much more biddable. But perhaps the bear was useful in other ways."

Sophie couldn't think of any particular uses for a bear. Finding honey, perhaps? They were supposed to like sweet things. There seemed like easier ways to find it though. Like asking an earth witch to charm a bee and follow it back to the hive. Which was something she'd learned about in her lessons at the Academe.

Just one of many things she'd learned that the Temple and all her instructors had never mentioned. Though whether that was because they didn't know or something that Anglion witches couldn't do or something they simply didn't wish to share, Sophie had no idea.

It had only made her more determined to learn as much as possible while she was here. When she returned to Anglion, she would have something to contribute if she could teach new skills to the witches there.

When. Not if.

It had to be when.

Outside the apartment, chimes began to sound, calling the students to the dining hall for dinner. She had arranged to meet Cameron and then they were going to the library once again to keep exploring the books there. "I have used up enough of your time, Madame. I should go." She rose, then bobbed a curtsy. "Thank you for your advice."

"My pleasure, child." She rose from the settee with the help of her cane. Riki stayed put but watched the older woman as she straightened. When she was standing, she peered at Sophie's face. "You look tired. Are you sleeping?"

"Yes, Madame. I am perfectly well." She lifted her chin. "Perfectly well" was not exactly the truth. She was always tired and her head began to ache about halfway through each day. But she hoped it would become easier as her understanding grew. "It has just been a long week. There's so much to learn. And the Illvyan makes it harder."

"Maistre Matin would allow you to use the reveilé," Madame Simsa. "Do you know what that is?"

"Yes. But for now, I am happier to do without." "Happier" wasn't the word. More truthful to say that the struggle of following her classes in Illvyan was the lesser of two evils when the alternative was allowing one of the sanctii to use magic on her. She had become more accustomed to seeing them now and then over the course of a day, but she still felt chilled around them. Actually letting one touch her was a frightening prospect. It would be like letting ice coat her skin. And that was before you added in the actual magical aspect of the experience.

Madame sighed. "I can't say that, in your place, I would not do the same. Hope is hard to let go of. Though why you would wish to run back to Anglion rather than stay here and fulfill your potential—bah! But I will not pester you about that. It is your life."

"Anglion is my home. My family are there."

"I understand, my lady. Go. Go and eat your dinner. Take your handsome man to bed and let him distract you from all of this for a few hours. You will sleep better and all of this"—she made a circling motion of her hand in the air in front of her—"is not going anywhere."

CHAPTER 7

Cameron returned from another hard session with Venable Marignon, hoping he had time to squeeze in a bath before lunch. The senior blood mage did not believe in going easy on her students. Or maybe it was just him that she drove so fiercely. After all, he was supposedly a full blood mage, so she shouldn't need to coddle him. Currently though, he was mostly a rapidly turning black and blue mage. So far, their training had mostly consisted of good old-fashioned hand-to-hand combat practice. There had been a few magical elements—he got the feeling she was still taking his measure in that department—but mostly she seemed to be enjoying succeeding in sending him crashing to the mat as often as possible.

This last session had been attended by other students as well, and that had almost been worse. The venable had decided to make an example of some of the differences in his fighting style. Which mostly involved sparring with him until she could lure him into a mistake caused by one of those differences, then delivering an excruciatingly polite dissection of the problem and what he'd done wrong to the assembled students.

Educational, but not good for his confidence.

Perhaps he should have a bath and a beer. He doubted they had iska in the Academe. Probably just as well. A glass of the northerners' favorite drink might have done him in entirely. But every part of him ached. Noon was surely not too early to begin drinking under those circumstances?

He was already pulling his robes—they didn't fight in the stupid things, thank the goddess, but he still had to wear them to and from his assigned classes—over his head as he entered their chambers.

Sophie was already there, sitting on the end of the bed. She held a sheet of paper in her hand, staring down at it, chewing at her bottom lip.

That didn't seem likely to be a good sign. He dumped the robe on the ground near the door as he kicked it shut behind him. "What is it?"

"Maistre Matin wants to see us after lunch," Sophie said.

"Again?" Cameron bit back a groan. "Doesn't that man have any other students to bother?"

He respected Henri but was beginning to find his frequent "requests" for Cameron and Sophie to attend on him irritating. The last few times had been to grill them about Chloe, on the surface at least. Cameron was fairly certain that he'd been trying to probe them for news of Anglion generally, but they'd been expecting this approach and had tried to limit the information they shared to the things they had read already in the textbooks on Anglion they'd discovered in the library. It had been gratifying to find those volumes were only a little thicker than their counterparts about Illvya back in Kingswell. The main difference seemed to be that they were freely available to the students here. He hadn't seen a complete text on Illvya until he'd joined the Red Guard. Now that he was here, he was rapidly coming to appreciate that it hadn't been so complete after all.

"He misses his daughter," Sophie said.

"Since we ran out of new information to divulge on that

subject several days ago, I hardly think that can be it," Cameron said.

"I know," Sophie said, sounding as reluctant as he felt. "But the alternatives aren't pleasant to contemplate. Madame Simsa told me yesterday that she didn't think the emperor would ignore us forever."

"I thought you talked about Tok. And familiars?" He and Sophie had been debriefing—for want of a better word—about their days each night, to share what they had learned. They'd discussed the ongoing problem with the raven. Cameron shared her reluctance to accept a familiar if that would mark her as different if they returned home. But he was starting to think that perhaps they would be foolish to turn down any chance of potential advantage. However, it was Sophie who needed to make the final decision. She was the one who would be bound to the bird, after all.

"We did. But the emperor came up in passing."

"Well, it's hardly news. So let's not borrow trouble. Maybe it will be the life of Chloe de Montesse part four that he wants." He didn't think so, but Sophie looked nervous enough that easing her mood for a few minutes seemed the right choice. If she was too worried, she wouldn't eat. She needed to eat. She still looked tired. He suspected her teachers were pushing her harder in the use of actual magic than Venable Marignon was pushing him. She was not yet fully trained in magic, so she was still developing her skills, rather than just learning how what she knew already differed from Illvyan practices as he was. Her power would also be of interest to them. It seemed unlikely they'd had a royal witch of her strength to study before.

He was not looking forward to the day when the venables decided to start poking around the bond he and Sophie shared. Bruises, no matter how bad, were preferable to that prospect.

"Well, at least we're allowed to dine first," he said. "Why don't you go on ahead? I need to bathe." He lifted an arm and sniffed, wrinkling his nose. "It's probably not polite to go see the maistre smelling like this." He tugged his shirt over his head, wincing as the movement tugged at aching muscles along the left side of his ribs.

"You're hurt," Sophie said, crossing the room to him.

"It's just bruises, love. They'll heal. Or I'll go to the healer, if not."

Sophie put a tentative hand along his ribs, where the bruise was blooming darkest. Given that the fresh bruises were layered on top of those he'd acquired in earlier sessions, even that light touch made the muscles throb.

"I could try," she said. "I'm starting to understand how healing works."

"Don't take this the wrong way, but I'd prefer not to be your very first patient." He grinned at her, turning a little so her hand fell away from his torso, then pressed a kiss to her lips. "Besides, you need to keep your energy up. No point wasting magic on me when there are others who can do it."

"I'm your wife." Her brown eyes looked worried again. "It's my job to take care of you. Lord Sylvain said men gain strength from the marriage bond. You shouldn't bruise this badly."

"Our bond isn't exactly traditional," Cameron pointed out. "And Lord Sylvain said it would protect me from illness. Not being repeatedly hit with training swords. Plenty of Anglion lords have died on the battlefield over the years. So there are limits to what the bond can do." He kissed her again, and she relaxed into it. "Don't worry. As I said, just bruises. I know what a cracked rib feels like. This isn't it." He crossed to the armoire to find a fresh shirt and trousers. "Go on ahead. Eat. Save me a place. I won't be long."

~

Mercifully, Henri did not prevaricate once Sophie and Cameron presented themselves at his office after their meal.

"I have received this," he said, lifting a stiff piece of heavy white paper from his desk. Sophie couldn't make out the coat of arms she glimpsed as he lifted it, but between the gilded edges of the paper and Henri's serious expression, she could only assume it was from the emperor.

She glanced at Cam. He smiled quickly, but if it was supposed to reassure her, it didn't really achieve the aim. Not when he immediately returned to watching Henri with the same expression one might use to watch a snake stumbled upon on a path.

"His Imperial Majesty requests your attendance at a ball he is throwing on fifth day," Henri said. "I assume you know how to interpret 'request' in this context."

"Show up or else?" Cameron murmured.

"Just so," Henri said. He put the piece of paper back on this desk with a sigh. "I was hoping he might be content to leave you alone a little longer. But at least he has given us some time to prepare rather than simply summoning you today. I shall see if I can find out if anything has happened that has encouraged him to haste. And why he has chosen a ball rather than an audience."

Given that they'd been here for more than a week already, it didn't seem overly hasty to Sophie. But she didn't know how quickly the machinery of the court moved here in Illvya. "Surely a ball is not an unusual event for an emperor to hold?"

"If it were his son making the announcement of a ball that has not already been expected by the court for weeks, I would perhaps agree with you. Alain can be . . . whimsical. His father, though, is not known for whimsy. Capriciousness, perhaps, but not usually in the vein of such frivolities as balls held out of season. For one thing, they annoy the ladies of his court who prefer time to prepare for such occasions."

"Am I to understand that you think the emperor is specifically organizing a ball for us?" Her lunch suddenly sat uneasy in her stomach.

"I suspect so," Henri said. "But as I said, I can find out more. It is not exactly what I had expected." He smiled a little grimly.

"And I would prefer to have some advance warning if he intends to do something foolish with you. We would not like to see your talents go to waste."

"I see," Sophie said faintly. She didn't want to ask what 'something foolish' might entail. Though the knowledge that the maistre might defend them offered a tiny scrap of comfort.

"In the meantime, you will both need suitable clothes. I have arranged an appointment with you at the best clothiers in Lumia, my lady. And my own tailor should be able to outfit you, my lord." He nodded at Cameron. "I've informed your teachers that you are to be excused from your classes this afternoon. There will be a carriage waiting for you downstairs and two of the venables from the blood mages to escort you."

She hadn't thought she could feel worse about this news but apparently she could. Why did they need an escort to visit a dressmaker?

"Are you expecting trouble?" Cameron asked.

Trust him to be practical. She took a breath. Between them, they could handle trouble. They had done so before. So far the score was far more in favor of the Scardales than those who tried to hurt them.

"Not expecting, no. But I believe in being prepared. Two blood mages should be enough. They know how to call for reinforcements quickly." He waved a hand in dismissal. "So go. Preparation, in this case, includes clothing. The rest we will deal with if I find out more."

It seemed to take no time at all before they were standing outside a small discreet-looking store in the midst of what appeared to be a wealthy part of Lumia. The people they'd passed in the streets were well-dressed, the gutters relatively clean, and the storefronts she glimpsed decorated with silk, velvet, and gilt, their large windows hung with finery. She'd been trying to match the streets they had taken with the mental map of Lumia she was forming in her head from the time she and Cameron had spent studying, but the carriage had moved swiftly and she'd lost her bearings.

Sophie stared at the names on the door mutinously. The gilded letters were surrounded by enough flourishes to take up half the pane of glass, but in the middle of the elegant script, standing out against the midnight blue velvet draped inside the glass, the letters read M & M DESIGNY, CLOTHIERS.

Simple enough. She needed a dress. So they had come to a dressmaker. The only problem was that she didn't want to go to the damned ball.

"If you glare any harder, the glass may shatter," Cameron said. He stood behind her, his body between hers and the pedestrians crowding the streets. The two blood mages who'd escorted them were still in the carriage. "That may not endear you to the dressmakers."

"As I don't really want a dress, that doesn't particularly concern me," Sophie said, trying to calm her nerves. Just a dressmaker. Something she had more than her share of experience with. Being a lady-in-waiting to a crown princess and then a queen involved a lot of clothes. Both hers and Eloisa's. She'd attended more fittings than she cared to think about. It wasn't a process she had ever particularly enjoyed. She liked nice dresses well enough, but when what was deemed suitable for her to wear had been so governed by protocol, it had seemed easier to just allow others to make most of the choices. She'd limited her protests to color selections she did not like and left it at that.

But it wasn't the dressmaking that had her feeling as though she might lose her meal there on the very elegant steps. It was the reason she required the dress in the first place.

Aristides Delmar de Lucien. His Imperial Majesty of Illvya. A man she had never expected to meet. Nor wished to, once she had found herself in his empire.

But apparently her wishes counted for nothing right now.

"I understand, love, but that doesn't change the circumstances. We can hardly say no to the emperor. No more than we could have refused such a request from Eloisa."

Even more so, to Sophie's reckoning. His Imperial Majesty was an unknown quantity entirely. Who knew what he might do if his will was thwarted. "Why is the emperor even interested?" she muttered. "Why can't everyone just leave us alone?"

"Because you were born to your parents and then you had the misfortune to stumble across me at the wrong point in your life," Cameron said, his voice tight.

She spun around, nerves retreating as guilt replaced them. She doubted Cameron was excited at the prospect of this ball either. And she was the reason he would have to endure it. "You were exactly the right point!"

His mouth twitched. "Be that as it may, this is the result. So, we should go inside before the Designys send a footman or whatever people have for servants here to chase us away from their doorstep."

"They won't chase us away. Not when the maistre requested the appointment."

"No, but no point being rude. They'll stick you full of pins during fittings and make you look like you're wearing a sack."

"I'd be happy to wear a sack. No one would pay any attention to me."

"Actually, I think the opposite is likely to be true." Cameron reached past her and tugged on the chain hanging from the neatly polished brass bell on the doorjamb. The chime was louder than the size warranted. Sophie peered a little more closely at the bell. Yes. There. A faint shimmer ran over the metal. Some sort of spell to enhance the sound.

Apparently the maistre hadn't been lying about the quality of the Designys' work. Anyone who could afford to pay a practitioner of the Arts of Air to bespell their doorbell was doing quite well for themselves.

The door swung inwards, revealing a young woman wearing a

deep blue dress that fit her perfectly despite its simplicity. Her dark hair was pulled up into a bun so smooth, Sophie wanted to reach and touch it to see if it were real.

"Yes?" the woman said, looking them up and down.

Sophie fought the urge to smooth out her skirts. Her dress was somewhat crushed after a morning of being hidden beneath her robes, but in her experience, dressmakers were more respectful to customers who behaved as if they were dressed for court, regardless of what they actually wore. "I am Lady Scardale. I believe Maistre Matin arranged an appointment for me?"

The woman's expression didn't change significantly but she nodded. "Yes, my lady. Welcome to Designys'." She looked past Sophie. "Is this Lord Scardale?"

"Yes," Sophie said. She wasn't sure who else the woman thought would be accompanying her to a dressmaker's appointment. "It is."

"Does he also require clothing?" The woman studied Cameron a moment, then ushered them inside with a graceful gesture. "We know some excellent tailors."

"The maistre has also made a recommendation on that front," Cameron said smoothly. "But thank you."

Inside the store smelled like gillflowers. Heady and rich. Sophie paused just inside the door, caught in unexpected memory by the scent. Her mother loved gillflowers, grew any number of them in the gardens at their estate. The striped pink flowers were a fixture in their house throughout the long hot summer months.

A wrench of longing tugged at her stomach. Home. Goddess, what she wouldn't give to be home.

"Lady Scardale?" the woman prompted.

Sophie nodded, forcing the memory from her mind. She stepped forward, the heels of her boots sinking into carpets so rich they muffled any sound of their footsteps. There were no dresses on display in the room. In fact it was close to empty. The only furniture was several low couches upholstered in striped blue and white silk, the blue several shades lighter than the dress their escort wore, and one small oval table standing near the wall farthest from them. The walls were hung with paintings of extravagant bouquets but she couldn't see any actual gillflowers. Was the scent another spell like the doorbell? She'd never heard of such a thing. Not that she could claim great knowledge of the Arts of Air.

The whole place was silent, the only sound the swish of Sophie's skirt over the carpet. Their escort's skirts ended a precise inch above the soles of the black leather boots she wore, as though designed to avoid precisely that effect.

The woman glided across to the table. Its mirror-polished surface held only a leather-bound ledger. Which was opened, their names written on one of the pages, and then closed again after the ink had been blotted.

"Please wait here a moment," the woman said. There was no time to respond before she opened a door that was so well fitted into the wall beyond the table that Sophie hadn't even noticed it, then vanished through it.

"Interesting style of service," Cameron said.

"Not so unusual. Haven't you spent any time with dressmakers before?" she said. In her experience, the expensive kind of dressmaker liked to make a performance out of the process.

"Tailors are more my thing."

"And tailors don't go in for superior attitudes, expensive furniture, and invisible flowers?" Sophie asked, turning back to wave her hand at the room.

"Not in my experience. The men who make the Red Guard's uniforms definitely don't," Cameron said with a smile. "I will confess to meeting a superior tailor or two when I had to get clothes for court. But no, there was a lack of invisible flowers. And empty rooms. Tailors tend to be full of shelves of cloth and pattern books."

"Pattern books are so dull," a male voice said from behind them.

Sophie turned. The woman in the blue dress hadn't returned, but in her place, a man and a woman stood by the table. They had identical bright blue eyes and hair an odd, almost bronze shade of blond. Not quite red. Not quite yellow. The woman's was curled and piled high on her hair whereas her... brother's—surely not a husband when they looked so alike—was cropped short. They wore clothes that were a testament to their skill. The woman's dress, a deep blue silk, was severely elegant. Her companion was more flamboyant, wearing a dark purple velvet jacket over a green shirt with a waistcoat embroidered with both those colors and black and silver. The colors may have clashed, but the garments were all made with the same elegance of line and skilled construction as the dress.

"You are the Designys?" Sophie asked.

"Yes." It was the woman who spoke. "I am Helene and this is Marx." She didn't explain further. She wore no rings though, so Sophie thought perhaps that her assessment of brother and sister was correct.

"And you are Lady Scardale," the woman continued.

"Yes," Sophie said. "I am Sophia Mackenzie. This is my husband, Cameron, Lord Scardale."

"You, sir, are enough to make me wish that I had taken up tailoring after all," said Marx, looking Cameron up and down. His voice was rich and rolling. The sort of voice that Sophie had heard amongst the actors who performed at court but had rarely encountered elsewhere. Was this a performance, too?

"Why didn't you?" Cameron asked.

"As I said, my lord, pattern books are dull. In my experience, most men lack a certain imagination when it comes to their clothes. Or else, where they have imagination, they lack taste. That seems to be the prevailing sin in the emperor's courtiers, at least. Women's clothing has so much more . . . scope." Marx smiled widely, revealing neat white teeth, then moved his focus back to Sophie. "And you, my lady, appear to be in need of some scope." He frowned suddenly, brow wrinkling. "Who made what you are wearing?"

"That hardly matters," Helene interjected. "She has come for ball gowns, not day dresses."

"Ball *gown*," Sophie said. "I only need one."

That earned her a head shake. "Oh no, Maistre Matin was quite exacting in his instructions. Three gowns. If you are pleased with those, then perhaps we can reconvene on the matter of other items to . . . supplement your existing wardrobe, my lady." It was clear from her tone that by "existing wardrobe" she meant something closer to "appalling rags."

The dresses that Cameron had bought her were hardly rags but they were not exciting. Nor, from the glimpses she'd caught of the clothes worn by the other students, were they at the forefront of fashion. She was content with that. Simple and serviceable made far more sense. After all, her clothing was concealed by her robes for most of her day. Clothes that blended in rather than stood out would be an asset if she and Cameron ever had to run again. So, even if Helene Designy's dresses were the most glorious creations ever seen, such clothes were currently of little use.

Besides, even if she were concerned with fashion, buying a wardrobe designed by the Designys would probably cost her several more of Eloisa's pearls. And they needed that money for other things. So she would be shopping elsewhere. She only hoped Maistre Matin was footing the bill for the day's acquisitions.

"Perhaps," she agreed, not wishing to be rude. Helene looked perfectly capable of stabbing a client who displeased her with pins, as Cameron had suggested. "But the gowns are our priority."

"You and half the noblewomen in the city," Marx said. "The emperor's whims are good for business. He rarely throws a ball on this scale at this time of year. Too many of the court travel to their estates during the summer to attend to harvest and other such rural mysteries. They don't generally return until well into autumn. So he has caught everyone off guard. But the maistre has asked so nicely, we have moved you right to the head of our queue, my lady."

"Thank you," Sophie said, tempted to ask for a list of the names of the women she had displaced. In Kingswell, securing the services of the various dressmakers who went in and out of fashion had been something of a blood sport amongst the ladies of Eloisa's court. If it was the same in Lumia, it might well be better to be forewarned about whose noses she might have put out of joint before she even met them. But asking would be futile.

"Shall we begin?" Helene said. She gestured gracefully to the door behind her. "Our fitting rooms are this way."

The fitting rooms were no less elegant than the store below. Just more busy. Here there was noise, though tones were still soft, voices carefully courteous. The woman who'd greeted them was introduced as Clara and was soon busy bringing bolts of fabric for the Designys' consideration.

Sophie, it seemed, wasn't going to be given much choice in the matter.

There were several other girls and women clothed in the same style dress as Clara moving around the space, presumably doing the same for other clients.

While Clara was still fetching fabrics, Helene whisked Sophie into a curtained alcove and asked her to remove her dress.

She refrained from commenting on the very plain chemise and underthings Sophie wore beneath her gown, but the arched eyebrow spoke volumes.

For a minute or so, Helene simply studied Sophie, every so often instructing her to turn, raise her arms, or stand in a slightly different position. Then she produced a measure tape from a pocket and began to wrap it around almost every part of Sophie's body, first over her corset and then without it. Her movements were brisk and practiced, pausing at the end of each wrap of the tape to note each measurement in a small leather-bound book with a pencil that disappeared into another pocket when she was done.

"At least we are working with good bones," she said at last after she had fastened Sophie back into her corset and helped her into her dress. "One could wish for a little more curve in the bust perhaps . . . ." Her hand sketched an absent line in the air that suggested more than a "little more" curve to Sophie's eyes. "But we can do much with corsets and structure to assist there." She snapped the book closed and opened the curtains.

"Marx," she called as she stepped out. "Come, consider these."

Sophie, following her, saw her pass the book to her brother, who opened it and glanced down at the rows of figures. He smiled, looking smug.

"This will do nicely." He passed the book back and came over to Sophie, tilting his head first one way and then another as he considered her.

"Now, my lady, from what we have been told, you have not been here long enough to know much of Illvyan fashions, let alone the court. You would hardly be able to see even what the women at the Academe wear under those dull robes. So the question becomes are you willing to trust Helene and me, or do you wish to see some examples?"

"Is there anything in current court fashions I should know about?" Sophie said. "Anything . . . risqué?" She knew enough about the whims of courts to know that very strange things could become popular. She'd been lucky in her time in Kingswell. The preference was for gowns that harked back to previous years, which had been a little cumbersome at times—though she had to admit the wider skirts on her Illvyan dresses were more so—but that was nothing compared to what she had read in her history books. Periods where women wore sheer laces with nothing underneath or fine silk robes that also left little to the imagination.

Marx inclined his head at her, expression approving. "No, my lady. The emperor has grown conservative as he has grown older. Not a bare breast or ankle in sight these days."

Bare breasts? Sophie couldn't stop her brows lifting at that.

"I think we'll stick to decently covered," Cameron added from where he stood to one side, observing. "Regardless of the fashions."

Helene nodded at him. "Of course, Lord Scardale. You will wish to make a good impression, not a scandal."

She and Marx started talking rapidly. Sophie struggled to follow. Her Illvyan classes had not included dressmaking terms. She was still working on the basics. So she really was going to have to put herself in the Designys' hands.

The conversation came to an end when Marx nodded decisively. "Yes. That exactly. Now, as to fabric." He walked over to the table where Clara was standing next to her stack of bolts and lifted one from the pile. A silk in a deep golden shade that reminded Sophie too much of Eloisa's coronation gown. He freed a length and then came back to Sophie to drape it around her.

"No," Helene said firmly. Marx nodded his agreement, to Sophie's relief. The process was repeated a dozen times, with the Designys making decisions rapidly on most of them. Two of the fabrics, an emerald green satin embroidered with black flourishes and a deep raspberry pink silk shot with silver, were ultimately dismissed. Which left a fiery red satin, a silk in a beautiful blue-green shade, and an unusual dark purple velvet, the color of the darkest part of twilight.

"These three are all excellent choices," Marx said.

"Yes," Helene agreed. "But for this first ball, it has to be the red."

"Isn't that somewhat bright?" Sophie asked, eyeing the fabric. "I thought the aim was to create a good impression, not a scandal." In Anglion, the red would be a bold choice indeed. Sophie couldn't actually remember seeing a court dress in such color. The court, as a whole, didn't wear much red. Perhaps because they were constantly surrounded by the color in the coats of the Red Guard.

"A good impression but also a strong one," Helene said thoughtfully. "You do not want the court to think you are an Anglion mouse, seeking to hide away. They are quick to sense weakness and pounce. This color is not weak. And the cut of the dress will ensure you do not offend any sensibilities. Besides, if you are studying earth magic, which I think from the tinge in your hair you are, you have a limited time to wear this shade. It would not go so well with earth red hair. Which in your case is a pity as it flatters your complexion brilliantly."

Was that a compliment? Sophie relaxed a little. Perhaps the Designys could pull this off after all.

"So," Marx said. "That is all we need you for today, my lady. Tomorrow morning, one of the girls will come to the Academe with the muslin and make any adjustments. Then a final fitting or two the day before the ball."

"That seems very fast."

"Your maistre is paying us well," Helene murmured. "The other two dresses can wait until next week. But the deadline is not moveable for this one."

"Then we will leave you to your work." Cameron came over to stand beside Sophie, bowing slightly to the clothiers.

"Yes, thank you," Sophie said. "I'm sure the dress will be perfect."

"Of course." Marx sniffed. "Ours are never anything less."

CHAPTER 8

The dress—gown, really—was indeed perfection. It fit Sophie like a glove, the belled skirts falling in layers of pleats and tucks in the rear before spreading in a small train, making her waist appear tiny. The sleeves were also shaped by pleats to curve around her arms then fan at the cuffs. The triumph though, she thought as she studied herself in the mirror, was the neckline. Which was deeper than she was accustomed to. But it was also edged and shaped by cunning folds that made it appear that she was revealing more than she actually was.

The Designys had sent a maid with the gown, who had dressed Sophie's hair, coiling it in sleek waves around her head. Somehow, they had procured hairpins beaded in a heavy gold that matched her betrothal ring and large teardrop earrings fashioned from the same metal.

The gold gleamed against her skin. Any other jewels would have been overkill. The gold and the dress were enough to make her status clear without being ostentatious.

The maid had also painted her face, the makeup heavier than it would have been in Anglion, her lips a shade that matched the dress exactly and a black substance lining her eyes.

She spritzed Sophie with a bottle of perfume that was heavy and spicy, the scent warmed by an element Sophie didn't recognize, before declaring her work done.

Cameron, when he was readmitted to the chamber, did a gratifying double take at the sight of her.

Indeed, his blue eyes turned heated and she held up a warning finger. "You cannot rumple me. I have no hope of recreating any of this. So stay there and let me admire you instead."

Whoever Henri's tailor was, he had done an admirable job. Cameron wore sleek black trousers and a long jacket of black satin, embroidered at cuffs and collar with a filigree pattern in black thread. It was lined with the same shade as Sophie's dress but otherwise was a stark contrast. The white shirt beneath was very bright, the black cravat stuck through with a pin in heavy gold like Sophie's jewels. Only this also had a ruby—or a very good imitation of one—winking in the head of it, adding another flash of red. "You'll do," she said, reaching for her fan. She'd seen Cameron in evening clothes and his uniforms many times, of course, but there was something about this particular suit that seemed to make him seem taller and broader than ever.

It was difficult not to walk over to him and do some rumpling of her own.

But that would have to wait until the end of the evening.

When they walked down to the carriage that was waiting to take them to the Imperial Palace, Sophie was relieved to find Maistre Matin waiting for them at the foot of the stairs, also dressed in formal clothes. His were black and silver and blue, and suited him well.

"Maistre, are you coming with us?" He hadn't mentioned it before. Maybe so she and Cameron would pay closer attention in the protocol lessons they had been subjected to. Those plus the fittings plus the several hours trying to learn the fundamental principles of Illvyan court dances had turned the past few days into a nightmare of activity. They had both missed several of their classes, a fact neither of them was happy about.

With any luck, after the ball, things could return to some semblance of normality. They would meet the emperor, hopefully convince him that they offered no threat, and go back to their studies at the Academe.

She could hope but, in truth, she knew it was unlikely that things would be so simple. Henri's spies—or whatever they were —at the court had not been able to discover any information on what had triggered the emperor's sudden desire for this ball and this impending meeting between them.

Whatever the reason, it was a very well-guarded secret. A fact that made her wish the dress didn't fit quite so well. A few deeper breaths than she was currently able to draw might have quelled some of the nerves chilling her skin.

Or maybe that was the presence of Martius in the carriage with them. He had taken his physical form and sat with Henri opposite her and Cameron.

It had seemed rude to ask whether it was usual for sanctii to appear at court with the creature right before her. The chill in the air emanating from the demon was disquieting. As was contemplating exactly what might occur at the ball that would require Henri calling upon the assistance of his sanctii.

And that was before she considered that, other than the driver, the men riding at front and back of the coach were all blood mages.

To distract herself, she pulled the thick fabric covering the window of the coach door aside and peered out at the passing streets. It was near dark, the last of the light of the sun barely visible over the tallest of the buildings, and lanterns were blazing to life from tall poles lining the street. Some of them seemed to be the oil lanterns she was used to back home, but others were the same strange lights used in the Academe. A few were earth stones, she thought, but the carriage moved past too fast to be certain.

Maybe they marked a temple of some kind?

The map Cameron had purchased and the more detailed

ones they'd found in the library had indicated that there were several temples dedicated to the goddess and several other deities she had never heard of. She had to assume they were imports from some of the countries annexed by the emperor. The largest of the temples to the goddess was by the palace, the others scattered throughout the city. But she was yet to see a devout or a prior anywhere near the Academe. She hadn't spotted any when on their trips back and forth to the Designys.

Would there be any at court? She couldn't imagine that the priestesses of the goddess were completely excluded from palace life here.

Though, if any were to be in attendance, she wasn't looking forward to crossing paths with the temple again.

The main road that led to the Imperial Palace bisected Lumia neatly. It also, judging by the dull throb of power she could feel far below the carriage, ran along the path of a ley line.

Which would explain why the main temple was near the palace, and at least provided some comfort that if she needed to use her powers tonight, she would be able to.

The road grew wider, lined with houses rather than businesses and tall trees spaced between the metal lampposts. As the houses grew larger and more ornate, it became clear they were nearing the palace.

Sophie's hand tightened on the fan the Designys had sent with the dress, but she was determined not to let the anxiety churning through her get the better of her.

This was not her first time at court. She might be a stranger but she was not a salt-shallow country girl new to the ways of nobility. The emperor's court would be large and the courtiers unknown, but people were not so different here. Likely the politics wouldn't be either.

Abruptly, the houses ended and the carriage slowed to pass through the gate of a high stone wall. Beyond lay not the forecourts and outbuildings of a palace but parklands.

The throb of power beneath her feet faded as they drove

through the gates, which suggested the road they now followed had diverged from the ley line. The loss of the connection was unnerving, making her feel exposed. She stared at the window, watching for any signs of trouble.

Lamps still lined the road. More ornate but spaced farther apart so the carriage moved through darker stretches between the pools of light. At first the light from the lamps made it difficult to see what lay beyond the paved edge of the road, but gradually her eyes began to adjust to the pattern of light and dark.

In the dimmer patches between the lamps, glimmers of light winked in and out, suggesting that more lamps existed in the depths of the grounds, perhaps lighting whatever paths crossed the ground shaded by the darkened shapes of trees several degrees taller and larger than those that grew in the city streets.

The carriage slowed to a more stately pace, the horses' hooves crunching sedately along the graveled road. Obviously not the done thing to rattle along the emperor's private roads at the same pace one might a public thoroughfare.

When they reached the boundaries of the park, the land abruptly opened out, free of the trees, and instead tamed into far more formal terraces and flower gardens. The horses' pace slowed again as they reached the end of a long tail of carriages circling up to the palace to deposit their distinguished occupants at the entrance. The line was long enough that Sophie couldn't make out where it ended when she chanced leaning her head outside the window.

She sat back onto the carriage seat, snapping her fan open and closed with impatience.

She would just have to wait. Neither Henri nor Cameron offered any conversation, and the silence, combined with the weight of the fathomless black gaze of the demon opposite her, weighed on her. She didn't want the quiet. It would only allow her nerves to multiply anew as they waited to reach the palace steps. But it seemed if the quiet was to be filled, she was going to have to be the one to fill it. "How many people will be attending tonight?"

Henri stirred at her question, his expression changing from distant to alert. "Five hundred. Maybe six. That seems the likely upper limit at this time of year. There will be those who are at their country estates and who will not choose to return at such short notice. If the emperor had announced his reason for the ball, or your attendance, I imagine that number would be higher. As it would be if he'd waited to summon members of the other imperial courts."

Five or six hundred? It was hard to imagine so many people gathered for a ball. And that wasn't even the full number of the court? The court at Kingswell probably numbered two hundred and fifty people when all the nobles and the courtiers were in one place. Eloisa's coronation had been larger as it was also attended by members of the Red Guard not on duty, those who held senior ranks in the various bureaucracies that formed around the court, and representatives of the three Arts. Not to mention the wealthiest merchants and traders and guild heads. But she doubted it had been more than four hundred at most.

Six hundred and not at full capacity. And this was just one of the imperial courts. The largest, of course, but it was beginning to sink home just how large the empire was. And how many people must be involved in the business of administering it.

"I guess we can be thankful that he wasn't willing to delay," Henri said. "If the emperor had decided to gather nobles from the other courts, the crush would be unbearable. The palace is large but it isn't truly designed to host a ball for several thousand people." He spoke almost absently.

Was such a number really nothing for him to be impressed by?

Perhaps not when he was master of a school of nearly a thousand students. Though it was easier to a rule a school than it would be to preside over so vast a court, particularly one filled with nobles from countries that had been subjugated by force.

The emperor must be formidable.

She should remember that.

The maistre's answers to her casual question had quelled her desire to ask any more. She stayed silent as their carriage slowly progressed in the queue. At one point, Cameron reached for her hand and she let him take it, the warmth of his skin a small antidote to the rapidly widening sea of nerves chilling her. Or maybe that was just the cold she felt from Martius sitting opposite.

The sanctii gave no indication that he was at all interested in the proceedings. He didn't speak to Henri. He barely moved, even when the carriage shifted beneath them. The stillness only made him more disconcerting.

After a small eternity, the carriage halted. The door opened and one of the blood mages extended a hand to assist Sophie in her descent. Her feet had barely settled on the paving stones before a servant of some kind dressed in magnificent silver and gold livery came bustling up to them. Tall, his brown hair clubbed back in a neat braid, he positively gleamed in the lamplight, the embroidery on his long jacket and down the sides of the black trousers glittering under the lights, the pattern of suns and stars shining like the real thing.

He clicked his heels and bowed to Sophie, then straightened and waited, his posture hardly concealing his impatience, while Cameron and Henri also climbed out of the carriage. Martius didn't join them.

The man bowed low to Henri. "Maistre. Welcome this evening. His Imperial Majesty wished me to greet you. He offers his regrets that he cannot see you immediately. But I will escort you to the ballroom so you can enjoy the festivities." He straightened, looking past Henri to Sophie, green eyes flashing a hint of curiosity before he concealed it again with a carefully neutral expression.

Festivities. Not her choice of words. Tonight would be a trial to be endured, not a lighthearted evening. Too many possible missteps lay before them for her to relax.

"Maistre?" Cameron queried softly.

Henri smiled reassuringly. "Everything is well, Lord Scardale. Let us proceed."

Apparently in the palace they were returned to being Lord and Lady Scardale. Well, perhaps that would help. She knew how to behave as Lady Scardale. Or as a court noble, at least. She actually hadn't had all that much time to become accustomed to Lady Scardale before they'd fled Anglion.

But she knew how to pull formality around herself like armor, even if she did not have the sure grasp of protocol here that she had in Queen Eloisa's court.

She and Cameron moved after Henri and the servant, past a steady stream of people walking up a central carpet laid over the marble stairs rising to the entrance to the palace.

The servant moved swiftly, taking them to the right of the queue. Other liveried servants and nobles alike melted out of their way. Whoever this man was, he was no mere footman or usher. The difference in the quality of his livery versus some of the others they passed confirmed it. The other servants were also splendidly outfitted, but the layers of gold and silver in the cloth of their clothes weren't quite so excessive, the embellishments simpler.

Nor did anyone else wearing the white and gold sport the jewels that dangled from each of their escort's ears and encrusted the buckles of his shoes.

Sophie tried not to crane her neck and gawk like that very salt-shallow girl she had told herself she was not.

The palace was huge, the ceilings vaulting something like forty feet above their heads. The floor was white marble laid in massive square tiles, softened by carpets that whispered like silk under their feet. She suspected the walls were marble as well, but they had not been left bare.

Illvyans didn't seem to approve of bare walls. Here, like the Academe, the walls were decorated. But not merely inlaid with painted tiles. That would be far too simple. Instead, they were gilded and adorned, the gold and silver and carved wood and jewels picking out fantastical scenes of flowers, plants, and animals twining up the walls toward the ceiling arches.

Lamps hung from golden brackets set at a height about two feet above Cameron's head. As they passed each one, the brackets dipped slightly, dropping the lamps lower to better light their way. Sophie flinched at the first one but then stopped to study the second as it lowered toward her. It had a faint feel of magic about it but she couldn't tell exactly how it was done. She stepped back and the bracket rose again. It was a neat trick. Though, given that there were also huge crystal chandeliers hanging above them, she wasn't entirely sure why they were needed. Still, the combined light spilling down from both walls and ceiling made the scenes on the walls sparkle and glisten.

It was a setting designed to make whoever walked its halls feel small and insignificant, a mere grain of wheat in the vast fields of the empire.

Sophie had to admit it succeeded. But she was determined not to let her discomfort show. Arranging her face in an expression as perfectly serene as she could manage, she followed the maistre to their destination.

CHAPTER 9

She'd never walked onto a battlefield but as Sophie walked into the foyer of the ballroom, waiting with Cameron and Henri so they could be announced, she wondered if the uneasy mix of fear and feigned bravado and trying to remember all the things she was supposed to do was similar to what a soldier might feel taking his place in the ranks before a battle.

Cameron would know, but if any of this was at all familiar to him, he gave no sign. He seemed to be perfectly at ease, his forearm steady under her hand.

Though there were some limits to his charade. Men trained to fight, as he had been, were rarely truly relaxed, and this was not the environment to foster that. His back was poker straight, his expression somewhat watchful, as he studied the vast room before them with practiced eyes.

It was not permitted to come armed into the presence of the emperor, a fact that Cameron had not been pleased to discover when Henri had told him. If Sophie had to guess, she would say that Cam was busy identifying any objects in the room that could be used as potential weapons. Possibly those worn on the bodies of the people thronging below as well. He could probably tell her where all the exits and entrances were by now as well.

His watchfulness was more than a little comforting. Cameron always said she was more powerful than him, but she was still untrained. He might be the lesser mage, but he was far more likely to be of use during any trouble that may arise than she was.

And now here they were. Entering the fray. Where there was little way of knowing what may happen. Victory or disaster. Either seemed possible. And the latter seemed more likely. Not wanting to borrow trouble, she resolutely put that possibility out of her mind and focused back on the scene before her.

Henri had not exaggerated the numbers. The ballroom was huge, yes, but it was also heaving with people. Women in gowns every color of the rainbow and men in a similar range of hues. Perhaps the majority of the men wore black—to stand out all the better against the silver and gold and white walls, perhaps—but everywhere she looked, long coats in many other colors stretched across broad and less broad shoulders.

She supposed the mirrored panels lining the lower ten feet of the walls were intended to add to the sense of space in the room, but with so many reflections moving and shifting in them, it only increased her sense of being completely surrounded. It was all she could do not to clutch at Cameron's arm as they moved forward. If he could pretend to be calm, so could she.

They reached the top of the long staircase that curved down to the main part of the room and paused while the servant announcing the guests boomed their names across the room. She fancied that the noise rising from below hushed slightly as the words "Scardale of Anglion" floated into the air.

Certainly there were numbers of curious upturned faces watching their descent. Henri murmured low-voiced comments, putting faces to some of the names they'd been busy memorizing since the emperor's invitation had been delivered. Senior courtiers, mid-level nobles. They didn't encounter anyone with a more exalted status. The length of the staircase gave her a chance to take in the entirety of the room. It sprawled off to the either side of the stairs, so large it was hard to take in.

To the right, people were dancing, pairs spinning and turning under the chandeliers. To the left, people were strolling or standing, conducting conversations or flirtations or goddess only knew what. There were low sofas and tables scattered around but far too few to accommodate all the people here. So most people gathered in small groups, the women's fans waving against the heat so many bodies in one place were sending forth.

From their vantage point on the stairs, the heat below was palpable. The heavy red satin, already warm, suddenly felt far too weighty. Then again, even the thinnest of muslins would be too much in this room. She snapped open her own fan, trying to raise a breath of a breeze. She supposed she should be grateful that there was no fashion for wigs in Illvya. She'd worn one to a costume ball thrown by King Stefan once in high summer and had never felt so uncomfortable in any other piece of clothing in her life.

Just the memory of it made her head itch. Which was a distraction from the heat, at least.

In the distance, beyond where the courtiers were mingling, there was a sudden oasis of space. The white marble floor changed abruptly to black and gold, the pattern like a rayed sun, fanning forth from the raised dais near the very edge of the room where an unmistakable throne sat in solitary splendor. The dais was framed in gold that seemed to melt down to join the sun pattern on the floor. Between the curved lip of the dais and the edges of the black marble where the long spokes of the sun design reached their limits, two long tables stood draped in blinding white and gold linens, set with sparkling crystal and golden flatware so they glittered like the rest of the room. They were set to either side of the throne so they—and whoever might sit at them—formed a gauntlet of a kind for anyone approaching the throne to pass through. Though currently no one occupied any of the chairs.

Likewise the throne stood empty. Where was the emperor, then? Mingling with the court? She doubted it. There would be far more guards in the room if that were the case. Was he still behind the scenes, hidden away in an audience chamber somewhere attending to urgent business? Or waiting to make a grand entrance?

That seemed more feasible. Unless of course, he was the type to try to slip in to a room.

The palace itself didn't raise her confidence in the likelihood of that possibility. It was designed to awe and overwhelm, to display the wealth and power of its occupant to the very best effect.

And to remind everyone of their place firmly beneath the feet of the emperor.

She would wager that the man did very little that would not serve to reinforce that message but she would have to wait until she met him to find out if she was right about that.

"Should we dance?" Cameron asked Henri. "Sophie and I?"

Henri pursed his lips. They'd moved forward at the end of the staircase, slowly moving through the crowd rather than deliberately aiming toward either the dance floor or the assembled throngs of gossiping nobles.

"I'm not sure," he said finally. "It is unusual for the emperor to be absent from his ballroom."

"So it would be bad form?"

"Not exactly. As you can see, many people are dancing. I just feel it might be prudent to await the emperor's arrival. You don't want him to be kept waiting if he decides to summon you." Henri's eyes went absent for a moment, the pale blue almost shimmering in the lights reflecting off every surface. For a moment Sophie thought there was an echoing shimmer across the black of his suit, but then it vanished.

"Perhaps we should wait," Sophie said. There was something

to be said for blending in to the crowd of dancers at the other end of the room, but there was no point trying to camouflage themselves if being extracted would only draw attention.

Cameron nodded in assent, looking enquiringly at Henri. "Maistre, we are in your hands."

As he spoke, a liveried servant came up to them and offered a tray of drinks in tall stemmed glasses. The liquid fizzed slightly, its pale green color unlike any wine Sophie was familiar with. Henri reached for a glass

"Campenois," he said. "From Partha." He sipped. "Try it, it is delicious."

Sophie reached for a glass, more to be polite than for any desire for alcohol. She touched it to her lips. The flavor was herbal and faintly sweet, the bubbles fizzing gently over her tongue. The maistre was correct. It was delicious. And would be far too easy to consume quickly. She lowered the glass and turned her attention back to the room as Henri slowly moved through the crowd, angling toward the area where the dais stood.

She was about to ask Henri to tell her who some of the people in the crowd were when a woman in a brilliant blue gown stepped into his path.

"Maistre Matin, how delightful." She dipped her head. The weight of the sapphires and diamonds looped around her neck and wrists and hanging from her ears would have possibly sunk a small boat. Henri bowed deeply in response to her greeting. Who was this woman? Someone of high rank, surely, to earn that bow?

"Venable du Laq," Henri said. "It is always a pleasure."

She was a mage?

Sophie covered her surprise by offering a curtsy as well.

"Venable, may I present Lord and Lady Scardale?" Henri said as Sophie rose.

"Indeed you may," she replied in a tone that made Sophie think that her crossing their paths hadn't been an accident.

Her face in a carefully pleasant expression, she studied the woman. She was taller than Sophie, though not by much, her hair a mass of black and brown and red streaks. A combination Sophie hadn't seen since the last time she'd seen Chloe de Montesse. Earth witch. Water mage. Maybe other powers. Venable du Laq was not one to be underestimated. Her face was sharply beautiful, eyes the color of sapphires studying Sophie just as intently as Sophie studied her. It was also carefully painted, making it hard to judge her age. Not old, certainly. Definitely older than Sophie herself though, to hold the rank of Venable. Perhaps more toward Chloe's age.

"Lord and Lady Scardale, this is Venable Imogene du Laq, wife of the Duq du Laq," Henri said.

"Your Grace," Sophie murmured as Cameron bowed. Venable du Laq, Henri had said. Not Her Grace, or Lady—she was forgetting just now what the correct title for the wife of a duq was. Interesting. Did her rank as a venable take precedence?

"Her Grace works for the emperor," Henri continued. "As one of the *corps de sages*. They are part of the Imperial Guard."

Imperial mages? She knew they existed. But for some reason she'd assumed they would be battle mages, like the Red Guard. Was Venable du Laq also a blood mage, then? Sophie shot Henri a sideways glance. It seemed this battlefield contained more potential dangers than she had thought. "That sounds fascinating," she said, forcing enthusiasm into her voice. "I would love to hear more."

Venable du Laq's red-painted lips smiled broadly. Though it was a court-mannered smile if ever Sophie had seen one, hiding whatever true emotion she may have been feeling. The cascading diamonds and sapphires at her ears sparkled under the lights as she tilted her head slightly. "Well, aren't you a bright one?" She gave Sophie a curiously intent look. "I should be glad to tell you of my work. Perhaps in return, you can share some knowledge of your homeland with me. One hears such curious things."

"Oh, we're not so interesting," Cameron said. "I'm sure there are far odder places in the empire." His voice was as polite as the venable's.

"Perhaps, but those are all places I could go if I chose," the venable returned. "Though perhaps your presence here may herald the beginning of better things between Anglion and Illvya."

Did she know something about the emperor's intentions toward them? Aristides seemed to have kept his views—along with his reasons for summoning Sophie and Cameron—close. Close enough to keep them from Henri's spies at least, but this woman worked for Aristides. For his mage corps. It was hard for a ruler to keep secrets from his own guards for too long. Though Eloisa had certainly managed to hide her affair with Cameron from hers. And he'd been one of them. She'd even kept that secret from her ladies-in-waiting. Or from Sophie, at least.

Sophie cut that line of thought off before it distracted her. Cameron was hers now. Eloisa was far away. She needed to keep her attention on more immediate dangers. Like the woman in front of her. Her gut said that Imogene was not to be trifled with. And not to be trusted. But perhaps she could be useful. "I would be delighted to talk to you sometime," she said. "I have only met some of the venables who work and study at the Academe so far. I would like to know more of you."

The venable's smile turned more sincerely pleased. "Excellent." She turned her gaze to Henri. "But I think I have taken up enough of your time. The maistre is looking impatient with me."

"With you? Never?"

Venable du Laq tilted her head. "That is kind of you to say, Maistre."

For an instant, Sophie thought her eyes looked sad.

"And did these charming Anglions bring you any news, Maistre?" Her voice had lost a little of the polished edge it held.

Henri's lips pressed together. Sophie thought perhaps he wasn't going to answer the question, but then he said, "Only that she is well, Imogene."

She? Chloe? Had this woman known her?

Had they perhaps been friends? If that had been the case, wouldn't Henri be offering more information than merely that Chloe was well? Most likely. The only conclusion then was that he didn't want her to know. Noted.

Before Venable du Laq could ask anything more, the servant who'd escorted them earlier pushed through the group standing nearest to them and stopped next to Henri, looking intent.

At the sight of him, the venable's expression turned to a court mask again, that glimpse of something more human locked away. "Louis," she said politely. "What brings you into the throng?"

The servant smiled tightly at her. "Duquesse, Maistre, good evening," Louis said. "Lord and Lady Scardale, my Imperial Master requests your company."

One of Venable du Laq's dark eyebrows flickered upward briefly.

"You, too, Maistre Matin." Louis smiled politely at Imogene. "I'm sure Her Grace will excuse you all."

"I serve at the pleasure of the emperor," Imogene said. "I'm sure my husband must be wondering where I have gotten to."

Sophie almost snorted at that. From what she'd seen of the woman in this brief time, it would be a brave man who expected her to dance attendance on him as his wife. Which meant, perhaps, that they should take the man who did command her loyalty and attention even more seriously.

The venable bobbed a shallow curtsy. "Maistre. Lord and Lady Scardale. I hope we meet again." She didn't say anything to Louis as she turned and began to move away from them.

Headed on a path that would take her toward the area where the dais stood, Sophie noted. Imogene clearly did not intend on missing out on anything important that might be about to happen. There was also clearly not a lot of love lost between her and Louis. But that was not so uncommon. Senior servants often had to perform whatever unpleasant tasks their masters set them. In a court like this, the more unpleasant tasks would include denying access or information to the nobles and courtiers. A loyal and unbribable servant was valuable but often not well liked by those who couldn't get around them.

This particular loyal—and presumably unbribable—servant was starting to look impatient.

"Lead on, Louis," Henri said, and the three of them followed him as he walked through the crowd. It was somewhat easier than their earlier progress had been. The people tended to fall away, clearing a path for Louis and for the three of them following in his wake. It only confirmed Sophie's suspicions of just how senior Louis might be amongst the emperor's functionaries.

They walked past the dais. Sophie had half expected to see the emperor sitting there, but apparently whatever he wanted now was not business to be conducted in public. They followed Louis beyond the dais to the far end of the room where he opened a door and led them into a corridor beyond.

There were guards standing by the door on the corridor side. It seemed likely that wherever they were now within the palace was off-limits to anyone not invited.

They moved briskly down the corridor, passing several more sets of guards, which only reinforced her theory. So where exactly were they going? She tightened her fingers around Cameron's arm. He reached over with his free hand to rest it on hers. A brief touch of reassurance. Whatever was happening, they were there together.

It was a comfort, if a small one, as her nerves, forgotten while talking to Venable du Laq, returned and multiplied with each step along the plush silk carpets.

Their final destination became clear when they reached a larger set of doors shielded by not two but six black-clad guards standing at either side of it, like a rank of well-armed ravens. Two of them moved in unison to open the doors.

The room beyond was less formal than the previous audience

chamber. It was decorated in shades of pale blue and green and lacked anything resembling a throne. Which was a relief. But it also wasn't empty. A tall, dark-haired man stood near the center of the room.

"Maistre Matin, Lord Scardale, Lady Scardale, *Eleivé*," their guide intoned with a bow even deeper than that he had greeted them with at the carriage.

The man waved impatiently. "Very good, Louis. Leave us now."

There was unmistakable command in that voice. Which left her in little doubt as to who this man was. She followed Maistre Matin's example and curtsied as low as she could in the dress as the maistre bowed.

"Well, Henri, what have you brought me this evening?" The voice was a rich low baritone.

"Your Imperial Majesty, may I present Lord and Lady Scardale." Henri bowed again, straightened, and then gestured Sophie and Cameron forward.

Aristides Delmar de Lucien was dressed in layers of gold-embroidered white satin, lace, and jewels, his dark hair bound back with more jewels and his hands glittering with rings. But the finery was not what commanded attention. No, that came from the sheer certain command in his clear gray eyes. Here was a man used to having his every wish fulfilled, his will obeyed, his world ordered perfectly according to his needs and wants.

And what Sophie suddenly understood as that gray gaze met hers was that, when it came to herself and Cameron, he was not yet decided what those wants and needs may be.

"Lord and Lady Scardale. Welcome. I am glad you could accept my invitation to attend tonight," the emperor said.

His tone was pleasant, as though they had indeed had some choice in the matter, instead of being compelled by his request.

Sophie curtsied again. "Your Imperial Majesty is too kind. We had not looked for such an honor."

"Indeed. That makes two of us. I find myself wondering what

I have done to deserve the arrival of such distinguished . . . . guests on my shores," the emperor replied.

That was a question with no immediate easy answer. Sophie rose from her curtsy and stayed silent.

"We did not intend to cause Your Imperial Majesty any trouble," Cameron said.

Aristides tilted his head at that. A jewel swung from his ear. A single enormous black pearl, she realized with a start. She had not thought that Illvyans wore pearls.

Was this why Martius had not accompanied them into the palace? Had he remained in the carriage? Sanctii weren't always visible, after all. She couldn't feel the chill in the air that would have told her one was close, so she had no idea.

"Regardless of intentions, I thought we should deal in person," the emperor said. "To keep matters simple."

"Simple, Your Imperial Majesty?" Henri asked. Was that a slight note of alarm in his voice?

"To lay matters out," came the cool response. "These two are not the only Anglions seeking our shores lately."

Sophie clamped her lips together to stop the gasp that rose in her throat but the emperor must have heard something. His gaze swung back to her.

"Indeed, Lady Scardale. An unexpected honor. We received a request for a diplomatic party to be admitted to Lumia not two days after your arrival. Several days ago, that envoy—envoys—arrived. They are very concerned with your well-being, it seems."

They? Who? Her mind was reeling. Anglion had sent people to Illvya. To . . . retrieve Cameron and her? To what end? To bear them home to safety? Or to finish the job started at the palace? She clasped her hands, worried they might start to shake.

"I have reassured them that you are unharmed," the emperor said. "But they seemed insistent on seeing for themselves." He smiled a little.

It wasn't a pleasant expression. Anglion was in no position to insist that the Emperor of Illvya do anything. In fact, the country spent a good deal of its time, money, and resources on ensuring that the emperor had no influence in Anglion at all. Some limited trade occurred between the empire and the island nation, but other than that relations were cool.

The might of the empire should be able to crush Anglion, but as the Illvyan imperial forces traditionally used water magic and sanctii to quickly subdue nations they wished to conquer, they had, so far, not been successful. Anglion remained protected by the breadth of ocean between its shores and the mainland. By the vast depths of salt water the sanctii could not cross.

And yet, she was to understand that they had sent people seeking her in the face of the knowledge that all that such a mission could possibly do was focus the attention of the empire back on Anglion?

"May I ask who these envoys are, Your Imperial Majesty?" Cameron said carefully.

"As to that—"

The doors behind them were suddenly flung open. "Father!" a voice cried. "Our guests grow impatient."

She couldn't resist looking, though it was a breach of protocol to do so. Luckily she didn't have to turn away from the emperor for long because the young—though perhaps not quite so young as the petulant tone suggested—man ignored the three of them completely to join his father. Crown Prince Alain, it seemed, didn't care much for protocol either. Or to notice lesser mortals than himself.

"Alain, I asked you to wait," Aristides said, sounding displeased.

"They are very insistent," the prince said casually, as though he didn't hear the rebuke clear in his father's voice. He looked very like his father, though his eyes were a dark and impenetrable shade of brown rather than gray. But they shared the dark hair, the rangy build, and the angles of cheek and jaw and nose that framed their faces like blades.

"You are the Crown Prince of Illvya. It doesn't matter how insistent they are," Aristides said, his tone quelling. "But perhaps you and I will discuss that later. Shall I present you to our other guests?"

Sophie had the feeling that the crown prince knew very well who they were. And that he'd forced himself into this discussion prematurely. But if the emperor wished to behave as though this was all perfectly normal, then they had to follow his example.

"Of course," Alain said. "I would be delighted."

His gaze was firmly on Sophie, and she found herself suddenly wishing for a neckline that had been constructed a little less daringly as his expression warmed.

She didn't dare look at Cameron. Punching the crown prince was not an action that would be to their advantage.

So she channeled a version of Madame Simsa's—or maybe it was Domina Skey's—imperious stare. The one that said you are an insect beneath my shoe and I could crush you if I was so inclined. She didn't sense any hint of magic rising from the prince. The room, though, was well warded, making even the deep throb of the ley line that still ran beneath their feet feel muted.

"My son. Crown Prince Alain Phillipe Delmar de Lucien of Illvya," Aristides said with a short sweep of his hands that encompassed the prince. "And this is Lord and Lady Scardale. Sophia and Cameron, as I understand it. Henri, you have met before."

The prince's lips drew back, revealing very white teeth. The overall effect was somewhat wolfish, though Sophie wasn't sure if the expression was aimed at her or Henri. He clicked his heels and bowed shallowly. "The Anglions! An unexpected pleasure."

To hide her instinct to roll her eyes at the comment, Sophie curtsied again. Cameron followed her example.

"Or should I say *some* of the Anglions," the prince continued.

Sophie straightened a little faster than strictly polite at that. The prince was still smiling at her. The more she saw that smile, the less she liked it. The emperor was clearly dealing in politics, and that was to be expected. The son, however, seemed as though he would be more interested in stirring up trouble. Not a welcome trait in a man who would someday rule an empire. His father should put him to work. He was already married, but that didn't seem to have turned him into a sober, fatherly type. So. What to do with a bored princeling? Send him to govern a distant country or two? Give him a war to fight?

Anything to take him far away from her. Hopefully her antipathy toward him didn't show. She rarely took an instant dislike to anyone, but apparently the crown prince was an exception. Well, his father was not yet old. Only in his forties. The prince had a long wait ahead of him for any true power. And if she was wary of the son, then best to make sure that she did nothing to offend the father.

"To think we go for so long with nary a visit from your little island and then such a crowd appears at once," the prince said, expression serious but voice amused. "I'm sure it will be a joyous reunion for you all."

That depended entirely on who the envoys were and who had sent them. She wasn't going to ask. It was the emperor's information to share or not.

"Alain," the emperor said warningly.

The prince bowed. "Father. Shall I fetch the ambassadors?"

Aristides nodded. "Yes."

Alain smiled and left the room. Sophie tried to look calm as she stood waiting for him to return. The emperor was silent, and she could hardly question him further. Cameron moved a little closer to her, offering silent comfort.

She turned her mind to considering who Eloisa may have sent. It was difficult to know. It was difficult to believe that the queen had sent anyone at all.

The amount of meticulously cautious negotiation and compromise that had taken place in the palace at Kingswell each year when the preparations for the annual trade delegations to Illvya were being planned had been staggering.

To have a delegation decided upon, assembled, and sent in a few days was unheard of.

That she was the reason for it to occur made her more ill at ease about being in the Imperial Palace than she had been before.

When the door opened again, the sound of it startled her, even though she'd been braced for it. She turned, abandoning protocol once more, to see who accompanied the prince. Four men came in behind Alain, filing in quickly to stand to the prince's left as he took up position by his father's side.

She recognized all of them.

Rigby Lancefeld—Barron Deepholt—who had been one of King Stefan's advisors and still served in that capacity to his daughter, stood closest to the emperor, leaning on the cane he always used. Next to him, Sir Harold Lenten, who had once headed King Stefan's personal guard. He had long since retired from service, though the long jacket he wore was the distinctive shade of red worn by the Red Guard.

Beside Sir Harold, standing slightly back from the line, was a tall, thin, intense-faced younger man Sophie thought was Sevan Allowood, a courtier and distant cousin to the young Barron Nester who stood above Sophie in the line of succession.

And lastly, and most surprisingly, was James Listfold, heir to the Erl of Airlight. Cameron's sister-in-law's brother.

Cameron took half a step forward, then checked himself as Sophie tightened her grip on his arm.

Sophie watched as the Anglions all bowed to Aristides. She'd forgotten in her few weeks away from court life how much time one wasted in all the endless acts of deference to rank and power.

When they were done, she turned slightly to face them. Technically, given her position in the line of succession, she outranked all the men. In a situation where she wasn't in attendance on the queen, they owed her courtesy, not the other way around.

She stared at Barron Deepholt. Who slowly, reluctantly, bowed to her. The others followed suit.

Well. That was a small victory. They still acknowledged her rank. Perhaps that was a good sign.

"These gentlemen were desirous of assuring themselves of your well-being, Lady Scardale," the emperor said. "Quite insistent, in fact." He spoke Anglish, his voice barely accented.

Who had taught him to speak like that? Oh, for a longer acquaintance with the emperor so that she might know what the small changes in his tone signified.

Or, for that matter, know what any of this signified. None of the four men looked particularly relieved to see her. James had smiled quickly at Cameron when they had first entered, but he was now stolidly blank-faced.

The lack of warmth did not bode well for the outcome of the meeting. She made herself wait. Better not to speak when she did not know what the right thing to say would be.

"We are grateful for their concern," Cameron said when it was clear she wasn't going to respond.

"Did you expect anything less from Her Majesty?" Barron Deepholt asked. His voice was deep, like his name, the rumble of it familiar. The sound of Anglish spoken by a native—something she'd heard from no one but Cameron since they'd come to Lumia—made her suddenly long for home.

These men were her chance to return. If, indeed, that was what they were truly offering.

"Well, Lord Scardale?" the barron prompted. "Did you not think Her Majesty would be keen to assure herself of the welfare of one of her own ladies-in-waiting? Not to mention a member of the succession?"

Cameron glanced at Aristides. Was he deciding how much of their story he wished the emperor to know or waiting to see if the emperor would intervene in the conversation?

But the emperor didn't speak. Merely watched with those gray eyes that gave no clue as to what the mind behind them might be thinking.

"As we were attacked the last time we were in Her Majesty's palace, it is difficult to form any expectation at all," Cameron said.

Aristides' mouth twitched fractionally. She wondered what explanation he had been offered previously by Henri—and the Anglions—about what had brought Cameron and her to his country.

Perhaps not a full one. Not that Cameron had revealed all the details yet.

"Her Majesty had nothing to do with the attack," Barron Deepholt protested.

Cameron shrugged. "That is a matter of her word."

The barron's face was reddening. "As your attacker did not survive the encounter, there seems little other evidence to offer. Is the queen's word not good enough for you, a sworn member of her guard, Lord Scardale?"

Sophie stilled. What would Cameron say to that? Would he mention that they had questioned the man before he died? That he had told a tale of being hired by a woman wearing brown and smelling of temple incense? A plausible enough tale, given the Domina's dislike of Sophie and her lack of binding. Plausible enough to make them flee.

"Let us say that hearing her word secondhand currently presents a dilemma," Cameron said neutrally.

Which left Sophie none the wiser about what he might be thinking. Only that he was taking a more aggressive stance with the delegation than she might have expected. He had been the one counseling caution, that they should not do anything that would endanger their ability to one day return to Anglion whilst in Illvya.

The barron squared his shoulders, bushy eyebrows drawing down. "The queen wishes you and your lady wife to return with us to Anglion."

Sophie's breath rushed out of her. That blunt statement contained no assurance as to what might happen once they set foot on Anglion soil, no evidence that the queen was worried about them. Just a bald expression of Eloisa's will for them to return. But then again, Barron Deepholt had never been one to mince words.

"And what evidence do you offer that you are actually here at the queen's behest, Barron?" Cameron asked.

Deepholt tapped his cane on the floor, which sent the long black coat he wore rippling around him. "Who else has the power to send a delegation to Illvya?"

"Be that as it may," Cameron said. " I would prefer to see proof that you speak for her."

"Her Majesty can hardly travel to Illvya," Sir Harold blurted.

Aristides raised his hand before Cameron could respond to that. "Lord Scardale, I am satisfied with the credentials the ambassadors presented me. They would not be here were I not. You may trust they come in service to your queen."

They could. If they trusted the emperor. But that wasn't a point they could argue. Sophie focused on the barron. "In that case, I'm sure she sent you here with messages."

All four of the Anglions turned their gazes on her. James looked faintly approving. The others, far less so. The barron didn't answer. She straightened her shoulders. "Did the queen send a message for me, milord? Or my husband?"

By right, it would come to her. But Eloisa and Cameron had been . . . intimate once. Sophie would once have said that she and Eloisa had been friends, too, but that was before the attack on the palace in Kingswell that killed King Stefan. Before Eloisa had been near-fatally injured. Before Sophie and Cameron had been bonded out of wedlock, Sophie unwittingly stealing the queen's lover in the process. Even if Cameron was a man Eloisa could never have married.

Before Domina Skey's influence over the court had expanded so rapidly.

So she knew nothing, really.

Barron Deepholt snapped his fingers toward Sevan Allowood. Sophie hadn't noticed the leather folio the younger man held earlier. But now he extracted an envelope from it, passing it to the barron. Sophie recognized the seal. Eloisa's. The same wave and crown device her father had used.

Seals could, of course, be forged.

The barron held the envelope out. She didn't reach for it. After a beat, Henri stepped forward and took it, passing it to Sophie.

"The queen would find your distrust distressing, milady," Sir Harold murmured.

"Queen Eloisa has never valued fools, Sir Harold," Sophie replied. "She does not teach her ladies to be reckless." And Sophie's time at court had, on occasion, demonstrated exactly why caution was to be favored over bold action.

"You think we would snatch you from the depths of the emperor's palace?" Barron Deepholt sputtered.

A little too indignant, perhaps. Though she didn't think they would attempt such a blatant violation of the emperor's hospitality, there were other things that could be passed by contact. Poisons. Or charms to make her believe what they said. Illusioner's work. Rare, but possible.

"Perhaps now would be an opportune time to remind you all that you stand under my hospitality. And my protection. *All* of you," Aristides said dryly.

A reminder that any attempt to take the Scardales by force would be ill-received? Or simply a caution for them all to maintain some semblance of civility?

Either way, she bobbed a quick curtsy of recognition at the emperor and then focused back on the seal.

Normally she would have asked Cameron for the loan of his dagger to open it. But here, he stood unarmed. Aristides, as though anticipating her lack, clicked his finger and one of the guards stepped forward, offering her a small blade.

She slid it beneath the wax, then handed it back somewhat reluctantly. A weapon would have been a comfort.

The paper she pulled from the envelope was heavy and a familiar weight and color. Sophie had penned enough notes on Eloisa's behalf to recognize the stationery the queen used. The sea blue ink was the color she favored as well.

Sophie studied the words on the page. The hand appeared to be the queen's. But the written words were unyieldingly formal. Stiff. They conveyed little more than what the barron had said. The queen wished for Sophie and Cameron to return to court. To be "restored to their rightful place" with all due haste.

It was no more comforting than the barron's message, for all that it appeared to be genuine. "Rightful place" could be interpreted in a number of different ways, entirely dependent on how the queen currently viewed them.

Wordlessly, she passed the letter to Cameron, who scanned it, then refolded it without comment.

The barron held out his hand, clearly expecting Cameron to pass the letter back to him.

Sophie lifted an eyebrow. "Are you requesting to read my personal correspondence from the queen, milord?"

He hesitated, then nodded.

She smiled tightly. "Request denied." She had the feeling if she returned the letter she might not see it again. Besides, she wanted it to be checked for anything hidden in the paper or ink. She turned to Henri. "Perhaps you could keep this safe for me, Maistre?" Taking a chance that the Anglions were unlikely to tackle an Illvyan mage.

Henri nodded and then made a small gesture in the air.

Martius suddenly appeared beside him. To a man, the Anglions stumbled back before they caught themselves, staring at the sudden manifestation of their worst nightmares standing by the maistre's side. Henri handed Martius the letter, said something in the sanctii tongue, and then the demon disappeared again.

"Really, Maistre?" the emperor murmured. Sophie couldn't agree more. That wasn't exactly what she had been thinking of when she'd asked Henri to take the letter.

Involving a sanctii was hardly going to make the Anglions view her with any less suspicion. But it was too late to act as though she was as shocked as the others at the sight of Martius.

"My apologies. I beg Your Imperial Majesty's indulgence," Henri said, bowing low.

"Most people would request permission before an act, not after," the emperor remarked.

Henri nodded in acknowledgement as he straightened but didn't appear to be terribly contrite.

The four Anglions still stared at the place where Martius had stood, faces pale and panicked.

"Are there any other messages?" Sophie asked. The chill Martius had left in the air was fading but still enough to make her want to shiver. She was determined not to react. Perhaps she wasn't doing her cause any good by demonstrating she was accustomed to sanctii, but so far the Anglions had not done anything to give her any real hope that it would be safe to return home.

Maybe she was being pessimistic. Cameron might have a different view. But so far, her instincts said she was in danger. Even the presence of James Listfold seemed more likely to be a means to try and compel Cameron's compliance than anything else.

"Barron Deepholt," she repeated as no one replied. "Do you carry any more messages for us?"

"Th-that was a demon," the barron stuttered.

"It was a familiaris sanctii," Henri corrected. "They are not uncommon here."

"But—" The barron's expression turned from upset to appalled. "Lady Scardale, have you . . . " He trailed off, as though unwilling to even speak the accusation.

"Lady Scardale is an earth witch," Henri said firmly. "She knows nothing of water magic."

The barron almost shuddered at the words. He clutched at his wrist, where he usually wore a heavy metal band studded with black pearls. It had been the fashion amongst the older men of the court. But his wrist was bare.

None of the party wore any pearls, in fact. Had they attempted to be polite? Or had they been warned not to. What, then, had they made of the emperor's choice of jewels?

"Even so—" the barron began.

"Even so, what?" Cameron interrupted. "My wife has done no more magic here than she would have back in Anglion."

"But she has kept company with a man who consorts with demons."

"In my time here, I have observed little consorting of any kind," Sophie interjected. "And demons—sanctii—are not slaughtering people in the streets. Not everything we have been taught about them is true, it seems. As you will have seen for yourselves since you arrived."

"This is true," James said, speaking for the first time. Sevan Allowood shot him a look of disgust.

"That does not change the fact that demons are an—" the barron started to say, but the rest of his sentence was cut short by the simple mechanism of Aristides clearing his throat. All attention turned back to the emperor.

"Gentleman, you have delivered your queen's request. I believe it is only fitting that Lord and Lady Scardale be given time to consider their response."

The expression on Barron Deepholt's face made it plain that he didn't think there was anything to consider. But he didn't argue.

"Now, I believe I must join my ball before the entire court

explodes in a fervor of curiosity about my whereabouts. We shall announce the presence of your delegation as a renewed sign of hope for improvement of relations between our two countries, and then we shall have an evening of entertainment."

Clearly anything else was not going to be a possibility. Beside the barron, Sir Harold looked like he was going to have an apoplexy, and Sevan Allowood was still looking most unhappy. James' face had returned to standard courtier neutrality, though he alone seemed to be focused on Sophie and Cameron rather than the emperor.

But before anyone could speak, the doors opened once more and the emperor's guards filed back into the room.

CHAPTER 10

C ameron escorted Sophie back to the ballroom, walking behind the emperor and his guards. The members of the Anglion delegation followed in their wake, and the space between his shoulder blades itched with the weight of the glares he could only imagine they were directing at him.

As first meetings went, what had just transpired was not promising. The lack of any assurance about what kind of reception awaited them if they returned to Anglion was disturbing. Disturbing enough that he was fighting the urge to take Sophie and vanish into the night once more. To run, to put it bluntly.

Only the knowledge that they would be unlikely to make it past the palace gates, let alone the city limits, kept him trying to come up with an alternative plan.

If the tightness of Sophie's grip on his arm was any indication, she was as upset as him. Goddess. He wished they could stop for a moment. Talk. Form a plan. But the emperor was moving and they must move with him. And then be swept up in whatever came next.

The party walked into the ballroom and the noise died

almost instantly, the musicians cutting off mid-note and the chatter of conversation silenced.

The emperor seated himself on the dais and proceeded to make a short speech in which he welcomed the Anglions, while not distinguishing Sophie and Cameron from the envoys.

His pronouncement caused a shocked murmur of response that rippled and spread across the room before silence descended once more.

"We need to—" Sophie started to say, but before she could complete her sentence, the crown prince strolled across from where he had been standing to the right of his father, bowed very elegantly to Sophie, and asked her to dance.

Ladies didn't refuse requests from crown princes to dance at their father's balls. Not even royal witches. So Cameron had no choice but to watch Sophie walk the length of the room, the crowd opening up to let her and Alain pass before closing behind them again, and then take her position on the dance floor.

"Easy," Henri said softly from beside him. "Don't glower so. At this precise moment, a dance with Alain might be the safest place for her. It is a clear sign of the emperor's favor, that he has sent his son to partner her to open the ball."

"That doesn't necessarily help up when it comes to . . . ." Cameron lifted his chin slightly in the direction of the barron who stood with Sir Harold and James—how was he going to get a moment to try and talk to James?—off to the left of the dais. The three of them were trying not to look uncomfortable and not entirely succeeding.

"They are displeased with you and you wife, I gather. You cannot do anything to change the fact that you came here. So perhaps it is not so bad that they be reminded that the emperor is protecting you, as he said?" Henri replied with a shrug. "For now, best we find you a dance partner as well so it doesn't look quite so much as though you are plotting how to punch the crown prince on the nose."

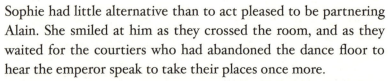

Sophie had little alternative than to act pleased to be partnering Alain. She smiled at him as they crossed the room, and as they waited for the courtiers who had abandoned the dance floor to hear the emperor speak to take their places once more.

Alain complimented her dress and made other small talk before the musicians started to play, but once they began, he merely stepped forward and swept her into the dance. The music swirled around her, the room spinning into a dizzying whirl of couples circling and swaying. Thankfully the hours spent with the dancing master earlier in the week seemed to have imprinted some memory of the steps on her feet and she was able to keep up with the prince, the movements of the dance easier once a partner who knew entirely what he was doing had control over her.

After the initial burst of concentration required to find her place in the rhythm, she managed to remember to look up at her partner.

"You dance quite well, Lady Scardale," Alain said.

Was there an unspoken "for an Anglion" implicit in that statement? "Thank you, Your Imperial Highness. I have always enjoyed dancing."

There. Polite chitchat. She would behave just as though she were at a ball at Kingswell and she had no greater concern than making sure that Eloisa was enjoying herself and that she herself danced with whomever amongst the court she had been told to dance with or who happened to ask her.

She wouldn't have picked Alain though, if she were choosing a partner. She watched his face, ready to react, but he appeared more interested in watching those around them. Seeing how they reacted to his choice of partner? Or perhaps trying to catch glimpses of himself in the mirrored walls?

Aristides had been dressed as befitted an emperor, but his clothes had been designed for elegance and authority. Alain's approached something closer to gaudy. The gold embroidery twining around his sleeves in patterns of snakes and some strange bird she didn't recognize was heavy enough that she wondered that he could even lift his arms for the dance. And where Aristides had chosen white as the base for his clothes, beneath all the embellishment, Alain's jacket was a poisonous shade of green.

He danced well though and didn't let her falter as they moved through the steps of one dance and then another. But on the whole, she would have been happy to trade his perfect dancing for a partner who was less accomplished but more . . . well, not attentive. She didn't want the prince's attention. But it would be far more pleasant to be dancing with a man who saw her as a person, not a game piece to be manipulated.

Though truly it would be far more pleasant to be almost anywhere else, so maybe her partner didn't matter overmuch.

The strains of the tune altered, morphing into a different, slower melody. The dancing master had warned them about this, that Illvyans often danced four or five long dances without stopping before they changed partners. There were no clocks on the walls of the ballroom, so she was just going to have to grit her teeth and keep dancing as long as the music lasted.

Once she had done her duty with the prince, then perhaps she would be able to fade into the background as much as possible for the rest of the ball.

Though, as she watched various degrees of speculation and curiosity spark on the faces of the dancers moving past them, she wasn't so sure that would be possible. The crown prince had deemed her worthy of notice. So had the emperor by inviting her to attend the ball in the first place and announcing her status as an honored guest. Unless the Illvyan court was wholly unlike the Anglion one, there would be a flood of those desperate to learn more about her and Cameron, and equally desperate to determine if any connection to them could be used to an advantage. She would not lack for partners.

"Such deep thoughts," Alain said abruptly, his gaze returned to her. He spoke Illvyan, though to his credit, he didn't speak at the rapid-fire pace of the couples around her. "Are you always so quiet when you dance, Lady Scardale?"

She made herself smile up at him. "Forgive me, Your Imperial Highness. I was merely enjoying the spectacle. Such a beautiful room." She widened the smile. "And I need to concentrate, unfamiliar as I am with your music." Not to mention trying to keep track of the snatches of Illvyan that she caught as the dance took them within close range of the other couples. As well as holding herself ready to translate whatever Alain himself might say to her.

Perhaps she should have requested the reveilé after all. Court intrigue was always difficult enough without trying to navigate it in a language she wasn't sure of.

"Well, you make it look effortless," the prince replied. Then he smiled at someone over her shoulder, and the amusement lighting his eyes sent an uneasy shiver down her spine. "But perhaps I can do something to make you feel more at home." He rotated her with a few quick steps and she found herself face-to-face with Sevan Allowood, dancing stiffly with a blond woman gowned in pale green. Sevan's eyes narrowed on Sophie, his expression stiffer than his steps.

"A friendly face, mayhap," Alain said. He nodded at Stefan's companion. "Lady du Plutars, it has been too long since I had the pleasure of your hand on the dance floor. Perhaps you would indulge me by changing partners?"

Goddess. She couldn't think of anything less likely to make her feel at home than having to dance with Sevan, who had spent much of their audience with the emperor glowering at her and Cameron.

But she doubted the prince would care to hear her objections. Before she knew quite what was happening, Sevan's partner had stepped out of his arms and the prince deposited Sophie neatly into them.

Conscious that doing anything but complying would cause a scene, she raised her arms to the required position and felt Stefan's hands close around her. One over her right hand, another at her waist. His skin felt oddly chilled despite the warmth of the room. Perhaps he was as nervous as she.

"Sir Allowood," she said politely as they swung back into the pattern. She wasn't entirely sure that was his correct title. He was a cousin to Barron Nester but a distant one, and not an eldest son, unless she was remembering the particulars incorrectly. He didn't stand in line to inherit either title or wealth and worked as some sort of clerk for the queen's revenue collectors.

Exactly the kind of younger man who often focused on climbing the ranks at court with ruthless ambition by making themselves useful to the monarch or the senior nobility. In Sevan's case, by attaching himself to the treasury. And volunteering for a delegation to Illvya was exactly the kind of task which might appeal to a man trying to distinguish himself. Which would explain his presence amongst the envoys better than his tenuous connection to Barron Nester.

So politeness would seem prudent.

"Lady Scardale," he returned. He stared down at her, dark eyes cold as his skin.

She remembered the look of disgust he'd given James earlier. This man was not her friend. Should she play the meek mouse or try to find out what in the goddess' name was behind this so-called mission to reclaim her and Cameron? Perhaps treading a path somewhere between the two would be wisest.

"That was neatly done," she said, nodding in the direction of the prince's back, revolving away from them.

Sevan's grip tightened on her hand. "If you imagine I can influence the crown prince of Illvya, then you are mistaken, milady."

"Oh," she said. "I don't think it was you. Did the barron make a request? Or did the crown prince come up with the scheme?" That seemed more likely. She didn't see why Alain would wish to do the barron any favors. But this was the second time he'd forced the situation. The question, then, was whether he was manipulating things on his own or at the behest of his father? The former seemed preferable. So far, the emperor had seemed neutral in this affair. It would be better if he remained so. No doubt he had his own agenda, but right now her instincts said she was safer under his protection than with the Anglions.

Which would have disturbed her far more if she hadn't more immediately pressing concerns. Like finishing the dance with Sevan and then getting far away from him.

So. Best to find out what he wanted. And he didn't seem to be readily volunteering the information. "After all, this is a fairly innocuous way of ensuring we have the opportunity to converse less formally."

Presumably that was what the emperor wanted. Or he wouldn't have thrown a ball to announce their presence in Lumia, let alone made public the news that he was receiving an unexpected Anglion diplomatic delegation. He could merely have summoned them to the palace to meet the envoys secretly.

Of course, she wouldn't put it past Alain to have arranged the meeting between Sevan and herself for his own amusement. From what she had seen of him, he was the type to find disruption diverting. She recognized the type. Eloisa had done her share of testing of her father's authority in her time as well.

Perhaps it was a failing of crown princes and princesses once they came of age. To be bred and trained to take the throne but not be able to do so until your mother or father died or otherwise vacated it must be an odd sort of limbo. Like the anticipation before one's Ais-Seann, waiting to see if you were going to have power or not. Only they remained in that state for years. Decades even.

Which might just incline one to find occupation and entertainment in other pastimes. Like court politics. Being in permanent waiting would be difficult to bear.

As was the current seething silence coming—or not—from

her partner. She wasn't in the mood to prevaricate endlessly. If Sevan was dancing with her when he so clearly disliked her, it was because he had been ordered or manipulated into doing so. "So, Sir Allowood, what are we to discuss?"

"If you believe that I wish to converse with a traitor, then you are also mistaken," Sevan said in a harsh rush.

Traitor? Sophie almost stumbled to a stop in the middle of the ballroom but Sevan's grip tightened—almost painfully—and kept her upright.

"I am no traitor," she hissed at him. "I fled in fear of my life. Someone tried to kill me."

"Yet here you are. Firmly ensconced in the court of your queen's sworn enemy."

Her mind was still reeling. Traitor? He thought her a traitor? Did the rest of the court? Or even the other envoys? Did Eloisa? "Exactly where you are standing, too," she pointed out.

"I am here because I was sent by my queen," Sevan said. "Not because I ran like a salt-cursed thief in the night."

"Well, there you have the advantage of me, sir," she said coolly. The initial shock of his allegation was fading into something colder. Not quite anger. Something far less emotional. As though the part of her brain that kept her alive had taken charge. "And the benefit of not having someone attempt to murder you in your bed."

"So you claim."

Sophie thought of the man they'd left dead in their room on the night they'd fled Kingswell. It was not a pleasant memory. "I do not claim it. It is the truth."

"The truth is a body and your defection."

At least he knew there had been a body. She and Cameron had wondered if someone—whoever was behind the attack—would attempt to spirit it away, leave no evidence of why they might have vanished. "Are you telling me that you think there is an acceptable reason for a man to sneak into my chambers at night? My husband already being there with me," she added.

"What possible excuse could there be? No one who meant well toward me would have done such a thing. And I have no reason to kill a man, let alone to lure one to my chambers and do it there. That would make me a most incompetent plotter, would it not?"

"And yet you did not remain to determine who he was or leave him alive so that he might be interrogated. Convenient. As it was to leave him dead and then turn up here."

She pressed her lips together. Arguing with the man wasn't going to change his mind. His words had the ring of the true believer about them. Whatever theories or arguments were being put forth in Kingswell to support her being brought home, he had apparently favored the ones that thought she deserved to be punished rather than rescued. In Sevan's mind, she had clearly been tried and convicted of some crime or other.

That meant that she couldn't trust him. Mostly likely couldn't trust any of the envoys. Even James, much as she could see that Cameron wanted to.

Barron Deepholt had been brusque but had stopped short of making actual threats, yet here was Sevan accusing her of treason in the middle of the emperor's ballroom. If he was acting on his own—or on the orders of someone trying to suborn the main diplomatic mission—or whether he just was clever enough to avoid letting slip the true mood of the court back home, she didn't know. Couldn't know.

So, softly, softly for now. Keep the Anglions circling around her. Do nothing to attract their suspicions or their ire while she and Cameron tried to extract more information out of them.

Maybe Henri could assist. Now that the existence of the Anglion delegation had been revealed to the court, surely information had to begin to flow throughout the palace. No court could keep secrets for long. Too many people jostling for status and favor. In those circumstances, information became currency for the advantage it proffered.

She would have to find a way to obtain some of that currency for herself.

The dance continued, the music changing again to a melody paced somewhere between the first and the second tunes. Sevan made no move to release her or slow his pace and let them retreat from the dancing, so she set her face to a smile and continued, mind racing with each step she took.

When the music finally faded to silence, she tugged her hand free a little too quickly for strict politeness but hid the move by reaching for the fan hanging at her side. She snapped it open, fluttering it rapidly, a barrier between her and the man still watching her with dislike and distrust. He couldn't reach for her again without drawing attention, so she dropped a quick curtsy.

"Thank you for the dance, Sir Allowood. It was most . . . instructive. But now I find myself in need of refreshment."

She whirled and retreated into the crush of dancers before he could reply.

∽

Cameron had lost sight of his wife amongst the milling whirl of dancers. Immediately after the crown prince had led Sophie away, Alain's wife, Crown Princess Nathalie, had stepped up and curtsied daintily before him. Unlike her husband, the princess was golden-haired and blue-eyed, coloring displayed perfectly in the shimmering gold gown she wore.

Also unlike her husband, Nathalie did not seem much inclined to talk. She responded politely to the few conversational forays he made but didn't attempt to lure him out herself. Was she annoyed about having to dance with an Anglion? Resentful of her husband dancing with Cameron's wife? Or was she just not talkative?

Whichever of the options was the truth, it was something of a relief to be able to focus on the dancing and not have to speak as well. Sophie had learned the Illvyan dances more quickly than

he had during their hurried hours of rehearsals. She had more
practice at dancing, he supposed. Most of the time when he'd
attended court balls, he'd been standing on the sidelines, dressed
in uniform and protecting Eloisa. That didn't involve dancing.

And tonight, the stakes were high. He didn't think literally
stepping on the toes of the crown princess was likely to win him
any friends. So he concentrated and tried to ignore the part of
him that kept looking for glimpses of Sophie's red dress through
the crowd.

By the time the seemingly never-ending set of dances came
to an end, he had no idea where Sophie was. He hadn't thought
it would be possible to lose anyone wearing a dress that color in
a crowd, but he'd underestimated just how many people were
filling the ballroom. But he could hardly charge into the mass of
people in search of her. He might not have spent much time
dancing at balls, but he'd spent plenty of time observing them
and absorbing the protocol. To abandon the crown princess
instead of escorting her back to the dais where presumably her
husband, not to mention the emperor, would be waiting would
be foolish.

If the encounter with the Anglion delegation had shown him
anything it was that they might well need the goodwill of the
emperor. Because it seemed goodwill from Anglion might be in
short supply.

He escorted the princess through the crowd, pretending he
didn't notice the guards who immediately began trailing them at
a discreet distance once they stepped off the dance floor. In the
Anglion court, the guards were present but they rarely stayed so
close to their charges.

What was happening in Aristides' court that would mean
the members of the royal family had to be more closely
protected? Was it the presence of the Anglions they didn't trust
or someone—or something—else? Of course, Stefan and Eloisa
had only ever had to worry about threats from their own
nobility—and it had been a long time since there'd been a move-

ment against the crown—and countrymen. They didn't rule a whole continent, or the many countries within it. They didn't have subjects who'd become subjects by force. Not in recent memory, anyway.

The princess murmured something polite to him as they reached the dais and then took herself off to stand with her ladies-in-waiting, who immediately clustered around her and began a whispered conversation. Which left him unsure as to what to do next. Looking for Sophie seemed the obvious choice.

He turned back to face the swathe of people, scanning again for a flash of bright red. Nothing. Next time he'd ask the Designys to provide her with a pair of the high-heeled shoes he'd seen some of the women wearing. That way he might have a better chance of spotting Sophie.

A servant offered a tray and he took a glass of something that resembled the wine Henri had made them try earlier. It had been pleasant enough and not overly strong. The last thing he needed was to overindulge.

He sipped it and watched the crowd, trying to see if there was a path he could take back to the dance floor that might contain fewer people.

It was an impossible task. The room was full to bursting no matter which direction he looked. After a minute or so, he gave up and just headed in a straight line from where he stood. He hadn't gotten very far when Barron Deepholt stepped into his path.

"Lieutenant Mackenzie," the barron said. "A word."

Cameron paused. He didn't think it was likely that the barron had anything promising to say to him. And now the man was just being rude, using his military rank and not his title. "I believe that's Lord Scardale to you, Rigby," he said, straightening his shoulders. He couldn't remember if the barron had ever given Cameron leave to use his personal name, but if the barron was going to play at forgetting the correct courtesies, so would he. After all, Cameron was brother to an erl and husband to a woman who also outranked the barron by wont of her position in the succession.

The barron scowled but nodded. "Lord Scardale. Forgive me. In all this excitement, I had forgotten about your sudden elevation."

Unlikely, but Cameron let it pass. Standing there trading insults with the man wasn't going to get the conversation over and done with any faster. "What do you want, milord?"

"I thought perhaps it wise if we spoke alone. Man to man, so to speak."

Cameron lifted a brow at him. He didn't know Deepholt that well. The man was maybe ten years younger than Cameron's father had been and hadn't been one of the late erl's group of confidants. And apparently the man shared the not uncommon attitude among male courtiers that women were not as capable as men. He'd never quite understood it, not when there was evidence in history about just what a royal witch was capable of. Eloisa wasn't the first queen to hold the Anglion throne. Not to mention that many of the men at court were married to royal witches.

Did the barron really think Sophie was just another silly lady-in-waiting who menfolk could pat on the head and send out of the room while they did business? He couldn't deny he'd met a few less than bright women at court, but Sophie wasn't one of them. And he'd met far more stupid men than women in his time at the palace.

"Is there more to discuss? You delivered the queen's message earlier." He moved away toward the outer wall of the room. The crowd was slightly thinner there. He didn't really want an audience for this conversation, even if the barron seemed to have forgotten just where they were.

The barron followed him, still looking displeased. They came to a halt again maybe thirty yards from the wall, where more of the black-clad Imperial Guard were stationed, standing at statue-like attention at twenty-yard intervals.

It was quieter there, but not by much. Out of necessity, the barron stood very close. The smell of sweat and heavy spiced cologne floated to Cameron's nose. It wasn't an altogether pleasant combination.

"I was hoping that you might be faster to see sense," the barron said. "You cannot be happy here in this . . . goddess-forsaken place, cut off from your service and your oaths."

"I believe the goddess has a strong following here," Cameron said mildly. "There's quite a sizeable temple not far from the palace. Perhaps His Imperial Majesty would allow you to attend a service there."

The barron shuddered. "No, thank you. Whatever they practice here, it isn't the path the goddess set for us. Not when they allow those . . . creatures to move freely among them."

Well, that was clear enough. What was less clear was what the man actually wanted. And how Cameron could steer him back to that topic. He shouldn't have mentioned the goddess. Not so soon after the Anglions had encountered their first sanctii. It was just as well that there didn't seem to be any more of them at the ball. Perhaps it wasn't the done thing. He made a neutral sort of noise, hoping the man might take it for agreement and return to the point.

The barron toyed with the heavy sapphire ring on his finger but before he could speak, a shortish man dressed in gray so dark it was close to black stepped out of the crowd to the barron's left.

For a moment, seeing the gleam of sweat on the man's forehead, Cameron thought the man must be drunk, but then he caught the glint of metal near the man's hand.

Knife.

He didn't stop to think, acting on instinct as he grabbed the barron, pulling him out of reach. The man in gray snarled and raised his arm, the knife clearly visible as he feinted at Cameron.

Fuck.

The blade was a good eight inches long. With a nasty hooked

tip. And Cameron didn't have so much as a dagger on him. He dodged the first swing, heard a scream from someone in the crowd but didn't move his gaze from the attacker.

Who came at him again, slashing in rapid succession.

Cameron dodged and rolled, aiming a punch at the man's knee as he moved past him. Weaponless against a knife, the best plan was to try and bring his attacker down, hope he'd lose his grip on the weapon. The attacker staggered but kept his footing. Cameron glanced around. People were falling back, forming a space around the two men. Out of the corner of his eye, he caught a glimpse of black moving rapidly through the crowd.

The guard, he hoped.

But before he had time to think anything more, the knife slashed again and he was stumbling back, narrowly avoiding the blade.

One of the guards reached his side, drawing a sword. Cameron started to fall back but a sanctii appeared out of nowhere, wrenching the blade from the guard's hand before backhanding the guard so hard the man flew several feet backward before crumpling to the ground.

The sanctii bellowed something, and then Cameron found himself facing a demon with a sword.

"Cameron, no!"

He heard Sophie calling his name. Then, just as the demon lifted the sword, another larger sanctii appeared—its coloring darker than the first—closed its massive arms around the first, and then they both vanished.

CHAPTER 11

Which left Cameron blinking in surprise at the man in gray.

Who lunged forward again with renewed ferocity. The appearance of sanctii fighting had apparently turned the crowd from half-wary to panicked. People were fleeing the fight, shoving and swearing to make their way. Through a gap in the heaving mass of bodies, he spotted one of the groups of low tables and chairs.

Finally. Something he could use. He reached for the ley line, found it with an effort, and sent the chair winging its way through the air, where it hit the man in gray in the back of the head and sent him slumping to the ground.

To his right, a flash of red. Sophie. He turned to see her fighting to stay where she stood against the tide of people trying to get away.

Two more black-clad guards appeared to Cameron's left, one of them dropping to his knees beside the man in gray. He felt briefly for a pulse on the man's neck.

Cameron turned back to Sophie, only to see a sanctii—the first one, he thought, rather than the second one—blink back into life only a few feet from the barron, who was standing frozen not far from where Sophie stood.

Goddess, no. The sanctii, whoever was controlling it, could not be allowed to target her. He had no idea how one tamed a demon, no idea how water magic worked, but he did know blood magic. And he knew the bond he and Sophie shared should make him stronger.

Acting entirely on instinct, he reached for the sense of her, and then used the answering surge of power to send the table flying toward the sanctii with even more force than he'd used with the chair. The power—Sophie's shared power—rushed through him like a flood, but the demon was too fast. It vanished and then reappeared just a foot or so away from him, reaching for him, fist swinging.

He lurched backward and the blow only grazed him, but it still felt as though he'd been hit in the ribs by a small tree. He stumbled, keeping his feet by some small miracle, and ducked by instinct as another blow came his way.

But before it could connect, Venable du Laq was there, yelling something in the rough language Henri used with Martius. The sanctii snarled at her, pivoting to lunge toward her. She snapped her hand in a strange gesture and another sanctii appeared. It had a slash of black across its eyes. Not the same creature who'd helped him before. It leaped toward the other demon, and then Henri was there as well, Martius joining the fray. The two sanctii both grasped the one who'd attacked. It struggled against them frantically and Cameron thought for a moment it was going to get away. But Venable du Laq made another one of those odd gestures and the captive sanctii froze as if turned to stone. Martius and the venable's sanctii looked at each other, and then all three demons vanished.

Cameron stood frozen, staring at the place where the demons had been, still geared for a fight that seemed to be over. Then guards in black surrounded him, several of them barking orders at once. Out of the corner of his eye, he saw Sophie being hustled away by Henri. He stepped forward, only to be stopped by a guard's hand on his chest.

He glared at the man. "I am going to my wife."

The guard shook his head. "You must stay here, my lord."

Stay? When there were sanctii battling in the middle of a ballroom? No. He needed to get to Sophie. He took another half step.

"Please, Lord Scardale. Just for a moment." A woman's hand on his arm.

He blinked, coming back a little from the battle haze and the thumping roar of his pulse in his ears. Then he focused on the woman in the blue dress.

"Venable du Laq," he said. "I wish to go to my wife."

"Soon," she said. "But the guards will have questions." She glanced in the direction Henri and Sophie had taken. "So do I."

"Questions? The man tried to attack the ambassador," Cameron said. He looked around but couldn't see Barron Deepholt anywhere nearby. Perhaps he, too, had fled.

"And you thought you'd stop him?" Another guard, a tall man with dark hair just turning gray at the temples and a blaze of gold and silver insignia on his uniform collar, stepped forward.

"Major." He nodded at Imogene, then turned an inquiring expression on Cameron.

"It seemed a good idea at the time," Cameron said, trying to absorb the information that Venable du Laq was not just in the Imperial Guard but a major.

"The room is full of guards," the man pointed out.

"The closest of whom was nearly thirty feet away. People can get very dead in the time it takes a man to travel that distance. Particularly through a crowd like this."

"I see." The guard studied Cameron a moment.

"You should be grateful," Venable du Laq said sharply. "His actions won Ikarus and me sufficient time to get close enough to contain that sanctii. Maybe you do not think one man could have done much damage before your men could act, Colonel, but believe me, one sanctii can do plenty."

Her tone was sharp. As the colonel outranked her, he wasn't sure what that said about the relationship between the emperor's mages and his regular guards. Or maybe Venable du Laq was just exercising her position as a duquesse to speak to almost anybody however she pleased.

"I am well aware, Major." The colonel bowed shallowly at Venable du Laq, which only confirmed that the woman's competing ranks complicated the protocol, then turned to Cameron again.

"Thank you," he said, clicking his heels together and performing another precise bow. "I am in your debt, M—"

"Lord Scardale!" Louis burst through the edge of the crowd. People had started to drift closer again now that the immediate danger was over.

Either Illvyans didn't scare easily or they were more interested in knowing what exactly had occurred than in safety.

"Are you all right, my lord?" Louis asked, brows wrinkling nervously as he looked Cameron up and down.

"Lord Scardale," repeated the colonel thoughtfully. "I see." He stepped back a little, scrutinizing Cameron with eyes so brown they were close enough to black. "Well, as I said, my lord, thank you for your assistance."

"Colonel Perrine, I must escort Lord Scardale back to his wife. I assume your men have things under control here?"

"Yes, Louis. You may tell His Imperial Majesty that all will be in order shortly."

"I'm sure he'll be asking you to explain it to him yourself," Louis said in an aggrieved tone, as though he was personally blaming the colonel for ruining what had to be an evening planned to within an inch of its life. Cameron felt a twinge of sympathy as the colonel's face went professionally neutral. He'd had to explain a fuckup like this a time or two to his superiors— though never, thankfully, to King Stefan or Eloisa—and it was never pleasant. Having that superior be Aristides de Lucien wasn't likely to improve the situation.

"Colonel," he said, aping the man's bow. He would have felt more at home saluting but he wasn't sure how Illvyans did that. He would have to ask Venable Marignon. "Perhaps we will meet again."

~

Everyone was jabbering in Illvyan around her and Sophie couldn't understand more than one word in five. Nor did she know where Cameron was. A fact that made her want to scream.

She could sense him in an odd way, like a tingling aftershock from the power they'd shared. She knew he was somewhere nearby, but right at that moment, nearby was not reassuring enough.

The dais where she stood with Henri and the emperor was surrounded by a solid ring of imperial guards. There would be no chance of breaking through to go and find her husband.

On the other side of the dais, the four Anglions stood. The barron was pale and sweating. Sir Harold and James were trying to get him to sit and drink a glass of something one of the servants had fetched. They spoke in low, urgent voices, but between the heated conversation Henri and Aristides were having and the far louder than before panic-tinged babbling of all the nobles still present in the ballroom, she couldn't make out their words.

She was ready to step in front of Henri and demand he speak Anglish to her when several of the guards moved aside and Louis, who had been sent scurrying away from the emperor's side when she and Henri had first returned, stepped through the gap, Cameron and Venable du Laq right behind him.

Heedless of protocol, Sophie picked up her skirts and practically sprinted to Cameron. "Are you all right?"

She looked him over frantically. No cuts in his clothing. No blood. But he was moving slowly. He reached out with his left arm and pulled her close to kiss her fiercely before he let her go.

"If you are done reassuring your wife, my lord," Venable du Laq said, "then I suggest you let me do something about those ribs."

Sophie's heart lurched. "Your ribs? You *are* hurt!"

Cameron waved his left arm. "Bruising, nothing more."

"Sanctii are strong," the venable said. "It could be worse than that."

"I've had a broken rib before. This doesn't feel the same. Not that it doesn't hurt, so if there is something you can do to ease it, Venable, I would be grateful," he added.

"Call me Imogene. Both of you. This is no time to stand on ceremony." She looked toward Aristides. "Perhaps we should continue this somewhere less public?"

The emperor shook his head. "No. No retreating."

He looked calm, but there was a tone to his voice that made Sophie think the emperor was quietly furious. He stepped forward. "Imogene, make sure I'm heard."

"Of course, *Eleivé*."

Aristides nodded and then motioned to the guards, who once again faded back to leave a break in the circle. Beyond, Sophie saw curious faces peering to see what was happening. A few worried ones as well.

"Music," Aristides called, and although he spoke in a normal voice, his words tolled through the room like a great stern bell. "This is a ball. The unfortunate distractions are under control. Let the dancing recommence."

He stepped back and the guards closed ranks again. But not before Sophie saw the courtiers start to move toward the dance floor. What the emperor wanted, the emperor got, apparently.

Cameron's hand slipped into hers. She squeezed it gently. She wanted nothing more than to pull him away from here and be elsewhere. She wasn't even entirely sure where. Just away.

Aristides had returned to the dais, seating himself on the

throne, expression stony. Louis bent to whisper a question in his ear and the emperor gestured him away with an irritable flick of his fingers. Imogene received a similar dismissal when she approached him. She came back to stand with Sophie, Cameron, and Henri, the silk of her skirts swishing over the marble with a vigor that suggested she was no happier than her emperor.

"I wanted to thank you," Sophie said. "For what you did."

"No more than my duty," Imogene said.

"Was that your sanctii? The one with the black around his eyes?"

"Yes. That's Ikarus." Imogene smiled tightly.

"And the other? The darker one that helped before you or Henri arrived?" Sophie asked, ignoring the disapproving expression she could see in the barron's face across the dais.

Henri and Imogene exchanged a look.

"What?" Cameron asked.

Henri looked over to the Anglions before turning away slightly so his back was to them. "I am not entirely sure," he said, speaking Illvyan.

Not eager to have the Anglions know what he was saying?

Sophie frowned. "Are there so many in Lumia that you do not know them all?"

Imogene shook her head. "No. We keep track of water mages. Particularly those bound to sanctii." She pressed her lips together. Then her expression turned considering. "Of course, you do shine so," she muttered. "But that should be of no matter." She paused. "But no, all the known water mages here tonight have sanctii I would recognize."

"How can there be a sanctii you do not know, then?" Sophie asked. "Does that mean there is an unknown mage? Was the man who attacked the ambassador a mage?"

"No," Cameron said. "He wouldn't have used a knife if he had magic. And I felt nothing from him."

"Then how?"

"That is something we shall find out," Henri said. "There is a theory that—" He broke off as Barron Deepholt approached the emperor's throne.

The man still looked pale, though two hectic spots of color sat high on his cheeks. Perhaps there had been more than water in whatever Sir Harold had been urging him to drink. "Your Imperial Majesty, I think we deserve an accounting."

Was she imagining it or did his voice quaver slightly as he spoke?

Aristides stared down at him for a long silent moment. "I believe the accounting is that you are alive and unharmed, thanks to the actions of Lord Scardale and others, my lord ambassador."

"But I was attacked!'

"Yes. Rest assured, Barron Deepholt, that we will bring those responsible to account."

Not justice, Sophie noted. Account. The facts would be gathered and then . . . what? A price would be paid?

The barron inclined his head. "Nevertheless, Your Imperial Majesty, it would be remiss of me to remain too long in your palace under such circumstances. Lord and Lady Scardale should accompany us back to the harbor so we can get underway."

Sophie stepped forward before Cameron caught her arm.

The emperor's gaze flicked to her before he focused back on the barron. "I believe, my lord, that you and your party will depart when I allow. As will Lord and Lady Scardale." His tone was flat, the anger that had been an undertone earlier rising much closer to the surface.

"But—"

"Enough, my lord." Aristides' voice cracked like a whip. "You are here as my guest. Trust me, you do not wish that status to change. You and your party may retire for the night. That is acceptable, given the distress you have faced."

The barron's face twisted. Behind him, Sevan Allowood took half a step forward before James clutched his arm and he halted, glaring at Sophie with loathing.

"But they were working with demons," he hissed, loud enough for her to hear.

"Shut up, Sevan," James said none too gently as he yanked the younger man back to his side.

"Louis," Aristides said. "See that Barron Deepholt and his party are escorted back to their chambers."

The barron—wisely—didn't venture any new objections. A squad of the guards broke off and surrounded the Anglions at Louis' direction.

As they marched away, Sophie let go of the breath she didn't know she'd been holding.

"May I attend to Lord Scardale now, Your Imperial Majesty?" Imogene said a little tartly.

Aristides made an impatient gesture. "Yes. Then I think it might be best if the three of you also retired for the evening, Maistre Matin. Take your charges back to the Academe. We will speak again soon enough." He looked around at Louis who hadn't followed the guards out of the room. "Show them to the white chamber so the major can work on Lord Scardale. Then fetch their carriage."

Louis nodded vigorously.

"And then," Aristides said, expression thoughtful, "I think perhaps that I would like to speak to my son."

It seemed to take forever before they passed through the palace gates and the wheels of the carriage bumped onto the cobbled road beyond. Safety. Or the illusion of it.

A very thin illusion. Not even the fact that Cameron had placed her between Henri and himself, all three of them sitting on one seat—cramped as that was—made her feel less exposed.

It was all she could do not to look behind them to watch the palace receding. To make sure no one followed. Not that no pursuit equaled any kind of certainty.

After all, the emperor's reach extended throughout the whole city—and the entire empire, for that matter. Though the emperor wasn't their immediate problem. No, that seemed to be the Anglions. Hopefully their reach went no farther than the walls of the Imperial Palace.

It would be foolish to assume that the Anglion court hadn't managed to develop some sort of network of contacts or spies in Illvya, no matter how small or tenuous. Though she found it impossible to believe that they could have placed anyone at the Academe.

No Anglion would wish to take on a duty that required entering the very heart of the magic that was forbidden to them. Where sanctii roamed freely. As did the mages who controlled them. No Anglion who wasn't desperate to survive, that was.

The reaction of the Anglions had proved that, both before and after the attack. She rubbed at her temples, exhaustion starting to set in now that they were safely out of the palace. She'd spent the time while Imogene du Laq had worked on Cameron's ribs half expecting to be summoned back to the ball-room. She'd kept silent, watching Imogene work, though part of her attention had been on the door, ready in case of another attack. There were questions she wanted to ask but she'd saved them for Henri, not wanting to inadvertently say something that might make Imogene decide that perhaps they did need to discuss things further with the emperor.

Cameron had asked again about the third sanctii and how it might have come to be in the ballroom. In response, Henri and Imogene had spoken quickly, their Illvyan reaching those speeds at which Sophie found it incomprehensible. As best as she could make out, they'd said something about a sanctii sometimes being able to ride the power used by a water mage when they brought forth a sanctii from . . . well, wherever it was the sanctii came from.

But she didn't understand the Illvyan—or water magic—well

enough to understand much beyond that. Or to know if the explanation made sense.

Apparently, Cameron hadn't wanted to ask anything more. He'd subsided back into silence as Imogene worked. To distract herself from worrying about him, Sophie asked Henri what "Eleivé" meant. She wasn't familiar with the term, and given that several people had called the emperor that over the course of the evening, perhaps she should be.

Henri had nodded at her question. "It means 'most high'. In an older version of our language. It is something the emperor is called by those he is close to. Or those he grants the privilege to. A less-formal term to be used in situations where it would not be appropriate to use his personal name, even if the speaker holds the rank or familiarity to do so. 'Your Imperial Majesty' is quite a mouthful, after all."

It was. So an alternative title made sense. She had filed the term away, though she doubted she would ever need to use it. By the time Henri was done explaining, Imogene had declared she'd done what she could and Louis and another small squad of guards had escorted them back to the carriage. And now they were free again.

At least for the night.

"What will they do to that man? The one with the knife?" she asked.

Henri grimaced. "I imagine they will extract such information as can be extracted, and then, most likely, they will execute him."

Even though she'd suspected as much, hearing it said out loud made her sorry she'd asked. But she didn't want to stick her head in the sand. The presence of the envoys had added so many layers of complication to the situation that she really had no idea how to start untangling it in order to reach a solution. All she could do was try to understand what had happened and what might happen next.

"Don't think about it," Cameron said. He also looked

unhappy with the thought. Though presumably it wasn't squea-mishness in his case. Maybe he was angry that he wouldn't get to do any of the interrogation himself.

Cameron shifted a little in the seat as the carriage slowed, one hand pressed to his ribs.

"Do they hurt?" Sophie asked. She was sitting as still as she could, not wanting to bump into him if she could avoid it. The fact that he'd been hurt made her want to both hit someone and cry. But she wasn't going to indulge either emotion.

He shook his head at her. "Nothing too bad. Whatever Imogene did back there eased them. Though I daresay I'll be happier when we're out of this carriage." The carriage jolted as he spoke and he winced. "Damned cobblestones."

"We'll get you examined again when we're back at the Acad-eme," Henri said. "Imogene is powerful but she never studied the healing arts particularly thoroughly. Her earth magic is not so strong. Her interests lie elsewhere."

He sounded vaguely disapproving. What exactly were Her Grace's interests if the man in charge of the Academe didn't approve? War? Espionage? Something else entirely? Imogene du Laq had used water magic and earth magic, and that little trick of amplifying the emperor's voice was most likely one of the Arts of Air. Was there anything she couldn't do?

It made her shiver. Trying to make it through each day in Illvya was like walking through thick fog, surrounded by things unknown and unimagined, hands outstretched in the hope it might prevent her from stumbling into something deadly. How could you protect yourself against something you didn't even know existed? And it didn't help when the explanations were offered in a language that was one of the things you didn't truly understand.

But that, at least, she could do something about. The night had held many surprises but also one truth: If she was going to survive here, she needed to master Illvyan as quickly as possible. She turned to Henri. "I want the reveilé."

Cameron jerked, head twisting. "What do you mean?" His knuckles where he was bracing himself against the carriage wall with the hand not pressed to his ribs went white.

Sophie focused on Henri. This was her decision, not Cameron's. "Can I have it?"

"I thought you wished to play things safe, to pursue only earth magic?" Henri said.

"The reveilé isn't me using magic," Sophie pointed out. No, it was a demon who would be wielding the magic. And aiming it at her. The snarling faces of the three battling sanctii swam before her eyes. So much power and strength. So inhuman. Could it really be safe to allow something like that to rummage around inside her head?

Her stomach clenched at the thought, but she had made up her mind. The vastness of the court and the frustration of not being able to understand all the conversations that had flowed around them had made it clear that her struggles with the language were a more severe disadvantage than she had supposed. Even without the attack and the sanctii, she would have reached the same conclusion.

She needed Illvyan, and the presence of the Anglion delegations meant that she didn't have the time to overcome that disadvantage the old-fashioned way.

"The Anglions won't take it kindly if they find out," Cameron said.

"Why should they ever know? I didn't ever speak Illvyan at court in Kingswell. The tutor my parents found for me died several years ago. For all they know I was fluent previously." She pulled the black cloak closer around her. Martius wasn't in the carriage with them, and she hadn't seen him since he'd appeared so unexpectedly in the ballroom, but she felt as chilled now as if he, rather than Cameron, was sitting beside her.

She couldn't get the hate in Sevan Allowood's eyes out of her head.

"If we are going to be returning to the palace—" There was

no "if." It was certain. Unless the emperor decided to send the Anglions back where they'd come from. Unlikely. And even if he did, she and Cameron had attracted Aristides' attention during the attack. Aristides had watched her very closely in those first minutes of confusion after the attack when Henri had dragged her back to the relative safety of the dais. As if seeing her anew.

Aristides hadn't struck her as a man whose attention was diverted easily once drawn. Eloisa shared that quality and she didn't rule over a realm anywhere near as complicated as the empire.

So no, she didn't imagine that the emperor would simply lose interest. Not until he had evaluated the situation and any threats or opportunities it might present. "When we return to the palace," she continued, "I need to be able to understand what is being discussed around me."

"Are you sure?" Cameron asked. He looked uncomfortable with the very thought of such a thing.

Well, that made two of them. But Cameron wasn't in her position. His Illvyan was fine. "I'm sure it's necessary." Need would have to stand in for certainty for now. "So, Maistre, will you do this for me?"

"If it is what you want," Henri said. His expression was troubled. "But not until the morning. You need to be well-rested. And you may change your mind with a little time to think on it."

She wouldn't. "Thank you, Maistre." She settled back against the seat, trying not to count each beat of the horses' hooves as taking her one step closer to safety.

CHAPTER 12

"I'm not going to question your decision," Cameron said, watching Sophie as she moved directly to the fireplace when they were safely back in their chambers. He undid the buttons of his jacket with care. The pain in his ribs had faded to a faint ache thanks to the expert ministrations of the Academe healer Henri had summoned on their return, but she'd warned him to be careful not to aggravate the injury anew. "But I want to understand. The ambassadors being there was a surprise, I agree. But also an opportunity."

Sophie hadn't taken off her cloak. She stood, hands stretched toward the flame, staring into them as though they held the secret solution to all their problems. He didn't know if she'd even heard him, so distant was the look on her face.

"Sophie, love," he said gently, moving to join her. "Are you cold? From the sanctii?" Or worse? Delayed shock, perhaps? The evening had been unsettling enough to give anybody fits.

She shook her head fiercely, dislodging several of the pins holding her hair in place. Strands fell around her face. He brushed them back. She had looked beautiful in the red dress. Glorious, in fact. But not entirely like his wife.

"No," she said. Then, "Yes. I don't know." She tugged at the large brooch holding her cloak closed at the neck. It was heavy gold like the other jewels she wore but unadorned by gems. Instead it had been formed to resemble a spray of small leaves, spilling down the fabric of the cloak. "And you—we—cannot take what Barron Deepholt said at face value."

Cameron thought about James' face as he had stood behind Sir Harold. He'd looked calm, but there had been none of his usual easy humor in his eyes. And there'd been no time to try and speak to him privately. Cameron wasn't even sure how he might go about arranging a meeting with James sequestered inside the palace.

Or even how to determine if he was there unwillingly. If he was there to somehow persuade Cameron to comply with the delegation's wishes, he would be watched. He and James had never been close, but one thing Cam knew was that James was very fond of his sister, Jeanne. Cameron was fond of her, too. She'd been his sister-in-law a long time now. The thought that his and Sophie's actions may have put their families at risk made his gut churn.

He'd known it was a possibility, of course. That their choice to leave might have repercussions. If the Domina had been behind the attack in Kingswell. Or worse, if the queen had.

He didn't want to believe that was true. Goddess. Eloisa had been his lover once. Could she truly want him dead now? Perhaps the true question was whether she was still the woman who had so charmingly coaxed him into her bed or whether that woman had vanished the moment the palace had been attacked and she had become queen.

"No, I agree, we need to proceed carefully. But Eloisa wouldn't have sent a delegation if she wasn't keen to bring us home." He didn't want to upset Sophie any more with the whirling suspicions in his mind. Not tonight. Not until he'd had time to think them through more carefully.

"Sevan called me a traitor," Sophie said. "Right there in the middle of the ballroom." She wrapped her arms around herself, shivering now. "His face. Cameron, I don't think I've ever spoken to him more than once or twice and he looked as though he hated me. As though he'd happily see me dead. I don't understand it."

A traitor? The shock of that word left him speechless. He'd known that their flight would cause trouble and the message from Eloisa had been terse, to say the least, but *treason*? If that term was being bandied around the Anglion court, then there could be no good outcome for Sophie. Or him.

He moved away from her, trying to think. Traitor. If that was truly what was being claimed . . . if charges of treason awaited them, then they couldn't return to Anglion. It could be fatal.

But would Eloisa do such a thing? Or did Sevan Allowood have some other game he was playing? His cousin stood above Sophie in the succession. His fortunes could rise with the young barron's. That might be reason enough for him to want Cameron and Sophie to stay in Illvya. Or to see them falsely charged if they returned to Anglion.

And he was just one candidate. There were others with cause to want to take advantage of the situation in Kingswell. A new queen, a palace recovering from attack. A succession radically altered by that attack. A perfect storm of events that could well prove too much temptation for anyone nursing a grudge against the royal family or Sophie.

If the word "treason" was being whispered there, then who was whispering it? Or perhaps the real question was who was pulling the strings at the palace. Eloisa? Or did someone else have control, manipulating the situation behind the scenes? Domina Skey was the most likely candidate for that honor.

She'd been uncomfortably close to the queen's ear since she had healed Eloisa after the attack. Though she had used Sophie's powers to do so. Did Eloisa know that? Or remember that she owed Sophie her life?

Part of him hoped it was the Domina. In theory, the earth

witches here worshipped the same goddess. But they didn't share the Anglion's horror of water magic. So whether or not the Illvyan priestesses would aid the Anglion temple if it sought to come after Sophie was an entirely unknown factor.

If they would, then he and Sophie would surely have to run again. But somehow, even if the temple had potential allies here, the thought of the Domina as their foe was still easier to swallow than Eloisa trying to kill them.

Of course, there had been no representative of the temple amongst the delegates. Barron Deepholt's wife was famously pious, but the man himself had never seemed overly involved in the religious community at court. That didn't mean, of course, that there were no other members of the party who were being kept out of sight. A temple representative may not wish to be seen on Illvyan soil or take part in activities such as balls, particularly one where sanctii may well be present. Though that begged the question of whether they would be comfortable setting foot on Illvyan soil in the first place.

His mind spun, trying to run through the possibilities. Presumably the Anglions had arrived by ship. Which ship? Goddess, right now he'd kill for a fast horse and a swift trip to the port. He was fairly certain he could identify an Anglion ship on sight. And if there was a ship, who was still currently aboard? Just the captain and crew? Or could there be other members of the delegation?

Goddess, he wanted to know. But he forced himself to stay put. Stay with Sophie. Who needed him whole and by her side. Besides, he didn't think Henri would let him get very far if he went haring off into the night. Nor would it do much good. One man couldn't take on a ship's company. Not even if he managed to find weapons enough to outfit an entire squadron. So even if he managed somehow to sneak aboard, what followed could only be disastrous.

He turned back to the fire where Sophie stood, watching him

pace. "I'm going to send a note to the maistre. Ask him if he can find out which ship the Anglions arrived on."

Sophie blinked. "Do you think it likely he can?"

He shrugged. "Possibly. We know what we are looking for now. Even if the delegation have concealed their ship somewhere or used an Illvyan vessel to come the last part of their journey, someone in the port will have noticed. Now that the emperor has revealed their presence, I'm sure Henri will be able to find a few looser tongues around than he did before."

He crossed to one of the two desks that had appeared in their room after they had commenced their studies and wrote the note quickly. It was late but there would be a servant around if he rang. Henri might be asleep, but the note would be waiting for him in the morning. He sealed the note carefully with wax and a ward strengthened with a drop of blood after pricking his finger with the point of his dagger.

It would have to be enough. For now.

When he'd finished, he looked around to find Sophie watching him with an odd expression on her face.

"What, love?"

"Your finger." She came over, pressing a quick kiss to his hand. "It reminded me of the temple. Of the offerings. It sounds odd, but I miss it."

"Not so odd. It was part of our lives back home."

"Do you think the maistre would let me go to a temple here in Lumia?"

Cameron frowned. "Not sure now is the best time for you to be roaming the city, love. The Anglions . . . ."

"You think they would hurt me?"

"I think they would be happy if an opportunity presented itself to let them snatch you away," Cameron said cautiously. "Though I cannot say what it is they might want from you after that."

Sophie shivered. "I think I'd prefer not to find out."

"You won't have to," he said. He pulled her down onto his

lap. "Not while I'm here to put myself between you and them. No one is taking you anywhere you don't choose to go."

From that angle, her dress gave him a most enticing view of her breasts. So be it. There was nothing more to be done until morning. And both of them could use a distraction.

"Did I mention how beautiful you look in this dress?" he said.

She looked startled but then smiled. "I'm not sure you did."

"Remiss of me. I am a terrible husband. Perhaps you would let me make it up to you?"

"I don't know. How exactly do you propose to do that?"

He grinned, then leaned down to press a kiss against the curving edge of her right breast where the red satin met pale skin. "Well, I thought I might start by removing the dress." He kissed the other breast, nipping gently. Then smiled against her skin when she gasped softly. "And then I thought I'd move on to showing you how beautiful I think you are without it on."

~

Cameron and Sophie were leaving their first class of the morning —Illvyan geography—when Willem waylaid them just outside the classroom.

The boy came panting up to them, looking relieved to have found them. He nodded at Cameron, then turned to Sophie. "Lady Sophie, the maistre wants to see you."

He would have missed the flash of apprehension in her eyes if he hadn't been looking for it.

"Of course. I'll go see him now."

Willem nodded happily. "Good. He seemed to be in a hurry when he asked me to fetch you." He paused. "They say there was some excitement at the emperor's ball. Is that why you were not at breakfast?"

The rumor mill in Lumia was definitely impressive. Goddess curse it.

"Everyone is fine, Willem. I simply slept late after the ball," Sophie said before Cameron could answer.

He knew that was a lie. Sophie had been too nervous to eat breakfast. He had been, too. Willem bowed but didn't immediately leave. His blue eyes still showed worry. "Do you need—"

"I know my way well enough to the maistre's office, Willem. You should go to your class." Sophie said.

"I'll walk with you, Willem," Cameron said, struck by a sudden idea. "I wanted to ask you a favor." He nodded at Sophie, who smiled in thanks and started away from them.

"A favor?" Willem said, Sophie apparently forgotten. "What kind of favor?"

Cameron walked a little farther down the corridor, away from the main body of students. "You said your father worked by the harbor, didn't you?"

Willem nodded. "Yes. His office is near the harbormaster's."

Cameron smiled at him. He was going to ask Henri to find out about the ship the Anglions had arrived on, but he didn't know if the maistre may be constrained from sharing anything he learned. So a little confirmation—or even additional information—couldn't hurt. "It sounds like an exciting place to work. All that coming and going."

Willem wrinkled his nose. "The ships are interesting, I suppose. But I don't like it down there. The harbor stinks."

"The harbor in Kingswell does, too, at times," Cameron agreed. "But still, do you know anyone there who knows about the ships? About arrivals and departures?"

"Of course," Willem said. "Are you trying to discover which ship the other Anglions arrived in?"

"How—" Cameron cut the question off. The damned rumor mill again. Well, the emperor had announced that there were Anglions visiting Lumia to the entire court. There was no way the news would stay secret for long after that if the Illvyan court was like the Anglion one. "Yes," he said simply. "I would be interested to know. The name of the ship and how many Anglions have come ashore."

"I will see what can be found out, my lord."

"Good. But discreetly, yes?"

Willem looked offended. "Of course. I do not gossip."

Sophie had barely made it one full corridor toward Henri's office when Tok found her and took up his usual place on her shoulder. The bird was unusually silent as she walked the rest of the way. Normally he cawed and squawked and made happy little grumbling noises when he found her but not that morning. Was he picking up her mood? She was tempted to ask, but she was still trying not to encourage him. The Master of Ravens had told her that some of the raven fams learned to speak over time. Indeed, on her first visit to the tower, one of the largest ravens she'd ever seen had squawked a grave "hello" in her direction as she'd followed the master into the first of the roosting rooms.

It had startled her and amused the master, but so far, if Tok could talk—and perhaps he couldn't being so young—he was hiding the ability from her.

He was still quiet when she reached Henri's office and knocked on the door.

Martius opened the door, which made Sophie flinch. At that, Tok did caw at the sanctii, flapping his wings briefly, feathers fluffing.

Martius' mottled gray face cracked in an expression that Sophie guessed was the sanctii equivalent of a smile.

"Little crow," the demon rasped. "She is safe enough. Be gone." He pointed down the corridor.

Tok squawked again, the sound edged with outrage, but he flew off in the direction indicated. Apparently even his defiance had its limits. Sophie couldn't blame him for that. She'd probably do whatever the demon told her to as well.

"Good morning, Martius," she managed.

The black eyes swung back to her. "Little witch. You may stay."

He stepped back and she walked into the room, trying to ignore the chill radiating from him.

Henri sat at his desk, a large leather-bound volume open in front of him. As Martius closed the door, he looked up.

"Sophie. Good. Are you well this morning?"

"Yes, Maistre. Quite well." Though she shivered as Martius came up behind her, and Henri frowned briefly before he stood.

"And are you still determined to take the reveilé?"

She nodded, swallowing against a throat suddenly dry as the dust on top of the ornate clock on the mantle above Henri's fireplace. He needed a more thorough maid, she thought, then had to choke back a laugh.

She was about to let a demon rummage in her head. She should worry about that, not about the quality of the service provided by the Academe's servants.

"And Lord Scardale? Is he in agreement?"

Sophie bristled at the implication that she needed Cameron's permission. "Quite frankly, Maistre, it is my decision. But yes, Cameron supports me in this." Reluctantly, but he'd agreed with her logic. That would have to be enough for now.

"Very well. Well, then. No time like the present moment." Henri rubbed his hands together briskly.

Was he looking forward to this?

Her hands tightened, clutching the sides of her robes. Now? Right now? She'd known that this was why he had sent for her, but apparently her body hadn't believed her brain.

"Nothing to be nervous about," Henri added. "Why don't you come over here and take a seat? Then Martius will be able to assess whether you are a good candidate for the reveilé. It doesn't work on everybody."

It was an effort to take a step. She kept her hands clenched in the thick black fabric of the robes, afraid if she let go they'd be trembling. Focusing on putting one foot in front of the other, she managed to walk the short distance until she stood beside the chair Henri had indicated. Sitting was easier—all she had to do was loosen the control that was keeping her knees locked and herself upright, letting herself sink onto the seat.

Henri peered down at her. "Are you sure you are well? You look pale."

Her mouth was dry. She licked her lips, trying to remember how to speak. "I confess I am nervous," she rasped, the words croaky.

"Would it help if I explained the ritual to you?"

"Yes, please." Her head felt light as she nodded. She had read about the reveilé but couldn't, at that moment, recall anything about it other than the fact that it was performed by a sanctii. That part was clear with Martius standing beside her and studying her with inky eyes, his expression indecipherable.

Henri rested against the edge of his desk. Trying to put her at ease? The fact that it seemed an unusually casual pose for the maistre actually had the opposite effect.

"Let me see. Where do I begin? You understand that I will not play a part in this ritual other than helping Martius to make the initial link?"

Yes. He'd explained that much the previous night. She nodded. She had no idea how a water mage might go about establishing such a link, so she was just going to have to trust in Henri.

"So. I will touch your temples. Then I will link with Martius. His hands will replace mine, and then he will give you the reveilé."

"How exactly?"

"That is something nearly impossible to explain to someone who isn't a water mage. And even then the concepts we use only bear a slight resemblance to the reality of what the sanctii is actually doing, I'm afraid. The best I can explain, the way the sanctii explain it, is that they can sense somehow the connections made by our brains. The pathways our thoughts and emotions take when we have them. They can also sense what certain parts of the brain do."

"Go on."

"Well, when a person is struggling at a task, say learning a language, or singing, or using a particular tool, the sanctii can sometimes see if there is a passage blocked in the mind that is preventing the necessary learning. And they can unblock it. In your case, because you have studied Illvyan, all the rules of grammar and the vocabulary should be there in your mind. So once Martius helps you find the right pathways, you should be fluent quickly. You will still have to practice and study, of course. There is only so much magic can do. The reveilé only improves the ease with which you understand and use the information you have. Unfortunately we cannot insert new information into someone's head. If we could, we could make a fortune. Or Martius would." Henri smiled wryly at that.

"But as it is, he can clear the way, and then you will practice. You should comprehend what is being said almost immediately as long as the words spoken are those you know. Your skill in speaking and your accent may take a little while longer to improve significantly. Everyone reacts a little differently. But again, nowhere near as long as it might take you to continue learning the language by rote."

It sounded like a vastly simplified explanation, which did little to ease her nerves. The thought that new information couldn't be placed in her mind was comforting, but she had to take Henri's word that this was true. But she couldn't think of anything more to ask, if Henri couldn't explain without going into arcane details she also wouldn't understand.

"All right," she said. She took two long breaths. "Let's get this over and done with."

Henri moved closer.

"Wait," she said as he moved his hands toward her. "Does it hurt?"

"Briefly," Henri said. "But you will be unharmed. Just stay right where you are and breathe."

Easy advice when you weren't the one sitting in her position. Still, it appeared to be one of those situations where there were no shortcuts. To obtain the result she wanted, she had to go through this part, pain or no.

She closed her eyes. That might make it easier. "I am ready."

Henri's fingers touched her temples. His skin was warm. Human. She made herself relax. Felt a throb of power from the ley line far below. Then the chill that was Martius moved closer and warm fingers were replaced by two points of pressure that felt like ice, not flesh.

The cold speared through her—not pain exactly, but something akin to it. She set her jaw against the sensation, fighting the urge to push it away as her own power flared in response and she had to tamp it down.

Martius made a small surprised grunt.

"Do you have it?" Henri asked.

"I see," Martius said. "Simple. And the other thing? That I could also fix. Do you want that, little witch?"

Sophie's eyes flew open. "What other thing?" She stayed still only because she had no idea what might happen if she broke the contact between them. "Maistre, what is he talking about?"

Henri shook his head. "I am not sure. If I were to venture a guess, I would say Martius is perhaps sensing something that results from the bond between you and your husband. In this case, fixing it would most likely mean removing it." He looked past her at the sanctii, said something in the harsh tongue they used.

Then he returned his attention to Sophie as Martius replied in the same language. "He seems to think so."

"Is that something he's done before?"

"Unlikely. Any such bonds formed here are done under controlled conditions by mages who know what they are doing."

The rebuke was clear in his voice but Sophie ignored it.

What she and Cameron had done hadn't been intentional but she wasn't going to give it up. Or let anyone else take it away from her. Not until she understood it. Until both she and Cameron understood it and could decide together.

"No!" Sophie said, voice firm. "Do not touch that." She glared at the maistre, given that she didn't want to move her head to glare at the sanctii in case it made something go awry and they had to start over. Or, worse, couldn't complete the spell.

"You heard Lady Scardale," Henri said. "Just the reveilé, Martius." His expression grew stern. Another flare of power vibrated beneath Sophie's feet. What was Henri doing? Compelling Martius to do only what was asked? Was there a risk he wouldn't limit himself to just the reveilé?

She was about to open her mouth to tell them to stop when a shard of ice seemed to spear through her brain and she couldn't think any more.

∾

By the time the agony receded, she became aware of someone pounding on the door. Then Cameron was there, calling her name, the familiar touch of his hands wrapped around hers lessening some of the chill that enveloped her.

She should open her eyes. But the pain in her head—now a dull roar rather than the initial splitting sensation—made it seem as though that would be a poor choice. The feeling that she was encased in ice didn't encourage her to be brave either.

"Sophie," Cameron said urgently, then, "What in the name of the goddess did you do to her?"

"Calm yourself, Lord Scardale. It is perfectly normal. She had the reveilé. She will be as good as new in no time at all. Better. Now she will be able to follow our pesky tongue with ease."

Henri touched her shoulder—or she assumed it was him as she could still feel Cameron's hands around hers. He said something in Illvyan, speaking at a rapid pace, the way native speakers did, rather than the slowed-down version he'd been using with her previously. Asking how the pain in her head was and whether she needed anything.

She understood it easily.

Her eyes did open at that. Then closed again as the light pierced her eyeballs like red-hot needles. "I understood that," she said. "Maistre, it worked."

"Indeed," Henri said. "Do you realize you just said that in Illvyan?"

From somewhere close at hand, Martius said something in his own language that sounded approving. But apparently the sanctii tongue was in no way related to Illvyan because it was as incomprehensible as ever.

"Yes," Henri said. "A job well done, my friend. You may leave now, if you wish."

Another tangle of syllables and then some of the chill on her skin eased. She cracked her eyes open a careful fraction. They still watered at the light, but she could only make out two blurry forms standing near her, not three. The nearest one was Cameron, who still gripped her hands tightly. Behind him, Henri leaned in, studying her.

"Lord Scardale, the best thing for your wife now is for her to rest. She can be excused from her classes for the rest of the day. Take her back to your chambers and put her to bed. Let her sleep it off and she will be as good as new in the morning. Better even."

Sleep sounded wonderful, so she didn't argue when Cameron lifted her in his arms and followed Henri's instructions.

CHAPTER 13

It didn't take until the next morning for Sophie to recover from the reveilé. She woke, sometime well past midday, to a clear head and no pain, even if she was still tired. But not tired enough to return to sleep.

She was alone in their room. She'd shooed Cameron out to his classes once he'd brought her back from Henri's office. There was no point in the two of them losing the afternoon. He could be learning rather than just watching her sleep. They didn't know how much longer they might have left there, after all. And their experiences at the ball had only driven home that the more they could improve their control of their magic, the better.

It was tempting to take herself off to her remaining afternoon classes, too, but she imagined if either Henri or Cameron saw her near a classroom she'd just be chased back to their room to rest.

There was food on a covered tray waiting for her and tea in a pot, still warm. She ate, starving now that she had recovered, and settled down with her tea and one of the Illvyan texts on earth magic that she had been struggling to read for her classes. To her delight, she understood it clearly now. The words, at least. The ideas about earth magic and how to use it were very different from those she'd been taught.

And the first few descriptions she read all began with some variation on "first, look for the connection to the ley line." Something which still baffled her. She had seen a ley line, of course, but only once when she was right on top of it in open countryside. Since then she'd been able to sense the lines but hadn't caught more than a glimpse of one from time to time.

Perhaps there was another text that would explain the concept to her in more basic terms. She pushed the book to one side. She could return to the library, look for one. That held more appeal than simply waiting for Cameron to return. It wasn't the same as going to a class where she'd actually have to use her magic. Reading hadn't hurt her head just now, so she couldn't see that it would in the library.

But she hadn't gotten very far in her journey to the library, which was on the far side of the Academe from their chambers, when she came across Madame Simsa.

The venable smiled at her. "There you are, child. I was just coming to see you."

"Madame?" Had she done something wrong?

"That fool Henri should have told me what he was doing this morning. There are ways to ease the pain after. For earth witches, especially." She gestured at Sophie. "Are you well?"

"I feel a little tired. But my head no longer hurts."

Madame Simsa nodded in approval. "Good. Then you can escort me back to my chambers and tell me all about this ball last night. There are the most peculiar stories circulating." She looked amused. "I thought it best to hear an account from a reliable witness."

There was no polite way to refuse such a request. And, Sophie realized, Madame Simsa was the perfect person to ask about the ley line connection. Much simpler than searching for another book to explain it.

She offered her arm to the older woman. "I am more than

happy to walk with you." She wasn't sure she would recount everything that had occurred at the ball—she would be keeping Sevan Allowood's accusations to herself for the time being—but she could find out what the venable had been told and at least correct the worst errors in the rumors.

As they turned to retrace their steps to the nearest staircase, Tok came swooping down the corridor and landed on Sophie's shoulder. She eyed him with resignation. The look in his eye he cocked at her was remarkably satisfied.

"Still sticking to his choice, then," Madame said.

"Yes," Sophie said. But she turned to the topic of the ball, asking Madame Simsa to tell her what she had heard as they walked.

By the time they reached the venable's apartments, Sophie wasn't sure whether to laugh or cry. The basic facts, that there was an Anglion delegation on Illvyan soil and that there had been an altercation, were in place but the details varied wildly. Madame Simsa had told her three different versions of the fight, none of them near the truth. The worst of the tales involved ten sanctii and twenty people dead at the end of it.

She saw Madame Simsa settled on one of the sofas in her tiny sitting room and then took a seat on the chair opposite. Riki had bounded onto the sofa to sit beside Madame Simsa as soon as she had settled in place, standing on her lap to pat her face and then climbing up on the back of the sofa to watch her like a small furred sentry. The smell of the monkey—an animal smell, sharper than the fur of a dog or a cat—mingled with Madame Simsa's dusty floral perfume and the papery scent of the books piled everywhere was becoming familiar.

It didn't take her long to sketch out the bare facts of the ball.

Madame Simsa looked concerned by the end of it. "These Anglions, they want you to return?"

"So it would seem."

"And do you want to return?" The older woman tilted her

head at Sophie. "Speaking for the Academe, we would be sorry to lose one with your talents."

"Anglion is my home," Sophie said gently.

"A home you ran from," Madame Simsa retorted, eyes sparking. But then she sat back with a slump. "Though I can understand the wish to return. But are you sure you will be safe?"

"At this stage, that is . . . unclear. But I don't want to burn bridges before I have to. I have family there. Cameron has family there."

"Of course. You must consider carefully." Madame Simsa settled back against the sofa, reaching absently to stroke Riki. "I do not envy you the decision."

Sophie would prefer that she didn't have to make it either. And she didn't want to talk about it anymore. It wasn't what she had come to discuss.

"I met Venable du Laq at the palace," Sophie said.

Madame Simsa frowned. "It seems it was a very busy evening. I'm beginning to be sorry I missed it."

Sophie couldn't tell if she was serious.

"And how was the duq's wife?" Madame Simsa asked in a tart tone.

The duq's wife. Not Venable du Laq. Or Major du Laq. Or Her Grace. Or even Imogene. It seemed Madame Simsa was perhaps not inclined to favor the emperor's mage.

"She appeared well," Sophie said. "She was helpful, in the end. She said she would like to talk more with me."

"I'm sure she would," Madame Simsa said with a click of her teeth that was distinctly disapproving.

"She seemed friendly. She helped Cameron during the attack. I had assumed the imperial mages would all be blood mages. Are there many who are not? "

"A decent number," Madame Simsa said. "It is a popular choice for some. And as for her ladyship helping, well, she may have assisted Cameron but surely a water mage and several sanctii becoming involved didn't do anything to warm the hearts of your Anglions."

Sophie made a face. She couldn't deny that. "They didn't seem that warm to begin with. And I, for one, am in favor of my husband remaining alive. So I am grateful to Her Grace."

"And the Anglions?"

"They were alarmed by the sanctii but I'm sure they will be fine. It may reassure them that the sanctii aren't exactly the danger we are taught." She hoped so. Otherwise, Madame was correct, the sanctii would not have helped Sophie's cause.

Madame Simsa pursed her lips. "Well, maybe, I suppose. But hear me on this, child. Imogene du Laq is not to be underestimated. She was always ambitious. She has succeeded in satisfying some of those ambitions as evidenced by the position she now holds. And by the man she married. Who is one of the few people I have ever met who may be more ambitious than his wife. The du Laqs are powerful, Sophie, and they will use what they can to grow even more so. I would advise you to tread cautiously. You are a tempting prize to the likes of them. They will use you to their ends if you let them." Madame Simsa hesitated. "Granted, Imogene can likely tell you more of what has happened at court since your Anglions arrived and about the work of the imperial mages than we here at the Academe can. But I would be careful about what you request of her. I would not like to owe her a debt."

"Thank you, Madame. I will be careful." She remembered then something Imogene has said. "Venable du Laq called me a bright one. I thought she might be commenting on my dress but later she said something about me shining. It was after the trouble with the ambassador, when she and Henri were talking about the third sanctii." She frowned, trying to remember the words. But between the late night and the reveilé, her memory of the conversation was not so perfect.

"The third sanctii?" Madame Simsa's white brows shot up. "The one working with the man who attacked the ambassador?"

"No, there was another. One she and Henri did not recognize. They were talking quite fast in Illvyan and I didn't understand all of it." She shook her head. Now that she'd had the reveilé, it would be useful to be able to go back in time and listen to some of those conversations over again. "You would have to ask the maistre. But do you know what Venable du Laq might have meant?"

"I expect she meant your connection to the ley line," Madame Simsa said matter-of-factly. "You are rather dazzling to the gaze."

Sophie rubbed her temples. Ley line connections. Again. Another thing she had to learn. But she had wanted to ask Madame Simsa about them and here was her opportunity.

"Are you feeling well, child? The first few days after the reveilé can be fatiguing, I gather. And, as I said, there are ways to ease the pain if it has returned."

"It's not that, Madame," Sophie said. She shook her head, then made a frustrated noise. "It's just . . . just that I feel as though I'm never going to catch up. Ever since my Ais-Seann, it's been one thing after another and I seem to be running behind, never quite able to regain control." Right now, it felt as though she never would. And that was not a feeling she enjoyed. "This is hardly how my life should have gone."

"Life rarely follows a plan in my experience. But I will grant, from what I know of your story, you do seem to have had a difficult few months."

With no hope of that difficulty ending any time soon.

"And now you are coping with it all in a strange place. It is natural to feel unsettled," Madame Simsa continued.

"I don't feel unsettled." Or not merely that. "I feel . . . I feel as though my hands are tied and I can't even see the rope to begin working out the knot. I seem to know so little compared to the students here. In Anglion they don't even teach us to see this connection to the ley line that you all seem to take for granted." Her voice had risen and she took a deep breath, trying to reach for calm as Tok squawked on the sofa beside her. It was not Madame Simsa who was the cause of her frustrations.

"Well, that part I expect I can help you with," Madame Simsa said, her tone calm. The sort of tone mothers used to soothe fractious children.

Part of her didn't wish to be soothed. But a larger part wanted to listen. If Madame Simsa could teach her to see the ley line connections, then some of the gap she felt between what she knew and what she needed to know in order to survive would be narrowed.

"I would be grateful if you could, Madame." She reached out and stroked Tok's wing. The smoothness of his feathers was oddly comforting. As was the gentle tap of his beak against her hand when he bent his head to push it under her fingers. She transferred her petting to his head and he made a happy little sound.

Beside Madame Simsa, Riki chattered softly. "Hush," Madame Simsa said. Then she smiled at Sophie. "Very well. So. Ley lines. We shall begin." She smoothed out her skirt, then frowned and stood.

"What did you see the first time you saw a ley line?" Madame Simsa peered over the back of the sofa as though looking for something. Then straightened, turning back to Sophie. "You have seen a ley line, yes?"

Sophie nodded. "Yes. The morning of my Ais-Seann. We were in a field and it was like a river of light." A glittering golden river. Like nothing she'd ever seen before. The need to touch it had been irresistible. If only she hadn't given in to its call, her life would have been very different.

But then again, blaming the ley line or her lack of willpower was futile. She could equally blame those who had attacked the palace, the reason that she and Cameron had been in that field in the first place. Or Eloisa, who'd sent her and Cameron to Portside that morning, or the duty colonel who'd scheduled Cameron to duty or . . . well, any one of hundreds of people, probably. It had happened. Perhaps it was even the will of the goddess. There was no point wishing for change that could never be made. She needed to focus on those changes she could control. Like her magic.

"A field?" Madame Simsa turned to peer over the back of the sofa. She made a satisfied noise and stood again, a lacy woolen shawl in her hand. "One day soon, I think you need to tell me that story, child."

Do not blush. Sophie focused on the memory of the ley line itself rather than the forbidden, wonderful, frantic, power-drunk sex that had come after it. "A river of light," she repeated. "Is that important?"

Madame Simsa sat back down, settling the shawl over her lap. Riki stretched her paw toward the shawl and the venable tapped it gently. "This shawl is for me, you silly beast. You have fur to keep you warm." The monkey retreated, looking indignant. Madame Simsa turned her gaze back to Sophie. "Understanding how you see the ley line helps me to clarify how best to proceed. Everyone sees the flow of power in their own unique way. The sanctii say it's because every person's mind is different, which I suppose makes sense." She paused. "Have you seen the ley line here?"

"I can feel it," Sophie replied. "Like water flowing beneath my feet. The power feels very deep. But no, I haven't seen it. I thought perhaps I caught a glimpse in the palace grounds but the carriage was moving too fast to be sure."

"So nowhere in Lumia? Nowhere since you arrived in Illvya?"

"No." Sophie hesitated. She and Cameron had spent their first hours on Illvyan soil in a cave. Then they'd gone straight through a portal. She'd felt the magic in the cave but there had been no sign of it. But she didn't want to explain that to Madame. She owed Captain Jensen her life. She wasn't going to betray the route he used for his smuggling. "Is that bad?"

"I don't think so. Not if you can sense it."

Sophie shifted in her chair, frustrated. "But if I can feel it, why can't I see it? If you Illvyans can, why can't I?"

"Perhaps because you were not taught to do so," Madame Simsa said, one hand smoothing the shawl. "It could be as simple as that. Or there may be another reason. That is what we will determine."

It was something of a relief to hear her matter-of-fact tone. It didn't sound like she thought Sophie was lacking in any way. "What does the ley line look like to you?"

"Like a strip of night sky floating just above the ground. Dark with tiny pinpoints of light, like starlight. When someone has a connection to the ley line, it's as though I see faint stars around them as well. In your case, the stars are plentiful. And not so faint." Her mouth quirked and Riki chittered at her. She shook her head at the monkey.

"So I should see the connection in a similar way to how I see the ley line itself?"

"Most likely. But not always. We shall experiment." The venable pushed up to her feet and set the shawl back down on the sofa beside her, where Riki reached for it once more. She shook her head at the fam. "If you chew that, I will not be happy with you, my friend." She shook her head once more. "If you take a familiar, child, do not choose a monkey. Troublesome beasts."

Riki chittered at her, looking indignant.

"Well, if you would behave, I would not have to say such things." She considered the monkey. "Actually, you can come with us." She turned to Sophie. "Come. I do not think these rooms are the best location to test my theories. We need something a little closer to the earth."

It seemed she meant that literally. She led Sophie back down to the grounds, heading in the same direction as they had for her testing. Tok rode on Sophie's shoulder and Riki ambled along at Madame Simsa's feet, keeping pace surprisingly easily for a not-so-large creature. Once they were outside, the monkey went on ahead, leaping up on window ledges and climbing tree trunks a few feet before dropping back down to catch up to them again.

They were definitely heading in the same direction as the testing. Only this time, they continued on beyond the row of small stone buildings. Sophie found herself in a small strip of garden that ran the length of the wall that formed the Academe's boundaries.

"I'd take you into the park beyond but Henri would likely throw a fit," Madame said, coming to a halt.

Sophie didn't want to confess that she wasn't overly keen on the idea either. Not after what had happened at the palace. Not only was the presence of the Anglions unnerving, but the fact that there were those in the court who seemed to hate Anglions so strongly as to attack them in the emperor's presence was disturbing to say the least.

Anglion was hardly in a position to threaten the empire. Why should Illvyans care about it? She understood why Aristides might wish to complete his empire, but she didn't see what real benefit adding Anglion to his list of conquests brought him or any other Illvyan. Certainly not any that would justify attacking Anglions in the emperor's presence.

"You would be safe enough, child. I doubt your Anglions have anything up their sleeves that could get past Belarus."

As though his name had summoned him, Belarus appeared beside her. Sophie managed to keep her reaction under control as the chill of his presence hit her. "Hello, Belarus."

The sanctii nodded at her. Madame Simsa made an impatient gesture. "Come along. You, too, Belarus. While you are here, you may as well be useful." She walked about ten feet farther along the fence line. "Here should do."

Sophie stopped obediently, not at all sure what they were doing. "What do you need me to do?"

"We're standing right on top of the ley line, child. Can you feel it?"

She could. She hadn't noticed it before, distracted with wondering what they were about to do. "Yes."

"Can you see it?"

So far she saw nothing but grass. "No."

"All right. What about in Anglion? Did you see the ley line all the time?"

"No. A few glimpses when I was outside. Never inside a building. My tutors always said the power runs deep through the earth."

Madame Simsa shook her head at that. "Now that is just silly."

"Madame?"

"The power runs through the earth, yes, but it is also on the surface. Maybe this is the problem you have. Your mind has formed an image of the ley line as something like an underground river. So it doesn't expect to see it above ground."

"That doesn't explain why I saw it out in the open the first time," Sophie objected.

"This was the day of your birthday? The Ais-Seann?" Madame Simsa said. She spoke the last two words hesitantly, as though they were unfamiliar on her tongue.

"Yes."

"Then perhaps it was the surprise of it all. You didn't know that you were going to see anything and you just saw what was there."

"Is that likely?"

"I'm not entirely sure," Madame Simsa said. "It's not as though I have a lot of experience dealing with the wrong-headedness of Anglion-trained witches. You can't even pronounce the words correctly. Ais-Seann. Bah."

"What do the Illvyans call it?"

"An ascension. As it should be. Your language has mangled it."

A-sense-see-on. A rising. A claiming. That was what her brain told her the word meant. And said slowly, the pronunciation was, in truth, not so different.

"How many Anglion mages have you met?" Sophie asked curiously.

"Two, not counting you and Cameron. There was a blood mage here for a while when I was a student but he moved on. And then there was another earth witch." Madame Simsa frowned, as though trying to remember. "Maybe twenty years ago. She wasn't very strong, not of the royal line or whatever you call it. But she and her husband—who had no power at all—had somehow fallen foul of the temple."

"The temple?" She hadn't heard of such a thing. Not of the temple driving someone out of the country. It was true that she had heard of them pursuing witches they thought were straying beyond the bounds of earth magic, but she couldn't imagine what a weaker witch could do to draw their attention.

"Yes." Madame Simsa nodded vigorously. "I'm sure that was it. Well, it usually is, isn't it? The kinds of things that make people want to flee their country are limited. Crime. Politics. Love. Religion. Those would be the four I can think of."

"Which one was it for Chloe de Montesse?" Sophie asked, unable to help herself.

Madame Simsa's expression turned sad. "That one was politics. And not even her own. Her husband—he always was an idiot." She looked up in Sophie. "Don't marry for looks. Make sure they have a brain in their heads." Then she smiled. "But you seem to have done well for yourself in that department. Your Cameron has a sensible head on his shoulders. A pretty one, too. But Charl de Montesse, well, he lacked the former. He became involved in some plot or another. The details were kept rather quiet after the event. He was arrested. Charged with treason. And at that point, Chloe ran. I doubt she was involved, but treason has a way of splashing onto those surrounding the one who commits the act. Such contamination can be fatal. Charl paid with his life. So I don't blame Chloe for wanting to save hers. Even though it was terribly hard on her mother and father. Aristides, at least, did not seem to think that they may have been involved. Henri kept his position. But lost his daughter for all intents and purposes."

Sophie swayed suddenly, feeling faint. Treason. Sevan's words came back to her. Traitor. Was that what had waited for her if she returned? Disgrace? Or death.

"Are you feeling all right?" Madame Simsa asked, peering at her. "The reveilé is draining. We can wait."

"No. We can't." Sophie straightened her shoulders, willing the dizziness to recede. "And I am fine." She wanted to know more about Chloe. And about the earth witch Madame Simsa had mentioned. But she wanted the magic first.

"You were saying something about a river," she prompted.

"Yes. If you have been picturing a river, deep below the earth, then that may be why you can't see it now." Madame Simsa turned to Belarus. "Does that sound reasonable?"

"Possible," the sanctii said.

"That's not encouraging," Sophie said. Belarus didn't offer anything more.

Madame Simsa shook her head. "All we need to do is change how you think about it. That may solve the problem."

"And if it doesn't?"

"Then we will try a different approach. Or send you back to class with the younger students."

"I'm not sure how many more classes I can take in a week," Sophie said.

"You'll find it easier now that you can understand the language more easily."

"I hope so." Anything to lighten the load would be welcome. "So, how do I change how I see the ley line."

"Practice, I expect." Madame Simsa glanced around, then moved a few steps to her right, standing with her back to the high stone fence. "Now. Come stand here with me. We're right above the line here, which should make it easier."

Sophie stood where she indicated.

"Good. Now close your eyes. Feel the ley line."

She did as asked. Let her eyes close, found the power again where it rushed and roared below her.

"Now. Picture what you saw the first time you saw the ley line. Your river of light."

She nodded when she had.

"And picture that river deep beneath your feet where you feel the power."

"How do you get a river of light underground?" Her brows drew together as she tried to take the image of the ley line in her mind and place it far below her.

"Imagination, child," Madame Simsa said, sounding a little impatient. "We are trying to alter how you see this, remember. So just try. Do you have it?"

"Yes," Sophie said. "I think so."

"Good. Now. When you draw from the ley line, what do you think about?"

"I just . . . reach for it."

"Anglions," Madame Simsa muttered. "All right. So in Illvya, we would say that part of your power is touching the ley line always. Not a large part but some. When you want to draw on it, that connection grows stronger . . . wider, for lack of a better term. Does that make sense?"

"I suppose so. What happens when someone isn't near a ley line?"

"Well, there are ley lines and then there are ley lines. There are small ones that cross between the larger ones we use," the venable said. "And the connection stretches. You've never not been able to use power when you wanted it, have you?"

Sophie thought about it. "No. But then again, I'm not sure I've ever been terribly far from a ley line when I wanted to."

"Well, in truth, you never are. So remember that. Now. I want you to reach for the ley line as you would usually do. But try and picture a connection. Imagine the roots of a tree sinking down to the river. Or a well. Whatever makes sense to you."

A tree? That seemed to make sense. Particularly if, as Madame Simsa had said, there were ley lines all around. There'd been a giant oak tree blown down in a storm at their estate the year she turned fourteen. The exposed roots at its base, gnarled and twisted, had been huge. And that hadn't even been the whole of them. Peering over the edge of the hole where the tree had stood, there were still broken roots in the earth. They had to be sunk deep to withstand the force that had taken the tree. She formed the image in her head. A grand oak tree, with herself standing as the trunk. She sent her power down, trying to imagine a root spearing through the earth. A single one to start with. More seemed needlessly complex.

When the surge of the ley line touched her, she saw the root sink into the light. "I see it."

"Good. Now imagine the light flowing back up that connection. Filling it, moving toward you and surrounding you. Keep your eyes closed. Just watch it. Count to fifty in your head."

She couldn't imagine what she must look like, standing there in bright daylight, eyes closed, watched by Madame, her monkey, and the sanctii. And Tok, somewhere. He had abandoned her shoulder for once.

Concentrate. The numbers ticked themselves off in her head. And the light she imagined flowed upward. Filling the roots and the tree she pictured and then spilling out and down onto the earth beneath her feet. The image of flowing light moved smoothly. Steadily. Until it was almost boring to contemplate. Forty-six. Forty-seven. Forty-eight. Forty-nine. "Now what?" she asked as she finally reached fifty.

"Now open your eyes and tell me what you see."

That seemed straightforward enough. But she hesitated to actually open her eyes. What was she going to do if this didn't work? It felt like just one more thing that could go wrong. Perhaps one thing too many.

A small thing maybe, but that might be the tiny thing that broke her.

"Sophie? Are you all right?"

Was she being ridiculous? Well, she couldn't stand there with her eyes shut forever. She opened them. Saw the glittering light of the ley line laid over the grass. Saw too, thin threads of it stretching to Madame Simsa, to Riki, to Belarus and, just visible in the air, a thin shining line leading to Tok perched on the wall. A similar fine line of light linked Madame Simsa and Belarus.

"What do you see?" Madame Simsa asked. "Anything?"

"The ley line. Right there." Sophie pointed at it. "Like it was at home."

"Is that all?"

"There are lines from it to you. And to Belarus and Riki. And to Tok. They glow like the ley line."

"Tok?" Madame Simsa looked briefly surprised, but then she shook her head. "Never mind. Those lines, those are the connections. If you see someone with one of those, then they have magic."

Sophie looked again. The thread of light to Madame Simsa was bright but the one to Belarus was even brighter. "Can you tell how much power they have from what you see? Belarus, his connection seems brighter than yours." She remembered what Imogene had said. About her being bright. Was that what she had meant?

"Some can. I can a little. The brightness can indicate that, how strong a link the person has to the lines, which is a close enough correlation to their magical strength for the purposes of this discussion. Or it can show how much magic a person is using. If someone who appears faint to you normally grows brighter, then it means they are using their power. It depends how sensitive you are to the ley line. Or how strong your own magic is, to put it another way."

So Venable du Laq saw her as strong? That was useful to know. Useful and a little alarming. She stared at the line connecting Belarus to the golden stream running along the earth. Had the brightness faded a little? "It's not as bright now."

Madame Simsa shrugged. "You weren't concentrating as hard. You will have to practice. Use the visualization. Eventually it should become second nature and you will be able to see it whenever you choose."

She could see how it would be helpful. Being able to identify those around you who could use magic against you. "I wonder why they don't teach us this in Anglion."

"I expect because they think it's water magic. Which it is not," Madame Simsa said. "But the water mages were the first to use the skill. They needed to monitor the sanctii—"

Belarus interrupted with a disapproving grunt.

Madame Simsa smiled at him. "Perhaps "monitor" is the wrong word. But no matter what you call it, the water mages worked out how to do it."

"I don't understand, if it isn't actually water magic . . . ."

"For that you'd have to ask one of the Anglion dominas, I imagine." Madame Simsa frowned. "We do not know enough about how Anglions run their lives. I'm sure His Imperial Majesty gets some information, but if he does he holds it close. Though perhaps one of the temple here could tell you more about the initial schism between Anglion and water magic. They must have records that go that far back."

"We were taught that the water mages were dangerous. Power hungry. That their demons—sorry, Belarus—were killers."

"And we are taught that the Anglions are uncivilized rebels," Madame Simsa said. "I know that is not true. You know now that the sanctii do not slaughter people in the streets."

That was not the same thing as they did not kill people ever, Sophie noted. But she understood the point. "Yes. So I want to understand more about what happened. It might help me decide."

"Decide?"

"Whether it is safe if I return home."

CHAPTER 14

Cameron watched the students and mages sparring before him and shifted uncomfortably on the bench. He understood the rationale for Venable Marignon not wishing him to train today. Earth witch healing was useful, but the body still needed time to catch up with what the magic wrought. The pain was gone but the ribs would still be healing and it wouldn't do to aggravate them. And as he watched Ranulph, one of the older students, land a solid blow of a heavy wooden training sword against his sparring partner's ribs, he was grateful it wasn't him. But still, sitting on the hard, wooden bench wasn't the most comfortable position and seemed to aggravate the lingering faint ache in his ribs. Discomfort aside, the main reason for wishing that he was doing something more active than observing was that observing didn't take the same degree of concentration that fighting did.

Which meant that he had far too much time to sit and think.

He'd thought so much his head was aching with the twists and turns and endless variations of situations and possibilities. And he was still no closer to knowing what he and Sophie should do.

It should be simple enough.

The offer to return home should have been irresistible.

That was clearly what the delegation had been expecting. For them to leap at the chance to return. Or be stupid enough to do so without stronger reassurances from Eloisa.

But lacking those reassurances, the decision was far from simple. Indeed, the sensible position, a position that would have been unthinkable a few short weeks earlier, would be to remain in Illvya. After all, alive was better than dead. And if Sevan Allowood had dared to call Sophie a traitor to her face, there were clearly those in the court who wished his wife to be the latter. Probably him, too.

But remaining in Illvya wasn't a guarantee of safety either. Aristides would decide if Sophie—or Cameron himself—were of any use to him. If they were, then no doubt he would set about ensuring that he obtained whatever benefits they represented. It didn't necessarily follow that he and Sophie would also benefit from the process.

Damned if they did and damned if they didn't, perhaps.

Which left the thorny issue of determining which form of damnation to embrace.

What he wouldn't give for five minutes alone with James.

Surely Jeanne's brother would give him the courtesy of the truth?

He pushed the thought aside for what had to be the twentieth time that day. He couldn't get to James, no matter how much he wished he could.

It went without saying that he couldn't simply present himself at the imperial palace and demand to speak to him. And the kind of magic that dealt in secret messages and illusions of the kind that might allow Cameron to get some sort of note to James was strictly the domain of those who practiced the Arts of Air. Cameron had no talent for illusion, and though there were plenty of illusioners at the Academe, there were none he knew even part of the way toward the level of trust required before he would involve them in something that might just put him and James in danger.

Which left him with nothing to do but watch other people work off steam. Which did nothing to improve his temper. He glanced at the clock hung on the opposite wall. Nearly time for this, the final lesson of the day, to end. Hopefully when he returned to their chambers, Sophie would be recovered from the reveilé. He hadn't wanted to leave her there alone but she had insisted.

He shifted again on the bench and looked toward the door. Perhaps Venable Marignon would not mind if he left a little early. But before he could act on the thought, the door swung inwards and Colonel Perrine and Imogene du Laq entered.

Most of the students came to sudden stumbling halts, pausing to stare at the vision of the black-clad colonel and the duquesse, who also wore a high-collared black dress and jacket. The clothes, far more decorous in design than the dress she had worn at the ball, were no less striking. Her collar bore two gold suns. Emeralds the size of his thumbnail graced her ears, sparkling as she turned her head to survey the room.

Venable Marignon, who had been assisting one of the younger students with some sword work, looked up, face annoyed, obviously ready to order them all back to work when she spotted the visitors.

Her expression didn't exactly alter, but the focus of her irritation clearly shifted from the students to the pair from the palace. She straightened and strode across the room. The bow she offered Imogene was shallow. And brief.

"Colonel. Your Grace. To what do we owe the pleasure?"

"We were looking for Lord Scardale," Colonel Perrine said. "We were told we would find him here."

Venable Marignon's mouth pursed. Then she tilted her head toward Cameron. "Over there. He is not training today thanks to the goings-on at the palace of yours."

Colonel Perrine inclined his head. "The palace is very grateful to Lord Scardale for his assistance."

"Hmmph. If that's true, then perhaps you could show that gratitude by letting me get on with my class."

"Of course, Verite, dear," Imogene said in an overly sweet voice. "We did not mean to intrude."

If they hadn't intended to intrude they could have sent for him. He had no idea if it were common for members of the Imperial Guard to visit the Academe. Presumably a number of them had trained here. But once sworn to the emperor, he knew from his lessons that they owed their allegiance to Aristides only. Judging by the various degrees of hero worship and awe on display on the students' faces, many of them hoped one day to also make that oath.

Venable Marignon turned from Imogene and snapped, "Back to your drills," to the class before returning to the center of the room. The students sprang back to their positions. Apparently fear of Venable Marignon's famous temper outweighed the novelty of visitors. Even imperial guards.

Imogene nudged the colonel's arm and the pair of them headed toward Cameron. He rose as they reached him, intending to bow, but Venable du Laq waved him off.

"Please, Lord Scardale, we can leave such things for the ball-room," Imogene said.

Which didn't stop Colonel Perrine from performing a shallow bow as he offered the envelope he held to Cameron.

"From my Imperial Master," he said.

That much Cameron had already gathered. He doubted anyone else was sending two members of the Imperial Guard to his doorstep.

He took the envelope. Between the thick paper and the black and gold wax seal, it was heavier than it looked. His thumb traced the rose-twined tower that graced the seal. An innocuous emblem for a not-so-innocuous man. "Am I going to like what this contains?"

Colonel Perrine shrugged. "I'm afraid I don't know what it contains."

"But if you had to wager?"

"Imperial guards don't wager, my lord."

Cameron turned to Imogene. "What about imperial mages?"

"I am a fair hand at cards," she said. "But I don't think this requires a wager. I imagine it contains an invitation to speak to the emperor again."

"An invitation or a command?"

"There isn't a large degree of difference when it comes to the emperor," Imogene said.

He hadn't thought so. The envelope suddenly felt heavier than before. "Am I supposed to open this now?"

"My orders are to wait for your response," Colonel Perrine said.

"Isn't that a little superfluous?" Cameron asked. "If I'm unlikely to say no?"

The colonel's mouth twisted in appreciation of the point but he merely shook his head. "I have my orders, Lord Scardale."

"Cameron," Cameron said automatically. He thought he might get along well with Colonel Perrine if they ever got to deal with each other on an unofficial basis. He was the kind of military man that Cameron was used to.

"Not while I'm on duty, my lord."

Ah. He should have known. In the colonel's place, Cameron would have responded the same way. "I'd prefer to discuss this with Sophie before I respond."

"Well, that shouldn't be a problem," Imogene said. "We have also sent for your wife."

"She's in our chambers."

"Apparently not," Imogene said. "But someone has been sent to find her."

What did they mean Sophie wasn't in their chambers? She was supposed to be sleeping off the goddess-damned reveilé. His jaw clenched and he relaxed it with an effort. As far as the venable and Colonel Perrine knew, there was no reason for him to be worried about Sophie's whereabouts.

"I'd also prefer not to discuss whatever there is to be discussed in front of an audience." He gestured toward the class. Just in time for the end of class chimes to sound. The thuds and grunts of the practice session turned to chatter and laughter as the students broke off their matches and began gathering up their gear.

Venable Marignon was particular about the state of the training rooms, but she had her pupils well trained and about three minutes after the chimes had sounded, the room was empty of students. Verite hesitated by the door, looking at him with a quizzical expression, as though offering to stay if he wished.

Tempting, but he didn't think Colonel Perrine or Imogene meant him any harm. For one thing, if they wanted to kill him, it would be far easier within the walls of the palace than here. Well, it might be just as easy to kill him here, but it would be far more difficult to explain the act to Henri and the rest of the venables. And for another thing, he wanted to know if they'd managed to learn anything from the attacker they'd taken into custody the night before.

He shook his head slightly at Verite and she hitched a shoulder in acceptance, then closed the door behind her. Almost immediately it opened again and Sophie walked in, Willem trailing behind her. Tok shot through the gap between door and lintel, circling the room to caw at Cameron before winging back to Sophie to land on her shoulder.

Imogene's dark brows lifted. "I didn't know you had a familiar, Lady Scardale."

"I don't. This one is just nosy," Sophie said, but she made no motion to dislodge the bird. Willem, on the other hand, she sent on his way with a smile of thanks and a firm assertion that he needed to get to dinner on time.

The boy looked reluctant but left. Cameron wondered if he'd

had time to send word to the harbor yet. Or go himself. He hadn't thought about how Willem might go about obtaining the information he'd asked for. He didn't want the boy to put himself at risk. He should warn him to be careful.

Sophie joined Cameron, sending him a questioning look before turning her attention to Imogene and the colonel. Her curtsy was quick but deep enough to be polite. "Your Grace, Colonel." She paused for a moment, studying Imogene, and he wondered what she was looking at.

Cameron passed the envelope to her. "Apparently His Imperial Majesty has done us the honor of requesting our presence again."

"Interesting that you know that already with the seal unbroken," Sophie murmured.

"Call it an educated guess," Cameron said.

"Let us see," Sophie said. She didn't have a dagger or one of the small silver knives ladies often used to open seals, but she managed well enough with a fingernail. Her expression, as she scanned the piece of paper she drew out, didn't alter. "Tomorrow night," she said. "Well, that will make Madame Designy happy. I doubt she'd appreciate it if I wore one of her creations to court two days in a row."

"Helene? I wondered if your gown was her work. Is she making you others?" Imogene said.

"Yes. I shall have to let her know we have an accelerated schedule."

Cameron had no idea why they were discussing evening gowns when there were bigger issues to deal with. "May I see that?"

He scanned the elegantly written script, but it offered no additional clues as to why the emperor wanted to see them again. Simply stated a place and time for them to appear.

"Any ideas as to what he wants?" he asked Colonel Perrine.

"I believe there is to be a continuation of discussions

between yourselves and your compatriots," the colonel said, looking thoughtful.

"Why the delay?"

"I believe the emperor wanted to give your chief ambassador a little more time to recover from the shock of last night," Imogene said.

Time to recover his temper more likely. The barron was not a man to take insults to his dignity—or his safety—lightly. He'd be looking for someone to blame for the attack. Which wasn't likely to improve the attitudes of the delegates toward Cameron and Sophie. After all, they were safer targets for his wrath than the emperor.

"Very well." He looked down at Sophie, who seemed resigned as much as anything. She knew as well as he did that they couldn't refuse the request. "Then you may tell your master that we will be delighted to accept his gracious invitation."

Colonel Perrine dipped his head in acknowledgement.

"Did you learn anything from the prisoner?" Cameron asked. Perhaps the colonel might not be able to answer him, but it would be foolish not to ask.

"Not much. He was paid. But whoever did so set it up well. He didn't know who it was. He received his instructions and his down payment via written messages brought by common couriers."

"What about the sanctii he used?" Sophie asked.

"He had been given a scriptii to call it."

Cameron frowned. He hadn't considered that possibility. "Can you trace the mage who made it?"

The colonel shook his head. "Perhaps. If we had it. But we didn't find it on him. The sanctii may have taken it. Or it may have been spelled to destroy itself when used."

"But Martius and Ikarus took the sanctii away with them."

"Yes. They overpowered it. They returned it to their realm. But no one can compel a sanctii to reappear here other than the mage who bound it. And our sanctii cannot compel it to answer them either. We do not know much of how their society works, but we do know that."

"So you would need the mage who controls it. And if you have him—or her—then you probably don't need the sanctii."

"Exactly," Imogene said. "And the sanctii was just following orders, presumably, so under our laws it has done no wrong. The normal punishment for a water mage who broke the laws would be to have the bond dissolved before any other punishments are meted out. The sanctii returns to their realm and the mage faces the consequences of their actions. I believe the Academe keeps track of the names of sanctii who have been associated with mages who have proven troublesome in the past."

"Why are their names important?" Cameron asked.

Imogene shrugged. "Some mages would think it safer, not to try to call such a one when they are attempting to form a bond."

"Some?" Sophie said.

"Others think that having a sanctii who has been bound previously is useful. Like having a trained soldier rather than a raw recruit. Of course, a trained soldier usually knows some of the loopholes in the rules. And a sanctii whose bond has been sundered knows full well that that is possible. But depending on the skills of the previous mage and what they worked on, there are those who would still take the chance. Sanctii live longer than we do. Why waste all that experience?"

"I didn't know that," Sophie said.

Neither had he. But it made sense. Unkillable demons probably did live a long time. And that wouldn't have been something that Anglion would be keen for its citizens to know about.

"So essentially you found nothing?" He tried not to let the frustration he felt seep into his voice but wasn't entirely successful

"We are still investigating," Colonel Perrine said, posture stiffening. "But no, so far, we have no answers for you or the barron."

"And the other sanctii? The one who helped Ikarus and Martius?"

Imogene shook her head. "Of that one there has been no sign. And Ikarus will not say more than he does not know why she was there."

"She?"

"Apparently she was female," Imogene said. "Which makes her somewhat rare. As I said, we don't know much about sanctii, but we do know there are more males than females. Or more males that answer to bonding than females. There is only one female bonded in all of Illvya itself that I am aware of. A handful or so more in the rest of the empire. Not that I know all the sanctii in the empire." She touched one of the emeralds hanging from her ear. "I am coming around to the theory that the reason she was there, Lady Scardale, was because of you."

～

Her? Sophie's heart thumped as she stared at Imogene in astonishment. "What would a sanctii want with me?"

"I do not know," Imogene said. "But we found no traces of the types of magic that might call a sanctii to the ballroom. No scriptii. No charms. I looked. So did some of my other colleagues in the imperial mages. Ikarus looked, too. He knows nothing. He says he didn't recognize her. Martius also claims ignorance. But something attracted the creature."

"But it was Cameron who the sanctii helped. It didn't even come anywhere near me," Sophie protested.

"As your main point of concern was, I imagine, right at that moment, your husband's well-being, I don't think that is an excluding factor. A sanctii usually acts on the wishes of the mage it is bound to."

"But I'm not bound to any sanctii," Sophie said. "Why would it do my bidding? How would it even know what my bidding was?"

"Why does that raven sit on your shoulder?" Imogene said. "Because it is attracted to your power. I can see you tell the truth that you are not bonded to it, but the potential is there. I can see the beginnings of a bond. All you would need to do would be to choose to complete it. Then it would be as solid as the link between you and Cameron." She nodded at the space between them and Sophie realized that Imogen could probably see the bond they shared. As she herself had seen the link between Belarus and Madame Simsa.

She couldn't see her bond with Cameron though. She hadn't asked Madame Simsa about that. About whether she could see her own magic. She hadn't so far, but then again, it was difficult to look at oneself from a distance without a mirror. And she hadn't encountered such a thing on her walk through the halls from the garden to the change rooms. She might not have noticed one even if she had, so distracted had she been by the suddenly changed world she walked through. One in which she could see glowing light around every other person who walked by.

She'd met Lia in one of the hallways on her way back from Madame Simsa's chambers. She'd found the light glowing around the other girl so distracting that all her answers to Lia's questions had been vague and possibly nonsensical. She was fairly certain that Lia thought she'd lost her wits and had been grateful when Willem had interrupted them.

And even now the light shining around Imogene and Cameron was distracting.

"But I don't know anything about water magic," she protested. "What would a sanctii want with me?"

"Not knowing is not the same as not having an aptitude," Imogene said. "Perhaps in Anglion you were merely an earth witch . . . ." She frowned, peering at the gap between Sophie and Cameron again. "Or maybe not just merely one, if I am reading that bond correctly, but given what I know of your country, I doubt anyone explained that to you. But we don't have time to go into that just now."

Sophie started to protest, then clamped her mouth shut. If she let Imogene finish, then she would know if the questions bubbling on her lips made any sense.

"What isn't a matter for another time is that I am sure you could, if you chose, learn water magic." Imogene looked at Cameron. "I don't know about you."

Cameron held up his hands. "I am perfectly happy being a blood mage, thank you very much."

"You are no more a mere blood mage than your wife here is solely an earth witch. You share some of her power. You might not be able to be as strong at her arts as you are at your own, but you could perhaps learn a little."

"Pardon me, but I'm not sure that learning a little water magic sounds sensible. Don't water mages have to exercise complete control over their sanctii?" Cameron asked.

"If they choose to hold a sanctii, then yes, strength is required to exert one's will at times. But not everyone rides such a line. Some water mages concern themselves with seeing and divination. And some with applying the things the sanctii teach us to improving the world around us. Those who make the fabriques and such."

Cameron looked intrigued by that, but he shook his head. "Regardless, this is a moot point if we return to Anglion. We cannot wield water magic there, nor would we have time to learn any before we departed. I imagine the delegation would be keen to leave these shores quickly once we decide."

"It would seem shortsighted to return to a place where you can only be a stunted version of that which you are supposed to be," Imogene said.

"Perhaps," Sophie said. "But Anglion is our home. Our families are there. And those are ties that cannot be easily dismissed." She glanced up at Cameron. "But we were speaking of the sanctii.

What does it mean if it did come because of me? Is it likely to turn up again? Is there any danger if it does?" The thought of a loose sanctii searching for her was enough to make a large part of her want to find some deep dark hole to hide in. There were just too many years of Anglion conditioning to overcome so quickly. An uncontrolled sanctii was a deadly one. Or so her instincts told her.

"It helped you—or Cameron—the first time. There's no reason to think it means you any harm."

"Then it could turn up again?"

Imogene's mouth twisted a moment. "I'm not entirely certain. Unbound sanctii very rarely appear. So, really anything is possible."

"And if I draped myself in pearls, will that discourage her?" Sophie asked.

"Maybe if you wore them floating in the middle of quite a large tank of seawater," Imogene said with a wry smile. "It is true that the sanctii cannot cross large bodies of salt water, but the amount of salt contained in a pearl wouldn't stop them. Despite what Anglion traditions might tell you. It's the fact that your country is an island that keeps you safe from them, not the pearls your court is so fond of."

That ruled out trying to figure out how to salvage what was left of Eloisa's pearls to wear. "So you're saying there's nothing I can do?"

"Try to be boring. She might lose interest." Imogene glanced at Tok, still perched on Sophie's shoulder, her expression somewhat skeptical.

"I'll keep that in mind," Sophie said. Given her current circumstances, she'd be perfectly happy to be boring. She just didn't think it was likely to happen any time soon. Which meant, she supposed, that she needed to keep her eyes peeled for stray sanctii. And send a note to the Designys to ask if they could have another of her dresses finished by tomorrow.

CHAPTER 15

"Is there a temple nearby?" Sophie asked as Helene placed pins in purple velvet with measured care.

The clothier's perfectly arched eyebrows lifted, her eyes widening. "A temple of the goddess?"

Sophie checked the habitual "what other kind is there"? Illvya, not Anglion. "Yes," she said with an encouraging smile. She already knew the answer, having found a temple nearby on Cameron's city map. But she wanted a simpler source if anyone asked how she had known where the temple was. It would be unwise to share how hard she and Cameron had been working to learn ways through the city. Besides, it would be interesting to know if Helene would help her.

Helene's nose wrinkled as she slid another pin into the sleeve of the dress Sophie wore. "I believe there is a small one in the square near Isle de Angelique. By the hospital there. That would be the closest. But do you not wish to see the main temple near the palace? It is very beautiful. Much more elegant than any of the smaller temples."

Elegance, apparently, was more important than what went on within the temple walls.

"Turn a little, please, my lady. Toward me," Helene said before Sophie could reply.

Sophie obeyed the direction. "A small temple is all I need." She wanted to understand more about how the goddess was worshipped in Illvya and ask about the history with water magic, as Madame Simsa had suggested, not to encounter whoever the Illvyan equivalent of Domina Skey might be. A small local temple was exactly what she needed. Now that her Illvyan was no longer a barrier, she could perhaps strike up a conversation with a devout or a prior. Find what she was seeking without drawing undue attention to herself.

"I just need directions." She made a small circling gesture with her hand. It had taken some convincing to get Henri and Cameron to agree that there was no reason she shouldn't go to the clothiers' salon for this final fitting rather than have Helene come to her. She had no idea what might happen at the palace later that evening. This might be the only opportunity she ever had to get information from an Illvyan member of the goddess' priesthood. Even though she had concerns about the envoys, if, in the end, Cameron wanted to return home, then she wouldn't let him go alone. If she was to return to Anglion, then she wished to be as well-armed as possible. Including learning some temple history that she doubted anyone in Anglion would ever volunteer.

"Stay still, my lady. This will only take longer if you keep moving. And you need this dress tonight, do you not? Every minute longer it takes me is a minute less for my seamstresses to complete the changes."

Helene's voice held an edge of irritation. Which, given how unflappable she had seemed on the other occasions Sophie had encountered her, might just be a measure of how tight the deadline for the dress was.

"Yes. I'm sorry." She froze back into position even though her arms were starting to ache. "But the directions?"

"You are not expected back at the Academe?" Helene asked. She paused again in her pin placement, brow wrinkling.

Had Helene been instructed to make sure Sophie didn't go anywhere else in the city? Goddess, she hoped not. She thought she could convince her escorts to let her stop at a temple, pleading devotion to the goddess. That was an argument that was difficult to deny amongst mages. From what she'd learned so far of Illvyan religion, earth witches were the most open with their belief in the goddess and the source of their power, but blood mages worshipped, too.

She needed to understand how the goddess' Illvyan adherents felt about their Anglion counterparts. Imogene had called the Anglion Temple corrupt, intent on retaining power over the people. Sophie didn't want to believe it was true, but Domina Skey had not scrupled to use Sophie's powers to heal Eloisa, even when it had drained Sophie near to breaking. Certainly her anger with Sophie and Cameron seemed to be due to the fact that Sophie could not be fully bonded to the goddess, which denied the temple whatever use of her power they might have had if the ritual had been completed as usual. It might have even led the Domina to try to kill Sophie. If anyone in Illvya could understand what threat Sophie might represent, it would be someone of the goddess' priesthood here.

But preferably someone with no need to play politics. The relationship between religion and the crown seemed more distant here, but it was unlikely that the two were completely severed. Not if many of the mages still worshipped the goddess.

She resisted the urge to rub her forehead, where a headache was setting in. If she moved, all she would achieve would be a torso full of pinpricks.

"No," she said, realizing that she hadn't answered Helene's question. "Not immediately." She smiled encouragingly, hoping to soothe whatever was concerning Helene. "The address?" she prompted again when Helene placed another pin.

Helene's shoulder lifted in a tiny motion that clearly meant something along the lines of "it's on your head," but then she rattled off a short set of directions.

Sophie had no trouble following the rapid-fire Illvyan, though she had taken care during her time at the salon not to reveal her improved language skills, making sure she still spoke slowly—not such an act when Henri had obviously been telling the truth when he said her comprehension would improve faster than her speech—and tried to keep her previously bad accent in place. She intended to let that slip a little in time. People would expect her Illvyan to improve when she was surrounded by the language so she should be safe if she let the pretense go gradually.

By the time Helene had completed her pinning and tucking on both dresses and Sophie was safely back in her own clothing, she was beginning to worry that the appointment had taken too much time and that her escorts would refuse her request.

But they didn't. They only nodded when Sophie said she wished to take an offering to the goddess, and when she repeated the address that Helene had given her, the carriage trundled off again. It didn't take very long. Soon enough the horses pulled to a halt and the taller of the two mages accompanying her opened the door and helped her out.

Sophie found herself facing a fairly nondescript red brick building, snug between two very similar structures. It was nothing like the temples back home which ran to marble and bronze and vaulting size, but there was a quartered circle inlaid in brass on the dark wooden door so she had to assume she was indeed in the right place.

The blood mages escorted her to the door but didn't follow her in when it swung inwards in response to one of them laying his hand on a brass plate beside the door, causing chimes similar to those in the Academe to sound from within.

Sophie entered slowly, expecting to be confronted by a brown-robed servant of the goddess. Instead she appeared to be alone. So who had opened the door?

She walked farther into the building and the door swung closed behind her, making her start. The room appeared to be some sort of entrance hall. Small. Painted white. Empty beyond the pair of lamps hung from the ceiling and another door marked with the quartered circle in front of her. But plain or not, it clearly sat above a ley line. The power hummed beneath her feet and made the floor glow. She stared at the door. In or out. There were no other options.

Out left her without answers.

In left her with . . . well, that remained to be seen.

As she pushed the far door open, a waft of spice and salt grass and sage came from the room beyond. The scent was as familiar as the smell of her mother's perfume. For a moment it induced a wave of homesickness so fierce that she thought she might burst into tears. Or worse, sink to the floor. But the sensation eased after the first eye-stinging minute and she tried to clear her mind of any thought of home as she passed through the door into the temple itself.

It was bigger than the façade of the building had suggested, not overly wide but running deep. Though, as far as Sophie could see, no other worshippers occupied any of the wooden benches. The ceiling was high, not domed like the temples of Anglion, and constructed from white-painted wood and plaster rather than bronze, set with panes of stained glass forming four quartered circles high in the ceiling. Each centered around a small opening to allow the smoke from the earth fires to escape.

Multicolored beams of light speared down from the glass, illuminating each of the fires. Three were small offering fires, complete with bundles of salt grass piled high in baskets in front of them, the nearest not far from Sophie, marking the beginning of the aisle to the altar, the other two set off to either side about halfway down the room. At the far end, near the altar, a larger earth fire burned, the flames a familiar medley of blue and green and orange from the salt-soaked logs that fed it.

The fires were so exactly like the ones from the temples she

had known in Anglion she was at the basket set before the
closest of them and lifting one of the bundles before she knew
what she was doing. She cradled the dried grass in her palm
gently, inhaling deeply. Salt and sage and the incense spices in the
oil added to the bundles. A smell woven deep through the
memories of her life. She breathed it again, greedily.

She hadn't realized how much she had missed it until now.
The scent and the comfort of the rituals she had grown up with.
Even if her relationship with the temple in Anglion had been
strained since her Ais-Seann had gone wrong, that didn't mean
she didn't still believe. She held the bundle closer to the flame,
then realized she had no blade to complete the sacrifice. There
was no sign of an offering knife.

"May I be of assistance, my lady?"

Sophie started as though she'd been slapped, jumping half a
foot, then whirled to see who had spoken.

"I am sorry, I startled you." The woman who spoke was
dressed in temple brown but her robes were an unfamiliar style.
More fitted. Shaped like a narrow-skirted dress with a long over
vest of some kind rather than an actual robe. The collar sat high
around the woman's throat, a bronze quartered-circle brooch
marking its center.

Her skin was nearly the same color as the dress, her hair a
few shades darker still. She was older than Sophie but not old,
and her eyes, a tawny kind of amber unlike any Sophie had seen
before, held a friendly expression. The ley light around her also
seemed to hold a faint amber tint. Or it could have been a trick
of the light. The ley light was faint enough that Sophie could see
that the domina was touching the ley line—though that might
be difficult for a domina in a temple to avoid—but also that she
didn't seem to be actively using any power.

"No, I'm sorry, I didn't hear you," Sophie said, offering a
smile and then a neat curtsy.

"I would not usually interrupt you at your devotions. But you
seemed to be looking for this." She held out her hand, palm up.

On it lay a simple silver blade, the polished metal reflecting glints of the colors falling from the glass above.

Sophie reached for it. "Thank you."

"We cleanse the offering knives several times a day," the woman said as Sophie stretched to pass the knife through the flame.

That didn't seem to require a response, so Sophie focused on the flame instead. She nicked her finger with the blade, dripped the blood on her bundle of salt grass, and with an unvoiced prayer that she and Cameron would survive all this, tossed it onto the fire. The flames flared blue and green from the salt grass and the oils anointing it and then subsided back to orange. She spent another minute staring into their depths, as though they might have some wisdom to offer. Finding none, she turned back to the woman who might be able to satisfy some of her questions.

"I have not seen you here before, my lady. Are you newly arrived in Lumia?"

"Do you know everyone who comes to the temple?" Sophie countered.

One side of the woman's mouth lifted. Sophie got the feeling that her attempt to avoid answering the question had not gone unnoticed.

"Many of them." The woman gestured at the empty room. "We are not so fashionable just now. The earth witches remember our great Lady but amongst those without power, well . . . ." She shrugged. "But I have not introduced myself. I am Domina Gerrard. I am in charge here."

In charge but tending the offering tools herself? Now there was something Sophie couldn't imagine Domina Skey doing. And this woman looked young for a Domina. But this was a smaller temple, so perhaps that was to be expected. "It is good to meet you, Domina," Sophie said with another bobbed curtsy. "How many serve the temple here?"

"Only ten," Domina Gerard said. "The priors and devouts

rotate between the grand temple and the others here in Lumia. Domina Davide and I are here permanently. Perhaps we shall come to know you, Madame . . . ?"

"Mackenzie," Sophie said and then fought the urge to curse. She hadn't wanted to announce herself as Lady Scardale, but Mackenzie was hardly an Illvyan name. At least she didn't think it was.

The Domina's eyes widened slightly but Sophie had no idea whether that was because she thought the name unusual or because she knew who Sophie was. "You are welcome in the Lady's house."

Well, if she knew who Sophie was, she was not immediately disapproving.

"Thank you." Sophie hesitated, unsure how to proceed.

"Would you like me to leave you to your devotions, or were you hoping to speak with someone?" Domina Gerrard said.

Well, one probably didn't become a domina without being able to read people a little. "I had a question," Sophie admitted. "Do you have time to speak with me now?"

A nod. "I have an hour or so before I need to prepare for our evening devotions." Domina Gerrard glanced around the empty room. "As we are alone, we can speak here if you are comfortable. I doubt we'll be interrupted. But we have other, more private rooms within if you prefer."

The thought of retreating deeper into a strange building—a temple—was not appealing. Goddess only knew what wards might lie within. She had no doubt the blood mages were waiting for her at the outer door. She didn't want to be farther from their aid should she need it. Not that she had any reason to think that Domina Gerrard meant her harm, but Domina Skey had taught her to be wary.

"I am happy to speak here. It's a beautiful temple." She gestured toward the ceiling. "The glasswork is lovely."

Domina Gerrard smiled. "Thank you. It is not as spectacular

as some, but I am fond of it." She moved over to the nearest of the wooden benches and settled on it.

Sophie sat beside her, leaving a little space. She folded her hands in her lap. The small cut left by the offering blade still stung, a welcome reminder of where she was and who she was speaking to. And also a reminder not to let her guard down.

"Before we begin, perhaps it will simplify matters if I tell you that I know who you are, Lady Mackenzie. Or who I think you are. I will confess, your Illvyan is better than I expected."

She could keep up her pretense but it seemed a lot of effort for little gain. "News travels fast, it seems," Sophie said, sidestepping the issue of her language skills.

"Yes. His Imperial Majesty saw fit to inform Domina Francis when the Anglion delegation arrived. Which required that he also inform her of your presence here in the city. A fact he had neglected to mention until that point. Not all news travels fast when the emperor wishes otherwise. But we were told to watch for you."

Sophie stiffened. "Watch for me?" The ley light around the domina hadn't changed.

"In case you came to the temple. Domina Francis thought you may have questions. Or need assistance."

"Domina Francis is domina of the temple near the palace?" Sophie hazarded. Illvya's Domina Skey in other words. Who wanted to offer her . . . assistance? Interesting.

Domina Gerrard nodded. "Yes. She has been for quite some time now."

"And are she and the emperor . . . close?"

"She makes her views on things known." Domina Gerrard smiled. "Sometimes His Imperial Majesty listens."

Some of the tension in her spine drained away. That didn't sound like the same kind of disturbing influence that Domina Skey had gained over Eloisa. Not that that necessarily meant Domina Francis was to be trusted, but it was not a point against her, at least.

"From what I have seen of the emperor, that would seem to be all that one can hope for," Sophie said.

Domina Gerrard's smile widened. "Yes. I had not had the honor very often. Which suits me. But you did not come here to talk about the emperor." She cocked her head. "Unless you did?"

"No. Not the emperor."

"Then ask. I cannot promise to answer everything, but I will answer what I can."

Answer and perhaps obtain some answers of her own? Answers to questions on the mind of Domina Francis perhaps. But Sophie hadn't expected not to have to pay some sort of price, and she doubted she could tell Domina Gerrard anything about the Anglion temple that Aristides de Lucien did not already know.

"I wanted to ask why the temple here accepts water magic. At home, we are taught the sanctii are anathema to the goddess. But here that is not so."

"You didn't want to start with a simpler question? Let me warm up a little?" Domina Gerrard said, shaking her head gently. "But no, I expect not. Let me start with a question of my own, then. What were you taught about why the goddess forbids water magic?"

Not enough. She tried to recall what exactly she had been told. Her lessons had included so little about Illvya or water magic. But there had been only a basic outlining of the history. Other than that, the temples services and teaching reinforced the message that water magic was evil. The tale of why it was had been couched in a lot of flowery temple-ese from what she could remember.

"To paraphrase a little," she began, "mostly that, a long time ago, water mages tried to suborn the temple. That the goddess blessed those who stood against them to protect her. And, when they were successful, the water mages were driven from our shores. And the kings and queens of Anglion since have kept us free by ensuring they do not return."

One of the Domina's eyebrows lifted. Something in her eyes told Sophie that this recounting was both unexpected and perhaps a little amusing.

"Well, that is part of the tale, I suppose," Domina Gerrard said.

"What's the other part?"

"Ah. That part is a little more prosaic and a little less mystical." Domina Gerrard's fingers strayed to the quartered circle on her collar. "I am no particular scholar of temple history, it has never been a passion of mine, but I will tell you what we are taught. You would have to go to the main temple to look at the records themselves. I believe it was four, maybe five hundred years ago now, but our archivists are somewhat fanatical about maintaining such things."

"So old," Sophie murmured. She couldn't imagine it. Yes, there were buildings in Anglion older than that—after all, the country had been settled for a thousand years or more, if what she had been taught was true—but books were rarer there than here in Illvya. And more tightly controlled. She had no idea how far back the temple records in Anglion might go but she did know that no one outside the temple would be likely to be allowed to look at them.

"Yes, they have ways of making paper last longer than it should. Don't ever ask one how though. It will lead to a long and boring lecture about various chemicals and the proper manner of storage. But that is off our topic. So. History. Let us say five hundred years ago. Illvya was an empire, but only a small one. We controlled three, maybe four of the other countries on the continent. And Anglion was free, as it is now. But back then, the emperor at the time decided that the de Luciens needed more toys to play with. He began pushing to expand the empire. Which made many countries, including your own, unhappy. I don't know if Anglion was within the emperor's sights at the time. In fact, it's difficult to imagine it was when it was well-defended and the sanctii couldn't travel there over the sea. Trade between the two countries was more open than now, but neither country welcomed water mages from the other.

"At the same time, your king—his name escapes me just now —was . . . well, shall we say, not an exemplar of men. And he had the lack of sense to fall in love with two women. And while perhaps no one expects complete fidelity from a king, in this case, neither of the women he loved was his queen. One was his brother's wife. The other, I am sorry to say, was a temple domina. A high-ranking one.

"Now the domina knew the king could never marry her. But she favored the brother's wife, an earth witch, over the current queen, a water mage. The king's brother was also a water mage. The king, however, was a blood mage. So a brother who could command a sanctii was, conceivably, a threat."

Sophie wasn't sure she liked where this story was going. "And was his brother a threat?"

"He wasn't given a chance to be. The king and the domina formed a plan to perform an *augmentier*. I assume you know what that is?"

"A binding."

"Yes. Such things are supposed to be voluntary. Somehow they convinced the brother's wife to agree to a binding as well."

"Three people can be bound?"

"Not usually. I have heard that sometimes a water mage who shares a bond with a sanctii may also bond with a husband or wife, but such things are discouraged. When it is tried between people, the usual outcome seems to be that while two of the three are strengthened, the third is more often weakened. Not something most mages would wish to endure, however fleetingly."

But royal witches were bound three ways, Sophie thought. To their husbands and to the temple. She clamped her jaw shut against the question that sprang to mind. She'd hear the story out first. Then decide what more was safe to ask. "And what happened after the binding was performed?"

Domina Gerrard shook her head. "Nothing good. The king managed to kill his wife and his brother. Claimed they were plotting against him. Plotting with Illvya to bring Illvyan mages to Anglion so they could summon sanctii and invade. He started hunting down water mages and their families with the help of other blood mages within the nobility. Many of whom had earth witch wives. Who were suborned into also being bound for the good of the country. Eventually the water mages were dead, along with whole chunks of families who showed talent for such things or fled to the empire. The king married his brother's widow, and since then Anglion has forbidden water magic and bound its royal witches to strengthen their husbands."

Even those without magic. Sophie wasn't sure she could feel her fingers anymore, she was clenching her hands so tightly. The temple had felt warm a few minutes before, the flames from four fires and the sunny day outside making the air pleasant. But now she wanted to shiver.

How much of what the domina had told her could she believe? Probably not the entirety. Illvyans had their biases just as Anglions did. But something had happened. And as much as it would be pleasant to believe that the goddess had forbidden water magic to her followers, the more mundane explanation offered by the domina seemed far more realistic.

Somewhere outside the temple, she was vaguely aware of a bell tolling. Which meant time was passing. If she stayed much longer, the mages outside would come looking for her. She rose. "Thank you for your time, Domina Gerrard. And for the history lesson." She bobbed a curtsy, the obeisance to the temple engrained in her. It was honor to the goddess, not the woman herself, she reminded herself as a small surge of rebellion flared within her at the movement. Though if the goddess allowed Anglion witches to be weakened to prop up their husbands, then perhaps that respect was unearned. But was it the goddess or those who purported to represent her? "I hope I can come and speak with you again."

Her head throbbed suddenly, reminding her that only yesterday, she had let a demon teach her Illvyan. Things were moving
far too quickly. She needed time to think. To untangle lie
from truth.

And the most urgent truth she needed was what the Anglion
delegation knew about what would happen to her if she returned
to Kingswell.

~

"What are you reading?"

Sophie looked up as Cameron came into their room late on
fourth day. He'd been to bathe after his last class as he often did.
The sight of him in his shirt and trousers, hair damp as he
rubbed at it with a towel, made her smile. She closed the book,
putting it back on the table in front of her. "It's that book on
bindings that we found in the library." They had little spare time
left over from their studies, but they were still determined to fill
in the gaps in their knowledge where they could.

Cameron came over and picked up the book. "On the Art of
Augmentiers," he said, reading the title. "Anything useful?"

"Hard going," she said, eyeing the book. It was, as the
majority of the books here were, in Illvyan. The reveilé had
helped greatly with her understanding, but it still took concentration to understand the ideas being set out in the book. "But
promising, I think. Maybe you can help me after dinner?"

He shook his head. "No studying tonight."

"What?" she said, alarmed. "Has something happened? Did
Henri say something to you?"

"No. Nothing's wrong," he said. "I just thought maybe we
could take tonight for ourselves. It's been nothing but study and
. . . ."

Discussions about what they should say to the Anglions
when they returned to the palace. They had spoken of little else
in the moments they'd had alone. And the best approach they

could come up with was to try and keep the relationship as cordial as possible, while trying to find out if further reassurances as to their safety should they return to Anglion could be obtained. There seemed to be little else they could do.

If that were so, maybe Cameron was right. Maybe they should take some time to just be. Or pretend to just be, at least. While they could.

"What did you have in mind?" she asked. Almost as soon as the words had left her mouth, the door chimes sounded. "Goddess, no. Now what?"

Cameron smiled. "I think that will be our dinner."

"Dinner?" She blinked, startled. They'd eaten every meal in the dining room so far.

"I asked Willem and he arranged it," Cameron said, crossing to the door.

Sure enough, when he opened it, one of the servant girls wheeled a wooden trolley into the room. Sophie couldn't see what was on it because the various plates were hidden under neat china covers, but it smelled wonderful.

"Thank you," she said to the girl as Cameron showed her out and then came back over to Sophie.

"Hungry?" he asked.

She shook her head. "Not just yet. Come and sit with me." The light was beginning to fade outside the windows and she reached toward the earth stone on the table, intending to light it. Then stopped and reached out her hand to Cameron instead. "You do it," she said, nodding toward the stone.

"I'll try," he said, wrapping his fingers around hers. They had been experimenting a little with this, her trying to teach him some of the basic earth magic skills she knew and vice versa. Madame Simsa had taught them how to ward the bond, and it had seemed a logical step to progress from that to this. Just small things, things that could be useful. Nothing too noticeable. She felt the pull on the bond between them, felt the steadying weight of Cameron's power meeting hers. Felt it flare stronger as he drew some of that power to him. The earth light began to shine and he grinned at her.

"There!"

"Success," she agreed happily. Their previous experiments hadn't always been successful. She leaned forward to kiss him quickly, felt the quick flare of desire through the bond. Then the echoes of it in her own blood. Which only intensified what she felt from Cameron.

Dinner could wait. She pulled back, glanced over at the bed, then drew on the bond, aiming the power at the quilts, sending them slithering to the floor in a satisfying heap.

"Sophie?" Cameron said.

"I think we should work up an appetite," she said, standing. She tugged at his hand.

He rose quickly. "I think I like that idea." He pulled her to him, bent to kiss her. She gave herself over to the kiss, wanting to stop thinking.

Cameron kissed her slowly, each touch of his lips on hers considered, as though he was intent on memorizing the shape of her mouth. The warmth of him flowed over her, through her, making her feel half-drunk with it. She started to tug at the buttons of his shirt, breathing in the scent of soap and clean skin. Of Cameron. She slid her hand across his chest as the shirt came apart, sliding it over his nipple. He groaned softly against her mouth, his kiss turning hungry as he lifted her, carrying her over to the bed to place her on her back against the mattress.

She waited to feel the comforting weight of him sinking down on top of her but instead she felt his hands at her skirts, pushing them up and then drawing off her underthings. She widened her legs, unable to stop the movement as his hands slid back up her thighs.

"Wider, love," he said, and his hands pushed against her. Then his head came down and she felt the first stroke of his tongue against her, like a streak of quiet lightning. She arched up against him but his hands held her still, held her open to him so all she could do was lie back and let him do what he wanted. It wasn't that difficult to submit, not when each new touch made her head spin and her heart pound as the pleasure built within her.

He added fingers to tongue, making her moan. So good. But she wanted more.

"I want you," she gasped, hands tugging in his hair.

"You have me," he said, lifting his head but not stilling the movement of those clever, clever fingers.

"More," she said. "All of it. All of you."

He laughed, and for a moment she thought he was going to draw things out, resist her urgings. But then he stood, shucking his clothes as she watched. She was too hungry for him, too focused on just him to worry about her own clothes. He was glorious in the last fading edge of light through the window and the paler golden glow of the earth light on the table behind him. The perfect statue of a man, muscles carved down his body in lines a sculptor couldn't have bettered.

"Come back here," she said, and his lips curved upward.

"Whatever milady wants," he said, crawling onto the bed.

"Milady wants you," she said as he lifted her farther up the bed, working at her dress with the fingers that had been torturing her not long before. She wriggled and lifted cooperatively, eager to have those hands back on her as soon as possible.

When she was naked, he smiled down at her. "That's better." He ran a hand over her right breast, fingers catching her nipple. She sucked in a breath. But she wanted him too much to let him delay. Her hand closed over his cock. Stroked it once, tightened as she heard the gratifying groan that escaped him.

"We were talking about what I want," she said, stroking again. "I want this. You. Now."

He didn't argue. Merely swung himself over her, his mouth finding hers again as he slid home. She wrapped her legs around his hips, pulled him closer as he moved inside her, feeling each retreat and return of him like her heartbeat. Let him fill her. Fill the world and chase everything else away so there was only pleasure and Cameron and the rhythm between them, the pulse of heat that seemed to spiral through the bond and through her and back to him. Always back to him, even as the pleasure and the pressure built and she knew she was about to tumble over into that place where there was only sensation. Even then, as she fell, she held onto him, the one who could take her there, unwilling to let him go. Wanting him to follow her, which he did with a moan that might have been her name.

When she surfaced from the pleasure-washed fog of it, she was lying curled around him, holding him tight. "Only you," she said fiercely. No matter what happened, the two of them would face it together.

CHAPTER 16

She was going to have to start wearing cooler gowns. Sophie lifted her water glass and sipped, schooling herself not to gulp the icy liquid down. Instead she held the glass curled inward a little so that some of its cool surface pressed against her wrist. Across the table, Barron Deepholt watched her and she forced a smile.

Why the emperor had thought that sharing a meal might make things easier between the Mackenzies and the Anglion delegation escaped her. Perhaps it may have done if things had been more informal. But here, in what was probably a small room for this palace but one that was still large by other standards, seated around a table laid with silver plates, gilded china, glittering crystal, flowers, and candles, with the emperor himself seated at its head, the mood was anything but informal.

And the room was hot. Lamps and candles burned everywhere. And worse, the candles were held by cunningly wrought stands that seemed to operate on the same mechanisms as the brackets holding the lamps they had seen on their first visit to the palace. They moved as food was served or people moved, adjusting their height or the stretch of their arms to keep the light close to each person. The chamber had no windows in its beautifully tiled walls, so there was no way for the heat to escape. The door only opened when the servants came with yet more food, and even then it didn't seem to offer any relief. Sophie was half tempted to ask Henri, who had accompanied them again and was sitting on her right between her and Cameron, to call Martius. The sanctii chill would be welcome.

But if the sanctii would increase Sophie's comfort, he would likely have precisely the opposite effect on the tempers of the Anglions seated opposite. So she would sit and sweat and hope there were not many courses left in the meal. There had already been four. The servings of each were small, but the tension of their situation left her without appetite and it was an effort to take a bite or two of each to be polite.

A servant appeared on her left and placed a tiny plate with a few perfectly sliced pieces of beef on it, drizzled with a dark sauce.

Her stomach rebelled at the thought and she sipped more water as everyone else set to eating.

When she put the glass down, Aristides said, "Do you not favor beef, Lady Scardale?"

She shook her head. "It looks delicious, Your Imperial Majesty. But I cannot eat too much or I will strain the seams of my dress. Not to mention its corsets. It would not do to have the Designys baying for my blood for ruining one of their creations. Who would make the rest of my wardrobe?" There. Just the kind of inane, slightly amusing chatter that she had been able to babble in endless torrents back in Kingswell.

Aristides smiled slightly. "Indeed. My daughters and daughter-in-law tread very carefully with their favored clothiers. Whereas I just pay the bills. It seems to keep the peace well enough."

"Exactly," Sophie said. Aristides wore a coat of silver-embroidered satin that was more elaborate by far than anything anyone else in the room was wearing. How did he keep his tailor in good humor? Or perhaps it was the task of the tailor to please the emperor rather than the other way around. Aristides definitely used his clothes as a reminder of who he was, and Sophie didn't want to imagine how much work went into each item. His tailor —whoever he was—must get heartily tired of white, silver, gold or black. She half smiled at the thought.

"And call me Eleivé," Aristides added. "'Your Imperial Majesty' is cumbersome at times, and it seems you will not be a stranger at my court."

She almost dropped her knife.

Across the table there was a clatter of china and she looked across to see Sevan Allowood scowling at her, the plate before him shoved out of place. Beside him, James leaned to whisper something in the younger man's ear. Which only earned him the honor of having Sevan's ill-tempered expression turn on him.

The exchange between the two men distracted her enough from her surprise. Henri had said only those close to the emperor used Eleivé. So why was Aristides inviting her to do so on only their second meeting? Was it a genuine courtesy or a way to drive a wedge between her and the Anglions?

On the face of it, Aristides was facilitating the relationship between them. But the seating arrangements were hardly conducive to easy conversation. Not with the four Anglion envoys on one side of the table and she, Henri, Cameron, and Imogene on the other. The emperor should have mixed his table more thoroughly if he wanted them to mingle. But she found herself grateful he had not. She would have spent the meal wondering if Sevan was about to knife her in the ribs if she had had to sit next to him. But still, arrayed as they were, the two sides facing off against each other, she didn't see how they were to come to any sort of agreement.

Down on Cameron's right, Imogene murmured something softly and Sir Harold smiled briefly in response. The imperial mage wore black silk embroidered with coils of silver that seemed somewhat serpentine to Sophie. Three strands of dark red rubies circled her throat and matching stones hung from her ears. Her hands sparkled with rings that were almost as magnificent as those Aristides wore. She looked beautiful and very Illvyan, somehow. She also looked cool. Sophie wished she knew her secret. She was certain her own face was turning pink in the heat, a color that would clash with her gown, but Imogene gave no sign that the room was anything more than comfortable.

Perhaps water mages could siphon off some of their sanctii's chill if they needed. That would be a handy trick. She watched Imogene smiling at Sir Harold and at Cameron, trying not to turn her head too much to show her attention had wandered from the emperor. She wasn't entirely sure why Aristides had included Imogene in the party. Had he thought another woman in the room might make Sophie more comfortable? Or that the presence of an Imperial mage might remind the Anglions to behave? Or did protocol simply demand a balanced number at the table?

Though the table was not balanced anyway to an Anglion eye, even leaving aside the uneven numbers of men and women and the strict delineation of envoys and the rest of them. The order of precedence was wrong. James should be seated next to the barron, who sat to Aristides' left as Sophie did to his right. Instead, Sevan sat there, despite the fact that he was the lowest-ranked member of the delegation. The lowest ranked in the room, in fact.

Perhaps Aristides found it amusing to seat him opposite Henri. Sevan had had the strongest reaction to the sanctii's presence at the ball. In Aristides' place, Sophie thought she would be trying to broker peace at the table rather than provoking friction. Unless, of course, he did not wish for her and Cameron to choose Anglion. Which was a thought that only added another stray piece to the seemingly never-ending puzzle she was trying to solve.

At least she could now see that none of the Anglions had any connection to the ley line. She'd been startled earlier to see a very faint thread of ley light coming from Aristides. She would have to ask Henri what power the emperor had, though judging by how thin the line was, it seemed unlikely it was a strong one.

But in this room, the Anglions were of more interest. Sir Harold, who was a blood mage, showed no signs of currently touching the line. She wondered if he hadn't thought to try it here, or whether he hadn't been able to connect with it. She had known that the barron had no magic, nor did James, but Sevan Allowood was more of an unknown. But he had no sign of the ley light's glow around him. Hopefully Cameron could see that now, too. She'd taught him what Madame Simsa had taught her. He didn't see the line the same way she did and had told her what light he saw was faint, but he had been able to see the connections.

He'd shared her confusion as to why they had never been taught to see this way in Anglion. Even if there was no perceived use for it for an earth witch, it was difficult to argue that a blood mage would not benefit from being able to judge his opponent's abilities and intentions by examining their connection to the ley line.

She had also recounted the tale that Domina Gerrard had told her about the schism between the Anglion temple and the water mages before they'd slept. He had been skeptical as to whether or not the domina had been telling the whole truth but also troubled, as Sophie was, by the story.

He had even asked her again if she wanted to dissolve their bond. A discussion she had ended by deciding that they both needed to stop thinking quite so hard for the night and distracting him into making love to her again. The memory didn't make her feel any cooler.

"Try the beef," Aristides said. "The sauce is an Illvyan delicacy."

"Herbs aged with wine and spices," Henri said in a reassuring tone. He'd been identifying foods for her in soft-voiced comments throughout the meal. She no longer needed someone to translate difficult Illvyan for her, and they were speaking Anglish anyway. But she appreciated having him there. And wasn't that a turnabout? That she was comforted by the presence of an Illvyan mage when faced with her own countrymen.

Out of deference to the emperor, she cut a small piece of beef and swiped it through the sauce. The tangy sweetness of it was pleasing, but she still found it hard to chew and swallow with Sevan glaring at her. Something about his gaze was chilling. Perhaps she should ask to sit next to him after all. He might counteract the stifling warmth of her velvet dress.

She sat through the next three courses, eating as little as possible, making small talk with the emperor and Henri, and responding to the two or three questions the barron directed at her. When Aristides pushed his chair back from the table after the servants cleared the bowls of the last of the courses, a salad of some kind, she almost let out a sigh of relief.

The emperor waited until the servants had offered finger bowls and heated cloths and then been shooed silently from the room by Louis, hovering near the door. At Aristides' silent nod, Louis also left the room, closing the door firmly behind him.

In his wake he left near silence, only the faintest of hisses from the oil burning in the lamps above breaking the quiet. All eyes were fastened on the emperor.

Who smiled. Not a particularly comforting expression.

"Now that we are all refreshed, we shall talk a little before the dessert courses," Aristides said.

No one offered any disagreement on this point. It was, after all, what they were all there for.

"I believe you have all been informed of the status of the investigation into the events at the ball. As yet we have no suspects, though my guards"—he fixed his gaze on Imogene a moment—"continue to work to uncover those who committed this act. But for now there is nothing more to say on the matter." This time his gaze moved to the barron. Who looked down and drank a hasty gulp of wine.

"Which I believe leaves us with the topic we were discussing at the ball." He turned to Sophie. "It is only fair that you know that a second Anglion ship has moored itself off our coast."

"Another delegation?" Cameron said, sounding disbelieving.

"No. A courier, it seems. Bearing only messages. Which were delivered to the barron and his party."

Sophie had no doubt that the messages had also been examined by the Imperial Guard or whichever branch of Aristides' forces had responsibility for guarding the harbor and the sea beyond.

Aristides lifted his wineglass. Drank. "Your queen also sent a message to me. In which she reiterated her desire for Lord and Lady Scardale to be returned to her."

"Was there a message for us?" Sophie asked. If Eloisa had sent something—anything—more informative than her previous letter, then perhaps she would know the way forward.

Barron Deepholt shook his head. "Not amongst the papers given to me. It is as His Imperial Majesty has said. Simply another request for you to return to Kingswell, where you belong. There was nothing addressed directly to either of you."

Sophie wished she believed him. But it seemed unlikely that Eloisa would send a second ship with exactly the same message. Delegations between the two countries were usually painstakingly negotiated. If the ship's arrival hadn't been expected, then something had happened to precipitate it. But apparently the barron wasn't going to be telling her what that something might be. She wondered if Aristides knew.

If he did he was keeping his cards close to his chest. Politics. She was starting to loathe the very concept. She turned back to the emperor, hoping her expression was politely enquiring.

"There was nothing in the queen's letter to me either," Aristides said. "Though you are welcome to read it if you wish."

A generous offer. Which meant that he most likely spoke the truth and there was indeed nothing in the message other than a renewed request for their return. That didn't mean there hadn't been other letters, of course. But if there had been and he wasn't telling her about them, he was hardly going to show them to her.

"Thank you, Eleivé, but that is not necessary." She straightened her shoulders, looked at the barron. "Forgive me, Lord Deepholt, but without further reassurances from the queen, I find myself unable to accede to Her Majesty's request."

"You refuse?" The barron sounded shocked.

"Not a refusal. I am merely stating a condition. The emperor says there is a second ship. Send it back. Ask Queen Eloisa to write with her word that my husband and I are safe if we return to Anglion. Then this conversation can continue."

"You little—" Sevan started to spit, rising from his chair, but James gripped his shoulder and shoved him back down.

"You will show respect, Allowood," James growled. "Lady Scardale is one of the heirs. You will show her respect or I will teach you how."

Sevan subsided, but the chill that speared through Sophie as their eyes met was colder than ever.

"Lord Scardale," Barron Deepholt sputtered. "Control your wife."

Cameron, who had been gazing at Sevan, every line of his body a promise of hurt if Sevan made another move toward her, turned his head slowly to the barron, blue eyes blazing. "I believe, milord, that you have forgotten that my wife technically outranks me. As she does you."

"Goddess be damned as to rank," the barron said. "You have the means—" He snapped his mouth shut suddenly. Coughed. "She is your wife," he continued. "She made vows, did she not?"

"I don't recall anything about her having to obey me in those vows. However, I distinctly remember the part where I vowed to be her shield," Cameron said. "Which means I would not allow her to return to a place which will not guarantee her safety after an attempt on her life, even if she wished to go."

The barron was turning an unbecoming shade of red-purple.

"You cannot disobey the orders of your queen!" He fairly bellowed the words.

Aristides cleared his throat and the barron froze. Silence fell once more.

"I believe Lady Scardale's request is a reasonable one, Barron. After all, it is only a matter of a few more days for the ship to return to Anglion and then bring us back your queen's response. Hardly any time at all. Perhaps you should return to your chambers and write the request. I'm sure the rest of your companions would be glad to assist you. I will lend you one of my fastest couriers to take the message to the ship."

The barron looked like he wanted to argue but apparently thought better of it. He nodded once but did not speak.

"Excellent," Aristides continued. "Venable du Laq, perhaps you would care to give Lord and Lady Scardale a tour of the palace, seeing as though our other guests have to retire to take care of this business. They did not get a chance to see much more than the ballroom the other night, and it would be a pity for them to miss it if they are leaving us soon. Maistre Matin, stay with me, if you'd be so kind?"

Imogene rose with such speed and a murmured "As you wish, Eleivé" that Sophie rather thought she had been waiting for just such a suggestion. But if the alternative was to stay and be berated by the barron, then she had no trouble at all choosing to follow in Imogene's black and silver wake and leave them all behind.

~

"Venable du Laq," Cameron said somewhat stiffly once they were all safely out in the hallway and the pair of guards standing outside the dining room had resumed their posts at the door. "Do you think, before you start this tour, that you might show us somewhere I could have a brief word with my wife?"

Sophie looked up at him, startled. He sounded . . . angry beneath the formality. Angry at what? At her?

"Of course," Imogene said. She glanced quickly at Sophie, then back to him. "There is a receiving room this way." With another glance at Sophie, she led them to a door a few hundred feet or so down the corridor. "In here. I will wait for you. There is also a bathroom, if you wish to refresh yourselves."

"Thank you," Cameron said. Then to Sophie, "After you."

She was tempted to stay out here with Imogene. But if Cameron was in a temper about something she may as well find out now.

Cameron closed the door behind them. The soft click of it sounded loud in the otherwise silent room. It was as described. A small room furnished with several groups of chairs and small sofas, arranged around an unused fireplace. Only one of the lamps was burning, the light a little dim. But it was also blessedly cool after the dining room.

Decorated in pale greens and yellows, it was the sort of place a princess might sit with her ladies to while away the hours or to receive callers. Not unlike the rooms she'd spent so many hours attending Eloisa in while the queen did exactly that. It just needed the familiar sound of women's voices and the scent of fresh tea and cakes and flowers to complete the picture. Instead, it held just her and, looming behind her though she had not yet turned to face him, one large and seemingly irritated northerner. True, he smelled better than tea and cakes, the scent of him as alluring ever, the effect heightened by the fresh spice of the cologne he'd splashed on when he'd donned his evening clothes. But on the whole, right now, she'd prefer to be back with a group of friends and with nothing more taxing on her mind than pouring tea correctly and untangling skeins of gossip along with the embroidery threads for a few hours.

But wishing for such things wasn't going to make them so.

Lifting the side of her skirt to make the movement easier,

she turned back to face Cameron. "You have something to say, milord?"

His eyes were very blue. She knew that look. Hadn't seen it directed at her before. "Goddess, Sophie. What were you trying to achieve, telling them like that?"

What? That was what he was angry about? "I said what we agreed. That we need more information. Assurances."

Cameron shook his head, the movement a quick snap from side to side. "Not in that manner. We need diplomacy, not burning bridges. This was supposed to be a decision we made together."

She threw up her hands, still not understanding what had him so upset. "It *is* a decision we made together. To proceed with caution."

"You call that cautious? A flat refusal?" He sounded incredulous.

"I didn't refuse. I asked for reassurances. I bought us more time." She scowled at him. "You know as well as I do that they aren't telling us everything. That something else is going on."

"And you may have destroyed any chance we had of finding out exactly what that may be."

"Oh really? You think they're just going to roll over and tell us everything? Did you have too much wine with dinner?"

He glared at her. "I think that if we had acted as though we were leaning toward going with them, I may have gotten a chance to speak to James alone."

He hadn't mentioned that in their conversations. Why not? "What makes you think he would tell you the truth?"

"He's Jeanne's family. My family. Or close enough to."

"And what if they're threatening him in some way? Do you expect him to choose me over his family? Over your family?"

"He's an honorable man."

"Honorable men do terrible things at times. Especially when their loyalty is pulled in more than one direction." Like Cameron's was right now, she realized. Between her and his home. Between the vows he'd sworn and maybe what his heart truly wanted.

"James wouldn't."

"He's not your brother," she said. "He owes you no particular loyalty."

"But you do," Cameron snarled. "And you just plowed on and as good as refused them without consulting me. It was foolish. You need to learn to think." His eyes were a blaze of blue.

"I am thinking. And not just with wounded pride or whatever it is that has you so wound up. I'm thinking that most of the options I have I don't like, but there are some I like less than others."

"And now you may have taken some of those options away. You should have asked me first. You have no experience with this kind of thing. You're so young."

"I have spent more time in the thick of court politics than you have," she retorted. "I was at court watching Eloisa and King Stefan. You were off being a soldier."

"Exactly. I understand tactics."

"And I don't?"

"Judging by tonight, no."

She was growing tired of being surrounded by men who thought they knew what was best for her. Or that she should want what they thought she should want. "I'm not going back there to be bound and contained and dealt with as they please," she snapped.

"Is that what you care about, your freedom?"

"I care about my safety. And yes, my freedom. You heard the barron. He stopped himself but he was about to tell you to use your marriage bond to make me obey you in some way. Because he doesn't bloody well know that we're not bonded in the traditional way. He thought you could compel me to do what you wanted. Which tells me that at least some of what Domina Gerrard told me is right. It tells me that there is reason for Domina Skey to hate me beyond the fact that I stand too close to the throne. I'm a royal witch who can't be controlled by her husband. But perhaps you'd prefer that not to be the case? Is that what you want, Cameron? For me to go home and let them turn me into something close enough to your slave? If they let me live, that is. Or perhaps you're planning on being a repentant widower? Or maybe you'd prefer to leave me here and go back to your nice peaceful simple life. Back to Eloisa's bed? Tell them you left your dangerous witch wife behind. All you have to do is ask. I know you didn't want this bond. I won't keep you if you want to go. But I'm not going back until I know exactly what they want of me." She was breathing too fast, her heart hammering in her ears, hands curled into fists at her side.

Cameron looked . . . frozen. Not giving her any clue as to what he might be feeling. About whether or not her fears had any basis. Not stepping up to deny or to offer comfort or apology. The sight of him made her heart crack a little. It was too much. She had meant what she had said. She wouldn't keep him against his will. Couldn't bear it, in fact. But then, she had no idea if she could bear it if he went either. And amongst all the other battles she seemed to be fighting, all the dangers around them, she didn't think she had the strength for this one. It was the one that could most easily destroy her. Cameron might just be the biggest danger of all.

And if she stood there one minute longer and waited for him to tell her he was leaving, she would break. "Do as you please," she said, letting the fear turn the words to anger rather than show him the hurt he'd dealt her. She headed for the door and he let her go.

CHAPTER 17

Cameron splashed cold water on his face and dried it, staring at himself in the mirror. His reflection looked as though it was spoiling for a fight.

"You just had one, you idiot," he told it. "With the wrong person."

He bent again and applied cold water a second time. Maybe it could wash away his anger. Or at least the words he'd thrown at Sophie. The words she'd thrown back at him. "Do as you please," she'd said.

None of it pleased him. Maybe that was the problem. No good options and no way to find a solution. He'd never liked not being able to solve a problem set to him.

But none of his training had prepared him to be set as the toy wedged between two angry rulers. Or an angry wife.

She pleased him. He knew that much. And he hated that he'd given her cause to doubt that. Sophie had made no secret of the fact that she felt guilt over the manner of their bonding and that he'd had to marry her. He thought she loved him, but somewhere within the foundation of that love was a small thread of doubt, waiting to trip her up.

He'd yanked hard on that thread just now. Goddess only knew what damage he'd done to the new-forged trust that formed the heart of their marriage. He'd never considered that a good marriage was a fragile thing, woven day by day by the acts of two people. In one so new as theirs, the threads were so fine to be near invisible, like a single strand of the silks Jeanne and his mother embroidered with. It took time and space to strengthen them into something that could bear the strain.

He'd seen a little of that with his brothers. Seen also, between his parents, what happened when the only things holding a marriage together were obligations and the constraints of society. His parents had been partners in the business of running the erldom and yes, they'd had children, so they had shared a bed at least three times. But there'd been little affection between them, other than the absent fondness you might have for something familiar in your life that made it easier. He'd never seen any sign of love in his parents. Or anything resembling the passion he shared with Sophie. Certainly his father had not seemed to be overly affected that his wife had died when she did. He'd simply moved his mistress nearer and shoved the burden of actually running the household onto Jeanne. As Liam's—the heir's—wife, Jeanne could hardly have shirked the duty.

Is that what he wanted his marriage to turn into? A loveless obligation? A resentment of the bond that held them together? She'd offered again to release him. It was entirely possible that here in Illvya she could find out how to do exactly that without his participation. Could set him free if that's what she decided she wanted.

The thought made his blood run cold.

He was worse than an idiot. He didn't want to be free. He wanted his marriage to be one of love like those his brothers had built with their wives. He wanted Sophie. Nothing else.

And he owed her an apology.

"Fix it," he muttered at his reflection before leaving the bathroom. But he'd no sooner opened the door of the receiving room, intent on finding out which way Imogene and Sophie had gone, when one of Aristides' silver-clad servants came around the corner of the corridor.

"Lord Scardale?" the man asked.

"Yes." What now?

The man offered an envelope. "For you, my lord."

As soon as Cameron took it, the man turned on his heel and headed back in the direction he had come, moving rapidly. Whatever was in the note, apparently it required no response.

He scanned the corridor. In the distance, the guards still stood outside the door of the dining room, which suggested Aristides was still inside with Henri. No doubt plotting whatever step came next in this game that was playing out around him and Sophie.

But at least they were safely out of the way for now. Other than the guards, the corridor was deserted.

Good. But still, he didn't want the guards watching him reading a note. They would no doubt report that the servant had spoken to him if they had seen the exchange—and if they hadn't, then Colonel Perrine had a problem on his hands—but he didn't need to speed the news that he had received a message on its way to Aristides' ears. Nor did he want to be interrupted while he read whatever this message was, so he went back into the receiving room, closing the door and leaning against it to ensure he wouldn't be disturbed unexpectedly.

The envelope wasn't sealed with wax and the paper itself bore no imprinted coat of arms or any other clue as to the writer's identity. A simple single sheet of plain white paper of no particular quality, folded neatly into quarters.

He unfolded it. It was marked with a single line of text.

THE BARRON'S TALE IS NO MOUNTAIN. HAVE CARE.

There was no signature. And the hand was careful, almost a perfect example of the script in the books his tutors had taught him from as a child. As though the author had deliberately scrubbed it of any sign of personality. It had to be James though.

He rubbed his finger over the words.

The truth and mountains, these things cannot be altered.

It was a northerner saying. One of those that had little meaning, really. But in the north, to say of something that it was no mountain meant it was not to be trusted. Or that it was an outright lie. No one else in the Anglion party was from the north. Nor was anybody else likely to be sending him a warning. Sir Harold had retired by the time Cameron had joined the Red Guard, so he had no reason to offer Cameron any favor. As for Sevan Allowood, well, that seemed as likely as Cameron growing wings and learning to fly.

So James. And a warning. That the barron was not telling them all there was to tell. He'd known that much already, but he hadn't known how important what was being held back might be. Important enough for James to risk his neck, it seemed.

Danger, then. Some kind of threat. And he was here while his wife wandered around the palace with Imogene du Laq and goddess only knew how many other people. Unguarded.

That was his fault. But one he could rectify.

He hoped.

Ignoring the chill in his guts and the hairs tingling at the back of his neck, he shoved the note into the inner pocket of his jacket.

Then left the room to find Sophie.

Sophie almost stumbled into Imogene when she left the receiving room. Only the other woman catching her arm stopped them colliding.

"Sophie? Is everything well?"

"Perfectly." It was a lie and no doubt Imogene could tell, but she didn't care.

"Where is Lord Scardale?"

"He wanted a moment to refresh himself," she said flatly. "He said to go on without him." She had no idea if Imogene had just heard everything that had been said between her and Cameron. Maybe the room was warded, maybe it was not. It didn't matter. She just needed to be somewhere away from him.

She waved in the direction they'd been walking before they had stopped. "Why don't we continue our tour? I'm not sure Cameron is all that interested in architectures and furnishings and such anyway."

Imogene blinked but then nodded, as though accepting the change of topic. Or accepting Sophie's wish not to discuss what had just happened. The mage smiled at her. "Oh, I have something better to show you than furnishings. Come, I'm sure your husband can find us when he's ready. I've learned in my years that it is often better to do as one wishes and let one's husband catch up or not."

Sophie imagined that any man married to Imogene might well decide that it was easier to let her take the reins a certain percentage of the time. And besides, she had no idea if the du Laqs' marriage was based on politics or affection. There had to be at least some of the former in it. If duqs were anything like erls, then they weren't completely free in their choice of spouse.

"That sounds very wise," she said. "So, show me your better thing."

She had no idea what Imogene's better thing might be. But whatever it was, it took quite some time to travel through the palace. They walked through a series of grand hallways and corridors, down several flights of stairs and then through what Sophie suspected was a tunnel used by servants. Imogene had paused a time or two to point out features of the palace, but when Sophie had kept her responses brief to these explanations, she'd given up and picked up their pace.

When they emerged from the last hallway, Sophie wasn't even sure they were still within the main building of the palace or whether they were now in one of the outbuildings she assumed must surround it. The hallway was much simpler, lacking the elaborate decorations of the palace, and the floor was gray stone tiles rather than marble. The ceiling still soared far above their heads, so wherever they were, it was still a large building. In her experience, palaces and other grand houses were usually surrounded by a network of stables and workshops and military barracks and servants' quarters and storehouses. Even the Academe had some of these. There was no reason to assume that Aristides' palace would be any different. This building could be almost anything. But before she could ask where they were, Imogene stopped in front of a pair of extremely tall doors. Exceedingly so. They must have been twenty feet tall or more.

But if the doors were large, the room they led into was enormous.

It would have fit several of Aristides' ballrooms within it easily. In the middle of the room, a hive of activity centered around a framework of scaffolding that held a . . . well, she wasn't entirely sure what.

"What is it?" Sophie said, staring up at the massive structure, Cameron and everything else forgotten for a moment as she looked up in wonder at the object resting in a vast frame above them. It reminded her of the hull of a ship, only fashioned from wood and leather and metal, joined together by some means she couldn't even begin to fathom. But instead of masts and rigging, there was . . . nothing. Not that she could see. She could see people climbing around the frame, balanced on scaffoldings or dangling over the edges on complicated rope and leather harnesses.

"Something new," Imogene said, eyes shining as she gazed upward as well. "I call it a *navire d'avion*."

Sophie parsed the Illvyan carefully. "A ship of air? But how can a ship float on air?"

"Ah. Well, that is a very good question. Very good, indeed. But come, let me show her to you."

Her? The thing didn't look particularly female to Sophie, but Anglion sailors referred to boats as female. Perhaps Illvyans did as well.

"Please," she said and followed Imogene across the room, intrigued.

The workers they passed bowed or curtsied at Imogene. Men and women, Sophie realized. Working with wood and metal and leather. Boatbuilding in Anglion was a male occupation. As were most forms of carpentry. Women got to furnish the insides of houses and palaces, not decree what they should look like outside.

The navire only grew larger in scale as they approached it. Imogene led her over to a row of long tables set up about fifteen feet from the outer edge of the scaffolding. A wide roll of paper lay flat across the surface of the center table, its corners weighted down with a china cup, a smaller hammer, and two large iron bolts. Drawn on it were diagrams of the structure before them, shown from various angles, both inside and out. Sophie had never seen such a thing before. She bent to take a closer look.

The drawings were skillfully rendered, the details intricate. She didn't understand all the markings and numbers that surrounded each diagram, but that didn't matter.

She pointed to the image that looked most like a completed ship's hull. It showed sails of a sort, though they protruded from the sides as well as from two masts in more usual places. "Is this what she will look like when she's finished?"

"Yes," Imogene said, grinning. "Is she not beautiful?"

The vessel looked more like the result of some strange mating between a giant fish and a ship. But there was an odd sort of elegance to the lines. Easier to see on the drawing than on the scaffolding-draped edifice before her. "Astonishing," Sophie said diplomatically. "But what will it be used for?"

"The empire is large. And travel is slow," Imogene said. She gazed up at the navire, expression hungry. "This will be faster. It doesn't need water or tides or good roads. Just a little wind." She looked back down to the image of the ship, her finger tracing its lines. "Wind and a little magic."

"Is that how it will rise into the air, magic?" Sophie looked from the diagrams to the giant bulk of the hull before her. There was nothing else that suggested how such a creation could do anything but crash to the earth.

"Yes," Imogene said. "The sanctii say it is possible. If we can find the right combination of powers. We have experimented with other means. There are gases that are lighter than air. That will float if contained."

"What's a gas?"

Imogene's mouth opened. Then closed. Then opened again, her expression horrified. "What do they teach you Anglions in school?"

"Reading, writing. Some arithmetic. Anglion history and geography. Deportment and various artistic and domestic pursuits for girls. Some magical theory if it is likely that you may manifest."

Imogene scowled. "No sciences? Nothing of the natural world?"

Sophie shook her head. "Not that I was taught. I learned some from my mother and father, of course. About herbs and crops and looking after the animals on the estate."

"Hmmph. What a waste. Do Anglions not think that girls have brains, too?"

"They know we have brains. But there are certain things that women do there and certain that men do. The magics fall that way, too. As the goddess—" Sophie caught herself. It wasn't as the goddess intended. Not to Illvyan eyes. Here, men and women could practice any of the Arts. There were a few male students in her earth classes. Outnumbered by the females, yes, but they were there. Just as there were female blood mages. The Arts of Air were taught to both sexes as well.

"I mean," she continued, "there are traditions."

"There are traditions here, too. But traditions may change and shift. And even tradition isn't a good enough reason for preventing someone from pursuing an interest or an occupation if they show a talent for it. I think you would be wise to stay here."

"It's not so simple," Sophie said. And now she was thinking of Cameron again. She didn't want to think about that. "Tell me what a gas is."

"I shall give you the simple version," Imogene said, "which is that everything around us in the world is made up of different substances that have different properties. All things can be broken down to these parts if you know how. Blood. Water. Dirt. People. We are all made of the same things. In different combinations." She smiled at that. "Air itself is made up of these things. In tiny, tiny quantities spaced far apart that . . . well, let us say they float, for want of a better explanation. Air is a gas. Things that do not float are called solids. Except when they're liquids. It has to do with the way the chemicals are held together. Which is overly complicated. So air floats and so do the chemicals within it. There are ways of isolating those chemicals, which gives you gases other than air. Some of them are lighter than air, as I said, so they will float in air. The trouble with those is that they also tend to be very flammable. The merest spark can set them alight. Which, when you build a structure containing metal, that will carry people who need fire for food and heating and wish to travel through skies that sometimes bring lightning, is not such a good solution."

"So, you want to find a magical way to mimic how those gases work?"

"Or to find another way to make the navire float." Imogene picked up the china cup. "If one could lift it." She held the cup in one hand and waved the other beneath it. "Push it up with more air. Or the power of the ley lines. Blood mages can move objects with magic. We just need a way to increase that power." She put the cup back down. "I will find it."

"Find what?" a voice behind them asked.

Sophie turned at the same time as Imogene. Cameron.

He still looked somewhat grim, the dark evening clothes turning him to something elegant but distant. She wanted to reach for him. She always wanted to reach for him. But no, she wouldn't give in to the pull of him today. Not until she knew how things lay between them.

"A way to power my navire," Imogene said, indicating the ship with a nod. She looked to Cameron, then back to Sophie. "To make it ride the air."

Cameron looked up at the structure. "Big."

"Yes. Once it is up, the air would help carry it. That's what the sails at the sides do." Imogene pointed at the picture and gave a rapid description of technicalities that meant nothing to Sophie. She wondered if Cameron understood any of it either.

"So the main effort is the initial lift. Then it is a case of ensuring it rides the winds safely. And then can return to the earth again, of course. Otherwise, the rest is for naught. I just need to find the right combination of powers." Her eyes narrowed thoughtfully. "How much work have the two of you done with your bond?"

"Not that much," Cameron said shortly. "Sophie, it's getting late. We should be leaving."

"Is Maistre Matin done speaking with the emperor?" Sophie asked, tone cool.

"I don't know," Cameron said. His tone suggested that he didn't particularly care, and Sophie bristled.

"Then perhaps we should stay here with Imogene until they send for us. I, for one, am interested in her creation. I've never seen anything like it."

"I doubt anyone has," Cameron said. He paused a moment, staring up at the navire as if trying to decide something. Sophie waited. If he was going to start another argument, then he could return to the Academe alone.

Eventually Cameron shook his head and his shoulders

dropped a little. "Forgive me," he said. "It has been a trying few days. I find myself eager for sleep tonight."

She wasn't sure if his apology was directed at her or at Imogene. If it were her, then it was a start, but he had somewhat farther to go before she might contemplate forgiving him.

"I find imperial dinners often have that effect on me as well," Imogene said with a half smile. "And the navire can wait another day." She turned to Sophie. "Your husband is correct. We should go back, find the maistre." She grinned suddenly. "If the emperor asks you about his palace, just tell him you found it all magnificent. He doesn't need to know that we spent most of our time here."

Sophie rather suspected that Aristides was fully aware of what Imogene was showing them. Even if the navire was Imogene's invention, she was an imperial mage and presumably was working on such an undertaking on the emperor's behalf. She wouldn't be showing it to anyone the emperor didn't wish to know about it.

But she might as well play along with the pretense. At least until she had a better idea why they were being shown the ship. That part she needed to think on a little longer. Had Aristides decided that she and Cameron were likely to stay in Illvya? Was the ship supposed to be an enticement? Or a warning? A display of the powers of the empire? After all, one use for a ship that floated through air might be to reach an island nation more easily. Attack on a front that they couldn't necessarily defend.

Was he warning her that Anglion would eventually be within his grasp?

She didn't know.

Something else to worry about. Which was entirely what she didn't need.

~

"Do you really want to go back and help Imogene with that . . .

whatever that was?" Cameron asked when they were waiting at the front entrance to the palace for their carriage to be brought around. Henri was a little distance away, talking low voiced to Imogene.

"It's interesting," Sophie said. "I'd like to know more about it."

"You do realize that such a thing is a weapon of war?"

"I'm not entirely an idiot," she said tightly. "So yes, it occurred to me. And yes, it also occurred to me that if they make it work, then perhaps it would be Anglion that Aristides would be turning his attention to."

"Good," Cameron said, and then, "I have never thought you were an idiot."

"Just a young naïve fool who didn't know what she was saying, then?"

He winced. "I owe you an apology."

"Yes. But I'm not sure I'm yet in the mood to hear it." She wrapped her cloak more tightly around her. The wind had gone strong since they had arrived at the palace and the scent of rain hung in the air.

"I deserve that." Cameron glanced toward Henri and Imogene. "But what I also wonder is whether that thing could travel far enough above the sea that sanctii wouldn't be affected by the salt water below them. A ship full of sanctii would make a very effective invading force."

Sophie's eyes widened. She hadn't thought of that. "Wouldn't it be easier to just ship a troop of water mages over instead?"

"Maybe. But that depends on whether the solution to how to make that thing fly ends up involving sanctii or not. If it does, then you need them."

She shook her head. "It seems unlikely. But I don't know enough about water magic to be certain how sea water even affects them."

"Something I think we need to find out," Cameron said. "I

—" He broke off, a smile abruptly appearing on his face. "Maistre Matin. Are you ready to depart?"

Sophie turned to see the maistre approaching them rapidly. And, in the distance, the sound of iron-shod hooves approaching. Any further speculation would have to wait.

CHAPTER 18

They were about halfway back from the palace before anyone spoke. It was Henri who finally spoke. "Another interesting evening. I will give you this, Lady Scardale. Life is not dull with you around."

"It used to be," Sophie said with a sigh. "I look forward to the time when it can be again."

"And have you thought about what you will do if your queen will not provide these reassurances you seek?"

Sophie shrugged. "I imagine at that point we will need to make a choice."

"Just so. You are, of course, both welcome to continue at the Academe. Your teachers speak well of your skills." Henri smiled at her. "We always need mages who are strong. We would be more than happy to complete your training. Or enhance it, in your case, Lord Scardale."

"What happens after the Academe?" Cameron said. "We can't stay under your roof forever."

"Well, that would depend on what interests you developed during your studies usually. Some of our students stay on as staff,

of course, or to immerse themselves in the study of magic itself.
Others join the imperial corps. A small number of earth witches
decide to dedicate themselves to the temple of the goddess. But
there are those who go out into the world and find occupation
for themselves. Who work in trades where magic is an advantage, such as those who make the fabriques, or become healers,
or join the households of nobleman. There are options. Mages
are respected here in the empire. You and your wife will not
starve, Lord Scardale, if you remain here. True, you will not be a
member of the Illvyan nobility. Not unless you distinguished
yourself in some way that might cause the emperor to reward
either of you with a title, but that doesn't mean you can't have a
prosperous life. A successful one."

"A safe one?" Sophie asked.

"Ah. Well, as to that, I am no farseer. No man or woman can
see their future clearly. And no life is without risk. But the risks
here are no greater than in Anglion, surely? For one thing, I
believe our skills in healing and other matters are somewhat
advanced compared to yours. That should improve your
chances."

What wouldn't improve their chances would be to remain
the center of royal intrigues. But it was difficult to see how they
could remove themselves from that position. It might become
easier once they made a choice between two countries, but right
now she didn't think that either monarch would want her to
stray too far from their control.

It felt like stepping from one cage to another. True, the
Illvyan cage was somewhat more spacious. And it offered more
options. Along with less chance of execution as a traitor, for a
start. But it was still a cage if she couldn't avoid becoming a tool
for the emperor to manipulate.

She leaned back against the carriage seat, suddenly
exhausted. Cameron beside her was a large warm presence but
less comforting than he usually would have been. He said he

owed her an apology. And maybe he was sorry for what he had said. That didn't necessarily mean that he hadn't meant it at the time.

Which cut her as surely as though he had taken a blade and stabbed her. But that was something else she couldn't do anything about. She was getting very tired of feeling helpless.

Her eyelids drifted closed and she was nearly asleep when the carriage suddenly jolted, sending her crashing against the wall.

"What was—" She didn't get a chance to finish her question. Because something flashed in sudden brilliant orange in the window beside Cameron and the carriage went tumbling through the air like a child's toy tossed in temper.

The world turned around her dizzyingly, and all she could hear was the splintering of wood and smashing glass and the shrieks of horses. She thought she heard Cameron call her name and reached for him, but they were still tumbling and her hands closed on empty air.

She could feel him through the bond but as she was tossed through space, she couldn't grasp exactly where she was, let alone him. She tried again but just as she thought she might have him, her head cracked sickeningly against something and the world went dark.

When her eyes opened, it was to the sensation of hands closing around her, tugging and pulling. It took a moment to remember. Carriage. Explosion. Falling.

That explained the pain in her head and the blurriness of her vision. The hands pulled again and she wriggled, trying to help them, but couldn't free herself. Until it registered that there were voices accompanying the grasping hands, and that they were speaking Anglish, not Illvyan. The voice closest to her said clearly, "Get the witch, let the other two die. They do not matter."

The hands around her wrists tightened, yanked at her a third time, the pressure harder, jerking at her shoulders. The fabric of her cloak, which she hadn't fastened, ripped and tore away, and then she was sliding upward despite trying to resist.

"Let me go," she screamed as her side scraped over something rough, but whoever had hold of her didn't stop and soon she tumbled out of the carriage and onto the cobblestones with a thump that stole her breath.

She gasped, then sucked in a breath as she started to push herself up.

"Stay still, witch," a low, harsh voice rasped, and she looked up to find a gun pointed at her face. The man wielding it wore a hooded cloak and had covered his face with some sort of black cloth tied around it, but his intent was clear enough.

Where was Cameron? Or Henri? She turned her head, pretending to shake it slowly as if to clear it.

The street they were in seemed empty, the buildings closed up and dark. Not an area with houses, then. But in a city as large as Lumia, someone should be around. Someone had to have heard the commotion caused by the carriage. Someone would surely call for help. There was a city guard as well as the Imperial Guard. Where were they?

The partially shattered carriage lay on its side about fifty feet away, the two horses fallen beside it. One was struggling to rise, whinnying hoarsely in distress, hopelessly tangled in its harness and held down by the weight of its companion, who lay motionless. To the left of the carriage, a fire danced on a patch of the road, burning and spitting sparks. Pieces of debris littered the street, some of them on fire. A chunk of something that might have been a door lay just a few feet from her, cracked and half-destroyed. She shuddered. So much damage. She was lucky to have survived.

"We should go." A second man joined the man with the gun. His face was covered, too, but he wore no cloak. His clothes were dark but simple, she thought. Plain jacket, shirt, trousers. Short boots. He bent down and she tried to scramble backward out of reach, but her feet couldn't find purchase on the stones and slippery velvet, and she only made it a foot or two before he grabbed hold of her wrist and hauled her to her feet.

She struck at him with her free hand. "Let me go!"

"Quiet." The gun swung round to face her.

Now that she was standing, she could see beyond the carriage. About a hundred feet past it stood a second carriage with a team of four, the horses dancing a little nervously in the smoky light, and a driver seated ready.

Goddess, no. She wasn't going wherever they were planning to take her.

She reached for her bond with Cameron. She could feel him but couldn't see him and he felt quiet, like he did when he was asleep. Unconscious? Hurt? Both? She couldn't say. But she needed some of his power. She had no other weapon at her disposal.

Pulling on both the bond and the ley line she could sense somewhere off to her right, she tugged at the chunk of door on the street and sent it arcing up to smash into the man holding her. He let go as the wood hit him, falling back with a shocked "Oof." He fell backward and she heard a crack that she hoped was his head hitting the stones but she didn't stop to look. Instead, she lunged for the gun.

The hooded man, attention drawn to his comrade for a second, didn't dodge immediately or fire, thank the goddess, and her hands closed around the weapon, trying to wrench it free.

"Bitch." The hooded man swore and swung a fist at her face. Pain arced through her head, bursts of light spinning in front of her eyes, and she started to fall forward. The action pulled the gun down but she somehow managed not to let go of it, instead trying to push it around so it faced her attacker. There was a sudden deafening sound and something stung her arm. The hooded man cursed again, falling back, clutching at his right thigh. For a moment she thought she'd been shot, as her arm throbbed painfully.

But if she had, it couldn't have hit anything too vital because she was still standing. She drew a breath, screamed, "Help me, please," as she reached for the ley line again, intending to try to send another piece of debris against her attacker.

Instead, suddenly, there was a sanctii between Sophie and the man in the cloak. She saw his eyes widen in horror above his mask, then he lifted the gun. The sanctii roared something in its own tongue and the gun suddenly . . . vanished. The man in the hood turned and bolted for the carriage, his motions panicked. The carriage had already begun to turn around, the driver having obviously decided that retreat was the order of the day. The sanctii roared again and stepped forward as though it intended to give chase.

"No," Sophie yelled. "Please. There are others here who need help." Her attacker in the hood showed no sign of turning back. In fact, as she watched, he reached the carriage and scrambled up beside the driver as the turn was completed.

The sanctii turned back to Sophie. Under the dim light of the streetlamps it almost looked like part of the road itself, the color of its skin blending into the shadowed cobblestones. Its black eyes reflected the light of the fire. It was the sanctii from the ball, she realized. The one who had defended Cameron.

"Please," she said, then started to move back toward the fallen carriage as the one containing the men who'd attacked them clattered away down the street, the driver whipping his horses into a gallop. "Please, I need help."

She glanced around. The second man was lying motionless on the cobblestones, seemingly no threat. So. Cameron and Henri. She turned and ran back to the wrecked carriage, ignoring the pain in her arm. Bending, she stuck her head through the shattered hole in the side of the carriage facing her, peering into the dark. There was no one inside and she pulled back, skirting around behind the carriage. With no knife, she had no way to try and cut the surviving horse free. She had to focus on Cameron and Henri.

Was the sanctii following her? She didn't look back. As she reached the other side of the carriage, the first thing that caught her eye was someone lying in the street about fifteen feet beyond the carriage itself. Henri. The figure was too short to be Cameron. And it seemed very still. Her footsteps quickened, even though her legs didn't want to entirely obey her, tremors running through them and the rest of her, the shivers enough to set her teeth chattering.

When she reached Henri, she saw his chest rise and fall. Slow, perhaps, but steady. Unconscious. But alive. There was no blood on his head or anywhere that she could see, though his cheek was scraped and part of his hair soot-blackened. She patted him down quickly, feeling for broken bones the way she'd seen her father do with animals that had fallen or gotten themselves trapped somewhere. All the while her mind was screaming at her to find Cameron. But she couldn't leave Henri until she knew he wasn't seriously hurt.

But her hurried inspection found nothing and with a sigh of relief, she heaved herself back upright and turned back to the carriage. At first she didn't see him, his evening clothes blending into the near-black shadow cast by the ruined carriage. But then her eyes found a paler patch amongst all the black and it resolved, as she squinted, into a head. Cameron's head. Soot-stained like Henri's, which was why she hadn't seen him immediately. He lay on his stomach on the cobbles, his head turned to the side so only half his blackened face was visible.

"Cameron." It was more breath than word but it was all she could manage against the fear suddenly gripping her throat and heart. "Cameron."

She had no recollection of moving but suddenly she was by his side. He didn't move when she called his name or when she started to frantically pat him down as she had Henri. His breathing was slow and, to her eye, not entirely steady. There was a gash on his forehead that had bled everywhere but she had brothers. She knew head wounds were misleading and blood was no longer pouring from it, so it couldn't be that deep. Of course, his skull could be cracked beneath the cut, but she didn't have the knowledge to determine if it was or to attempt to heal such an injury.

No other cuts revealed themselves as she continued her inspection, though the sleeve of his jacket was ripped almost clean off. Relief had begun to flood through her until she came to his left foot. It was tangled through the wheel, which was half off the axle, listing at a drunken angle. But not just the wheel, his foot was caught on something else that she couldn't quite see. She slapped a hand on one of the cobblestones closest to her, calling earthlight, but the glow wasn't strong enough to help much. Part of the underside of the carriage was buckled and twisted, and she couldn't make out exactly what had caught Cameron's foot.

When she wrapped her hands around his shin and tugged gently, Cameron moaned and, worse, the carriage itself moved, creaking alarmingly. Goddess. If she pulled something the wrong way, she might just send the entire weight of the carriage crashing down on him.

He moaned again and she glanced back, but his eyes were still closed. The sensible thing to do would be to wait for help, but what if the men who had attacked them regained their courage and decided to return for a second attempt to take her? She'd be helpless. Cameron and Henri, more so. She'd heard the men say they didn't need "the other two." And they had guns. What if they returned and decided to put a bullet through Cameron's brain?

She scrubbed a hand over her face to brush away the tears that threatened to fall. When she blinked them clear, she saw a pair of thick gray legs beside her and looked up to see the sanctii.

It hadn't left. Thank the goddess. Sanctii were strong, weren't they? Could the creature lift and hold the carriage so she could try to release Cameron's foot? She stared up at the impassive face. "His foot is caught. I can't pull it free because the carriage is broken. It might fall. Can you lift it?"

The sanctii tilted its head. Then turned to face the carriage. It leaned forward slowly, its body bending gracefully in a way that seemed impossible with the rocklike skin, and inspected the carriage much as Sophie had. When it straightened, it turned back to Sophie.

"Help," it said, nodding and stretching its massive hand toward her.

She didn't know what it wanted. Did it need her to stand? The chill radiated off its skin like an icy wind but she forced herself to ignore the sensation. She put her left hand on Cameron's leg, wanting the comfort of something warm and human, and lifted her hand to place it in the sanctii's.

There was a sensation rather like a lightning flash or her world being turned briefly inside out and then put back again. Everything whirled around her and she closed her eyes, willing herself not to vomit. When the nauseous sensation faded, she opened them. To see the carriage seemingly suspended in air about six inches off the road.

"What—" She stopped. This wasn't what she had meant when she asked it to lift the carriage, but what was done was done. And there was no denying the carriage was lifted. She'd never heard of a spell to make something float. She had no idea what the creature had done, but this wasn't the moment to waste any time asking questions. "Thank you." She nodded at the sanctii, and then pulled her hand free and crawled back to the wheel.

Cameron's leg was raised with the rest of the carriage. The angle looked uncomfortable but not dangerous. It seemed the sanctii had been careful to consider the tolerances of the human body when it had decided how high to lift the carriage.

She slapped more of the cobblestones, lighting them up, though the magic seemed to come slowly and made her head spin slightly again. With the carriage raised, she could see more clearly. One of the springs that eased the carriage's ride was twisted around the axle and Cameron's foot. If she could unwrap it, then she should be able to ease him free. But the thing was made of coiled steel nearly half an inch thick. She doubted she was strong enough.

Easing back, she turned to look at the sanctii. "Can you help me again? Please?" She patted the cobblestones beside her. "There's a spring holding his leg and I'm not strong enough to shift it, I think. But you may be. I don't think it needs magic. Look." She pointed at the spring. The sanctii knelt next to her and peered down to look through the wheel, curving its upper body into an awkward crouch.

It—no, *she*, Ikarus had said the sanctii at the ball was female —looked back at Sophie and then reached forward and tapped the carriage. Which rose obediently another half a foot into the air, dragging Cameron's leg upward.

"Careful," Sophie said, only stopping herself from trying to tug the creature away with an effort. She had asked her to help. She needed to trust her. The sanctii reached through the wheel with both hands. Metal groaned and Cameron's leg twisted slightly. Sophie leaned in to support it and as the sanctii moved back, his foot came free of the wheel and she was able to lower it to the ground.

"Thank you," she said to the sanctii. "Thank you, I—" The carriage suddenly crashed to earth, sending up a cloud of dust and splinters. Sophie heard a creak and looked up to see the wheel toppling toward her, but then the sanctii's hand was there. She caught the wheel, pushing it back toward the carriage, where it stayed.

Sophie stared at the creature, unable to think for a moment. Indeed, the world began to spin a little again, as though she had reached the limits of her strength. But as she fought the dizziness, she heard the sound of hoofbeats in the distance. Ikarus appeared next to the carriage and the sanctii who had helped her winked out of existence as though she had been a figment of Sophie's imagination.

As Ikarus bellowed and vanished, too, Sophie allowed herself the luxury of giving in to the demands of her body and slid into darkness.

CHAPTER 19

Sophie startled awake as a hand touched her gently. A voice murmured, "Easy, Lady Scardale. You are in the Academe. You're safe."

The soothing voice wasn't enough to reassure her. She pushed up to a sitting position, scanning the room. It looked like the Academe. In fact, it seemed to be the healing room where Cameron's ribs had been attended after the ball. The woman standing beside her was the same dark-skinned, gray-eyed earth witch—Rachelle—who had worked on him then.

Cameron. "Where is my husband?" she demanded, suddenly frantic.

"He's still unconscious," Rachelle said, stepping back so Sophie could see Cameron lying on another bed like the one she occupied. His face was clean and there was a bandage over the cut on his forehead. "But I have examined him. He does not seem to have any serious injuries. A wrenched knee, which I have attended to, though it will be a little sore for a few days."

"Then why isn't he awake?"

Rachelle shrugged. "He has quite a bump on his head. But there is no crack in his skull and no bleeding within that I can sense. In such cases, sleep is the best remedy. It may do more harm than good to try and wake him. If he hasn't roused by dawn, I will consider it."

"What time is it now?"

"Just after three," Henri's voice said from the other side of her. "You were out for a while yourself, Sophie."

She twisted to face him. "You're awake."

"Yes, fortunately." He smiled briefly, the expression followed by a wince which caused him to reach up to rub his temples gingerly. He had also been cleaned up, though there were still traces of soot staining the silver of his hair. "All three of us are fortunate, I think. Though I will confess my memory is somewhat hazy. I remember the carriage, then being here. But not what happened in between. Which Rachelle here tells me is common. Do you remember?"

Memories of grasping hands and a gun suddenly flooded through her. Her breath caught and she had to fight to breathe, panic flaring anew.

"Sophie?" Henri said.

She pushed the fear away. "Yes. I remember. Mostly. There was an explosion. The carriage flipped. They tried to take me."

"Take you?" Henri said, startled. "Do you know where?"

"I assume to the harbor." She hesitated, but there seemed little chance that she would be returning with the Anglions now. Not after they'd attempted to take her by force. "They spoke Anglish, Maistre."

Henri nodded, face grim. "I suspected they may have. I will inform Venable du Laq. She is waiting outside to speak to you."

"Imogene is here?" Sophie shook her head. "I thought . . . ." It was blurred, the memory. If it had been Ikarus at the end, and Imogene and the guard had found them, then why were they here, not at the palace? "She brought us here?"

"I understand we were slightly closer to the Academe than the palace when she found us," Henri said. "And I suspect that as we were attacked leaving the palace, she was being prudent. It would take quite a force to get to you here. She is rather keen to talk to you and report back to the emperor. Who, I imagine, will then wish to speak to you himself. But I have already told her that none of us is going anywhere until morning at the earliest and that she can convey that to the emperor."

"And she agreed?"

"It helps that Cameron is still not awake, I think. We will see what happens. She may be able to sway Aristides. She amuses him, I think. And she stands up to him. He likes that." He looked at her meaningfully. "Though he will pretend he does not. But he has enough sycophants to appreciate those who are more honest."

That might be true, but she couldn't picture herself taking Aristides to task any time soon. She would leave that to Imogene. Who had a sanctii at her back to shield her from imperial temper. Maybe the emperor wouldn't want to annoy Ikarus.

Ikarus. Who had found her at the carriage wreck.

"Ikarus came," she said slowly. "I remember that. But not Martius?"

"No. Martius wouldn't be able to. It is one of the limitations of the binding. If a mage bound to a sanctii is unconscious, the sanctii returns to their realm. It means they aren't bound here while we sleep, which would be boring for them, I'd imagine. But more practically, it also means that you cannot seek to seize a mage's sanctii by knocking out the mage. Of course, it also means the mage is left unguarded in such circumstances, but those who created the binding spells thought that perhaps a safer option than the alternatives."

"Alternatives?"

"Someone else seizing the sanctii. Or an enraged sanctii slaughtering people in defense of his unconscious mage. In truth, it isn't something that has often been tested. At least not in recent times. We are more civilized these days, it seems." He peered at her. "How are you feeling?"

"Tired," she said, which was understating the situation. Her body was weary in a way she hadn't felt since she'd first arrived in Illvya. A bone-deep kind of tired. She wanted little more than to lay her head back down on the pillow and sleep for a day or three. But that would have to wait. "But otherwise all right, I think." She looked to Rachelle, who nodded confirmation.

"Rachelle, would you leave us a moment?" Henri said. "Perhaps you could let Venable du Laq know that I will be out to speak to her shortly."

Rachelle nodded and left, though her expression was somewhat curious. As she pulled the door closed, Henri moved to lock it behind her. Then touched the door itself as though checking the wards.

"Ikarus said there was another sanctii. The same one as the ball?" he asked, turning back to Sophie.

"Yes," she said. If he already knew, then there was little point denying. "It helped me. It scared off the Anglions. Then helped me free Cameron. His foot was trapped in one of the wheels. I don't think I could have freed him by myself." She didn't mention the floating carriage. That seemed like something best left for another time given Henri already seemed worried about the strange sanctii. "When Ikarus came, it—she. They said she was a she, didn't they?—left. Perhaps because she knew there was nothing more to do."

"Perhaps. Though I am more interested in how she knew to come in the first place."

Sophie shrugged helplessly. "I do not know."

"Were you working magic?"

She had been. Using blood magic through the bond. It wasn't something she wanted to explain just now either. "Maybe." She rubbed her forehead slowly. "It's all a little jumbled in my memory. All I know is she helped me. I would have probably been on a ship back to Anglion by now without her. And I don't know what would have happened to you or Cameron."

"No," Henri agreed. "But her behavior is unusual. We don't know what she wants. So I would caution you to be wary if she appears again. You are not a water mage, after all. Sanctii can be dangerous."

She started to nod, then stopped. "And if I wanted to become a water mage?"

"Does that mean you are staying in Illvya?" Henri asked.

Sophie turned to look at Cameron, lying so still in the bed. "I cannot see how we can return now. But Cameron would have to agree, of course."

"Of course. Assuming he did, then I would have no issue with you adding water magic to your studies, if you show an aptitude."

"I could have a sanctii?" she asked. She wasn't entirely sure where the words had come from. Other than that twice now, a sanctii had stood between either her or Cameron and death. And that she wasn't entirely sure she wouldn't feel a lot safer in this very moment, even in the heart of the Academe, if she had one by her side. She shivered again.

Henri pursed his lips. "It takes many years of study to get to that point, Sophie. The bond is a complex thing and a difficult magic. Not all water mages attempt it. And, in your case, we would need to study the augmentier that you share with Cameron. To understand what impact another bond might have upon it.

"Multiple bonds can be unpredictable. They are extremely rare for that reason, other than those who take a petty fam and then later a sanctii. That seems safe enough. We think because an animal fam is not adding its own magic to a bond. Just its strength. If you stay, perhaps you could consider putting Tok out of his misery before you worry about a sanctii. Willem had to put the damned bird in a cage to stop him from trying to peck the window above the door there to pieces when they first brought us back, apparently."

"He didn't hurt himself, did he?" Sophie said, guilt flooding her.

"The bird is fine. Willem has a few scratches, I believe,"

Henri said. "He will survive those. But if you don't wish to bond with Tok, then I think we will have to send him elsewhere if you stay. He shows no sign of giving up his affection for you."

"I will think about it," she said. If she stayed, there seemed little reason to continue to deny the bird. His company had grown on her over the last few weeks.

"Good. Now, I think it would be best if we let Imogene in before she tries to batter down the door in her own manner. Which is likely to be far more effective than Tok's. And we cannot simply shove an imperial mage in a cage until morning," Henri said with a grin. "Then you can bathe and change and perhaps get a little sleep. Rachelle will watch over your husband."

Sophie glanced down at the mention of a bath. Until now she hadn't paid any attention to her clothes, but her purple gown was torn and stained with soot and dirt and other things she didn't want to think about. It smelled. The rest of her probably did, too. A bath and a little sleep sounded very tempting.

"Very well," she agreed. "But I'd like a minute alone with my husband first."

"He is unconscious," Henri pointed out.

"Just a minute," she said.

Henri shrugged. "All right. But do not take too long. The emperor needs to hear your story."

She nodded and climbed cautiously off the bed when Henri left the room. Made her way over to Cameron's side, moving carefully against the lingering aches in her body. Cameron's face was clean now, and too pale to her eyes. She put her hand on his chest, felt the reassuring rise and fall as he breathed.

Goddess. She could have lost him. They'd fought, and then he could have died. The sudden rush of fear caught in her throat, stealing her breath. She couldn't lose him. She wouldn't lose him. He was what mattered. "I'm sorry," she whispered, bending to kiss him. "And I love you." He didn't stir and she stayed there a few seconds more, trying to convince herself that Rachelle was

correct and that he would be fine with just a little more rest. The
bond felt quiet but otherwise normal. Nothing to indicate
anything amiss. So she would just have to trust that it would be
all right. Then she could tell him again so he would hear her. She
kissed him again and then left to find Henri and Imogene.

The conversation with Imogene hadn't taken long. Sophie had
told her what she remembered of the attack and of the sanctii's
help, again leaving out the part about the carriage floating. She
had a feeling that would only draw the conversation out, and she
wasn't sure she wouldn't pass out again if she had to keep talking
much longer.

Imogene hadn't looked entirely satisfied, but she had left to
report back to Aristides when Henri declared that Sophie
needed to rest.

The bath that followed restored some of Sophie's energy,
making her feel less wobbly and disoriented. She headed back to
her chamber intending to sleep, but once there, she couldn't
bring herself to lie down. Instead, she decided to return to the
healing rooms and sit with Cameron. If worse came to worse, she
could always sleep there, if she needed to. After all, the healing
rooms had plenty of beds.

The Academe corridors were deserted, as was to be expected
at something close to four in the morning. Even though she
knew she was as safe here as anywhere in Lumia, she wanted to
walk faster, the silence around her disconcerting.

The creak of a door swinging open as she passed it made her
shy like a horse, leaping sideways, heart pounding. When she
recovered, she shook her head, tempted to laugh at the over-
reaction.

Until the darkened doorway suddenly burned with light.

"Is someone there?" She hesitated. After the night she had

had, her first instinct was to run, to scream for help. But if there was only another student inside, she would feel foolish indeed. She reached for the ley line, just in case, not entirely sure what magic might help her in the empty corridor but unwilling to be entirely unprepared. One hesitant step toward the door. Then another.

"Hello?"

A figure appeared in the doorway. She bit back a scream. Too tall to be human.

It beckoned to her. "Come."

It sounded like the sanctii from the carriage—at least she thought it did. Where it stood, silhouetted in the light in the room, she couldn't be sure. Sanctii voices didn't have the same variation as a human's. Though she knew her ear was untrained when it came to distinguishing sanctii. Most likely they were all unique once you knew what to listen for.

"Come." The sanctii spoke a second time.

It was either do as requested or flee. Was there any point fleeing a sanctii? They could move far faster than humans.

She moved to the door, then into the room as the sanctii retreated. Under the light of the lamps, it was clearly the same near black sanctii who'd saved her.

"What are you doing here?" Sophie asked. And how had it infiltrated the Academe's wards?

"Find you," the sanctii said, sounding matter-of-fact.

"Why?" Curiosity was beginning to chase away her fear of the creature. Henri had warned her to be careful, but she didn't get any sense of danger from the sanctii.

"You need."

"I need what, exactly?"

The sanctii tapped its chest. "Help. Bond."

Sophie felt her mouth drop open. A bond? The sanctii wanted a bond? She took a step back without thinking. "I'm sorry, but I really don't know anything about water magic. Not even the basics. It's not possible."

The sanctii's dark eyes were unreadable, but she shook her head. "I know."

She knew it wasn't possible, or she knew water magic? It had to be the latter. If she knew it wasn't possible, why would she be asking?

"I'm sure you know water magic. But that doesn't help me. I need to know what I'm doing before I could even consider a bond."

The dark forehead wrinkled slowly. "No. Can learn."

"Yes, but that takes time. Magic is hard for humans. It's not safe if you don't know what you're doing. A bond is very hard." She wondered if the sanctii understood. The others seemed to. "Besides, I have a bond. An augmentier. With my husband. The maistre says it would take time to understand that, that we need to study it before I could have another."

"This?" The sanctii reached out and plucked at what was seemingly a blank patch of air near Sophie's right elbow.

A sudden pulse of power hit her. Apparently the sanctii could see the bond. "Yes."

"This important?" The wrinkles on its forehead deepened, looking like crevices carved shallowly in granite.

"Yes. Very. Precious even." In the distance she was vaguely aware of Cameron. Not quite awake perhaps, but he had stirred in response to whatever the sanctii had done.

"No hurt."

"What does that mean?" Sophie asked.

"Bond. No hurt if teach."

Teach? "Wait. Do you mean something like the reveilé? You can show me water magic that way?" If that was an option, why didn't the Academe know about it? Or maybe they did know and there were very good reasons it was an option not taken.

The sanctii nodded. "Same."

"But why? Why help me?"

"You need. I saw."

"Saw? I don't understand."

"Too hard to explain in this tongue," the sanctii said.

That might just be the longest sentence she'd ever heard a sanctii use. But regardless, this couldn't be a good idea, could it? She gripped the back of her neck, rubbing at aching muscles, trying to think. "I don't think this is a good idea." She hesitated. "I don't even know your name." Why that mattered, she didn't know, but it seemed wise to have some knowledge of the creature. If only to help when she tried to explain all of this to Henri.

"Elarus."

"I'm Sophia. Sophie."

Elarus nodded. "Yes."

"You know who I am?"

"Yes."

The sanctii still watched her. Sophie wondered if she found this conversation as frustrating as Sophie did, unable to speak easily in Illvyan.

"And it was you who helped my husband at the palace. At the ball?"

"Yes."

"Why?"

"Saw you. Saw need."

Well, that was clear as salt ash. But after tonight she knew she would not be returning to Anglion any time soon. Even though she'd said to Henri that Cameron would have to agree, she couldn't see how he could possibly disagree with her. Those men who'd tried to take her had been enemies, not allies. Wherever they had intended to take her, nothing good could be waiting. Anglion was no longer for her. Or Cameron. She'd told him she would let him leave. Maybe she would have to. But regardless, she would protect what was hers.

She stared at the sanctii, weighing the options. Learning water magic quickly. Why shouldn't she? "If you teach me, you want me to bond with you?"

The sanctii nodded. "Yes."

So. Knowledge with a price. Which was always the way, in

her experience. Tying herself to a sanctii. A being she'd grown up believing was a demon. Well, many mages before her had done it and survived. Even Anglions, once upon a time, it seemed.

If there was one thing she had learned in the last few days it was that sanctii were not to be underestimated. And that they protected their mages. It seemed the fastest way of keeping herself and Cameron safe. She couldn't command guards or an army to keep them safe. But she might just be able to command a sanctii.

Command? Was that the right word? Elarus was offering. She'd always thought a mage compelled a sanctii to form the bond. "Why do you want this? Isn't it a burden to one of your kind? To be controlled by a mage?"

"Your world. Different. Magic. Different. We help, we see." Elarus didn't sound perturbed by the thought. Which made Sophie wonder if the water mages were in as much control over their sanctii as they thought. Or whether, to a sanctii, a human life was just too short a period of time to be concerned with having to obey someone. Like taking on an apprenticeship with an obnoxious master, maybe. A short period of boredom in exchange for the knowledge and skills gained.

And, in truth, there seemed to be little risk to a sanctii in the bond. She'd never heard in any of the tales of sanctii being killed. Just of the water mages who wielded their power suffering various terrible fates.

But what she didn't know was what risks there were to her if she took what Elarus was offering. It might hurt her. Kill her. Or damage her bond with Cameron, regardless of what the sanctii said.

Cameron.

She thought of him, lying in the bed in the healer's rooms where she'd left him. If Elarus hadn't stopped the man with the gun, she might be dead, or Cameron might. And why would a sanctii help her only to try and harm her later? Other than a headache, the reveilé hadn't done her any harm. What would she risk to keep Cameron safe? She loved him, bond or no bond. If he didn't truly love her, perhaps it was best to know. If the bond was shattered, then he would be free to do as he chose. He could go home if he wanted to. If he didn't love her. And if he did, he should want to stay no matter if they shared a bond or not.

To keep him safe, she would let him go. She owed him that.

She extended her hand, tried to pretend she couldn't see it shaking. "Very well then," she said to Elarus. "Show me."

Elarus took her hand. Wrapped her long cool fingers around Sophie's. The pain when it came was far worse than the reveilé and seemed to last longer. She wasn't entirely sure she hadn't been set on fire or flayed or shattered into pieces. She heard herself scream, somewhere far in the distance, and then suddenly the pain ceased, leaving her a crumpled, sweating mess kneeling on the floor, panting for breath.

"There now, it is done," Elarus said, and Sophie realized she could understand the words that were not spoken in any human tongue.

She looked up at the sanctii, trying to slow her pounding heart, scrubbing the dampness of tears off her face. Her head ached like fire. But she climbed to her feet, standing somewhat shakily.

"Good," she said. "When I learn how to work with whatever it is you just dumped into my head, we can see about that—"

The door to the room flew open, crashing into a wall with enough force to make the lamps above their head dance.

"Sophie," Cameron roared from the doorway. "What in the thrice-damned name of the goddess did you just do?"

CHAPTER 20

His head was pounding like someone had used it as a target in sword practice as he stared at Sophie. And the sanctii standing next to her. Who looked remarkably like the one who'd been at the ball.

Who also, presumably, had something to do with the shrieking jolt of power and pain that had blasted down the bond, sending him bolting upright in the healer's room with only one thought top of mind—to get to Sophie.

The creature, looking at him through those black, depthless eyes, seemed unconcerned by his sudden appearance. Sophie, on the other hand, looked astonished. Astonished and . . . guilty.

"Yes, Lady Scardale, I would very much like the answer to that question as well." Maistre Matin shouldered his way past Cameron into the room and Cameron became aware that the Academe was rousing to life behind him, doors slamming and footsteps hurrying toward them.

Sophie's chin lifted. "Elarus offered to teach me water magic."

"Sweet suffering—" Henri broke off the words. "Do you have

any idea how dangerous that is? No. Of course you don't. Anglions!" He threw up his hands.

"What did you do?" Cameron repeated, stalking over to Sophie. She looked . . . well, a lot like he felt. Pale and blotchy. Her brown eyes squinting slightly as though the light hurt them. If she had half the headache he did, they probably did.

"I accepted her offer," Sophie said.

"Is that what I felt?" Cameron demanded at the same time Henri said, "You did what?"

"She taught me water magic," Sophie said, glancing up to the sanctii. "I think."

Henri started swearing in a low tone. The words weren't Illvyan or Anglion but they were clearly profanities. "You think!" he managed after a minute or two. "That could have killed you. Did you not stop to think that if this were a safe way to learn magic that we would not have to bother with this entire institution?" He waved his arms wildly as though lost for words.

"I thought there may be a risk," Sophie admitted.

"Why in the name of the goddess would you do such a thing?" Cameron asked. There was a padded chair to his left and he gripped its back, not entirely sure his legs would keep him upright. Could have killed her? He could have lost her? Forever? His head throbbed again and he pushed two fingers into the middle of his forehead where the pain was the worst. It did nothing to ease the sensation.

Why would Sophie risk her life? Let alone decide to learn water magic . . . which would mean that she couldn't return to Anglion.

The memories of the night suddenly crashed over him. The palace. Dinner. Sophie's declaration. Him yelling at her. A carriage ride, a flash of light, and then . . . nothing. Nothing until he'd woken up to the sensation that someone had just shoved a red-hot poker into his brain. In the healer's room. What had happened?

"I did what I needed to do to keep us safe," Sophie said. She was shaking slightly and he moved without thinking, gathering her into his arms and pulling her down on his lap into another chair. She smelled of the oils she liked to use in her bath, and sweat, and Sophie.

He could have lost her. His arms tightened involuntarily.

"Tell me," he said softly.

She shifted on his lap to look down at him. "What do you remember of tonight?"

"I remember dinner. And . . . after dinner." He reddened at the memory of their fight. "Then the carriage. Then . . . nothing." He frowned, shaking his head softly as though he could dislodge the memories and bring them forth, but his mind stayed stubbornly blank.

"Someone tried to blow up our carriage," she said. "They tried to take me."

She was trembling, he realized, and he pulled her closer, wanting to ease the fear in her voice.

"They spoke Anglish, Cameron. Anglish. They wanted to take me. Force me back, I think. I can't go back there. I don't think I'd live very long if I did."

Rage burned through him so white-hot for a moment it chased away any other sensation. Someone had tried to take her? To kidnap her? To drag her back to face some false charge? "I'll kill them," he muttered.

Sophie actually smiled at that.

He tried to let go of the anger. To tamp it down so he could think. Anger could wait. There would be time to use it. But not until he had the whole story of what had happened. And of what, exactly, Sophie had done. "Go on."

"Elarus helped me," she said. "Like she did you in the ballroom. They would have taken me if she hadn't come. They may well have killed you and Henri. You were both unconscious."

"So you let her teach you water magic to say thank you?" He still didn't understand.

"No, I did it because, as far as I can tell, having a sanctii is as near a guarantee of safety that we might be able to come by. Now that she's taught me, once I know what I'm doing, I can bond her and we'll be safe." She stared down at him. "I'm sorry, I know this means I can't go back. I'll understand if you want to."

"You think I'd go back there without you? Did that sanctii addle your brains?" He pulled her down and kissed her. "Body and blood, goddess damn it, Sophie. Body and blood. You're mine and I am yours. So I guess I'll get used to a sanctii if that's what you want. If you bond with her."

"If you bond her?" Madame Simsa said from the doorway. "What do you mean 'if'? Do none of you have eyes in your head? She and the sanctii are already bonded. What do you think made so much noise and woke half the Academe?"

Sophie twisted, mouth falling open. He was fairly sure his own expression mirrored hers. Madame Simsa was making her slow way across the room, her monkey at her heels.

"What do you mean?" Sophie said.

"I mean that creature bonded you somehow." Madame Simsa pointed to the space between Sophie and the sanctii—Elarus, was that what Sophie had called her? "Can't you see the link?"

What was she talking about? Link? He remembered then what Sophie had taught him. About seeing the ley line connections. The thought of using any form of magic made his head throb, but he made an effort. Sure enough, glimmering faintly like a row of stars hanging in midair, there was a line of power running from Sophie to Elarus.

"That's a bond?" He had no idea what he was looking at. He hadn't been able to see the bond between Sophie and himself when she'd taught him any more than she had.

"Yes," Madame Simsa said shortly. "Admittedly, it's a little different from the usual sanctii bond. I imagine that's because it wasn't Sophie controlling the magic when it was formed." Her gaze snapped to Sophie. "I should have thought that one accidental bond would be enough for anybody, child. What were you thinking?"

"Not accident," Elarus said abruptly.

Madame Simsa's focus moved upward to the sanctii's face, her expression cool. "Maybe not on your part. I won't ask you what you were thinking because I'm sure you won't tell me. Sophie, did you know what she intended?"

"I agreed that we would bond, once I knew the magic," Sophie said slowly.

"Never bargain with a sanctii," Henri said. "They are cunning." He snapped his fingers and Martius appeared. "Martius, can you tell me if there's anything untoward in the link Elarus here has formed with Lady Scardale, please?"

Martius looked at Elarus. If Cameron wasn't mistaken, the male sanctii's expression was distinctly unimpressed. But he said nothing, just kept staring, then turned back to Henri. "No. For female, no."

What the hell did that mean?

"Very well," Henri said. "That is one problem solved." He scowled at Sophie. "Lady Scardale, you will refrain from attempting anything even vaguely resembling water magic. Elarus may have given you the knowledge, but that doesn't mean you understand it well enough to use it with any degree of safety. You can commence your studies tomorrow. For now, I suggest we all try to get a few hours' sleep. Tomorrow is likely to be a long day if it starts with a visit to the palace."

The palace? Why—he understood suddenly. Aristides would want to know what had happened in the attack on the carriage. Kings, in his experience, didn't react well when people declared to be under their protection were attacked. He doubted emperors were any different. What was more surprising was that they weren't at the palace already. He didn't know how Henri had managed to delay, but Cameron was grateful that he had.

"Excellent idea, Maistre," he said, shifting his grip around Sophie so he could stand with her in his arms. He wasn't entirely certain that he could carry her all the way to their chambers but he was damned sure that he wasn't letting go of her any time soon.

~

Cameron put her down just inside their chambers before he closed the door, triggered the wards, and stood with his back pressed to the wood, breathing loudly in and out, eyes closed.

"Are you feeling unwell?" she asked. She doubted he should be up and out of bed. He probably shouldn't even yet be conscious. That was her doing. As were the chills running over her skin. Though maybe she could lay the blame for those at Elarus' feet. But she was going to have to get used to that, wasn't she? Maybe with the bond, she would build a tolerance to the sanctii's' lack of warmth.

"Give me a moment," Cameron said.

"If you are unwell, I should call for Rachelle," Sophie said. There was more color in his face than there had been in the healer's rooms, but there were also shadows under his eyes and a bruise darkening the right side of his chin.

Cameron didn't open his eyes. "I am as well as a man can be when he has just been informed that his wife was almost kidnapped and then chose to ally herself with a . . . a sanctii."

"Are you going to yell at me again?" she asked. She probably deserved that much. And, quite frankly, she didn't think she had anything left in her right now for an argument with Cameron to upset her. "It's all right if you want to."

Cameron pressed fingers to the bridge of his nose. "I am currently trying to dissuade myself from either kissing you or throttling you," he gritted out. "So, a moment."

Heat flooded through her at his words. "I'm not sure I should give you a moment," she said. "After all, I have a right to be angry with you, too. You almost got yourself killed. For the second time."

His eyes opened. "Neither time was voluntary."

"My bonding with Elarus wasn't entirely voluntary either," she said.

"That is not necessarily a point in your favor. In fact, it is exactly that lack of good sense I am contemplating."

"I did what I needed to do," she said. "For us." She moved closer so there was only a foot or so between them, staring up into angry blue eyes. "Body and blood, remember? You can protect me. But I'll protect you, too. I don't care if that makes you angry."

His gaze darkened, his pupils flaring. "Oh, don't you?"

"No. Not if you're safe." Safe. Alive. Hers. She needed to prove to herself that was all still true. She stepped closer to him, put her hands on the buttons of his shirt, and yanked. Buttons scattered wildly and the material tore.

His arms closed around her, scooping her up as he moved across the room. She landed on the bed and he began shoving up her skirts, fumbling at his trousers as he did so.

"We haven't finished the discussion about your new . . . friend," he said as she spread her legs, suddenly desperate for him.

"I'm sure we haven't," she said as he moved over her.

He paused, one hand on the buttons at the neck of her dress. "She's not here now, is she?"

She hadn't considered that. She couldn't feel the sanctii anywhere. No chill cooled her skin. Quite the opposite. The lust boiling through her had her sweating. "Not as far as I know." She reached down and put her hand around his cock. "Do you care?"

"Not in the least," he growled, then took her mouth with his. She let go of him and he pushed into her with one sure thrust that pinned her back against the mattress.

It was almost too much, him so hard against her. It was perfect. She pulled her mouth free as she clamped her legs around his hips. "One more thing you should know, husband," she said, her voice as rough as his. "That part where I said I would let you go? I lied. You're mine." She sank her teeth into his shoulder. "Mine."

"I know," he said. "Just as you are mine." And then he began to drive into her, sending all thought of speech, all capability of coherent thought, out of her head. There was only the touch and feel and taste of him, until she was spasming around him, the rush of pleasure so fierce it almost consumed her as she cried out.

Some time later, Cameron rolled off her and reached for the quilt to pull over them. Neither of them made any effort to move farther up the bed. She wasn't sure she could move other than to turn and curl back around him.

"Cold, love?" he asked, sounding half-asleep.

"No. Not with you here." She giggled suddenly.

"What?"

"I think we found the cure for sanctii chill," she said. "Which may be fortunate."

"Oh, so my marital duties will include being your human bed warmer now?" he said, sounding amused.

"Didn't they already?" she said, laughing for real now. She may have done something stupid by bonding herself with Elarus, but with Cameron on her side, she was certain they could work it all out. Body and blood. The thought made her ache for him all over again. She rolled on top of him, raising first a surprised "oof" then, lower, a more approving reaction. She wriggled against him just as the door chimes began to sound.

Cameron groaned. "How much would you like to wager that Aristides has decided he isn't willing to wait until morning and wants to see us now?"

Sophie shook her head. "I try not to make losing bets."

"How much do you want to wager that I'd be perfectly happy to tell him to fuck off right now?" Cameron said, one large hand descending on her ass to hold her in place when she started to roll off him.

"As our aim right now is to remain out of prison and out of

the emperor's bad graces, I think I'll decline that bet as well,"
she said. She pressed a quick kiss to his mouth, then scrambled
free. "You can warm my bed later. I promise I'm not going
anywhere."

She hoped to the goddess, thinking of the possible ways
that an audience with Aristides could play out, that that
were true.

~

She'd insisted on being able to bathe and change again before
they answered Aristides' summons. She didn't have another of
Helene's dresses to wear and she wasn't about to attempt to
dress herself in the red satin so she took one of her simple day
dresses to the bathing chamber.

When she emerged, Madame Simsa was standing in the
corridor, a bundle of black cloth in her arms.

She thrust it at Sophie. "Yours."

Sophie shook out the bundle. A set of Academe robes.

"Put them on," Madame Simsa said.

"I'm going to the palace."

"Yes. So you may as well let them know what you are. If you
wanted a sanctii for protection, no point hiding the fact that you
have water magic. Or will have," Madame Simsa said. "Henri
wasn't joking when he told you not to use it yet. You could hurt
yourself. And others."

"I won't," Sophie said. She hoped she'd have no reason to try.

"Good. Then I'll see you when you return from the palace.
Henri will no doubt want you to study with Venable Pellesier,
but you'll work with me as well. That old goat doesn't know
anything about being female and a water mage. The fact that
your sanctii is female will probably give him conniptions."

"Does it make a difference?"

Madame Simsa snorted. "The answer to that question will
take more time than I suspect you have this morning. Go." She

gave Sophie a little shove toward the bathing chamber. "Put them on. And don't forget who you are."

Sophie obeyed, retreating inside to don the robes and settle them into place.

The robe was an odd weight on her shoulders. The fabric was light, made of fine wool in deference to the cooling season, but the folds and gathers and length of it meant that there was plenty of material to add to the weight. At least that's what she assumed was making it feel so cumbersome even though it was a finer material than her previous robe had been. That or the fact that, seeing the colors at her collar in the mirror, no longer solely brown for earth but blue as well, there was no escaping the fact that by accepting Elarus she had changed her life irrevocably. A royal witch who practiced the fourth art would never be welcome in Anglion, bound or unbound. Some, no doubt, would say it made her a traitor.

Well, so be it.

She scowled at the Sophie in the glass. "I choose myself," she said firmly, then grasped the robe and her skirts as she turned to leave.

"Lord and Lady Scardale," Aristides said gravely. "First let me offer you an apology for what has occurred in my city. Trust me, we are taking measures to exact retribution on your behalf."

"Thank you, Your Imperial Majesty," Cameron said, bowing slightly. "We are grateful for your concern."

Sophie kept her eyes on the emperor as she curtsied beside Cameron. His voice had been cold, holding the same thread of chained anger that it had after the attack in the ballroom. She found herself devoutly thankful that she was not one of the people facing his wrath.

The room they were in was unfamiliar but clearly Aristides' throne room. Large, immaculately decorated, and designed to focus all attention on the large golden chair the emperor currently occupied.

Its back formed the flares of a sunburst, spiking out around the emperor's head, framing his dark hair in gold that glittered in the light of the candles and lamps. The first signs of dawn had been lightening the sky when their carriage had passed through the palace gates, but the sky that showed through the windows set high in the walls was still mostly dark.

They weren't alone with the emperor. Not even close to it. Imogene, Colonel Perrine, and a number of other black-clad guards and imperial mages were arrayed to the left of the room —even Imogene was dressed in sober black, the close-fitting jacket and long skirt echoing the lines of the guards' uniforms. She wore black leather gloves, not a single ring or jewel in sight. Crown Prince Alain was also present, standing closest to the emperor himself, gazing back out at the room, his expression stony. Next to the guards stood a group of grim-faced older men and one woman who Sophie assumed were the emperor's counselors or whatever they called them in Illvya. Or representatives of the parliament, maybe.

Sophie and Cameron and Henri themselves had been told to stand directly in front of Aristides. To his left, looking none too happy, stood the Anglion delegation. James Listfold had tilted his head enquiringly at Cameron when they'd passed him, but the other three had barely glanced in their direction.

Barron Deepholt had both hands clasped over his cane, his knuckles pale where they clenched the wood, as he stood watching the emperor. Beside him, Sir Harold stood at sharply set attention that would have pleased the most exacting military inspector. James was also focused on the emperor, his posture that of a well-trained courtier showing respect to authority. Next to him, Sevan Allowood looked tired but somehow resolute, his jaw set. He was sweating lightly but Sophie couldn't fault him for that. The throne room was, like most of the palace, overheated for her taste.

After her initial glance at them, she made herself ignore the Anglions as they were ignoring her. She was glad of the robes and the enveloping folds that allowed her to grip the sides to hide the slight tremor in her hands. She could hide those but she couldn't quell the sick feeling in her stomach. No matter what happened here this morning, part of it was bound to be unpleasant.

Aristides lifted his gaze from the three of them and glanced around the room. "It is early," he said. "And I know some of you have been roused from your beds. But the matter brought before me was too urgent to wait."

Sophie's grip on the fine wool tightened. She could almost hear the words of her old deportment instructor telling her that 'ladies keep their hands clasped in front of them, Sophia, not scrunched in their skirts like a naughty child.' Right now, the rules of deportment could go to damnation.

"Last night," the emperor continued, "after departing the palace, it seems Lord and Lady Scardale and the Maistre of our Academe were attacked in their carriage as they traveled the streets of our city. An attempt was made to kidnap Lady Scardale."

She thought she heard a grunt of surprise from the barron, but it was quickly stifled.

Aristides was looking at her. "Lady Scardale, is this correct?"

"Yes, Your Imperial Majesty, it is. There was an explosion and our carriage was overturned. There were at least two men and a driver who tried to take me from the carriage while my husband and the maistre were incapacitated."

"And did these men say anything in particular?"

"Only that they wanted me." She wasn't about to repeat exactly what had been said. There was no need. She turned slightly, looking Barron Deepholt in the face. "They spoke Anglish, Your Imperial Majesty."

"You lie!" the barron exploded.

Aristides gestured sharply and the barron snapped his mouth closed with visible effort.

"Native speakers, Lady Scardale?"

"To my ear, yes, Your Imperial Majesty. They had no Illvyan accent that I could detect."

"And did you recognize any of their voices?"

"No. One of them spoke very low. They were trying to conceal their identities. They wore masks. And the one who seemed to be in charge had a hooded cloak. I didn't see their faces."

"I see. Was there anything you noticed that may identify them?"

"A gun fired into the cobbles, Your Imperial Majesty. A chunk hit my arm." She pushed her sleeve back to reveal the wound. Rachelle had cleaned it and covered it with some sort of clear paste that had set hard, but left it otherwise untended. At Henri's instructions, she'd told Sophie when she'd asked. Now she understood why. "I believe the man with the gun was similarly wounded. In the leg. His right thigh, if I remember rightly."

"Your Imperial Majesty, I must protest," Barron Deepholt stepped forward, the movement jerky. "These accusations are unfounded. Lady Scardale is trying to poison you against us."

"Oh? To what end, my lord barron?"

"So she does not have to return to Anglion, clearly." The barron thumped his cane against the marble floor. "Look at her, standing there in those robes. Flaunting her defiance of our temple."

"My lord," Aristides said quietly. "If Lady Scardale wishes to stay in Illvya, she knows very well that she has only to ask. There is no need for her to make up stories. I would not allow her to be removed from my realm against her will. I have offered her my protection. Which has been *violated*." The emphasis on the last word cracked through the room.

The barron swallowed. "Still, Your Imperial Majesty. Perhaps she has other outcomes she wishes to achieve."

"Such as? You have continually assured her of her safety in Anglion. What plot do you believe she has formed in the few weeks she has been my guest?"

"I—"

"As for her claims being unfounded, they are not. The scene of the crime was investigated by my own guard and several of my imperial mages. There is evidence of a magical detonation and, indeed, a bullet found in the street and, as I understand, damage to the street that a bullet being fire into the cobbles could cause. True, Lord Scardale and the maistre were unconscious for some of the attack, but they also remember the explosion."

"She's a traitor who wishes to take the throne," Sevan Allowood said suddenly. He stepped forward, shaking James off when the older man tried to haul him back.

"Indeed, Mestier Allowood? How curious. It seems an odd tactic to flee the country one is supposedly trying to conquer," Aristides said. "But perhaps you know something I do not?"

Sevan glared at Sophie but didn't say anything.

"Your Imperial Majesty, you must forgive my secretary. He is overcome," the barron said, sounding outright worried.

"But what could concern him? Did your ship bring bad news from home, my lord barron?"

What was going on? Aristides clearly was working his way around to a point. She just had no idea what it might be.

The barron shook his head, subsiding.

"As it happens, your secretary is of interest to this discussion. As is the rest of your party."

"Your Imperial Majesty?" Sevan wasn't the only one looking sweaty now. A bead of moisture was rolling slowly down the barron's forehead.

"Once my guard brought word from Lady Scardale that her attackers had spoken Anglish, you will agree that it is natural that my attention was drawn to the Anglions already within my palace. After you were summoned here this morning, my mages conducted a search of each of your rooms."

"Your Imperial Majesty! The rules of diplomacy state that—"

"The rules of diplomacy, my lord, are precisely what I wish them to be. In this case, I choose not to let them be a shield for a criminal to hide behind. If indeed a criminal is to be found amongst your party." Aristides beckoned to Imogene. "Major du Laq, did your mages find anything of interest?"

Imogene came forward. "Yes, Eleivé, we did." She unfastened a leather pouch hanging from the belt of her jacket and withdrew a handful of round white objects. Each one was marked with a black symbol that Sophie shouldn't have recognized—she had never seen such marks before—but part of her mind whispered "scriptii." The knowledge Elarus had imparted was there after all, even if she couldn't use any of it yet. "These were found in Sevan Allowood's room. Well-hidden."

"Liar!" Sevan shrieked. "Witch liar. You and your demon-loving kind are the only ones who could produce such things."

Sophie felt the chill rising off the scriptii. Much like the chill she had felt every time she had been near Sevan, she realized suddenly. She had thought it the effect of the obvious dislike he held for her. The fact that he might have a scriptii had never entered her head. "Your Imperial Majesty," she said. "I have seen a scriptii, or the remnants of one, in Anglion."

Aristides arched an eyebrow, as though inquiring what this had to do with Sevan.

Sophie plunged on. "I can feel them. Scriptii. Water magic, I guess. They feel cold to me. Sanctii, too. Those are worse, of course. At the ball, I felt cold near Sevan. I didn't think anything of it then. I wasn't looking for scriptii. Not on an Anglion. But it could have been. It felt like one."

"Is this possible, Maistre?" Aristides asked.

Henri, who had been staring at Sophie as she spoke, turned back to the emperor. He nodded. "Mages can have different sensitivities to the different arts, Your Imperial Majesty. I was unaware of Lady Scardale's, but there is no reason to doubt what she says."

Imogene nodded agreement.

"I have seen my wife do this, Your Imperial Majesty," Cameron said. "In the palace at Kingswell. The mages there said the same thing about what she was feeling."

"Leaving aside the matter of why a scriptii might be in your queen's palace, which we will return to, Lord Scardale, I am satisfied that your wife is telling the truth. Imogene, a scriptii could have summoned the sanctii in the ballroom?"

Imogene nodded. "Yes, Eleivé. And if it was on the Anglion, then we would not have been looking for it."

Sevan lunged forward suddenly, face twisted. He didn't make it very far before Ikarus appeared and tackled him to the ground. Sevan writhed and screamed, the sweat on his face pronounced.

"He looks sick," Sophie said to Imogene. "He's sweating. Could he have taken something? Poison? If he thought he might be found out?"

Imogene looked at her sharply, then turned back toward the guards. "Fetch a healer. Quickly." She ran across to where Ikarus held Sevan, muttered a string of low words, and placed a hand on Sevan's head. He stopped struggling and went still.

"Major?" Aristides said, staring at Sevan with distaste.

"Poison, Eleivé. I believe I have stayed its course."

Aristides gaze sharpened. "Good. Do not let him die, Imogene."

"No, Eleivé," she muttered, looking exasperated.

"And while you're there, perhaps you would be so good as to examine his thigh. The right one, was it, Lady Scardale?"

"Yes, Your Imperial Majesty."

Imogene produced a small knife and neatly slit Sevan's trousers open. There was a gash on his upper thigh that looked fresh to Sophie's eyes.

"So," Aristides said. "It seems we have found at least one of the conspirators."

"Your Imperial Majesty, I swear I knew nothing of this. After all, I was the one attacked at the ballroom," Barron Deepholt said, his face ashen. Beside him, James was staring at Sevan with something akin to disgust. Sir Harold merely looked ill.

The barron had a point, of course. He had been attacked. Though, if Sevan had been behind the attack in the ballroom, it seemed likely it had been designed to cast suspicion on her, she realized. Give the Illvyans a reason to send her home, perhaps? The barron could have been part of such a ploy.

"As to that, my mages will determine the truth. You will be questioned. You have my word that you will not be harmed if you are innocent, and that you will be returned to your ship and free to leave. If you are not, then you will be subject to the laws of this land. As will your secretary and the others on your ships."

The barron bowed acceptance. Sophie couldn't see that he had any other choice.

"Yes, Your Imperial Majesty. I do not understand why Sevan would—" He broke off. Whether because he didn't know what more to say or whether he thought it would be pointless to offer any defense of Sevan's actions, Sophie couldn't have said.

"Ah." Aristides expression eased a little. "Louis?"

The major domo approached, bearing a letter. "Eleivé." He deposited the letter in the emperor's outstretched hands.

"Perhaps I can shed some light. The document I hold is one of the messages that arrived on your second ship. It has taken me some time to confirm its contents, but it was addressed to your secretary. I will assume he did not share its contents with you, my lord. A pity. It seems not all has been peaceful in Anglion during your time here. There has been a breakout of some illness in the district of your Barron Nester. Quite virulent. It seems the barron and his younger brother sadly did not survive it. Nor did most of their household. Your secretary was kin to the barron, I believe?"

Barron Deepholt nodded slowly.

Sophie stood frozen. Kiaran Allowood dead? And his brother? But that meant that she . . . . She bit the inside of her cheek, trying to maintain some calm. Cameron had stiffened beside her when Aristides had made his announcement.

Something was very wrong in Anglion. Though her more immediate concern was when Aristides had obtained the letter. How long was the "some time" it had taken him to confirm the news?

"Perhaps he was afflicted by his grief," Barron Deepholt ventured. "Not in his right mind."

"Perhaps," Aristides said judiciously. "That remains to be seen. But I believe you will accompany Colonel Perrine now and submit to our questions. If you satisfy him, then you will be returned to your ship. You will return to Anglion. You will take my condolences to Queen Eloisa on the loss of two of her heirs. And convey Lady Scardale's regrets that she will not be returning to Anglion. Another blow, I'm sure. And Barron Deepholt?"

"Yes, Your Imperial Majesty?" The barron seemed to have shrunk half a foot.

"You will also reiterate to Her Majesty that the Scardales stand under my protection. And that I take that very seriously. Perhaps you will be able to use your experience to convince her of that."

The barron bowed so deeply that he risked knocking his head on the floor. "Indeed, Your Imperial Majesty."

Sophie had to grant him some points for maintaining a semblance of grace under pressure. She wasn't sure she would be able to remain calm if she was about to be dragged off to be interrogated by the Imperial Guard. She devoutly wished she never had cause to find out.

The room seemed very quiet as the Anglions were escorted out, only the sound of booted heels on marble breaking the silence.

When they were out of earshot, all attention turned back to the emperor.

Aristides shifted on his throne. "So, Lady Scardale, let me be the first to offer my felicitations."

"Felicitations, Your Imperial Majesty?"

"Barron Nester was above you in the line of succession, was he not? He and his brother. You have moved up in the world."

Sophie gestured at her robes. "That hardly seems relevant anymore, Your Imperial Majesty. The Anglions are not going to accept an Illvyan-trained mage as their queen even if something should happen to Queen Eloisa. Besides, there are others still above me."

"Your crown princess? Who has shown no power and no ability to bear heirs? Or the cousin? What is her name?"

"Penelope Fairley, Your Imperial Majesty," Cameron supplied in a voice that sounded half-strangled. Was he only just now starting to do the math in his head?

"Yes. Her. Past childbearing, as I understand it. Also with little power. And though I understand that by some reckonings your crown princess' husband could inherit, I do not think that is a move the Anglion court would accept if others of the royal line live. No, Lady Scardale, I believe that, until your queen remarries and has children, you are the next most likely candidate to hold the throne of Anglion should it stand vacant."

"Then I wish that the goddess may grant Her Majesty the gift of children," Sophie blurted. As soon as possible, she refrained from adding.

"It may not be that simple," Aristides said, and Sophie's blood chilled.

"Your Imperial Majesty?"

"Someone is playing dangerous games in Anglion, Lady Scardale. They tried to kill you. They seem to have succeeded in killing Barron Nester. Not to mention eliminating King Stefan and half your nobility in the attack on the palace at Kingswell."

Aristides, it seemed, was far better informed about Anglion than she had thought. It was a realization that was not comforting. Though she should not forget that one of the prime candidates for pulling the strings and sowing discord in Anglion was Aristides himself.

"Someone is manipulating your succession. Your very throne, perhaps. And that is a situation I find displeasing. Your country and mine have ignored each other fairly well for some time now. Anglion is of little strategic significance to us, after all. Though, granted, it is a country rich in resources. But whoever is behind these goings-on seems to have access to a water mage. And an Anglion with its own water mages may be a different proposition for the empire. It would not do for someone with such power to have the mind to start a rebellion against me. Or to try and claim territories on the mainland."

"I doubt such a thing has crossed Queen Eloisa's mind," Sophie said truthfully, grateful that she managed to speak without her voice trembling. Eloisa had never spoken of conquest. It was a rumble that had moved through the court a time or two under King Stefan, but anyone with half a brain dismissed such a scheme as absurd. Anglion was safest in isolation. The empire would respond to any encroachment with force Anglion couldn't hope to match. Nothing good could come of that confrontation.

"Your queen seems to be failing to protect her subjects," Aristides said. "Whether through a lack of ability or whether she is being manipulated, that fact seems unarguable. If she cannot keep her own heirs alive, then her reign is doomed."

"She is new to the throne, Your Imperial Majesty. And come to power in difficult times," Sophie said.

"Still, she should be able to prevent assassins making their way onto her diplomatic parties. Either she is being manipulated or her own attempts to play politics with her delegation fell short."

"I'm not sure I understand, Your Imperial Majesty."

"I believe Sevan Allowood was sent as a fallback, Lady Scardale. To kill you, if you could not be persuaded to return. Perhaps he will reveal the reason why when he is interrogated or perhaps he will not. But the fact remains that someone in Anglion seems to want you dead and your country unstable. I find myself in disagreement with both those choices. Your country needs a strong queen, Lady Scardale. One who can settle these matters. One who can perhaps bring a final peace between our countries and undo some of the less desirable aspects that have developed in yours."

Her mouth had turned dry as dust. Surely he didn't mean . . . . "You cannot be serious."

"I rarely joke, Lady Scardale."

She was going to faint. She was sure of it. She definitely couldn't speak.

"I will make myself plain. Lady Scardale. It seems that Anglion may be in need of a new queen. I am of a mind to give her one should the situation continue to deteriorate. Which leaves you with one question to answer, my lady. Will you take the crown if I offer it?"

She tried to form the words "absolutely not" but the muscles of her throat were locked with shock and the denial would not come. All she could do was stand there, frozen, beside Cameron, eyes locked with Aristides'. And, as the uproar the emperor's invitation caused faded to mere background, she knew only that, once again, her world had shifted beneath her, sending her tumbling once more into chaos. And that she had no idea whatsoever what to do next.

ABOUT THE AUTHOR

M.J Scott is an unrepentant bookworm. Luckily she grew up in a family that fed her a properly varied diet of books and these days is surrounded by people who are understanding of her story addiction. When not wrestling one of her own stories to the ground, she can generally be found reading someone else's. To keep in touch, find out about new releases and other news (and receive an exclusive freebie) sign up to her newsletter at www.mjscott.net. She also writes contemporary romance as Melanie Scott and Emma Douglas.

You can keep in touch with M.J. on:
Twitter @melscott
Facebook AuthorMJScott
Pinterest @mel_writes
Instagram @melwrites
Or email her at mel@mjscott.net

ALSO BY M.J. SCOTT

Urban fantasy

The Wild Side series

The Day You Went Away*

The Wolf Within

The Dark Side

*A free short story that's a prequel to The Wolf Within

Dark romantic fantasy

The Four Arts series

The Shattered Court

The Half-Light City series

Shadow Kin

Blood Kin

Iron Kin

Fire Kin

EXCERPT FROM SHADOW KIN
CHAPTER ONE

The wards sparked in front of me, faint violet against the dark wooden door with its heavy brass locks, proclaiming the house's protection. They wouldn't stop me. No one has yet made the lock or ward to keep me out. Magic cannot detect me, and brick and stone and metal are no barrier.

It's why I'm good at what I do.

A grandfather clock in the hall chimed two as I stepped into the shadow, entering the place only my kind can walk and passing through the door as though it wasn't there. Outside came the echoing toll of the cathedral bell, much louder here in Greenglass than in the Night World boroughs I usually frequent.

I'd been told that the one I was to visit lived alone. But I prefer not to believe everything I'm told. After all, I grew up among the Blood and the powers of the Night World, where taking things on faith is a quick way to die.

Besides, bystanders only make things complicated.

But tonight, I sensed I *was* alone as I moved carefully through the darkened rooms. The house had an elegant simplicity. The floors were polished wood, softened by fine wool rugs, and paintings hung on the unpapered walls. Plants flourished on any spare flat surface, tingeing the air with the scent of growth and life. I hoped someone would save them after my task here was completed. The Fae might deny me the Veiled World, but the part of me that comes from them shares their affinity for green growing things.

Apart from the damp greenness of the plants, there was only one other dominant scent in the air. Human. Male. Warm and spicy.

Alive. Live around the Blood for long enough and you become very aware of the differences between living and dead. No other fresh smell mingled with his. No cats or dogs. Just fading hints of an older female gone for several hours. Likely a cook or housekeeper who didn't live in.

I paused at the top of the staircase, counting doors carefully. Third on the left. A few more strides. I cocked my head, listening.

There.

Ever so faint, the thump of a human heartbeat. Slow. Even.

Asleep.

Good. Asleep is easier.

I drifted through the bedroom door and paused again. The room was large, walled on one side with floor-to-ceiling windows unblocked by any blind. Expensive, that much glass. Moonlight streamed through the panes, making it easy to see the man lying in the big bed.

I didn't know what he'd done. I never ask. The blade doesn't question the direction of the cut. Particularly when the blade belongs to Lucius. Lucius doesn't like questions.

I let go of the shadow somewhat. I was not yet truly solid, but enough that, if he were to wake, he would see my shape by the bed like the reflection of a dream. Or a nightmare.

The moonlight washed over his face, silvering skin and fading hair to shades of gray, making it hard to tell what he might look like in daylight. Tall, yes. Well formed if the arm and chest bared by the sheet he'd pushed away in sleep matched the rest of him.

Not that it mattered. He'd be beyond caring about his looks in a few minutes. Beyond caring about anything.

The moon made things easier even though, in the shadow, I see well in very little light. Under the silvered glow I saw the details of the room as clearly as if the gas lamps on the walls were alight.

The windows posed little risk. The town house stood separated from its neighbors by narrow strips of garden on each side and a much larger garden at the rear. There was a small chance someone in a neighboring house might see something, but I'd be long gone before they could raise an alarm.

His breath continued to flow, soft and steady, and I moved around the bed, seeking a better angle for the strike as I let myself grow more solid still, so I could grasp the dagger at my hip.

Legend says we kill by reaching into a man's chest and tearing out his heart. It's true, we can. I've even done it. Once.

At Lucius' demand and fearing death if I disobeyed.

It wasn't an act I ever cared to repeat. Sometimes, on the edge of sleep, I still shake thinking about the sensation of living flesh torn from its roots beneath my fingers.

So I use a dagger. Just as effective. Dead is dead, after all.

I counted his heartbeats as I silently slid my blade free. He was pretty, this one. A face of interesting angles that looked strong even in sleep. Strong and somehow happy. Generous lips curved up slightly as if he were enjoying a perfect dream.

Not a bad way to die, all things considered.

I unshadowed completely and lifted the dagger, fingers steady on the hilt as he took one last breath.

But even as the blade descended, the room blazed to light around me and a hand snaked out like a lightning bolt and clamped around my wrist.

"Not so fast," the man said in a calm tone.

I tried to shadow and my heart leaped to my throat as nothing happened.

"Just to clarify," he said. "Those lamps. Not gas. Sunlight."

"*Sunmage,*" I hissed, rearing back as my pulse went into over-drive. How had Lucius left out *that* little detail? Or maybe he hadn't. Maybe Ricco had left it out on purpose when he'd passed on my assignment. He hated me. I wouldn't put it past him to try to engineer my downfall.

Damn him to the seven bloody night-scalded depths of hell.

The man smiled at me, though there was no amusement in the expression. "Precisely."

I twisted, desperate to get free. His hand tightened, and pain shot through my wrist and up my arm.

"Drop the dagger."

I set my teeth and tightened my grip. Never give up your weapon.

"I said, *drop it.*" The command snapped as he surged out of the bed, pushing me backward and my arm above my head at a nasty angle.

The pain intensified, like heated wires slicing into my nerves. "Sunmages are supposed to be healers," I managed to gasp as I struggled and the sunlight—hells-damned *sunlight*—filled the room, caging me as effectively as iron bars might hold a human.

I swung at him with my free arm, but he blocked the blow, taking its force on his forearm without a wince. He fought far too well for a healer. Who was this man?

"Ever consider that being a healer means being exposed to hundreds of ways to hurt people? Don't make me hurt you. Put the knife down."

I swore and flung myself forward, swinging my free hand at his face again. But he moved too, fast and sure, and somehow—damn, he was good—I missed, my hand smacking into the wall. I twisted desperately as the impact sent a shock wave up my arm, but the light dazzled me as I looked directly into one of the lamps.

A split second is all it takes to make a fatal mistake.

Before I could blink, he had pulled me forward and round

and I sailed through the air to land facedown on the feather mattress, wind half knocked out of me. My free hand was bent up behind my back, and my other—still holding my dagger—was pinned by his to the pillow.

My heart raced in anger and humiliation and fear as I tried to breathe.

Sunmage.

I was an idiot. *Stupid. Stupid. Stupid.*

Stupid and careless.

His knee pushed me deeper into the mattress, making it harder still to breathe.

"Normally I don't get this forward when I haven't been introduced," he said, voice warm and low, close to my ear. He still sounded far too calm. A sunmage healer shouldn't be so sanguine about finding an assassin in his house. Though perhaps he wasn't quite as calm as he seemed. His heart pounded. "But then again, normally, women I don't know don't try to stab me in my bed."

I snarled and he increased the pressure. There wasn't much I could do. I'm faster and stronger than a human woman, but there's a limit to what a female of five foot six can do against a man nearly a foot taller and quite a bit heavier. Particularly with my powers cut off by the light of the sun.

Damned hells-cursed sunlight.

"I'll take that." His knee shifted upward to pin both my arm and my back, and his free hand wrenched the dagger from my grasp.

Then, to my surprise, his weight vanished. It took a few seconds for me to register my freedom. By the time I rolled to face him, he stood at the end of the bed and my dagger quivered in the wall far across the room. To make matters worse, the sunlight now flickered off the ornately engraved barrel of the pistol in his right hand.

It was aimed squarely at the center of my forehead. His hand was perfectly steady, as though holding someone at gunpoint was nothing greatly out of the ordinary for him. For a man wearing nothing but linen drawers, he looked convincingly threatening.

I froze. Would he shoot? If our places were reversed, he'd already be dead.

"Wise decision," he said, eyes still cold. "Now. Why don't you tell me what this is about?"

"Do you think that's likely?"

One corner of his mouth lifted and a dimple cracked to life in his cheek. My assessment had been right. He was pretty. Pretty and dangerous, it seemed. The arm that held the gun was, like the rest of him, sleek with muscle. The sort that took concerted effort to obtain. Maybe he was one of the rare sunmages who became warriors? But the house seemed far too luxurious for a Templar or a mercenary, and his hands and body were bare of Templar sigils.

Besides, I doubted Lucius would set me on a Templar. That would be madness.

So, who the hell was this man?

When I stayed silent, the pistol waved back and forth in a warning gesture. "I have this," he said. "Plus, I am, as you mentioned, a sunmage." As if to emphasize his point, the lamps flared a little brighter. "Start talking."

I considered him carefully. The sunlight revealed his skin as golden, his hair a gilded shade of light brown, and his eyes a bright, bright blue. A true creature of the day. No wonder Lucius wanted him dead. I currently felt a considerable desire for that outcome myself. I scanned the rest of the room, seeking a means to escape.

A many-drawered wooden chest, a table covered with papers with a leather-upholstered chair tucked neatly against it, and a large wardrobe all made simply in the same dark reddish wood offered no inspiration. Some sort of ferny plant in a stand stood in one corner, and paintings—landscapes and studies of more plants—hung over the bed and the table. Nothing smaller than the furniture, nothing I could use as a weapon, lay in view. Nor was there anything to provide a clue as to who he might be.

"I can hear you plotting all the way over here," he said with another little motion of the gun. "Not a good idea. In fact . . ." The next jerk of the pistol was a little more emphatic, motioning me toward the chair as he hooked it out from the table with his foot. "Take a seat. Don't bother trying anything stupid like attempting the window. The glass is warded. You'll just hurt yourself."

Trapped in solid form, I couldn't argue with that. The lamps shone with a bright unwavering light and his face showed no sign of strain. Even his heartbeat had slowed to a more steady rhythm now that we were no longer fighting. A sunmage calling sunlight at night. Strong. Dangerously strong.

Not to mention armed when I wasn't.

I climbed off the bed and stalked over to the chair.

He tied my arms and legs to their counterparts on the chair with neck cloths. Tight enough to be secure but carefully placed so as not to hurt. He had to be a healer. A mercenary wouldn't care if he hurt me. A mercenary probably would've killed me outright.

When he was done he picked up a pair of buckskin trousers and a rumpled linen shirt from the floor and dressed quickly. Then he took a seat on the end of the bed, picked up the gun once again, and aimed directly at me.

Blue eyes stared at me for a long minute, something unreadable swimming in their depths. Then he nodded.

"Shall we try this again? Why are you here?"

There wasn't any point lying about it. "I was sent to kill you."

"I understand that much. The reason is what escapes me."

I lifted a shoulder. Let him make what he would of the gesture. I had no idea why Lucius had sent me after a sunmage.

"You didn't ask?"

"Why would I?" I said, surprised by the question.

He frowned. "You just kill whoever you're told to? It doesn't matter why?"

"I do as I'm ordered." Disobedience would only bring pain. Or worse.

His head tilted, suddenly intent. His gaze was uncomfortable, and it was hard to shake the feeling he saw more than I wanted. "You should seek another line of work."

As if I had a choice. I looked away from him, suddenly angry. Who was he to judge me?

"Back to silence, is it? Very well, let's try another tack. This isn't, by chance, about that Rousselline pup I stitched up a few weeks ago?"

Pierre Rousselline was alpha of one of the Beast Kind packs. He and Lucius didn't always exist in harmony. But I doubted Lucius would kill over the healing of a young Beast. A sunmage, one this strong—if his claim of being able to maintain the light until dawn were true——was an inherently risky target, even for a Blood lord. Even for *the* Blood Lord.

So, what had this man—who was, indeed, a healer if he spoke the truth—done?

His brows lifted when I didn't respond. "You really don't know, do you? Well. Damn."

The "damn" came out as a half laugh. There was nothing amusing in the situation that I could see. Either he was going to kill me or turn me over to the human authorities or I was going to have to tell Lucius I had failed. Whichever option came to pass, nothing good awaited me. I stayed silent.

"Some other topic of conversation, then?" He regarded me with cool consideration. "I presume, given that my sunlight seems to be holding you, that I'm right in assuming that you are Lucius' shadow?"

I nodded. There was little point denying it with his light holding me prisoner. There were no others of my kind in the City. Only a wraith is caged by the light of the sun.

A smile spread over his face, revealing he had two

dimples, not one. Not just pretty, I decided. He was . . . alluring wasn't the right word. The Blood and the Fae are alluring—an attraction born of icy beauty and danger. I am immune to that particular charm. No, he was . . . inviting somehow. A fire on a winter's night, promising warmth and life.

His eyes held genuine curiosity. "You're really a wraith?"

"Yes."

He laughed and the sound was sunlight, warm and golden, a smooth caress against the skin.

"Is that so amusing?"

"If the stories are to believed, you're supposed to be ten feet tall with fangs and claws."

I tilted my head. "I am not Blood or Beast Kind. No fangs. Or claws."

He looked over my shoulder, presumably at my dagger. "Just one perhaps? But really . . . no one ever said you were—" He stopped abruptly.

"What?" The question rose from my lips before I could stop myself.

This time his smile was crooked. "Beautiful."

I snorted. Beautiful? Me? No. I knew that well enough. The Fae are beautiful and even the Blood in their own way. I am only odd with gray eyes—a color no Fae or true demi-Fae ever had— and red hair that stands out like a beacon amongst the silvery hues of the Blood. "That's because I'm not."

He looked surprised. "I know the Blood don't use mirrors, but you must have seen yourself."

"Maybe the Night World has different standards."

"Then the Night World needs its eyesight examined," he said with another crooked smile. "Gods and suns."

Silence again. He studied me and I looked away, discomfited, wondering what angle he was trying to work by flattering me. Did he think I could sway Lucius into granting mercy? If so, then he was in for a severe disappointment.

"What happens now?" I asked when the silence started to strain my nerves.

"That may well depend on you."

Liked it? Find out more about Shadow Kin and the other three books in the Half-Light City series at M.J's website (www.mjscott.net).

70067779R00202

Made in the USA
Lexington, KY
10 November 2017